JUDGEMENT DAY

JUDGEMENT DAY

Andrew Neiderman

OPEN ROAD

INTEGRATED MEDIA

NEW YORK

ISBN: 978-1-5040-7602-9

This edition published in 2022 by Open Road Integrated Media, Inc.
180 Maiden Lane
New York, NY 10038
www.openroadmedia.com

For My Family
The only reason to be

JUDGEMENT DAY

PROLOGUE

Warner Murphy believed he had good reason to admire himself in the gilded framed bathroom mirror. He wasn't a smoker and not much of a drinker, rarely partaking in a martini at lunch with a client or other attorneys, and he never had even experimented with drugs. He was athletic, religiously attending his sports club, and unlike most young attorneys he knew, was intelligent about what he ate. Practically a vegetarian, Warner took a lot of ribbing about his concern for his nutritional health, but unlike most, he hadn't gained any significant poundage to add to his high school weight at graduation. At just under six feet and one-hundred and eighty, he was buff with GQ styled dark-brown hair and stunning greenish-blue eyes.

Warner wasn't neurotic about it. He wasn't looking for any signs of age creeping into his thirty-four-year-old body and face when he examined himself in the mirror. As far as he was concerned, age had been put on a wait list. He couldn't even imagine the day he would dye his hair. He hadn't slowed down at all, and was still constantly admired for his boundless energy, which he knew came from his optimism and self-confidence as well as his healthy lifestyle.

However, he wasn't just admiring himself in the mirror this morning. He was looking to answer a question he had asked himself most of his adult life. Do successful people really look successful? Do they stand out in a crowd even before you get to know them or about them? Do their faces glow with power, their eyes reveal their new super-confidence, and their smiles give other dreamers hope? Do I have that look? Was it vain to wonder?

He searched his reflected image, trying to imagine the way others saw him. There was no question he attracted envy. It came with the territory. He expected it. He was very successful for someone his age, and while luck always played some role in the scheme of things, he had no reason to be surprised at his accomplishments. He didn't believe he was arrogant about it. In his mind false modesty was worse, and he was rarely condescending. He wanted to be liked and respected and he believed only the most self-centered jealous people would wish him ill-will.

But that didn't worry him.

They'll choke in my exhaust, he thought.

What was going to happen today was not that much of a surprise for him. The truth was that he had been anticipating it for some time. Was that arrogant or just self-confidence? For as long as he could remember, he was an outstanding student in high school, successful in sports and in his social life, always making a good impression, looking more mature and responsible. Without his parents pressuring him, he dressed better than his peers and was attentive to his hygiene. In college his concern for his coiffure, the sharp crease of his trousers, and the crispness in his shirts and cuffs drew some ridicule from his classmates. Some even avoided him, distrusted him because of it as if he were some DEA plant or someone the school administration depended upon for inside information about the rumblings in the student body, but he couldn't help himself. He always wanted to look and feel like a real winner.

Maybe it was his maternal grandmother's influence. She lived with them after his grandfather had died, and with his mother working almost full-time, utilizing her accounting skills in his father's modest limousine company, his grandmother pitched in when it came to raising him. She would brush his hair, straighten his shirt, brush off his pants, and make sure his shoes were polished and the laces tied well before she would permit him to leave the house.

"People say you can't judge a book by its cover. Don't believe it, Warner," she told him, her grayish blue eyes taking on that assured look of self-confidence he believed he had inherited from her rather than from his parents. For as long as he could remember, she was the most excited about any of his achievements. "First impressions are full of glue," she told him. "They stick on people's eyes and in their mind, and it's very difficult to get them to change opinions once they have them."

"Right, Grandma," he whispered to his image now. It wasn't the first time he had replayed her words and her looks in his mind and then had spoken to her. Sometimes, he thought he was working harder not to let her down more than he was working for anyone else, including himself, even though she was dead now for nearly ten years. She would never be dead to him.

And today she certainly would be especially proud of him rising to a full partnership after just over seven years at his law firm. Simon and James were afraid they would lose him. They knew other firms were pitching offers at him frequently. He had become something of a New York star as a trial attorney, almost all of his cases high profile, Page One stories. Even the district attorney was trying to get him to change sides. If his grandmother was alive, it would show in her smile, but she would also have that look that said, "I expected no less." She was like that even during her final days when she managed to attend his high school graduation and saw him deliver the Valedictorian address and have his scholarships announced.

He paused. He saw a tiny area on his jaw bone he had missed when shaving and went right to it, running his fingers over his skin searching for any other fugitive strands. He studied his teeth, making a mental note of his next dental cleaning, and then trimmed a little off his right eyebrow.

"I think you spend more time on your appearance than I do," his wife Sheila said from the bathroom doorway. "Don't you know vanity is a sin?"

He had a feeling she had been standing there watching him for a while. She held their daughter Megan's hand and the two looked in at him with almost the same expression, his five-year-old shaking her head with playful criticism scrawled across her face just like it was scrawled across her mother's.

He smiled. His angels.

Megan had Sheila's unique shade of golden-brown hair, borderline blonde, and she had Sheila's Wedgewood blue eyes. Friends called her a clone of her mother and kidded him about having little or nothing to do with her looks, but he saw his smile in his daughter's smile and smiled himself at the way she would study people, squinting a little just as he would do when she was just a little suspicious or skeptical about what someone had said to her.

"Now, now, don't be jealous, you two. Big day ahead," he said. "Gotta look the part."

"When don't you?" Sheila kidded. "I heard George Clooney is using your tailor."

She widened her loving grin, radiating her excitement. Her styled hair was silkily soft, thick and rich. He loved brushing his lips against it and then parting her bangs to plant a kiss on her forehead. Her child-like smile, full of trust and love, always rescued him from disappointment or depression not that either had much of a place in his life and especially not in this home this morning.

He straightened up quickly, taking on the posture of a commanding general.

"How dare you speak this way?" he kidded. "Don't you two know whom it is you are addressing?"

"Wait. Aren't you the attorney who is soon to be a full partner at Simon and James Associates? Four successful high profile defenses in a row the last two years alone, I believe. They know they have a winner and so do we. We're very proud of Daddy, right, Megan."

"He brought home the stars," his daughter said. Everything was measured in stars ever since she had begun attending Kindergarten.

They both laughed.

"Reservations at Le Grenouille?"

"Taken care of," Sheila said. "Just the two of us. I'm not sharing you with anyone tonight."

"Sounds dangerous."

"You have no idea," she said. "Give Daddy a kiss, Megan, and let's go, honey. You don't want to be late for school, and we don't want to make Daddy late for his big day."

Megan shot forward into his arms and Warner picked her up and kissed her after she kissed him. He set her down slowly and she ran back to Sheila. The two looked at him once again. Sheila blew him another kiss to add to the kisses she had given him this morning when they had made love.

"No better way to start celebrating," she had said almost the moment he had opened his eyes.

As they headed for the front door, he smiled to himself recalling every erotic second. From the way his male friends talked about their marriages, he knew his was something special. Passion seemed to be seeping out of his friends' lives the way air deflated from a pinhole in a tire. One day, they'd wake up in a marriage that had flat-lined. But that wasn't going to be true for him and Sheila. No one had a more perfect life.

Once again, he had pangs of guilt because of how confident and successful he felt. Maybe Sheila was right. Maybe it was vanity to believe he deserved it, but once again he reminded himself that he didn't pretend humility well and hated to see it in others. For one thing, it was easy to recognize false modesty, and any dishonesty, no matter how small, annoyed him.

He returned to the mirror and brushed out the small crease in his shirt and then went into the bedroom to put on his grey, pinstriped Armani suit jacket. He had it cleaned and pressed, for weeks anticipating this special day. He was actually getting a little impatient. The two senior partners had no idea just how close they had come to losing him. He paused to look at himself one final time in the full-length mirror.

"Go get 'em Murphy," he told himself. It was the same little cheer he muttered before taking an important exam in college and now stepping into a courtroom. With his smile of satisfaction and pride frozen on his face, he started out and turned left in the hallway to go to his den-office to get his briefcase.

They had a twentieth floor, two-bedroom apartment in one of East New York's more prestigious buildings. From the soft furnishings, to the elegant curtains and subtle but expensive accouterments that included the Lladro porcelain figurine collection, Sheila had done a great job of decorating, keeping it warm and cozy despite its size, marble floors and high ceilings. The area rugs were almost half his starting salary, a salary he had more than quadrupled, but he was proud that despite the luxurious upper East Side New York building with its private security and attentive maintenance, their jewelry and expensive watches, their designer clothing, their first class European and Caribbean vacations, there was nothing pretentious about them. Sheila was too grounded for that.

Like him, she had come from modest beginnings. Her parents had a successful, but small continental restaurant in the Hamptons. She was only in the sophomore year in NYU downtown when they had met that summer. He had just begun his career. If luck played any real part in his life, it was that decision he and two friends had made to stop at her family restaurant. She worked summers as a hostess. Her older sister was already married to a local dentist. He and Sheila had a storybook romance after that and once they were married, they had soared together, love birds embraced by the clouds of glory and success.

Was it possible to be happier, to be more self-satisfied? Really . . . was it arrogant to feel this way? This fear was haunting him more than usual this morning, but he was determined not to feel guilty about it, especially today. Besides, he was certainly no Icarus. He had no wings held together with wax and wasn't reaching for a heaven too high. Everything he was achieving was sensible, logical, but most important, deserved.

Just as he picked up his briefcase, the door buzzer sounded. He paused. She couldn't have left without her key, could she? Wouldn't be the first time, he thought, shook his head and called out as he walked toward the front door.

"Coming. What did you forget?" he sang.

It had to be Sheila and Megan. No one else in the building would be visiting this early and certainly not without first calling. They really weren't that friendly with the other tenants anyway. Certainly none of them would know about his impending promotion. They would be reading about it and afterward might offer him and Sheila congratulations, but there wasn't any woman or wife in the building with whom she sought close friendship.

Any guests or visitors coming from outside the building were announced first by the security in the lobby. In fact, there was a video image of them sent to the apartment's intercom that had a six-inch screen and the owner had to send back his or her approval before the visitor could get into the elevator. Everyone's image was kept on file with the time of arrival. The building's lobby had as many CCTV cameras as the lobby of a bank. He prided himself on the building's security and told friends, "We're safer than the gold in Fort Knox."

He went through the living room to the foyer and was surprised when he opened the door to face a tall, stout baldheaded man in a dark-blue special delivery man's uniform. It was a bit ornate with gold epaulets and gold cuffs. No matter how well he was dressed, however, this was disturbing. Whatever he was bringing, even a congratulatory note from someone at the firm or in his family, it should have been left at the desk in the lobby or a call up to him should have occurred to tell him something had to be signed with delivery. He didn't want to get Charlie Bivens, the morning receptionist, fired, especially today, but he would definitely lodge a complaint about this before he left for work. Details were always important to him. Success required it. As his grandmother would recite, *For want of a nail the shoe was lost.*

"Yes?" he said, not trying to hide his now quite visible annoyance.

The man didn't respond. His face seemed made of granite. Nothing moved, not his lips, not his eyes, and in fact his grayish brown eyebrows looked penciled on or embellished with some sort of eyebrow makeup. He reached into his oversize trouser pocket, took out a Pachmayr forty-five with a combat grip and pointed it at Warner, who had never been comfortable with guns. The forty-five looked like a small canon to him.

"What the hell . . ."

He felt his fingers weaken like five melting icicles and the briefcase drop to the floor.

"Move to the patio," the man said in a deep voice that seemed to come from somewhere below his chest. It was more like an echo.

"What is this? Who are you?"

Was it some sort of sophisticated robbery? He didn't care about the small amount of cash in the house, or even the jewelry. What more could the guy take? He appeared to be alone, but how could this happen in this building? Whatever he was planning, he would never get away with it.

"I want you to see something," the man said and waved the pistol. "I'm not going to ask twice. The next time I'll splatter most of you over the walls."

Because he deliberately spoke out of the right corner of his mouth, he sounded like someone trying to imitate a film noir gangster. Nevertheless, Warner felt the cold chill at the back of his neck, backed up and watched the man enter, closing the door softly behind him. He waved the gun again to indicate he wanted him walking to the patio.

"Let's go. Move it."

"What for? I don't understand this."

"You object? I know you're a lawyer, but it's not a request of the judge. I give the orders in this court. Move."

He had the gun pointed right at Warner's heart. There was suddenly the scent of burnt wood. It came from the man's hair and skin and it was a little nauseating. The coldness in his eyes seemed to chill the very air around them. He felt a small trembling start in his knees and move into his stomach. Reluctantly, he took a few steps toward the patio.

The man stepped forward and opened the patio door.

"After you," he said with only the suggestion of a smile. It was more like a sneer.

Warner stepped back.

"What is this? We're twenty flights up? What am I supposed to see? I'm not taking a step farther until you explain." He did everything he could to sound firm.

The man suddenly warmed his smiled and brought light into his coal black eyes.

"Maybe it's a banner in the sky." He looked at his watch. "Hurry."

"Huh? A banner in the sky?"

Was this man part of some sort of practical joke tied into the firm's way of congratulating him? What else could it be?

"Whose idea was this?" he demanded, now feeling brave enough to raise his voice. "The secretaries?" Maybe it was some of his friends from other firms. He knew one or two who were capable of something like this and who would enjoy hearing about how he almost pissed in his pants. "It's not funny."

"Sorry," the man said in a far softer tone of voice. He shrugged. "Don't get upset. I take my part seriously." He put his pistol back in his pocket. "It's a fake anyway," he added. "A stage prop I used in a play last month."

"Stupid," Warner said shaking his head. "Childish, in fact." He was still trembling a little from the shock of it, and he hated the fact that someone, part of a joke or not, had filled him with such deadly fear. "Someone's going to hear about this."

"Sorry I was so convincing. Maybe I'm a better actor than I think."

"Whatever," Warner said. "I don't find it funny. What if my wife and child were still home?"

"Oh, I waited."

"What?"

"We thought it was a little too PG-13 for your daughter so I waited for them to leave."

"It's not PG-13 or R. It's S, for stupid," Warner said, now assuming the tone of a trial lawyer pressing home his argument.

The man shrugged.

"Still, you don't want to miss it," he said, "and chances are, your wife and daughter will see it from below."

Unable not to be curious now, Warner stepped out on the patio and gazed around at the almost clear, New York spring sky. There were just a few clouds that resembled someone's puffed breath in freezing weather.

"So? Where do I look?" he asked, not hiding his irritation. He wasn't in the mood for any forgiveness.

"Turn right," the man said.

Warner turned right, but saw nothing unusual, nothing happening. There were just a few more clouds. He shook his head.

"Look, I . . ." he started to say, but was interrupted when he suddenly felt the man's arms around his legs from the knees down. The grasp was steely tight and in fact, slapped his legs together so hard and fast, his knees stung.

"What the hell . . ."

He was quickly lifted higher than the railing. Besides being embarrassed at how easily he was being lifted, he was absolutely shocked. A fist of panic closed around his heart. He pushed down on the man's shoulders to break free, but to no avail. In fact, his action only helped lift him higher.

"Let go of me!" he cried, squirming and feeling foolish. The man was handling him as if he was half of what he weighed and had a child's muscles. Pounding on his head didn't seem to bother him either. He hit him as hard as he could in the left temple, but it didn't even make him twitch and it felt like he had broken his hand. The panic brought more blood to his face as he was listed higher and higher. "What do you think you're doing?"

"Seeing if you can fly," the man said and threw him over the railing as easily as tossing a penny.

1.

John Milton was casually leaning against his black stretch limousine, his arms folded across his chest, looking up at Warner Murphy's building. He saw him flailing in the air like a wounded bird and begin his rapid descent. With all the traffic and usual noise, no one could hear his screams, no one but John that was.

"There's a fall worse than the descent into hell," he whispered. His ebony black eyes turned a shade of ruby as a soft smile rippled across his perfectly shaped, strong lips. His rich, light caramel complexion looked metallic in the late May morning sunshine. Although his hair was thick and richly ebony, it was the shade of burned wood in the sunlight. When he moved into shadows or darkness, his hair became more like his eyes, ruby.

Warner's body splattered like an egg on the roof of a parked S-class Mercedes sedan, blowing out some side windows that then exploded on the street and sidewalk. The shards danced like spilled diamonds over the pavement. It was the Mercedes that ironically was to take him to the office. Well, maybe not so ironic, John thought.

People walking on the sidewalk screamed, cowered or leaped up like they had stepped onto a bed of fire and then ran, assuming it was some terrorist bombing. The brakes of taxis and other automobiles screeched like a flock of wounded geese just peppered with the buckshot of gleeful hunters. Miraculously, there were no accidents, but the subsequent shouting of drivers and pedestrians resembled a chorus of mental clinic inmates ripped out of the comfort of their own quiet insanity and pushed into each other on a busy New York street.

John smiled at Charon, his Egyptian driver, when he came out of the coffee shop with two take-out lattes, holding them up as if they were torches for a parade.

"You missed it," he told him. Charon handed him his latte.

They both stood there gazing at the commotion, the shouts and screams intensifying as otherwise oblivious New Yorkers were now rushing to get a look and more people realized what had happened. The Mercedes driver had stepped out of the vehicle and was so shocked that he was having trouble keeping his balance. He looked drunk. He was certainly over the limit when it came to distress and fright. It brought a bigger crowd.

Voyeurism always pleased John Milton. It was like icing on a cake. It forever confirmed for him that evil, destruction and violence were fascinating for people, something that had long, long ago convinced him he couldn't lose. He smiled at Charon.

Charon was just under six feet five with wide, firm shoulders that strained the threads of his uniform jacket. He had a face that looked molded out of grayish brown clay, the face of a golem. He was a soulless shell with lifeless brownish-black eyes. Because of the glow behind them, they resembled two pinholes in the wall of castle Pandemonium inside of which flames burned eternally. One look at him and any observer would conclude those eyes had never reflected a moment of repentance, an ounce of regret or compassion. They were eyes that had grown accustomed to violence. They were orbs of indifference. Nothing surprised him or upset him. He didn't even blink.

"Not bad," John said after taking a sip of his coffee and holding up the cup. "I'll have to remember this café."

Charon said nothing. He didn't even nod. He continued to stare at the commotion and drink his latte, whereas John Milton's face was enflamed with excitement and pleasure. Off to the right they could hear the mournful scream of a police siren growing louder and then another and another resembling a chorus of the sleeping dead jolted into an undesired resurrection. A fire engine jetted out of its garage nearby, moaning like a Medieval beast of fantasy abruptly disturbed in its cave. More pedestrians snapped out of their robotic morning trek to work and turned toward or walked faster now toward the gruesome scene playing itself out like the final reel of some all too familiar movie.

Death in the city, all cities, was far more common than rural and suburban areas. It had the same instantaneous terrifying effect on witnesses as it did elsewhere, but because it was so ordinary here, even a violent death, it was practically shrugged off moments later. After all, traffic and business demanded attention, and like some impatient and aggravated snake, twisted and turned until it was back into the flow, the slow moving vehicles now trickling through the streets like spilled blood.

John brushed down the front of his navy stretch wool two-button suit jacket and tugged gently on his black tie. His black onyx ring seemed to catch a wandering ray of sunlight and glittered back at the mostly sunny sky as if rejecting it. He looked up but he didn't squint. To him the small puffs of clouds to the east looked like they had paused in their monotonous journey from one horizon to another so they could look curiously down at the shenanigans of these earthly creatures foolishly set loose on the world.

"Don't tell me Death has no sting," John told Charon and laughed. Charon continued to stare ahead and sip some more of his latte silently.

The special delivery man who had visited Murphy suddenly appeared in front of Warner Murphy's building, looked in John Milton's direction, and then started away. By the time he reached the South West corner of the block, he began to evaporate. Before he turned, he had completely disappeared.

John sighed.

"How wondrous are my works."

He looked at Charon who evinced the first signs of seeing and hearing by nodding slightly.

"Something like this puts me in the mood to cruise," John said. "But we have an appointment, do we not? We always have an appointment. Business is brisker than it's ever been, and I'm including the Middle Ages in my estimation. I'm actually overworked, but whom would I complain to, Charon?"

Charon nodded again and opened the door for him. Then he got in, put the coffee down in the holder at his side and started the engine.

"One more moment," John Milton commanded and gazed out at the first responders moving like ants around a glob of honey. "Death be proud for thou art mighty and dreadful," he recited, rewriting the famous poem by John Donne. "Okay, Charon. Onward. You just don't appreciate my sense of humor. I'm wasting my hot breath."

The limousine softly entered the flow of traffic and turned left at the first traffic light. As they made their way cross-town, John flicked on his stereo and began to play Carl Orff's Camina Burana. He watched the pedestrians and traffic through his tinted windows.

When they reached Eighth Avenue, they started downtown. The contrast between the properties here and on the upper East Side was stark. He looked out of his window like a visitor from another planet, amazed at the seemingly aimless movement of some people, the sprawling homeless bubbling in doorways or sprawled on graffiti scared benches, the occasional alcoholic clutching his bottle in a paper bag like some Neanderthal grasping precious rocks or bones, and the small knots of unwashed youth unfolding like fists up and down the sidewalks and moving in and out of people, knocking and bumping, resembling explorers searching for some reason to keep traveling.

Off in the distance, the trail of a military jet cut a seam in the blue sky.

John saw it through the moon roof and smiled.

"I'm back where I belong," he said. "Thank you for making it all possible."

His laughter, much louder now, trailed behind him like smoke and like smoke was caught in an uplifting breeze, it rose to the fifth floor of an apartment building, seeped through the opening in a bedroom window and woke Stoker Martin who groaned and slapped at the rays of sunlight jetting into his dingy bedroom like sharp darts, stinging his face and bare chest. He sat up quickly, coughed, choking on some sticky phlegm and looked over at Tanya Green. His ex-wife's hairdresser was always good for another New Year's Eve, as he put it. He had a lot to celebrate. It would take him, even with his wasteful ways and off-track betting, a good, long while to spend the money he had earned with two quick movements of his trusty right trigger finger recently.

He had been suspicious about this particular offer when it came. It sounded too good being nearly double his usual fee. How did this obviously very wealthy client find him? To be more specific, how did he or she find or know Skip who brought him the gig? He was always curious about that. How well known was he and what risks did that information out there bring him? When he voiced some concern because the amount of money actually frightened him, Skip came up with what he had to admit was a very clever way of protecting himself.

"Your employer will be waiting for you when you come out of the building," he said. "He's an asshole who wants to be sure you've earned your money. You'd think he'd avoid being seen with you."

"I don't like that, Skip. I like being anonymous. That's why I work with you."

"Right, except I came up with something I've advised done before with some of my other mechanics."

"And what's that?" Stoker asked.

"When you come out, you give him your pistol."

"Huh? Why?"

"Tell him he has to hold it for you. You wipe it clean, even the bullets. If he doesn't wipe it afterward, he's prints will be on the weapon."

"Oh."

"And he'll have it in his possession. If he ever gets picked up or accused and tries to lessen his involvement by fingering you, he's got a problem. He has the gun and he was at the scene of the crime."

"Not bad, Skip. Thanks. Good thinking."

"That's what I'm paid to do, good thinking."

Stoker nodded. Everyone was more than a little paranoid and rightly so. Skip was as D and D as the next guy. Deaf and dumb was as natural to the gang, as he liked to think of his shadowy friends, as natural to them as breathing.

Relaxing now, he lay back and smiled to himself. It always amazed him how his own thoughts amused him. The gang? How could he call these guys that? When would he stop being a teenager? Never, probably. He recognized that being a loner all his life, he secretly hungered for trustworthy friends, buddies, and especially a best friend. He couldn't even find that in a wife, but realizing that fact convinced him that selfishness was good and morality was an illusion imposed on the stupid.

When he took the time to really think about it as he was doing now, he realized that even the legitimate work he attempted for nearly eight years was lonely. He was naturally drawn to all things desolate and isolated. His one great accomplishment, besides his talent with weapons, was acquiring the skill and the license to drive the gas tanker, but the work meant hours on the road alone and stopping to eat at roadside restaurants, alone. He was talking aloud to himself all the time, and sometimes, even when he was among other people, he would slip and voice his thoughts aloud. It was pretty damn depressing having only yourself as a real friend, but who else could he trust?

Tanya groaned.

"Pull down the shade," she muttered. "Shit, Jesus, Stoker, what is it, six or something?"

He glanced at the clock on his night table.

"Nearly nine," he said.

She had her head buried under the blanket. Her legs were exposed up to the knees. Why in hell would you tattoo the back of your calves? Why would you tattoo any part of yourself you couldn't see easily? And her tattoos . . . lizards crawling up. It was creepy. What was worse than looking at the broad you were with the morning after? Mornings were slaps in the face as far as he was concerned. Fantasies, good dreams, and all the hope you harvested the night before and expected to fulfill the next day all popped like an overheated light bulb. Disappointment put the taste of the crust of burnt bread in his mouth.

He tugged roughly on the blanket, exposing Tanya's naked butt and then wacked it so hard, his palm stung. She cried out, her curses unleashed like damned up muddy water breaking free and rushing in every direction. He laughed.

"I'm getting up," he said. "I need a shower."

"You need more than a shower," she muttered. "You need sandpaper."

"Ha, ha."

He scrubbed his cheeks with his palms and walked to the window to look down at the Street of Scum, as he referred to it. "So why the hell don't you pick up and move out?" He asked himself in a loud whisper. "To where? Beverly Hills? Worth Avenue, El Paseo?" He knew all the high-priced, upscale famous streets, but he felt uncomfortable there, felt like a stranger, an illegal immigrant whenever he walked through any of them.

He had left home at seventeen and hadn't spoken to his parents for nearly twenty years. He didn't even know if either or both of them were alive. From time to time, he wondered about his younger brother Wade. He'd be twenty-two now. What could have become of him? He wasn't retarded. They called it something else, auto testic or something. He remembered the way he would look at him sometimes and wonder, do I have something wrong with me, too? Something not so easily seen?

Stoker never had much faith in his genes. His father was always struggling to make ends meet, even as a plumber with all the stories about plumbers getting such high fees. His mother worked odd jobs, sometimes in the public school cafeteria and sometimes in the local diner, both of them looking shop worn around the dinner table. They were aging so fast that it was frightening. It was like taking a meal with a pair of zombies. In the end what was he running away from? "Nothing much," he told himself. He had no regrets. "I have no regrets," he said.

"What?" Tina asked, turning to look at him. She had heard his loud whispers. "What are you mumbling about? You're always talking to yourself, and why the fuck are you standing there naked by the window? Anyone looking up from the street will see you."

"Who gives a shit?" he replied and went to take his shower.

In the bathroom, he stood before the mirror for a few moments and looked at himself. His face seemed to metamorphose into the shocked face of the man he had killed a week and a half ago. He saw the whole scene being replayed in his mirror as if it was a television screen. He had slipped into the building and then easily gotten into the apartment. There was his mark relaxing in his soft easy chair in this plush living room of expensive furniture and carpets, art that belonged in museums on the walls, cabinets of expensive crystal and one helluva nice media tower. He was listening to some classical music that to Stoker sounded like one note monotonously repeated. Classical music, except for that one with the cannons firing, always annoyed him.

The man wore a burgundy smoking jacket and had a tumbler of Scotch or something in his hand. His brown and gray hair was stylistically cut and he looked like he had a perfect tan. It was like destroying a work of art, Stoker vaguely thought. What was he, fifty-five, maybe sixty?

"What the hell . . ." the soon-to-be dead rich man said. "Who are you? How did you get in here?"

"Special delivery," he replied sounding serious. He loved it when he could use that line and loved the confusion on their faces. Could it be special delivery?

"What?"

There was nothing else to say. He pumped two thirty-eights into his handsome and otherwise contented face and then left the way he came, touching little even with his gloved hands. And how about those plastic bags over his shoes? Was that a brilliant move or what? He had seen the forensic unit wearing them on a television show recently.

He took them off outside of the elevator and slipped out of the building through a basement entrance. Outside, he came face to face with his employer as previously arranged. The guy looked like he was going to pass out. His lips were trembling so badly that Stoker thought he was freezing despite the warm temperature. He was dressed in a suit and tie and looked like he had just come from a business meeting.

"Mr. Martin? Skip sent me," he added as if that was those were the passwords.

"So?" he said.

"Is it done?" he asked.

"I didn't come here to play bridge," Stoker told him. "Here," he said. He was still wearing the gloves. The man looked at the weapon.

"I don't understand."

"You hold onto this, see. I'll come by for it in a few weeks."

He shoved the gun into his hands. The idiot almost dropped it.

"But . . ."

"Just do what you told."

"This is the actual gun?"

"What the fuck do you think it's a replica? Be careful with it. It's got a hair-trigger. You'll shoot off your dick."

He slipped away, clinging to the shadows and didn't even look back.

The scene shrunk into a pinhole and disappeared in the mirror.

Funny, how he remembered all the details of this hit more vividly than the others. Was that a sign of something? Could he have a conscience, after all?

He turned on the shower. It took a damn two full minutes to run warm enough to get into it.

"Why the hell do you stay here in this hell hole?" he asked himself. In the shower he muttered and complained to himself about other details in his life as well. His complaints were flowing as quickly as the water, a constant stream of regrets and accusations that went as far back as the day he was born. At this point it had become at least a weekly chant.

"You know, you're fucking crazy," Tanya said getting in beside him. "I mean that literally," she added reaching for his dick. "You fuck like crazy."

He laughed.

The sound of it reminded him of something . . . the laugh he had heard in his sleep.

The laugh that had woken him.

It came . . . from somewhere deep inside him . . . very deep inside him and it wasn't his laugh either. It was if there was someone else in there, someone else laughing and mumbling a stream of raucous thoughts, the stuff of which nightmares were made.

He wanted to squeeze and squeeze himself until all of it oozed out of his ears, mouth and nose, and left him white as a sheet flapping in the wind.

2.

Lieutenant Matthew Blake paused just inside the doorway of Warner and Sheila Murphy's apartment and closed his eyes immediately. His body swayed a little. He seemed to be saying a silent prayer. Detective John Fish nearly walked into him. He had gotten out of the elevator and followed Blake, but had his head down, thinking about the building's layout and security system.

From what they already had determined viewing recorded video of the lobby taken just before Warner Murphy's death, no one had entered the building other than receptionist Charlie Bivens to replace the night receptionist. The mailman hadn't arrived yet and the only people visible were residents leaving the property. The only anomaly was a five second black out on the lobby that Bivens said related to the computer shifting tracks. When measured against everything else, it didn't seem significant.

Fish so wanted to impress Lieutenant Blake with some new idea, lead or brilliant insight from the moment that he had been assigned to partner with him two weeks ago. In the NYPD, Matthew Blake was as famous as Sherlock Holmes when it came to his determination to solve crimes and bring down the evil that occurred in New York City. Fish knew that Matthew Blake had turned down promotions that would take him off the streets. Obviously, he enjoyed the work, the contact with people, and oddly enough, especially with victims. It didn't take Fish long to realize that Matthew Blake had a passion for solving crimes and bringing some closure to those who suffered a loss. Other members of the department Fish had met said Saint. Matthew, as they referred to him, had a religious fervor about solving crime. They warned him that Saint. Matthew kept a maddening pace.

Blake's last partner, Peter Thomas, had been a career man who had reached retirement age and opted for it, even though no one was pressuring him to step aside. All Fish knew was something dramatic had recently occurred and, although he wouldn't admit it or describe it, it spooked him. Some claimed he was on the verge of a nervous breakdown. He wasn't burned out. He was more like someone who wanted to leave through the fire escape and not the front door.

Lieutenant Blake wouldn't talk about it. Matter of fact, he wouldn't talk about anything personal or relating to other members of the division. Sometimes, it seemed as if he believed in was in a special division of his own.

Whatever his problems were, Fish thought when he heard about Peter Thomas abrupt departure, doesn't really matter to me. One man's problem is another man's opportunity or we wouldn't have doctors and lawyers, he had concluded gleefully; and opportunity, despite all the progress and inroads, was still not as available for African Americans or came at a much slower pace. He thought it, but would never voice it. Whiners and complainers didn't win much sympathy in a world where the ugliest actions of humanity were too often seen and felt. There was too much other injustice.

He nodded at the patrolman standing guard outside the door, who was also looking curiously at Lieutenant Blake. The long pause registered like a piano out of tune. It actually spooked him a little.

Blake seemed to shudder. He still hesitated. Both he and Fish had put on their plastic gloves and covered their shoes. Forensics was on their way. It didn't surprise Fish that they had beaten them to the apartment. The body had been taken to the morgue, and it was an unusually busy morning, two definite homicides, an armed robbery, and two rapes before noon in their precinct. Blake had muttered that it seemed it was raining down on them today, as if evil came in storm waves like the weather. He sounded like he literally meant it. He even had looked up as if he expected to see some unusual dark cloud hovering over the city.

"Something wrong, Lieutenant?" Fish asked. Matthew turned and looked at him as if he had just said the dumbest thing uttered anywhere, anytime. "I mean . . ."

"Relax, Fish. It's not going away."

"What?"

"The homicide," Matthew said nodding at the inside of the apartment.

"We don't know yet that it's a homicide," Fish offered meekly. "Do we, Lieutenant? If anything, on first look, it seems like suicide."

Had he missed something? Fish wondered.

Matthew Blake glanced at him again, this time with a stone cold expression.

"Taking your own life is still a homicide," he replied and finally stepped into the apartment. Fish shrugged at the patrolman who looked a little uncomfortable to say the least and then followed Blake in.

Anyone listening to the tone in his voice and seeing the expression on his face, might think Lieutenant Matthew Blake had resented John Fish replacing Peter Thomas, but from what Fish had experienced so far, he wasn't prepared to say Lieutenant Blake was hesitant about accepting him at his side. Admittedly, he wasn't overly enthusiastic about it. If Fish could characterize it at all, it would be an expression of indifference. It was as if whether he or anyone was there or not didn't matter much in Lieutenant Blake's view of things. He could almost hear him think the same word he had thought when he was told about Peter Thomas, "Whatever."

Fish wondered if Blake had even read his resume. The quality or experience of the proposed partner seemed to be of no concern. It was like putting another handkerchief in your pocket or something to replace the one that had been lost or put in the laundry.

Other officers in the division had already briefed Fish about Matthew Blake. Despite his success, there was something about him that irked many of them. Matter of fact, when they referred to him as St. Matthew, it sounded derogatory. They almost had Fish reconsidering whether or not it really was an opportunity to be partnered with him, despite his stellar record. No one could explain it in any terms that made sense to him. The closest anyone came, and it was sort of ridiculous, was Deputy Inspector Cullen telling him, "Blake has some psychic powers. It's not what you would call hunches or even a sixth sense. He seems plugged into something none of the rest of us are.

"But, it hasn't hurt anyone," he quickly added.

"You just wonder what the hell he does for excitement. The guy's thirty-four. He's not gay. He hasn't been involved with any man, but he hasn't been involved with any woman for the last four years either as far as I know. The man lives and breathes the job. He's the best example of a police vampire, someone who feeds on crime day or night. That's what Peter Thomas used to say. He swore the man never sleeps. So get whatever sleep you can."

"We checked the video replay, Lieutenant," Fish offered right after they had entered the apartment. "No nonresident can use the elevator without the receptionist green-lighting at the approval of a tenant, and all tenants have a special elevator key no matter what floor they are on. The receptionist claims that he didn't unlock the elevator for any guest before Murphy plunged to his death. He has to activate the button for the floor of the tenant they want to visit after the tenant approves them," Fish continued, checking off the points on his pad as Blake turned slowly and studied the apartment before looking back at him. "We viewed the tape to confirm what he said."

Blake knew all that. Fish was still impressed with the building's security system. "Never seen such security. It's more like a maximum security prison."

He looked up, expecting at least a nod. Blake was six feet two, broad shouldered, but lean and hard. He always walked with a steely spine and sat erect, head high. He hadn't been with him that long, but Fish had never seen him slouch. In fact, he never looked tired or bored. His energy was always under control. He reeked of efficiency which only made Fish more self-conscious about himself. At five feet eleven and a half and nearly one-hundred ninety pounds, John Fish wasn't insecure, but there was just something about Lieutenant Blake that made him feel smaller when he was beside him, even dreadfully inexperienced. Suddenly, he was walking straighter and was sucking in his stomach. He made a mental note to get himself into the gym more often.

But Lieutenant Blake's most striking feature was his eyes. He had piercing green eyes, extraordinary eyes that when he fixed them on someone, he seemed to look beneath that person's skin and into his or her very brain. Fish had learned that Blake was a master at interrogation. The hardest suspects acted like he made their skin crawl and not vice versa.

"He has instincts that ain't been discovered yet," Cullen had added to his description. It wasn't really a critical analysis. His voice was full of admiration, even some envy, Fish recalled. Actually, in the end, it reinforced his desire to be Blake's partner. So Lieutenant Blake worked hard and sincerely cared about victims of crime. So what? We should all work harder and have compassion, he thought. He was confident he would learn many things working with Blake, things he didn't know or more important, didn't realize that he didn't know.

"We checked the service entrance video, too, and no one entered that way all morning. I mean, what are you thinking? If there is a perp, he lives in the building?" Fish continued when Blake didn't even nod. Matthew's dark red eyebrows lifted. Fish thought it meant he had made a good suggestion. Finally.

"Possibly," he said. "Although . . . it feels like something else, Fish."

What the hell did that mean? Fish gazed around. Feels like something else? Nothing was disturbed in the luxurious apartment. It looked like it had just been cleaned. Everything was so neat and organized. There wasn't even a magazine out of place. It was a showcase. He ran what they knew through his mind. Once Murphy's wife had been notified of his death, she had not returned to the apartment. She had passed out and was taken to the hospital emergency room. Their daughter had been picked up by Sheila Murphy's parents and was with them at the hospital or at their Manhattan apartment by now. So no one else had been in this apartment since the death. What was it that Blake saw or felt that gave him the idea it was something more?

"What am I missing, Lieutenant? Why does it feel like something more?"

"Coincidence," Blake said.

"Coincidence? What coincidence?"

Lieutenant Blake didn't answer. He walked slowly, so slowly, through the apartment to the still opened patio door that it was as if he was tracing steps only he could see or something. He paused at the door, looked back at Fish, and then stepped out on the patio. For a while he just stood there looking out at the city. Fish approached him, standing just inside. He was a little acrophobic, maybe because at the age of two, he fell out a first floor window. Even though he had landed on a bed of newly piled leaves, it still had been terrifying. Your home was supposed to be a vessel of safety.

"You know what always bugs me about all this, John?" Matthew Blake said still looking out at the city, his voice taking on an entirely new tone, more like the tone of a young man in a state of wonder.

"What?"

"That no matter how terrible the incident is, whatever we're investigating, the city goes on as if nothing's changed. There's barely a hiccup. It's like it all glances at the crime, the victims, and then turns back to whatever. . . . I mean, except for the family of the victims and sometimes close friends, no one seems to notice crime. Oh, we have the cable networks concentrating on this or that horrendous act infinitum, but that's almost become nothing more than another television show to capture ratings. Makes it all pretty impersonal and for me, unreal.

"That receptionist downstairs, for example," he continued, "probably knew Murphy well enough to be a little disturbed and upset enough to bring up his breakfast when he saw him splattered on a car roof, but he's going to have his lunch and dinner and do whatever he does as if nothing's changed today. Maybe that's why evil has the upper hand."

Fish just stared. Was he supposed to contribute to this philosophical rant? Blake looked at him.

"Ever think about any of this, Fish?" he asked.

"Not like that," Fish said. "I suppose . . . you're right," he added, but he wasn't sure what Blake was right about.

Blake nodded and studied the railing. Then he touched it and Fish saw him close his eyes as if he were trying to draw up a vision. Was this what Cullen meant when he said he was plugged into something the rest of us weren't? It was weird all right. He couldn't help feeling a little uncomfortable. He looked back to see if the officer at the door was watching. He wasn't.

"He was struggling," Blake said. "But we don't have to wait for forensics. Check this out."

He looked back when Fish hesitated so Fish moved quickly onto the patio and looked at the railing. What the hell was he supposed to see? He shook his head.

"There's nothing unusual there. It looks recently polished."

"Exactly, Fish," Blake said. "No scuff marks, no sign of any shoes on these rungs. They're pretty clean. He didn't climb up and over. This railing is too high for someone to accidentally fall over it. Even a man that tall has to work a little at it."

"So you think he was thrown over?"

Blake continued to look out as if the answer was in the sky or something.

"He is or was a pretty big guy," Fish added. "Not the easiest man to heave over a railing this high."

"Exactly. Whoever did this had to lift him at least six feet or so. Imagine what such a man might look like." He looked around the patio and back at the door. "There's no sign of a struggle in this part of the apartment and nothing out here. No bleeding, nothing. It's all pristine," Blake said. "But he was thrown over," he insisted. "He was drawn to the patio or forced to it someway without disturbing a thread on the furniture in that living room. What happened to him had to have the element of surprise."

Fish nodded. At the moment, he couldn't think of any reason not to agree.

"What did you mean back there when you said coincidence?"

"Before you came on, Peter and I investigated a murder about a dozen blocks from here. We made an arrest. The trial is supposed to be held next month."

"So?"

"This victim, Warner Murphy, he was the defendant's attorney."

Fish just stared for a moment and then shook his head.

"That's amazing, but what's one thing have to do with another? Unless you think the district attorney was afraid he'd lose the case because of this Murphy and had him killed. You don't think that, do you?" He didn't mean to sound facetious but it came out that way. "I mean, I suppose someone who liked or even loved the victim hated Warner Murphy for defending the accused killer, but . . ."

"I don't know what to think yet, Fish, but what I've learned in life is that there's no such thing as a coincidence."

Fish didn't want to disagree, but Blake wasn't making any sense to him.

"Well, if you suspect something foul, I guess we should start on the other residents. See who knew him and who didn't."

"Yeah," Blake said. He shook his head. "But I don't think it will lead to anything."

How the hell did he know that? Fish thought.

"Why not? We've pretty much established that no one came up here through the lobby. If you think he was murdered, it has to be someone already in the building, doesn't it? Who else could get up to this floor? They'd have to slip past the receptionist and the CCTV and have that special elevator key. I'll review the video of the elevators. I guess another resident could have used the stairway."

"Maybe," Matthew Blake said, but he still didn't sound like he believed even in the possibility.

"Well . . ."

Blake turned as if he just remembered Fish was there.

"Go on. Check it all out. I'm going to dig around at his law agency and later see if I can talk to his in-laws and maybe his wife at the hospital, although that might have to wait. Call me if you come across anything interesting."

"Right."

Blake started out and then stopped and suddenly started to look at everything more closely. He went into both bedrooms and the kitchen and dining room before joining Fish who waited in the entryway.

"What?" Fish asked. Blake had a look on his face that suggested he had discovered something. "Were there signs of some struggle in another room?"

"No. But there's not a religious icon hanging on any wall in this house or on any shelf, not a cross, nothing," he said.

"Maybe they wear it around their necks. I do," he said showing his cross.

"I don't think so," Blake said. "I suspect religion is not important to them."

"Not unusual these days, Lieutenant. At least not organized religion."

"No, not unusual."

Then why mention it at all? Fish thought, but didn't say. What did that have to do with the man's death anyway? He wanted to ask, but couldn't. Blake was already out the door as if he had stumbled on a hot lead and for the life of him, Fish couldn't think of anything even remotely resembling one.

3.

Michele Armstrong paused in front of the entrance to 1 Hogan place and took a deep breath, as deep a breath as a high diver might take before leaping and soaring off the board. It was really the way she felt. She had been on the New York County District Attorney's team for more than three weeks, but she still couldn't shake off the feeling every morning that this was her first day on the job. It still had that new car scent. Everything, no matter how old it really was, looked and felt crisp and new to her, whether it was her desk, her phone or her computer.

After graduating from Cornell University and the New York University School of Law, Michele went to work for the Orange County, New York District Attorney's office and lived with her parents who had a refurbished farm house in Goshen, New York. She racked up a half dozen impressive convictions of violent criminals, two homicides in five years, and was recruited by the New York District Attorney. It was a stage upon which she always dreamed she'd play.

Michele's driving ambition always amazed and amused her mother, who had taught grade school for twenty years and as soon as she was eligible for retirement without penalty, took it. She often talked about being a lady of leisure as if it was genetic to the sex. Michele's mother wasn't always like that. She had started out ambitious and dedicated, but hardened, grew more cynical, and although proud of Michele's accomplishments, never hid her hope that Michele would marry well and calm down. Calm down meant stop pursuing your career as though there was nothing else worthwhile in life.

"Half the women you know and will know will resent you for being successful as well more than half of the men."

"We're not Islamic fundamentalists, Mom," she countered. Her mother shrugged.

"Most of those women don't complain, at least half of the ones I know."

Frustrated, Michele avoided arguments the way anyone would avoid a traffic jam. She looked for detours into new subjects, often so unimportant that she barely listened to her mother's comments. Why couldn't her mother look at her as something more than just another woman? Parents didn't look at their sons as just another man.

Nothing's changed since Adam and Eve walked out of Paradise and started the fashion industry, she concluded. She always liked to conclude a serious subject with a dry or sarcastic joke. In that way, she wasn't unlike her father. He was a master at moving smoothly from deeply serious topics to light, satirical subjects. His automobile customers loved it.

When it came to her career ambitions, her father never discouraged her. However, she would admit that he didn't pressure her to do any more or less. Wherever she settled, at whatever level, he would be satisfied. He owned and operated a successful Chevrolet dealership just outside of Middletown, New York, and at time seemed as married to that as he was to her mother, and as much a parent to his employees as he was to her and her brother.

Her younger brother Bailey worked with their father and just recently had gotten married to Amanda Morris, a girl in his high school class he had pursued unsuccessfully when they were younger. She had married her high school sweetheart a year after graduation, but divorced just under six months later and then had gone to Albany Business College. Soon after, with the help of some of her own father's influential friends, she landed a management position at New York State Electric and Gas. It wasn't long before Bailey started dating her. Michele was just warming up to her, wary that her brother might have been running on the steam of his high school crush and taken on more baggage than he knew.

However, none of that could hold her attention now. She had moved into the city rather than do an hour or so commute, and although she could afford a good apartment, had decided, when she was invited, to live with her aunt Eve, her mother's eccentric older sister, widowed with no children. Her mother didn't think she'd last a week living with her older sister. These days they rarely saw each other. Although they had similar physical features, two sisters couldn't be more different in temperament and priorities.

Aunt Eve owned a loft apartment in Soho and to Michele was quite entertaining, if not outright comical on the surface, especially the way she dressed in those tie-dye outfits, gaudy jewelry and exotic headbands. Ever since she and her husband were in a horrendous car accident, one that took her husband's life and left her in a coma for nearly two weeks, Aunt Eve was quite spiritual, and in fact, for the last four years had been and still was a practicing psychic. She had a devoted following and did readings three days a week in her home. The house was full of spiritual artifacts, herbal medicines, and talismans to ward off evil. Her supposed ability to channel the dead won her the moniker, *The Shirley McLaine of Soho*. Whatever, Aunt Eve was a great contrast with her mother and had a joyful, cheery temperament most of the time and was always encouraging. It was a delight to be with her.

As usual, she gave her a good luck charm again this morning before Michele left for the office. Today it was a magic eye amulet that she claimed had a "Good Eye to attract positive energy and ward off evil." Michele fingered it in her jacket pocket and entered the building.

"Hey, hey, hey," David Dugan chanted as she headed for her office. He was the Executive Director of Communications for the district attorney's office. One of the many so-called Wunderkind in this office, David at just thirty-eight had been a New York Times reporter and a congressional spokesperson before taking a job in a public relations firm and then gracefully moving into the district attorney's office when the opening arose and he was courted. He was a brilliant wordsmith and knew how to finesse any comment so as not to offend or cause any more attention than was necessary. In the short time she knew him, Michele thought he could convince God that Lucifer didn't mean to create a rebellion in heaven. He might refer to it as some sort of creative repositioning or something at a press conference at the Pearly Gates.

Ironically, however, David was somewhat awkward when it came to women, especially an attractive woman. He stumbled and stammered and often said silly things, rushing to hide his nervousness. Michele knew from the way she caught him looking at her that he thought she was very attractive. But it was exactly her beauty, her great figure and rich complexion that made her seem so unapproachable to him. How could it be that a woman like her was not at least being pursued by eligible bachelors, especially in New York? Unattached and look like this? Was she gay? Michele was the sort of woman whom any man thought was already booked for the weekend. It wouldn't occur to him that she was free.

"How was your weekend?" David asked her before she turned to go into her office. "I hope it was better than mine. Mine was a war zone between things going bad at my apartment, refrigerator dying, a toilet overflowing, and my mother's problems with my sister who broke up with her fiancé, and . . . forget it. I'll ruin your makeup with my list," he concluded.

Michele studied him for a moment, smiled and went into her office without giving him an encouraging word. He wasn't her type, not that she had settled yet on whom or what was her type. Maybe she was, as her mother often accused her of being, too particular and demanding. After all, compromising your ideals was the fastest way to any semblance of happiness. So wrote the modern prophets.

The moment she had entered her office, her secretary, Sofia Walters came rushing in, her large bosom lifting and falling like water balloons. The overweight thirty-seven-year-old dark-brown haired woman looked like she had just seen a ghost. Every feature in her face, however, was prone to exaggeration when something excited her, especially her hazel eyes. They looked like they might explode.

"You're up," she practically gasped.

"Excuse me?"

"You're up for it. I heard Mr. Barrett talking to Mrs. Rozwell minutes before she told me to have you go right to her office. You're being assigned your first case," she declared and clapped her hands together like someone trying to kill a fly.

"What do you know about it?"

She shook her head. Michele was a quick study. She picked up on Sofia's quirky ways quickly. She shook her head, but that didn't mean no, or I don't know anything. That meant what she knew impressed her in some way. It was more like "You won't believe it or something."

"What?"

"Murder case," she said. "A high profile one, too."

She smiled.

Michele hung up her jacket and straightened her skirt. She glanced at herself in the small makeup mirror she had brought to her office on the first day and then nodded.

"Well, let's go get it," she told Sofia and walked out quickly, her heart pounding with glee. After all, this was why she wanted to be here, wasn't it?

She walked down the corridor to Eleanor Rozwell's office. Rozwell was chief of the trial division and was all nuts and bolts and no window dressing. An emotionally harder woman Michele had never met. She made some of Michele's tough law professors look like pussies. She spoke so sharply at times that she could cut your ears. There was no nonsense in anything she did or said. It looked like she never relaxed, even when she left the job at the end of the day. Michele was convinced that Rozwell's husband had to be a wimp. No strong-willed man could live with a woman like her.

Despite all this, in some ways Michele wanted to be like her. She certainly wanted to have her dedication and self-confidence, but she also recognized that something preciously feminine had been sacrificed. She had no children. She kept herself to being more correct than attractive, her makeup applied with almost surgical precision. Her hair was always perfect, not a strand rebellious, and she dressed in conservative skirt and jacket suits that did little for her good figure. She was stern, but not manly enough to attract any ridicule. Michele's first impression of her was she was content only giving birth to successful prosecutions. Don't have any miscarriages and certainly, no abortions, not in the New York courts.

"Morning, Eleanor," she said entering after she had been announced and given permission. Eleanor Rozwell continued to write whatever note she was writing, her head down, her concentration unbroken. Michele stood there, almost at attention. It could have been a meeting in some military officer's office.

Slowly, Rozwell looked up and studied her for a moment as if she was making a final decision about her decision. A good three seconds passed. Michele didn't break her gaze, nor did she make the slightest nervous gesture.

"Mike thinks you're right for this," she began. A man named Elliot Strumfield was murdered a little less than six weeks ago in his home. The chief investigator on the case, Lieutenant Matthew Blake, always had someone in the frame from day one. Strumfield was the CEO of Strumfield Investments, a moderate size hedge fund. He and his wife Cisley have a penthouse apartment in the Waterford Building on East Sixtieth and First Avenue. All of the tenants are high worth individuals. There's an ex-secretary of state living there."

"I know of the building," Michele said, hoping to get to the bottom line a little faster. Instead of being annoyed by the interruption and the implication, Eleanor Rozwell smiled. She admired a no-nonsense, waste not a moment employee, whether it be a janitor or assistant district attorney.

"The security is pretty tight, as you can imagine. Strumfield, it appears, had discovered that his junior partner, Lester Heckett, had, over some time, siphoned off a few hundred thousand off the books. According to Cisley Strumfield, her husband had confirmed his suspicions, confronted Heckett and was on the verge of turning him into the police. Heckett had begged for a few days to restore the money. Strumfield gave it to him with the codicil he would resign, but Strumfield was shot twice in the head with a thirty-eight soon after. Very professional hit man style, not that I'm an expert on it.

"Nevertheless, Cisley reported seeing Heckett near the building just after the murder. She hadn't been home at the time and arrived what appears to be minutes afterward. A subsequent search of Heckett's apartment turned up the murder weapon. Of course, he denies having been there and says Mrs. Strumfield is mistaken. Unfortunately, she is the only one who saw him there."

"As I said, I know that building. Didn't Heckett have to sign in to visit, especially at that hour?" Michele asked.

"Somehow, he didn't."

"The receptionist doesn't recall him being there?"

"No, but he could have gotten past her. The receptionist at that time of day is a Mrs. Karey Ireland, sixty-two and relatively new on the job. It's the only small hole in this. Meaningless in light of everything else. He had the murder weapon in his house."

"Prints?"

"No, but the gun was in his possession."

"What about the bullets?"

"No. Maybe he wore gloves when he put them in."

"He didn't have a permit for it?"

"No." She grimaced as if she was swallowing bitter medicine. "There's no trace of the gun to him, but he could have gotten the gun from some illegal source. It's an unregistered weapon with the serial numbers filed off. Gangland style."

"I won a case once because of the fingerprints on the bullets," Michelle muttered, more to herself.

"Well this case is different. No case is the same."

Michelle nodded quickly.

"Was the weapon traced to any other crime?" Michele asked.

"No. At least not yet. The rest looks like a slam dunk. He has motive and not much of an alibi. Of course, Heckett claims he's innocent. He was surprised to discover the gun in his house and hid it, thus his explanation for his prints on the weapon. Naturally, he claims he's being framed. He hired Simon and James to represent him. They assigned a hotshot member of the firm reportedly about to be made a partner. His name was Warner Murphy."

"Was?"

"Warner Murphy seems to have committed suicide yesterday. Simon and James, we learned, are going to ask for a postponement and when they do, are probably going to get it, which is fine. Gives you more time to put icing on the cake. Here's the file," Rozwell said.

She didn't hand it to Michele. She just touched it and then lifted her hand away as if she was daring her to take it. Maybe, for some reason, she thought she might hesitate. Why? It did look like a slam dunk: motive, the weapon, opportunity, and identified at the crime scene, which was a nice thing for a brand new trial assistant district attorney to have.

She practically leaped forward to pick it up.

"There's going to be a full blown article on the case now, with references to Heckett's attorney's suicide and a more detailed look into the lives of the wealthy in New York. Talk to Dave Dugan about any press releases or answers to reporters' questions after you're up to speed. Good luck," she added and made a gesture with her pen that could not be misunderstood to be anything but, "Dismissed."

Michele clutched the file to her bosom, nodded and walked out. She held it like a prize she had won. After all, she was here less than a month and her name would be in all the New York papers and she would be on television with press releases. Her parents would be surprised, especially her mother.

She had gotten into law and had decided on being a prosecutor because she believed she could make a difference in the battle between good and evil, but she would be lying to herself and anyone who asked, if she didn't admit that vanity also drove her. Fame, even more than fortune as proven by the fact that she hadn't gone into some lucrative law practice, which she could have easily done, drove her as well as her desire to render justice and be an advocate for victims and their families.

What's the difference? she thought whenever she felt a little guilty about her vanity, if the final result was the same and the bad guy was punished? It's Adam Smith's concept of capitalism, the Invisible Hand. Serve yourself well and you'll serve others well.

Besides, she thought, it's the way we're all built; it's human nature, even since the first cave man scratched his name in a wall so he'd live forever.

She smiled at Sophia, tapped the file, and said, "Let's get to work."

As they announced at the trotter track her father loved to take her to, she declared with a little modification, "The horse is in the hands of the starter!"

It wasn't a race, but it was a competition and she practically luxuriated in any. It excited her. She was convinced that it was in her nature to be this way, and that, probably more than anything else, was what made her a different sort of woman from her mother.

4.

Kay Billups looked up from her receptionist's desk even before the door of Simon and James Associates was opened. It was odd the way something had seized her attention and taken her away from the thank you's she was writing to those who had already expressed their condolences through cards or baskets of flowers and fruit. Not only did this strange feeling take her attention away, but it brought a flush to her cheeks and quickened her heartbeat. It was like one of those movie moments when a character looks up just when a storm is about to blow out the windows of her home or something horrible was about to come crashing in on her. She was actually holding her breath.

There was a logical reason for these feelings, of course. She was terribly high-strung these days. Poor Mr. Murphy. What could have happened? And that beautiful wife and child . . . how devastated they had to be. She was still sick to her stomach thinking about them. From the moment she had heard the news, she felt as though she had been turned inside out. Her body felt raw and vulnerable and like everyone else in the office, she was constantly on the verge of tears.

The door opened.

John Milton stood there for a moment as if he was expecting applause on his entrance. Still without stepping forward and closing the door behind him, he gazed around the plush lobby, nodding at the large painting of a country lawyer holding up a Bible and saying something to convince a skeptical looking judge. The richly paneled walls in the lobby ran smoothly around and were complimented by the coco tiled floor. There were baskets of flowers and fruits on the dark cherry wood tables at the sides of the two settees and more baskets and cards on the tables in front of them. Recessed lighting poured a little too much brightness for his taste. He also thought the curtains on the two windows were blah, even drab. He nodded to himself, confirming that a great many changes would have to be made here. The firm owned the building so redecorating was inevitable.

Kaye continued to stare at him. She looked like she was afraid to utter a word. He smiled.

"Good morning," he said with a little more cheerfulness in his voice that would suit her anytime, but especially this particular morning. He closed the door and stepped forward.

"Good morning. Can I help you?"

"I'm sure you can. You look like someone dependable, as dependable as a mother."

Kaye didn't smile. What an odd thing to say, she thought. She wasn't in the mood for any humor today, dry or otherwise.

"Well, I am a mother, and as far as I know, quite dependable. What can I do for you?"

"I'm John Milton," he said. He said it as if he thought she should have known.

"Oh, yes."

Mr. James had personally informed her of John Milton's appointment. She could see in the senior partner's eyes that this was a very important man, at least to him.

"I'll let Mr. James' personal secretary know you've arrived."

"Thank you . . ." He looked at the name plate on her desk, "Kaye."

"Please, have a seat."

"Not necessary," he said. He looked up at the painting and shook his head. "Great painting. When you want to work wisdom into any argument, it helps to know your bible," he said.

"Yes." Kaye moved quickly to buzz Rose Bloom, Alexander James's personal secretary as if she wanted to get this man away from her as quickly as possible. "I have Mr. Milton for Mr. James," she said. She hung up and looked at him. "She's coming right out."

"Of course," he said. He looked around again, nodding to himself or for Kaye's benefit. She wasn't sure. "The lobby could use some vibrant color," he said. "These flowers are beautiful, but they're not going to be here long."

Kaye raised her eyebrows.

"They're not meant to be here long."

"Yes. Please don't mind me. Can't help myself. When I see wrong, I always try to right it."

"We're not in the mood for redecoration of the offices today. I don't know if you know, but . . ."

"Of course, I know. That's why I'm here," he said. "And I'm sorry. I'm sure, Mr. Murphy was well-liked."

"Loved," she corrected.

The door to the inner offices opened, not soon enough for Kaye.

"Mr. Milton?" Rose Bloom said.

"I am."

"Welcome. Please. Right this way."

"Merci," John said.

He smiled at Kaye, but the smile didn't warm her heart. It sent a chill up her spine. There was really nothing about him to encourage these cold feelings. She even felt a little guilty about it. So he was opinionated. So what? What lawyer wasn't? He was very good looking, stunning in fact.

There was even something impish about him. Even before this dreadful tragedy, this office could use some lightness once in a while, she thought. Everyone was so serious, probably because just about every case they acquired was very serious. They were, after all, one of the premier criminal defense law agencies in the city. No high net-worth individual who needed a criminal defense went anywhere else lately.

She wrote off her reaction to John Milton as part of the gloom that had settled like a heavy fog of soot over the offices and everyone in it and then went back to her thank you memos. She had volunteered for the job just so she could keep very busy and not think, and here she was, thinking.

On her way to her boss's office, Rose Bloom couldn't help but pause when they had reached Warner Murphy's office. His secretary, Nicole Joseph, looked up from her desk. She was wearing a black dress and had her dark-brown hair pinned up somewhat severely, John thought. Almost devoid of makeup and ashen-faced with bloodshot eyes, she reminded him of one of those hired Greek mourners he thought were quite amusing. She looked easily fifty. She's going to have to go, of course, he thought. The reverberations to any of his actions never seem to end. Nor, should they.

They stopped at Alexander James' office. Rose's desk and some file cabinets with another settee and two side tables, as well as another coffee table furnished her small enclave. There were some more baskets of flowers and fruits expressing condolences on the table, so many in fact, that there were some on the floor as well.

"Looks like Mr. Murphy had many friends."

"The entire firm does," Rose said, "and everyone knows what a blow this is to all of us in the legal world."

"Yes, How tragic," John said. "Tragedy is not an uncommon word in this world, but we never get used to it. It's always a big surprise as if all we were promised were rainbows."

He smiled. His eyes seemed to dance on the surface of hers. She nodded and opened the inner office door to announce him.

"Thank you," he said as he passed her to enter.

She caught a whiff of his seductive cologne and couldn't help the flutter under her breast. She surprised herself by closing her eyes and hesitating, and then practically had to lunge to close the door behind him and not look like some teenage girl instantly stirred by a fantasy.

John stood back against the closed door. He almost laughed aloud at the expression of doom and gloom the two senior partners wore. If they only know how useful those expressions could be. To disparage hope in the human heart was almost an unexpected pleasure. But then again, so many things were.

Alexander James rose first and offered his hand.

"John, we are very glad you've accepted our offer."

"You guys know how to wine and dine, but regardless, I knew I'd be happy here," he said, turning to Bill Simon, who was the taller and leaner of the two. Alexander was more rotund with thinning salt and pepper hair, but no gray in his eyebrows or goatee, which helped reduce the roundness in his face. His lips were a little too thick and he had a well-developed second chin. To John Milton he was a wonderful advertisement for gluttony. He could be the poster child.

Simon, on the other hand, was more Puritanical. He wasn't a terribly good-looking man. In fact he looked like a beardless Lincoln with that perpetual visage of a troubled heart and shoulders that sagged with the weight of the world's suffering sick and poor. He was less inclined to humor and very focused on his work. John Milton didn't trust men who refused even to consider desserts at lunch and dinner. However, it didn't take him long to realize that Simon was harder, more invulnerable, and clearly far more intelligent.

"Who wouldn't be impressed with your record of successful defenses and want to work here? There's a built-in cache with this firm. Just the mention of your firm's name makes prosecutors tremble. They know they have a terrific fight on their hands. It's perfect fit for me. You guys have done all the groundwork, laid the foundation. I can see great opportunity to build and expand. In a short time, we'll have need for a half dozen new associates. As I suggested at dinner, we should be defending corporations, attracting international business, have offices in other states.

"With all the new regulations enacted almost daily in this country and the expansion of existing laws and prohibitions, we have an endless well from which to draw new business."

He paused. He didn't want to overwhelm them. It was his biggest flaw, being too passionate about what he did, what he loved to do. After all, that was how it had all started, he thought and subdued a private smile.

"Please," Alexander said indicating the settee on the right. John sat and both Simon and James pulled two chairs up to sit in front of him. He felt like he had a box seat to a private play. Now, he couldn't help soften his lips into a slight coy smile.

"This looks like what they call a full-court press, no?"

Alexander smiled, but Bill Simon nodded.

"It has to be," he said. "We've got to move quickly, but we're impressed with your courtroom accomplishments, John, as you know. We feel confident that you'll be able to step in quickly."

"Ah, our unfortunate Warner Murphy, his current caseload. I suspected that was why you hired me so quickly."

"You were always on our radar screen," Bill said. "Matter of fact, Warner, Alex and I were discussing you just days before his tragic death. Warner, himself, did the background research on you."

"I was told someone was inquiring, yes," John Milton said. "The upper echelon of the legal community in this state, as in most, is smaller than most people think. I probably know just as much about each of you as you know about me."

He could see that the way he had said it made Alexander James a little uncomfortable. He suspected Bill Simon didn't know about his partner's sexual indiscretions. John Milton's favorite way to tease some of the priests, rabbis and Imams was to tell them Adam and Eve had no idea what new pleasures awaited them. Yes, there was pain, too, but in his way of thinking, it was obviously worth it.

"So you want me to pick up Murphy's caseload quickly, yesterday, matter of fact."

"Yes. The Heckett case in particular," Alexander said."Absolutely. It's very interesting. However, from our discussion at lunch, I had the feeling you thought Warner Murphy was thinking of a plea deal?"

"He was having some trouble building a defense for him and expressed that to both of us only days before his death."

"Maybe he did more; maybe he began to explore the possibilities with the district attorney's office?"

"Not that we know of. He could have done something off the record because he was depressed about his prospects of winning an acquittal. However, his depression was nothing like what it would take to have something like this occur," Bill Simon added quickly.

"It's never easy to understand an unexpected death," John said. "I suppose in a way all death is a surprise. We all think we'll live forever," he added with that wry smile he cherished.

Both senior partners nodded. When someone close to you dies or is killed, you can't help thinking about your own mortality. Such is the weakness in the human spirit, John thought. If they all thought they might live forever, I'd have an even easier time. Punishment in the afterlife would be an empty threat.

"Is there any more information about his suicide?"

The two looked at each other. He sensed their hesitation.

"You know something that hasn't been released yet?"

"We don't believe it was suicide, John. You know we had offered him a partnership. He had every reason to live and enjoy his life," Bill Simon said.

"Of course, but it's likewise true that none of us knows anyone deeply enough to understand all his or her actions," Simon added.

Probably your wives say that," John Milton suggested. Alexander almost laughed, but Bill Simon looked surprised.

"Why our wives?"

"Women are always more interested in the secrets we all bear in our hearts. It's part of the feminine nature."

"Is that why you're not married? You're afraid to have anyone know what secrets you carry?" Bill asked. John could sense that they had discussed his personal life.

He laughed.

"No. I simply haven't yet found the woman who could tolerate my obsession with my work," he said. "However, I will say we're all, men and women alike, always surprised at what someone we think we know is hiding inside him. I don't expect there's anyone who would want his whole life examined," he said looking more at Alexander James. He seemed to flinch. "I speak only for myself, but I certainly wouldn't. I'm sure that was true for Warner Murphy."

"Yes, but . . . for him to commit suicide? Now? At this point in his life?" Alexander said. "I can't buy it. You didn't know him as well as Bill and I did. He was practically a son to us."

"I am sorry," John said. "It's painful, especially when it's so unexpected, but my advice is don't commit to any theories about it just yet. I read the newspaper this morning. It seems impossible for anyone to have gotten up there to do him any harm, not with that sort of security, video, etc."

"The chief investigative officer on the case has doubts nevertheless," Bill Simon said.

"Oh? Well, some people commit suicide if their finances are in the toilet," he said.

"Warner's finances were and are just fine. The police have already looked into it."

"I see. As I said, there are other causes," John offered.

"So far, nothing's surfaced that would even remotely suggest any personal unhappiness. You know we were going to confirm his partnership the day he died. When the detective heard that, he was even more skeptical," Simon said more firmly this time.

"It's far from a closed case," Alexander added.

"Well, then let's leave it up to the police investigators," John said rubbing his palms like someone washing his hands. "In the meantime, let's talk about setting me up to work for you."

"Yes, well, you have our financial package."

"No, not that. I need to arrange myself here. I don't mind taking Murphy's office immediately, but I want to bring in my own personal secretary. She's been with me so long, she knows what I want before I do."

"Oh," Alexander said. "Nicole Joseph was here the day Warren began. We'd have to let her go. There's no other place for her."

"Exactly. I'd like my secretary here the day I begin as well. It's very important to me," John said with such a firm tone, even Simon's eyebrows rose. They both understood it was a deal breaker to say no.

"It's customary for the partners to staff the offices," Alexander offered as an act of resistance. John didn't respond. He stared at him coldly. "Of course, with these special circumstances."

"Exactly my point," John said. "These are special circumstances."

"Nicole is very familiar with the case," Bill Simon said as one more final attempt.

"My girl will be just as familiar with it in hours believe me. She's one of a kind. It's like a baseball pitcher who's comfortable with his own catcher. I'm sure you understand."

Alexander shrugged. Bill Simon looked a little upset, but nodded. He slapped his knees and stood.

"We're asking for a two week postponement."

"You don't have to. I'm fine with the schedule. You might call me a workaholic. Let's not give the prosecution any further reason to be optimistic. In fact, it will surprise and shock them a bit when we agree to keep on schedule. Keeps the pressure on them, too."

Alexander James smiled.

"I guess that will," he said. He looked at Bill Simon.

"You're putting a lot more stress on yourself, John," Bill said.

"Stress is what keeps me going at full speed, which is the only speed worth going," John said.

"Let me show you around," Alexander said. "You might as well meet Warner's secretary. Maybe you'll change your mind."

"Maybe hell will freeze over, but not in our lifetimes," John Milton said smiling. "Not with how busy this firm is and how busy it will become, eh?"

Bill Simon finally smiled.

"You have quite the sense of humor, John," he said. "I didn't realize it."

"You should see how I work it in a courtroom."

"I guess we will," Alexander said, "and quite a bit sooner than we had anticipated. Shall we?" he went to the door.

"Not a moment to waste," John said.

"Welcome to our firm," Bill told him and extended his hand. John Milton took it, and like the Chinese when they greeted their president, he took it with both of his.

"As I've been saying, I'm looking forward to making it an even bigger success than it is."

He followed Alexander James out and felt certain he could hear the sound of angels screaming.

And these weren't fallen angels either.

He imagined God putting his hands over his ears. The image was delightful.

Nothing brought more pleasure to his much too often sour heart.

Finally, he thought, finally I'm on a battlefield that fits my nature.

5.

Michele watched Matthew Blake enter the restaurant. She would have known it was he who had come into Roma Sparita even if she hadn't seen a photo of him in the file. His suit looked tailor-made for his sculptured body. Most of the detectives she had known looked like they took a college course in disheveled. However, even at this distance, Matthew Blake radiated a manly self-confidence that captured her feminine interest, and from what she could see, the interest of every other woman in the room. He had a classic face, the face you would expect to find on a Greek statue, but he also had that four or five day beard that was popular with young male models, movie and television actors today. She had to admit that she liked it. She was around too many cleanly shaven, neatly groomed men who radiated conservatism. There was nothing remotely dangerous about them, and with nothing dangerous, there was nothing exciting. At least, that was true for her.

Although he had never met her, he didn't pause at the host's desk to ask where she was sitting. She watched as he perused the room quickly and just started in her direction. She was in one of the imitation leather booths toward the rear of the sizeable restaurant, her briefcase on the seat beside her. She was sipping on a cranberry juice and soda.

"Ms. Armstrong?"

"Michele," she said extending her hand. He just touched it, but somehow sensually so that it was more of a caress, and then he slid into the seat across from her.

"Sorry I'm a little late."

"A few minutes. No problem. I saw you come in. How did you know it was I when you looked around? There are four other women sitting alone in this restaurant."

"I'm a detective, remember?" he said and smiled. He gazed around. "You just moved to New York, right?"

"Recently, yes."

"How did you find this place? I've been here a while and I wasn't aware of it. There's one with the same name in Rome in one of the piazzas in Trastevere."

"Trastevere? Where's that?"

"It's a rione, rione Thirteen in Rome."

"Rione? My Italian's a little rusty," she said and tugged on her left earlobe, just the way her father's favorite actor, Humphrey Bogart did in *Casablanca*.

"A Rome district. You should know the Latin word regio, meaning region. There's lots of Latin in law."

The waitress arrived.

"I'll have the same," he said nodding at Michele's drink.

"How does a policeman have all this worldly knowledge?" she asked, just a little stung by his comment. She felt her face flush a little. Whether he meant it or not, he sounded critical. Was he one of these macho guys who automatically assumes she would be inferior to a man in her position, one who would be more comfortable and confident if he was dealing with one of the male assistant district attorneys?

"I did a lot of traveling before settling in New York and still do whenever I can. So District Attorney Barrett assigned you the Strumfield case as your first dip in the legal sea?"

"It's not my first dip. I've been prosecuting in Orange County. And rather successfully, I might add."

"Yes, I know."

"But like everyone else from New York, you think you're special, is that it? Nothing that happens in the hinterland can compare?"

"I'm not from New York. But I do think New York's special otherwise I wouldn't be here, and my guess, neither would you."

She smiled. He wasn't someone easily cowered.

"Your right. I read your report. You don't speak like most of the policemen I know, and you certainly don't write like a policeman either," she added. "I never read a police report as vivid in detail. It's practically a literary work."

"We all have hidden talents," he replied and looked at the menu. The waitress brought his drink. "Have you chosen something?"

"The cacao e pepe pasta. I've had it a few times."

"Done. Please make that two," he said to the waitress and handed her his menu. Michele did as well and then reached for her briefcase and took out Matthew Blake's report.

"I see that Lester Heckett had replaced the money he took, but not until after he killed Strumfield."

"Clumsy attempt at a cover up. The damage had already been done. There are two other partners in the company, but neither as of yet has been willing to pursue embezzlement. Of course, Heckett now claims it was all done with Strumfield's verbal permission."

"Which his wife contradicts. But why wouldn't Strumfield have mention the embezzlement to the other partners and why didn't they know about it on their own?"

"Best I could tell was Strumfield really wanted to give him the chance to redeem himself. They go back quite a ways, were in college together, but as you see," he said nodding at the report, "from reading my interview with Cisley Strumfield, she insists he still demanded Heckett resign immediately after he restored the funds. The partners didn't review the accounts during the period of time in question. They depended too much on Strumfield to oversee everything. Richard Longine spends most of his time private jetting around for skiing holidays or beach holidays, and the other, Lawrence Kaplan, looks like because of family money, he fell into it all, and isn't really that swift when it comes to finance."

"How long did it take Strumfield to realize what Heckett had done?"

"According to Mrs. Strumfield, her husband had suspicions and about a week before he was killed, he had conducted a full audit privately."

"Why did Heckett think he could get away with it? He must have known Strumfield would realize what he was doing eventually."

"Most people who commit crimes believe they can get away with them otherwise they wouldn't commit them. He did have control of the movement of funds and there was a deep trust between him and Strumfield for some time. He didn't begin the company with Strumfield, but Strumfield took him in and made him successful. He was perhaps a little too dependent on the belief that Strumfield wouldn't think he would ever screw him?"

She shook her head.

"Still, that's a hole I'd like to fill before opening argument," she said. "He knew Strumfield for some time. I have to believe he knew he was going to discover the discrepancy eventually. Maybe, Cisley Strumfield is wrong. Maybe he did give him permission at first and then for some reason, changed his mind and demanded the money be instantly returned. His defense attorney could easily suggest it and plant that thought in the minds of the jurors."

"I can help you there. There's no logic to that. Heckett didn't invest the money in something. He didn't buy himself expensive cars, expensive jewelry or upgrade his apartment. He socked it away in a foreign bank account. Maybe he thought he was smarter than Elliot. Ninety percent of the time, ego gets people in trouble. Elliot Strumfield realized he had been robbed by someone he had trusted."

She nodded.

"Okay. I feel confident about the motive for the murder. Tell me about the discovery of the pistol."

"It was buried under some towels in the bathroom cabinet. Not a place anyone normally would keep a weapon of course, unless he or she was trying to keep it hidden."

"Didn't he have a maid or anyone who might find it?"

"Yes, but we got to it before the maid's day to clean. I think he knew he would be a suspect and hid it in haste expecting to hide it better later."

"Why didn't he just get rid of it?"

"Maybe it wasn't his to get rid of. Maybe he was told to hold onto it."

"Told? Who would tell him?"

"The actual killer," Blake said and sipped his drink.

"What? I thought you concluded he's the killer. I don't understand. What are you saying?" she asked with more hysteria in her voice than she would want. "We're trying him for murder."

"Calm down. He is guilty of murder. He just hired someone to carry it out."

She thought a moment and nodded.

"I have to admit that Eleanor Rozwell has those suspicions. She told me the killing had the markings of an expert hit and when I put that together with financial businessman . . . well, I didn't think it was part of economics one."

"Her instincts were correct. I have an amendment to my original report."

"Amendment? When was that submitted?"

"I'm submitting it now, especially after reading the forensic report and after I reviewed Heckett's background. There's no evidence he was familiar enough with guns to perform so perfect a hit. As you will see, forensic is estimating the killer was a good fifteen feet away from Strumfield, yet delivered two perfect wounds to his forehead, less than an inch apart. Because of the bullet's trajectory, we know the killer stood on that little landing from the entry way to the living room. If Heckett was doing the actual killing, he would have had to be closer. It would make more sense that he would get closer to be sure he didn't miss anyway. Whoever did it was confident of his accuracy."

"And you just recently came up with these conclusions? What took so long?"

"We're terribly understaffed. Budget cutbacks. I had two other murders, a rather violent rape, and an armed robbery resulting in a death in between. But I think what I'm telling you now about this case is valid. Lester Heckett didn't actually pull the trigger."

"You sound like you're working for the defense. I've handled some shootings. Maybe he was just lucky with his shots."

"No. Think about it. If Heckett went to Strumfield's house to kill him, he would have rung the bell and when Strumfield opened the door, shot him or very soon afterward. The killer surprised him which means he got in on his own. Heckett definitely hired someone, someone who was also expert about getting in and out unseen. He's an experienced killer. I'm sure of it."

"But up until now, we were claiming he was there. Cisley Strumfield is the eye witness. That doesn't make sense."

"She's not claiming to have seen him in the building, coming out of their apartment, anything like that. She saw him near the building."

"From the way this reads, she's implying she saw him leaving the building."

"The defense will argue she's assuming that. To be accurate, according to her exact testimony, he was walking away quickly."

"But, if he hired someone, then why was he there at all?"

"I don't think he was actually in the apartment for the hit, but he waited outside to have it confirmed. He might have been instructed to be there."

"Why?"

"It's my guess that was when the hit man gave him the weapon and told him to hold it for him. He would do what he was told. He was involved in a murder now and had laid out a lot of money."

"The money he stole?"

"Yes, but he had more."

He reached into his inside pocket and produced a paper folded lengthwise and handed it to her.

"What's this?" She looked at it and then looked up. "Statement from a bank in the Cayman Islands?"

"Exactly what it says. You can see he withdrew seventy-five thousand dollars. And if you check the date, it's a day before the killing."

She looked at it again.

"How do you know this company is owned by Heckett?"

"It is. You'll have to confirm it."

"How did you get the statement?"

"I went back and searched his apartment again and this time, I found the paperwork behind a print picture hanging on the wall in the living room."

"When?"

"This morning," he said. "I was working off the original warrant. No worries. I've been busy or I would have found it earlier. I'm involved heavily in another case. You know about Warner Murphy?"

"Of course, his lawyer. The suicide. It's been a headline story. Dave Duggan is figuring out exactly what I should say when asked about it. It's sure to come up."

"It's wasn't a suicide. I can't prove it yet, but it wasn't," he said with such assurance, she had to sit back and take it all in slowly.

"You think all this is connected somehow?"

"Somehow. I just don't have any idea yet, but there's something bigger happening here," he said.

"Bigger? How do you mean?"

"I don't know yet," he said and looked up as the waitress brought their food. He gazed down at his dish. "Looks just like it was in Trastevere," he said.

"You know the dish? I just thought . . . so you're well-traveled, you know Latin and you know what a restaurant specializes in. You're a little confusing, Lieutenant, or should I say surprising."

"Aren't we all?" he said and sipped his drink, his eyes reaching over the glass to softly caress her face.

She felt herself blush, but not from shyness as much as from the way her heartbeat quickened and her lips moistened. It was as if they were already passionate lovers who were at that early stage when neither could take his eyes off the other or not think of kissing and embracing constantly.

At least, that's what it felt like.

They both began to eat, but she couldn't help looking at him. Despite the work he did, he had an aura of calmness about him. He was unlike any other detective she had ever met and worked with. Did that come from his self-confidence? She couldn't recall any other man, detective or not, who sounded so sure of everything he said.

"I really don't understand the part about his being made to keep the gun. Why would the killer want that anyway?"

"You know that when we investigate a murder, there are two major things to determine immediately, the cause of death and the weapon. When you tie the weapon to a suspect, you're ninety percent there."

"I'm aware of all that."

"Sorry. I don't mean to sound condescending. My point is professional hit men know that as well. Ordinarily, they would dispose of the weapon. New weapons aren't exactly difficult to acquire in this country."

"So why would the hit man want it still around?"

"Think of it as an insurance policy. You hire someone to do the killing. He wants to be sure you can't turn him in or double cross him in some way, especially give him up if you're tied to the crime. So, he makes you keep the murder weapon. Maybe he claims he'll be retrieving it after it all blows over."

"Following that logic, why would Heckett do it?"

"Heckett's an embezzler, not a killer. He's afraid of the man he hired."

"Why didn't he wipe the weapon clean before he hid it? He's surely going to plead that he didn't know it was there or it was planted."

"We're not dealing with someone who's comfortable killing anyone or having them killed. He was rattled. I mean look how dumb, inexperienced he was about hiding it. The best he could come up with was under a pile of towels in the bathroom? Didn't he see The Godfather? At least he could have put it in the guts of a toilet."

She laughed and then paused, remembering a previous case and what she had said to Eleanor Rozewell.

"But the bullets had no prints on them."

"Which supports my theory. A professional wears gloves putting in bullets. Heckett never touched the bullets."

She sighed. It wasn't a fact she wanted to hear.

"How is it?" she asked, nodding again, but this time at the food.

"It's terrific. As good as the original."

"Original? You sound like you were there when it was first created."

He smiled.

"I do feel that way sometimes," he said.

"Have you always been a policeman, a detective?"

"In one way or another."

She shook her head.

"A detective who is himself a man of mystery," she said and reached for the report as she continued to eat.

"It takes one to know one so I practice disguising the truth."

"Which is probably another excuse for avoidance."

"Did you take a course in personal relationships or something?"

"Something," she said smiling. "Okay, let's look at your interview with Cisley Strumfield. She claims she was on the way home from the drugstore. She had taken a taxi back because she doesn't like walking alone at night. When the taxi dropped her off, she saw Lester Heckett walking quickly away. She claims she thought he had seen her and sped up. She was worried about it so she hurried upstairs and discovered her husband shot. She called the police immediately. You weren't the first on the scene, and you have a note here about the patrolmen traipsing too much on the crime scene."

"Fortunately, no one touched the body."

"Not even Cisley?"

"Not according to what she says there, right? She was so shocked, she nearly fainted and then went to the phone in the kitchen. She didn't come out of the kitchen until the patrolmen arrived."

"How long before you were there?"

"Medical examiner tells me about an hour and a half after he was shot. I would have been there sooner, but my last partner was having some personal issues and I had to deal with that first."

"Oh?"

"He's retired and I have a new partner." He looked at his watch. "We're going to rendezvous in an hour."

"Rendezvous?" She squinted. "Where are you from, Lieutenant Blake?"

"Genetically?"

"No, where were you born, smart-ass?"

He laughed.

"I can't wait to watch you cross-examine witnesses. Okay, but no jokes," he said as a prologue.

"Okay. No jokes. So?"

"Bethlehem." He waited a moment and then smiled and added, "Pennsylvania."

"Jesus," she said.

"My middle name."

"Now who's joking?"

"No, I'm serious. I usually leave it out of introductions and off documents if I can."

"Matthew Jesus Blake?"

"One and the same," he said.

"You seem . . ."

"What?"

"Like you're from somewhere else," she said. He sat back. "A detective who's a man of mystery," she emphasized. "I'll fix you," she added. He raised his eyebrows.

"Oh?"

"I'll have you meet my Aunt Eve and she'll check you out. She has special powers."

He started to laugh and stopped as if he believed Aunt Eve did have the potential to expose him. At least, that was how Michele took it.

"Maybe you should return to the report. Time's expensive for a man with my clock. They're raining crime all over my jurisdiction these days."

She looked at the report.

"Well, I'm confident we can tie Heckett to this murder. I mean, look at Heckett's alibi. Had a headache and was home all night. No calls, no visitors, no confirmation. He recently separated from his wife and lives on the West Side near Central Park, high overhead costs. He has two young boys, one twelve and one ten, so there's child support and alimony." She paused and then looked up. "Why did he embezzle the money if he had this much money in the Cayman Islands?" she asked, sounding more like she was asking herself.

"Is there ever enough for these people? I think he was preparing to leave everything, his upcoming alimony, child support, and unhappy situation at work. He wasn't making it fast enough in this economy. He had an escape plan and needed more. He might have taken even more than that, if Strumfield didn't smell him out."

She nodded.

"Can you get me some more on that, those plans to leave?"

"Yes," he said. "I have something for you now, but you'll have to figure a way to introduce it in trial if Heckett doesn't take the stand, which he probably won't."

"Did he buy or rent a house?"

"In Hong Kong . . . an apartment. I found the rental agreement," he said and handed it to her.

She looked at it.

"He went through an agency in the city. I can subpoena their records and call in the agent who processed it. No problem. Helps to further establish the motive. Very good work."

"Thanks," she said but she shook her head and looked troubled.

"What's wrong?"

"We're going to have a problem with this new twist you're presenting today, him hiring a hit man. When the defense hears or reads your amendment to this report and sees the hit man was an expert with weapons, which you claim Heckett wasn't . . . By the way, how can you be so sure of that?"

"You have most of his bio there. Heckett grew up in Manhattan. His father was a banker, loan executive most of his life. His mother was a nurse. He has an older sister who married a Canadian who owns a tour company in Vancouver. Guns weren't part of his growing up. He never owned a weapon. He never was part of a shooting club and was never in the military service. It's not brain surgery. The man was no expert with a thirty-eight. It's not easy shooting someone so accurately with a pistol from that distance."

She nodded, sadly.

"Unless we can prove he hired someone, Lieutenant, it could turn out to be true reasonable doubt. You'd be handing him his ticket home."

"You don't want me to distort the facts, do you?"

"Of course not. I'm just . . . it's my job to anticipate arguments an envision how those arguments might impact on the jury."

"I know. I'm going to get you the hit man before the trial starts."

"You are?"

"I have a lead," he said. "Don't worry."

"I'm not sure I can do that."

"What?"

"Not worry."

He nodded.

"Okay, worry, but I'll get him." He glanced at his watch. "I have to get moving. Sorry. I know they probably have a great dessert list here."

"Never eat it. Hate sugar highs," she said. He smiled.

"Likewise."

Her mobile vibrated.

"Excuse me," she said and said, "Armstrong." She listened for a moment. "What? Yes, that is surprising. I'm meeting with him right now, matter of fact. Yes, he's filled me in, but I think we need to talk. There's more information, an amendment to his original report. Okay. I'll see you then," she added and ended the call.

"Problem?"

"That was Eleanor Rozwell."

"So?"

"Simons and James are not asking for a postponement. They've replaced Warner Murphy already and the replacement, an attorney named John Milton, is on the case. Maybe he's read the forensic report and made the same conclusions you've made. He could have more time if he wants. He's either brilliant or arrogant," she added.

Matthew nodded and stood.

"More often than not, one cannot exist without the other," he said.

"Yes, but this gives you less time to find the so-called hit man."

"Worry," he said. "It motivates me."

He turned to leave.

"Wait," she called.

"Yes?"

"Something else you said . . . the attorney, Warner Murphy. You really suspect his death is some way connected?"

"I do, but I'm not sure about that yet, and I have nothing to go on except my instincts."

"You have a lot on your plate," she said. He smiled.

"So do you. Thanks for lunch," he told her and headed out of the restaurant.

She watched him leave and then sat back, glancing at the report and thinking about Lieutenant Blake's new information. What happened to her slam dunk introduction to the New York court scene?

Something dark and heavy had come rushing in and over her. It was as if all the light and hope was sucked out of the room for a moment.

She looked sharply, having the sense of someone watching her. She panned the room, studying every man and woman remotely gazing in her direction. Funny, she thought, I've never had this sort of paranoia when I was involved with any of my former cases, and yet it feels like more than just an overextended imagination. Shadows, eyes, voices, and even the clatter of dishes and the sound of the traffic outside seemed different. It as if she had stepped out of this world.

She shook her head.

"Get hold of yourself, Michele Armstrong," she muttered.

These were thoughts and feelings better left for Aunt Eve, she told herself and signaled for the bill.

6.

Alexander James thought he had died and gone to sex heaven when John Milton introduced his personal secretary. Why would a woman so startlingly beautiful with so vivacious a figure settle for a legal secretary's position and work at it for as long as John said she had when she could easily just walk onto any film set, get paid huge sums for modeling or capture the heart of any and all wealthy bachelors in moments? Of course, he suspected she might be John's girlfriend.

"Alex, this is Nora Adamson," John said. "She'll be fulfilling my personal secretarial duties here as she has at my previous firm."

Alexander rose quickly to come around his desk. He wanted to be closer to her. He was actually drawn to her more by her extraordinary almond shaped blue-gray eyes than her perfect figure with breasts that seemed to rise and threaten the buttons of her light pearl blouse with every breath she took. He felt held by those eyes, captured, and was unable to look away or in any way hide his fascination. He was rarely so obvious when it came to beautiful women, but right now he was practically panting. She held out her hand and he actually trembled when he brought his to it. Her fingers seemed to burn their way to his blood, carrying the heat not to his heart, but instantly down to his startled prick. He feared he was losing control of the pulsating threat.

"A pleasure," he said. He looked at John with an expression of feigned accusation. "How can you conduct any business with such a beautiful woman so close?"

John Milton smiled.

"It's a challenge. I'll admit, but Nora's talents go much deeper than her obvious beauty. She can see the weakness in a defense or prosecution almost as quickly as I can. And she has an incredible memory for details."

"Mr. Milton exaggerates a little, but thank you for the compliment, Mr. James," Nora said.

At least, he thought she had said it. It seemed more like a soft whisper, melodic, a caress of his ears, warming him like lips moving over his chest, down over his stomach and to the inside of his thighs.

And that perfume she was wearing . . . he had never smelled anything like it. It seemed to circle in his brain and make his lips salty and wet. He could spend the rest of the day, months even, standing here looking at her and taking in every detail of her very being.

"Please, call me Alex. We're like family here," he said. She was still holding his hand. He tried to swallow after he had spoken, but he couldn't. Every muscle in his body was tight and focused like the muscles of a panther about to strike. Something utterly primeval in him was threatening to burst out. The small pause of silence was thunderous.

"Alex," she said like some obedient slave. Now he couldn't keep his eyes off her full, perfect lips and the way she formed his name, holding the X-sound just a little longer. His name never sounded as melodic. How coarse and common was the way his wife Margaret pronounced it, often making it sound more like profanity, especially when she was either upset with him or disagreed with him. "Al'x," she'd say, sucking in the second syllable and grimacing as if it choked her. In seconds here he regretted his marriage and his spoiled children.

"Nora and I are going to start reviewing the file on Heckett and the case itself, Alex. I'll have some thoughts for you before the end of the day."

"Please," Alex said. Nora finally released his hand and strangely, it felt ice cold, just as cold as it would feel if he had stuck it in the freezer. He clasped it behind his back and rubbed it. "And don't hesitate to ask me anything," he told Nora.

"I won't," she said. Maybe he imagined it, wanted it, but he thought she had added, "ever hesitate." Her smile was blazing. She started to turn away. He felt panic.

"You explained our employees package to her, John?" he practically cried, hoping to hold her there a little longer.

"Nora doesn't need any explanations. If anything, she'll explain it to me," he added and then laughed.

Nora held her smile, but brought her right hand up slowly to the base of her throat. He nearly salivated at the way her fingers moved ever so gently across the base of it and then down to the top of her cleavage like a woman who was dabbing herself with perfume in preparation for a tryst.

"Yes, well, I'm here if you need me."

"Alex, you have plenty to do with the Marcus case. The man is too free with his comments to the press. You had better tighten the reins. I've had clients like that and practically had to tie and gag them before trial."

"I know. I know. Some people are their worst enemy," he said.

John smiled that wry smile he was rapidly becoming famous for here.

"Most people, Alex. Most people are their worst enemies."

He opened the door and Nora left, her body moving with a swing and rhythm such as he had never seen.

"What's wrong with you?" he asked himself as soon as he was alone. "Making a fool of yourself over a pretty woman."

"That's not just another pretty woman," he replied. She had him talking aloud to himself. For Christ sakes, stop acting like a teenager, he thought, but the prospect of concentrating on the Marcus file diminished rapidly. He kept looking up and envisioning Nora Adamson standing there. Finally, he sat back and closed his eyes.

In his fantasy, she had returned and without a word spoken between them, began to disrobe, pealing her clothes away with such grace and style that he saw nothing pornographic in the stripping. Naked, she walked around his desk and approached him. He turned his chair to face her and she knelt down, unfastened his pants and dipped her hands in smoothly, gently slipping her fingers into his briefs and cupping his testicles, her fingers stroking his stem. The blood rushed through it, hardening him. He wasn't this hard since his teenage years, he thought. It's miraculous. She brought her lips to the tip, but didn't take him into her mouth. She played over him, tasting him. He moaned. She moved to the inside of his thighs just the way he had imagined it earlier. She was working him ever-so-slowly. His heart was pounding, pumping, flourishing with his hot blood. His mouth filled with the salty taste of first kisses. His whole body was shuddering and then . . .

The intercom buzzed. He opened his eyes, the fantasy popping like a soap bubble.

"Mr. Broadstreet is here to see you, Mr. James," Rose Blum announced.

He looked down. His pants were open as he had fantasized only his hands were in his underwear cupping and stroking his testicles and penis and not some imaginary Nora Adamson. Shocked, he sat up quickly.

"One moment," he replied, his voice unable to disguise the panic.

He worked quickly to zip up and button up, but he could feel the sweat around his neck and knew his face was as flush as a newly blossomed rose. He reached for some water and wiped his face with his handkerchief.

What the hell had happened?

He took deep breaths and looked down. His erection wasn't receding. If anything, that part of his body was in a small rage. When he was a teenager and either he or one of his friends had an erection like this, they'd always chant, "Wear baggy pants."

There was no joking now. How was he going to stand up and shake Steven Broadstreet's hand? The man was too sharp of an investigator to not take note of the failure to do so. He hyperventilated, forced himself to think of the client and the file and started to feel some relief.

Until he looked down again.

How hadn't he noticed it the first time?

He had an orgasm.

"Jesus, Mary and Joseph," he chanted. If he could smell it, Steven would. The panic circled him like a tiny tornado. He felt his head spinning. He couldn't see anyone now!

He lifted his receiver.

"Yes, Mr. James?" Rose asked.

"Would you put Mr. Broadstreet on please," he said and waited. "Alex?"

"Steve, I hate to do this to you, but I need a favor."

"Sure, what?"

"Can you come back in say two hours? I'm deep into something here unexpected, something personal. If it's difficult, we'll reschedule another day."

"No, no problem. I'll come back," Steven Broadstreet said. "Are you all right? I mean . . ."

"Yes, I'll be fine. Thank you. Thank you," he repeated and hung up quickly.

Then he rose and went into his private bathroom. He stood looking at himself in the mirror. His face was still a little flushed, but it was calming. He began to take off his pants to do what he could to rescue the rest of the day.

Two doors down the hall, John Milton sat behind his desk looking at Nora Adamson. Neither had spoken a word since they had left Alexander James' office. John smiled.

"You did well, Nora. I'm as proud of you as a father could be."

Nora smiled, but she looked a little uncomfortable in her clothes, scratching her arms and squirming.

"Need a break?" he asked.

She nodded.

He closed and opened his eyes after a good ten seconds. Nora's clothes were neatly spread on the chair in which she had been sitting. Suddenly, there was a small movement under them and then, she appeared, stretching her six feet body before curling around her clothes. Her tongue protruded and her head swayed.

John Milton smiled, his eyes full of pleasure and happiness.

"Is there something wrong with me?" he asked one of his favorites. "I think you're more beautiful like this."

She slipped off the chair and snaked around his left foot, moving up his leg. He stroked her head. She lowered herself to his lap and he leaned over to continue reading the forensic report on the Strumfield murder.

His mobile vibrated and he dug it out of his inside pocket.

"John Milton," he said. He just listened. He never said goodbye. He closed the phone. "Houston, we have a problem," he declared. "Sorry, my love," he said. "I have something I must do."

She went into quick retreat back to the clothes and he closed his eyes, held them and then opened them to see Nora sitting across from him.

"I have to leave. No rest for the weary," he said.

"Tell me about it."

"Now, now, no regrets, my dear. Regrets sound too much like remorse and you know how I feel about that." He stood up and looked around. "This is such a dull office. The whole place is as dreary as heaven. But fear not, sayeth I. It shall not be long before we change it."

Nora laughed and stood.

"Work on that detective's interview of Cisley Strumfield. Unravel it for me."

"Okay," she said. She took the papers and started out.

"Oh."

She turned.

"Don't do anything more with our Mr. James today. I don't want him to get a heart attack. Too soon," he added and laughed.

She smiled and left.

He pulled out his mobile and speed dialed Charon.

"I'll be right out," he said. "We have an appointment."

Charon never said hello and never said goodbye. The line went dead and Milton put his phone in his inside suit jacket pocket.

On the way out, he paused to speak to Kaye Billups. Anyone could see she wasn't comfortable speaking with him, but he was now an associate. She had to be as pleasant as she could be, even though the man disturbed her in ways she didn't understand.

"And how is our mother Kaye doing this afternoon?" he asked.

Her lips trembled.

"I'm fine," she said.

He looked around the lobby.

"I miss those flower baskets, don't you? They added so much color."

She couldn't speak. She looked down at her keyboard.

"How many children do you have now, Kaye?" he asked.

She looked up quickly.

"What do you mean, now?"

He smiled.

"How many children do you have?" he repeated.

"I have three boys and a girl. And they're all healthy and doing well."

"I'm glad. They're wonderful once you get over the shock of their being born," he said.

She had no reply. She watched him walk out and sat back.

If she didn't know better, she would think that he knew about her abortion in college.

Of course, that was ridiculous.

Wasn't it?

John Milton looked back at the agency entrance from the elevator and thought, she'll be the first who's going to want to go once he takes over or perhaps, she'll go sooner.

But that's how it should be. Her replacement was waiting to join Nora.

In time, they would all join Nora.

How perfect this all was now, and just when he was starting to get bored with the battle.

The elevator door opened. He got in and pressed the button for the lobby. Then he looked at his reflection in the metallic walls. It was distorted, but he could still make out a pair of wings melting.

When he stepped out, he looked like someone who had just heard very bad news. His rage propelled him past other visitors to the building and other employees of businesses that had their offices here. No one spent more than a glance on him. Something made them turn away quickly.

By the time he stepped out, he was calm again. He smiled at the doorman and then slipped into the rear seat of his limousine. Charon closed the door and he sat back, preparing himself like a fireman, to put out some smoldering ashes. He conjured up Stoker Martin and then told Charon exactly where to go.

It really was like a game of chess after all.

And he was about to say, "Checkmate."

7.

On entering the loft apartment, Michele heard what was now familiar chanting coming from the dining room. She saw it was lit only with candles and paused in the doorway to look in at her aunt holding hands with two other women, all with their eyes closed, their voices in a chorus of "ooommm." Her aunt sat at the head of the table and was wearing an indigo headband with an eye at the top of her forehead, a multicolored tie-die one piece, and rings of bracelets with different crystals on both wrists. She nodded gently, keeping her eyes closed, but letting Michele know she knew she had come home. Smiling to herself, she continued to her rather large bedroom on the west end of the loft. Half of her bedroom was her home office.

When her aunt heard that Michele would seriously consider moving in with her, she had the space redecorated. The two large windows with industrial frames were softened with the newly installed light walnut paneling carried over the frames. Beige cotton curtains were hung and an electrician was brought in to update the outlets and provide a high speed broadband and Wi-Fi service. Another two telephone lines were also brought in, one for a dedicated fax and another for Michele's landline. That was it when it came to updates, however.

The light fixtures were all bought at antique shops. They didn't match, but they all had character and style from the 1950's. Her aunt already had the working juke box that used to play its records for nickels and quarters. She thought Michele would enjoy having it in the far right corner and moved it into her bedroom. She had asked her if she wanted her own television and Michele had told her it wasn't necessary. She liked to read herself to sleep. To soften it further, her aunt bought two large light pink area rugs.

"Pink," she told her, "will calm and relax you. It neutralizes disorder and you'll need to come home to it every day from the work you do."

"Thank you, Aunt Eve," she said.

"I know you're skeptical, dear, but you'll see."

It did give her a good feeling. That was all she was prepared to admit.

She dropped her briefcase next to the desk chair and then plopped herself into the dark blue heavy cushion easy chair that her aunt said she had rescued from some charity's thrift shop in which all sorts of donations, including furniture, were donated for sales. There was just one tiny rip under the left arm, but the seat was still remarkably firm. Her aunt was certain someone had died in it, and it was donated to the charity simply because of that. Michele knew her mother wouldn't permit it near her home, much less take it in and use it even if that story was only a rumor. She would drive an additional five miles to avoid passing a cemetery.

"How do you know someone died in it, Aunt Eve?" she had asked.

"The dead leave something behind, a stain in the form of a shadow."

"Only you can see?"

"There are others who can see it. I just happen to be one, yes. If you don't want it in your bedroom . . ."

"No, that's fine," she said. "It's very comfortable."

"I thought so," her aunt said smiling.

Actually, her body felt like it was comfortably softening and settling as the tension began to dissipate. Late in the afternoon, she had a concerned session with Eleanor Rozwell and District Attorney Barrett. The information she had brought back after her lunch with Lieutenant Blake wiped some of the confidence off their faces. She could sense that Michael Barrett especially had wanted her to have a comparatively easy first prosecution. She was, after all, prosecuting for the first time in New York City.

She was even more convinced now that New Yorkers believed everything was different there. They had an arrogance about it. Whether it was restaurants or theater, this was where the best came and where you would experience the best. That applied to jurisprudence as well. In their eyes, a murder case trial in New York jurisdictions outside of the city were just not as intense or as complicated. For one thing, the media coverage was better because just as the best came to the theater to perform or to restaurants to cook, the best came to television and newspapers to cover the stories here.

Both the district attorney and Eleanor Rozwell made it clear that her performance in court would be reviewed with the same cold scrutiny employed when critics reviewed an actress or a chef. Being hard, even cruel and sarcastic was almost required. She assured them both that she still felt quite confident and she wasn't thinned-skinned. She didn't want to mention Blake's confidence about finding the hired killer and tying him to Heckett. That was her ace in the hole, or the closer in a deal, as her father might say, but it was better not to rely on it or let the D.A. think she was doing just that, relying on something and not working hard herself.

She sat back and closed her eyes. Now that she was home and away from the case, even for a little while, she could think about other things. She realized that since her lunch with Lieutenant Blake, she had been feeling different, and it had nothing to do with the case. She was feeling different in the sense that she was thinking about things she hadn't thought about for a while, namely sex and romance.

Her mother wasn't all wrong about her fixation on her career. During her time in the Orange county district attorney's office, she had two relationships, both lasting just short of a year. One was with a young doctor, Abe Curtis, who had just joined a family practice in Middletown, New York. They met at a charity function. Her mother was ecstatic when she heard she was going on a second date with him. She was practically planning the wedding. But between her work schedule and his, they began to drift apart and his ultimate complaint about her was basically the same complaint she received from her next great fling, Ray Mallen, the owner of a large heating oil company, a company he had inherited from his father-in-law.

"You're always somewhere else, Michele. Often, I'm afraid, when we're making love," he told her. "Not good for my ego."

She couldn't deny it, but worse, she couldn't prevent it. Even if she forced herself to stop thinking about her current prosecution when she started out on a date, she always slipped back into it, either because something said reminded her of something she had read or heard related to her case, or some vision of the defendant flashed across her mind and roused her anger and passion. It was Abe who had told her on the day they basically broke up that he wasn't sure if her dedication and ambition was a curse or a blessing.

"I've always been ambitious and determined, but I knew from the day I decided to go into medicine that if I didn't learn how to compartmentalize, I wouldn't have a personal life. You need to get there, Michele, if not with me, than with someone else or you'll just burn out."

Were they both right? Was there something wrong with her? She remembered the discussion of Moby Dick in her college sophomore American lit class. When they discussed the character of Captain Ahab who now lived primarily to get revenge on the white whale, he was characterized as a monomaniac because of his obsession with that and that only. It was technically a form of psychosis. Was that happening to her?

Maybe to prove that wrong as much as anything, she thought romantically about Blake now, not that she could prevent it. He had incredible eyes and so confident a demeanor. It was easy to feel safe with him, and despite her need to be independent and strong, as independent and as strong as any man in her position, she couldn't deny a desire to be with someone like him, someone who would be there to protect her.

Did that make her weaker? Couldn't you still be dependent on someone else for something in your life? If we're so independent of each other to the point we don't need each other, what was a relationship, a German Confederation? Equal parts that combined to have more buying power or something?

On the other hand she was guilty of making sure the men she was with knew she could be independent. Maybe she was too strident about that. There were silly little things she didn't let Abe or Ray do for her, like step forward to open the door, get to her chair at the table quicker and pull it out for her, and even get to the car door to open it for her. Both had odd looks on their faces when she moved quicker and did these things for herself. Abe went so far as to say, "Are you trying to make me obsolete?" In the beginning, they could laugh about it, but as they saw each other more and more, those little things began to take their toll, chip away until they were almost escorting each other to everything like two acquaintances and not two people in a passionate romance.

"Serves me right for wanting to play baseball rather than play with dolls," she muttered.

She opened her briefcase and took out the folder Eleanor had given her with information about her opposing counsel, this John Milton. When she read the description of his early life, she was amazed that he had reached the level of success he had. Look at all he had to overcome.

Apparently, his biological mother was a prostitute in New Orleans, and apparently she had either died or disappeared immediately after his birth. He was an orphan until he was nearly eight and then adopted by a Cajun family in Houma, Louisiana. He graduated from Tulane University and practiced law in New Orleans at two criminal defense firms before passing the bar in New York and working at a small firm in Albany, New York.

She noted that his adoptive parents were both deceased and the law firm he worked at in Albany was gone. It had only one other attorney, however, and apparently, after Milton left, the attorney, Robert Lial, suffered a stroke and retired. By then, John Milton had racked up an impressive record of defenses. When she perused them, she concluded it was no wonder Simon and James hired him to replace Warner Murphy.

She read some of the news stories about the cases John Milton had taken on. Some of them were defenses of clients accused of the most heinous crimes like the grandmother accused of deliberately suffocating her own grandson. Her daughter and son-in-law had turned her into the police, but John Milton won an acquittal despite their testimony. In fact, reasonable doubt was built around the possibility the daughter was the murderer. From what she read, he seemed to be quite good at confusing the testimony of prosecution witnesses and carving a clear path to reasonable doubt in all his victories. None of the cases he had taken were easy defenses. If anything, he seemed to search for the most difficult.

There was a headshot of him at the end of the file. He looked too young for the career he had already had. He was certainly strikingly handsome. He had eyes, that even in a photograph, seemed alive and able to follow her. It was surely her imagination, but she thought his lips moved ever so slightly, lips that were enticing, suggestive.

I'm working too hard, she thought and quickly closed the file just as she felt her aunt's presence and looked up to see her standing there, looking at her with an unusually serious expression on her face.

"What's wrong, Aunt Eve?" she asked.

"I saw a dark shadow hovering over you just now," she said. "You're troubled. Is it this new case you're trying in court?"

She sat up quickly, fighting the urge to look around. Her aunt could spook her sometimes, and she could certainly spook herself. Lately, she was always looking behind her, and it wasn't simply because she was living in a big city now. She had been doing that back home, too, especially when she took on a prosecution. Maybe she should see a therapist. She wasn't just being careful anymore. She was growing paranoid.

"It's turning out to be a little more complicated than I anticipated, yes, but I'm fine. I'll handle it."

"Or it will handle you," she said. "Have you met the defendant yet?"

"No, I won't until the trial, Aunt Eve, and I might not say a word to him or him to me, unless he decides to take the stand. I'll be talking plenty about him. Don't worry about that."

She nodded.

"Sometimes, people affect you with their negativity. Stay out of his aura."

Michele laughed.

"I won't get that close. Don't worry."

Her aunt narrowed her eyes. Whenever she did that, Michele couldn't help feeling her aunt really was special in some way. She wasn't a total kook.

"There's a lot of interest in this case," Aunt Eve said, looking like she was reading a crystal ball.

"Yes, it's a high-profile victim, very wealthy and successful. The defendant is part of that world, too. There's going to be a lot of coverage in the media."

"No, there's something more," she said. "Something bigger."

Michele smiled.

"Like what, Aunt Eve?"

"I'm not sure, but I feel it. I feel deeper vibrations. Be careful, Michele. Trust no one."

"Right. Now you send just like your sister."

She snapped out her trance instantly.

"Well, I'll have to make sure that doesn't happen too often," she said and they both laughed.

"Let me take you out to dinner," Michele said feeling new energy. "We'll go to your favorite gypsy restaurant in the East Village."

"And I predict we'll both be very satisfied," Aunt Eve said.

Michele watched her leave, buried the file on John Milton in her briefcase, closed it, and then rose to shower and dress. As she took off her clothes, she found herself visualizing Lieutenant Blake again, fantasizing about him, imagining his fingers undoing her blouse, unzipping her skirt and his lips brushing across her forehead, down her nose to her lips. She actually moaned thinking about it and then was abruptly ripped out of her erotic thoughts by the landline ringing. For a moment she just stared at it angrily and then, thinking it was her mother for sure, lifted the receiver roughly, nearly pulling it apart.

"Hello," she said. "I'm fine," she was about to add the moment she heard her mother's voice, but the words got stuck in her throat.

It was Lieutenant Matthew Blake.

"We're going to have to make a deal with this man," he said.

"Excuse me? What man? Surely not the defendant?"

"No, the hired killer. He'll turn on Heckett to get a lesser sentence once I corner him."

"Why do I have to make that decision now?"

"I'm close," he said. "I want to get this all neatly packaged for you."

The way he said, "for you," actually made her blush. Despite enjoying that feeling, she reacted the same way she did whenever anyone professionally involved with her made a pass at her. Her instinct was to consider it insulting, taking a liberty, thinking that somehow flattery or flirting was more important to her because she was a woman.

"Of course," she said pedantically, "Heckett is still the target. He paid for the murder. He initiated it and in my eyes and I hope the eyes of any juror, he is really the one who pulled the trigger."

"The irony here," Blake said, "is that the trigger man has committed more sins. We'll have to talk about all that one of these days," he added.

Was he suggesting a future for them beyond the Strumfield case?

She hit him with one of her favorite Professor Baker quotes. Baker was one of her law school teachers. He had a sharp wit and a great sense of irony. He was actually a little impish and loved irritating his students playing the devil's advocate.

"Morality is a luxury the law often can't afford," she replied.

Lieutenant Blake didn't laugh. Somehow, she knew he wouldn't.

"He's always counted on that," he said.

"Who?"

"Satan," he said.

She waited to hear him laugh, but he didn't. He didn't sound like he was kidding at all.

"Never met him," she said.

"Yes, you have. Many times. We all have. I'll be in touch very soon. Hopefully with some good news for you," he added and hung up before she could respond.

Nevertheless, she held the receiver against her ear for a few moments as if she could hear him talking after he had gone off the call. She caught the image of herself in the gilded oval mirror had aunt had put up on the wall. She was standing there naked holding the phone, and call it her wild imagination, or call it suggestive thinking, but she would swear that just for a moment or two, there was a dark shadow hovering over her, just as her aunt had described.

It lingered and then moved on to become one with a shadow in the corner, a corner she would avoid.

8.

"How do you know that creep?" Fish asked Blake when they left the fifth floor walk-up in the South Bronx. "I feel like we just took a dip in a sewer."

He inhaled deeply to clear his lungs of the stench and what he was certain were dozens of airborne infections. He couldn't help but imagine the nests and lava of every known insect inside those walls. The building was rotting from the inside out.

"That's where they live, the sewer," Blake muttered.

"He looks like somethin' wiped off the bottom of a shoe."

The informant was anemic looking with cloudy dull brown eyes, thinning nearly orange hair, a piece of his right earlobe missing and a rather ugly sore at the right corner of his thin, pale lips. He coughed a lot, too and spat into a ragged faded green towel. Fish didn't want to touch anything in the rat's nest, least of all him. Blake seemed unaffected, practically oblivious. His tone of voice when he questioned him was gentle, concerned, the voice of a clergyman, not a hard ass policeman.

"I thought you spoke to him pretty kindly."

"He's to be pitied, yes," Blake said. "You drive."

Fish got behind the wheel.

"I'm curious," he continued before he started the engine. "Really? How do you find somethin' like that? I hesitate to call him somebody."

"A friend of mine, a priest, Father McGukian, recommended him."

"Recommended him? That sounds like he was helping him get a job."

"In a sense he was. He thought I might help him on the path to salvation."

Fish smiled and started the engine.

"I get it," he said pulling away from the curb. "By being an informant, he thinks he's compensating for a life of sin. Balancing the old scale of justice."

"Something like that."

"This priest convinced him to cooperate?"

"That and an occasional fifty and those groceries," Blake said.

"Well, if he confessed his sins to this Father McGukian, Father McGukian isn't supposed to share that information, right?"

"He didn't share details. He just pointed me in the right direction. A good priest is not too much different from a good lawyer. They know how to split infinitives."

"Whatever. I've worked with some informants. They're usually trying to squeeze out of somethin' or another. I never saw one this down and out. And I never brought one a bag of groceries."

"Kindness and charity can unlock many a shut door. You can get more with honey than vinegar, Fish."

"I'm not going to find out that you went to seminary school first, am I?"

"You're a detective," Blake said. "Figure it out."

Fish laughed.

"Have you heard of this other guy, the guy he fingered? Skip Tyler?"

"His name's come up, but I haven't had the pleasure of an introduction."

"Right. The pleasure. This job is full of perks. Whatever you believe, Lieutenant. I sometimes wonder how anyone could like this job?"

"You think of whom you're protecting or whom you're getting their deserved justice."

"Sometimes it feels more like pest control. Doesn't it get to you?"

"What?"

"The slime, the underbelly, what my grandmother called the rust of the human soul?"

"Sure. That's when I go upstate and bathe in Nature. I just have a higher tolerance than most."

"Probably challenges your faith."

"On the contrary, it strengthens it, Fish."

"Don't get it."

"When you know your enemy well, you know his strengths and weaknesses and you know how to conduct battle. Your faith is your searchlight."

Fish looked at him. He expected to see him smiling, but Blake looked deadly serious. He nodded. Saint Matthew. Makes sense.

"Okay," he said. "I'll investigate your past and find out who you are."

"Let me know what you find out. I've been trying to find out who I am for years."

They drove on. Fish was getting more courageous about digging into Lieutenant Blake's life, but it was still like pulling nails out of cement. He still had the feeling that any moment, he would tell him to mind his own business or concentrate on their work and not him. Did the guy have any friends? No one at the precinct seemed to know and none there fit the bill.

After a few more minutes and a few more turns, Fish felt more relaxed.

"At least we're searching in a better neighborhood."

They drove to more upscale apartment buildings off Pelham Parkway in the Bronx following the directions Blake's informant had given them. The parking was horrendous however and they had to double park. This time Fish put the bubble light on the roof and turned it on.

"I had a nightmare about a parking enforcement officer giving me a ticket in the cemetery for being under the tombstone too long," he said and Blake finally laughed.

"You have a great sense of humor, Fish. It's refreshing."

"No shit?"

"Don't get too needy, Fish. I have only a few compliments to spend on anyone a day."

"I believe that," Fish said and Blake laughed again.

Maybe he was making some headway and that initial wall of un-certainty and concern between two police partners was breaking down. At least, that was what Fish hoped.

They checked the names on the apartment house directory and pushed the buzzer for Skip, real name Barry Tyler. There was no response, but an elderly lady stepped out of the building and Fish delib-erately caught his foot in the door to keep it from closing. She looked at him sharply. He quickly reached into his inside jacket pocket and took out his identification.

"Worry not, ma'am," he said showing it to her.

She shook her head.

"That's what makes me worry," she replied and walked down the short stoop of cement steps. Fish and Blake started to enter when Blake reached out and squeezed Fish's upper right arm, actually squeeze it pretty hard. He turned sharply.

"What?"

Blake nodded at the street and Fish looked. He saw a black Chrysler Town Car pull away from the curb.

"Who's that?"

"I'm pretty sure it was Tom Beardsly."

"Tom Beardsly? Why do I know that name?"

"He was that FBI agent who killed those two innocent civilians in a shoot-out last summer in Manhattan, down in Wall Street. Big story. One of those people was some international financier, a philanthropist and close friend of the mayor. It was headline news in the Wall Street Journal."

"I remember. So that was Beardsly?" he asked. He was really asking, what the hell does it matter? What's it have to do with any of this?

"Yes," Blake said. "He free lances as a private investigator for attor-neys these days."

"Attorneys. So? This is a big city, right? Legal issues on every corner. Oh, I get it, coincidence again, huh?"

Blake didn't reply. He looked very thoughtful for a moment and then walked into the building quickly and went to Skip Tyler's apartment which was on the first floor. He started to push the buzzer and stopped. The door was not quite closed. He looked at Fish and then opened the door. They both stood there a moment listening.

"Tyler?" Blake called. He looked at Fish and then took out his pistol. So did Fish.

They moved through the living room, glanced in the kitchen and then turned right to approach the bedroom. That door was open, too, and Skip Tyler was on his back on the bed looking up at the ceiling. He was in his briefs, his arms at his side in crucifix fashion. Below his left hand was a syringe. They saw the preparations for heroin on the nightstand. Tyler's eyes were wide open, a look of surprise and terror on his face.

"Overdose," Fish said.

"I don't think so," Blake said. "Let's get forensics up here. I can see a bruise on his right wrist," he said walking around the bed.

"Tryin' to find a vein maybe?"

"No" He studied the bruise a moment. "It's not a trauma from a needle puncture. It looks more like he was grabbed, tightly." He looked at Tyler's naked chest closely. "There's another here. I think someone put his knees on him and held him down. It looks like he was struggling. The syringe was injected and Tyler stop resisting. We'll get it officially confirmed. You call. I'm looking around," Blake said.

He returned to the living room and sifted through some papers and looked in drawers. Then he paused and looked at a corner of the sofa where he saw a mobile. It was still powered on. He went to contacts and then put the phone in his pocket.

"They're on their way," Fish said. "Find anything?"

"His mobile. I want to check out some numbers. The names on the phone book are obviously just tags, code for some of his deadly contacts. You stay. Don't go back in the bedroom but check out the rest of the place."

Fish had the feeling he was being given busywork.

"Maybe your desperate informant got money from someone else first, Lieutenant, someone who wasn't happy with a deal Tyler made."

"No. He'd be afraid I'd find out. Besides, it feels . . . like something more to me than just an argument. Someone came here deliberately to get him off the chart."

He started out.

"Lieutenant?"

"What?"

"You think that ex-FBI guy had something to do with this?"

"Remember my motto," Blake said.

"Enlighten me. I forgot."

"There's no such thing as a coincidence," Blake said and walked out.

"How could I have forgotten?" Fish muttered.

Outside, Blake took off the bubble light, got into the car and started to call in the telephone numbers. When the names began coming back, he wrote them down. All of them were of some interest, but one in particular shouted out at him. He had almost gone after this man because of another killing. The dates of the calls to this guy were close enough to murders he either had investigated or knew about. One date particularly interested him. It was just before the Strumfield murder. He started the engine and drove off slowly, planning a strategy.

He smiled to himself.

Perhaps he will be able to put a smile on Michele Armstrong's face before long, too. Suddenly he realized, that had become very important to him, and not just because he was helping her do her job either.

9.

Stoker Martin sat at the bar in Ernie's Tavern and fingered the hundred dollar bills in his left pocket. Of course he knew it was stupid to carry so much cash on himself, but ever since he was a kid, he enjoyed the feel of money, especially a great deal of it. Just looking at numbers in a bank book or on a brokerage statement never satisfied him, no matter how big the numbers were. Anybody could print numbers on a paper and claim to be rich, but he could pull out a wad of hundreds and fifties and instantly widen eyes and raise eyebrows if he ever wanted to. No one could convince him that seeing so much money didn't still impress everyone, even in the age of credit cards. They still had scenes with suitcases loaded with bundled dollars in movies, didn't they? He could see people in the theater smile or look envious. They didn't react as vividly when numbers were mentioned or viewed on a page.

As nutty as it sounded, he also liked the scent of money, even coins. He fantasized filling a bathtub with hundred dollar bills and submerging in it. He got so he seriously planned to have Tanya take a picture of him doing just that, maybe next week. The only thing that made him hesitate was he wasn't sure it was a good idea to let her know just how much he really had. She knew he was flush most of the time, but she surely never imagined how rich he was becoming. And she never asked any questions. She was the kind of girl who always closed her eyes when violent scenes came on in a film.

He looked about the tavern to see if anyone was looking at him in particular. He wasn't stupid about it. He didn't show the money in public. He could feel it in his pocket, but he wouldn't exhibit it, especially in a place like this. In his wallet he kept the money he would spend, and he kept that in fives and ones, barely totaling fifty dollars.

Ironically, he was proud of the fact that he had never robbed anyone. It seemed beneath him to do that. Any idiot could figure out how to rob someone of whatever he carried and most petty thieves weren't capable of pulling the trigger. They were simply bullies with courage propped up with a gun or knife. Victims were cowards, on the other hand. If they put up any resistance, the creeps would probably high-tail it. Yeah, there was a little gamble involved, but there was always what he called a fail-safe point, a moment when you realized this creep could pull the trigger. Then and only then would you gave in. He was confident he had the ability to see that. He looked in the mirror, didn't he? The thought brought a smile to his face.

Of course, the way you dressed and carried yourself also invited these creeps. If you look like a wimp, they'll come after you. The trick was to look tougher than they were. In fact, you should look like you might rob someone yourself. That would keep them away. Of course, that meant he shouldn't carry a weapon until he was on a job. He could be just as interesting to cops as he was threatening to crooks, and one thing you didn't want to be caught carrying in New York City, especially, was an unlicensed concealed weapon. He didn't even have them in his home. Skip provided the weapon. He liked the fact that it couldn't be traced to him. Of course, now this was especially true of the last job.

"Part of the service for my ten percent," Skip had kidded, but it wasn't a joke to him. He expected that kind of service and preparation. He took more precautions than a boy scout.

Maybe I should run a survival course for people like me and people who lived in urban areas, especially these tough neighborhoods, he thought. Make it a side job. Who better to teach it than someone would cut your throat or put a bullet in your head for the right price?

"Another?" Ernie asked.

Stoker checked the time. He was going to pick up Tanya at eleven tonight. He was tempted to forget about it. She would talk his ear off until he stuck his dick in her mouth and even then, she would mumble some final words. Like he was ever interested in her work or her customers or for that matter, anything she had to say. It was time to dump her and go for someone with a little more class. With the money he had and could spend, he deserved someone younger and far more educated. Maybe he would spruce up his wardrobe and start hanging out where professional working women would hang out. He could pick up one of those high-priced escorts or something.

The clump talking behind him let out a loud laugh as if they had just heard his plan. You? Find someone with class? What would you talk about, driving a gas tanker? The last book you read was the phone book. You don't even know the name of your Congressman. He glanced at them disdainfully. And then, enviously. Maybe if he thought back to grade school, he would recall having a group of friends like that. It was times like these when he was struck and struck hard and deeply at just how much of a loner he had become. The work required it, he rationalized and turned back to Ernie.

"Yeah, one more, but that's it," he told Ernie. "I don't want to be arrested for WUI."

"WUI? What's that?"

"Walking under the influence," he said.

Ernie smiled. Stoker shook his head in disgust. Ernie was five feet ten and about twenty-five pounds overweight at least, but he had a great personality for a bartender and owner of a tavern, always able to at least appear interested in whatever his customers had to say, even if what they said was clearly stupid. He would have made a great politician, Stoker thought, but he did have a lucrative tavern, always busy with a tribe of regulars who had turned it into their private tee-pee. Here they argued politics, business, and whatever tabloid story led the headlines. There was always a lot of chatter and laughter. It had a friendly, warm atmosphere and was as close to an English pub as any American bar could be. If Stoker was being truthful, he'd have to admit that was what drew him here. Maybe he wasn't part of any click, but he could at least pretend to be. He could even join in their laughter from time to time.

It was such a simple place, barely decorated with some old movie posters in frames, some wall sconces, the usual plaques and licenses, and some pictures of Ernie's family. Ernie and his son ran the bar and his wife and daughter-in-law manned the kitchen to produce the simple menu that satisfied those who wanted something to eat as well. Occasionally, Stoker had some of their fish and chips. In his own way, Ernie Stratton was a success.

But what disgusted Stoker and what he criticized Ernie for was his bad teeth. He was missing at least two on the lower right and three on the upper left. When he smiled, he looked like someone from the hills in *Deliverance*, Ernie's favorite movie. Ordinarily, that would be enough to discourage would be customers, but many of the people who came in here weren't that better looking and also were missing some teeth. In fact, he probably had the best set of dentures of anyone in the joint.

"What if I paid for your dental work?" Stoker offered when Ernie brought him his third vodka and cranberry juice.

"Who needs it? I ain't goin' to be in magazine ads or movies and my wife loves me just the way I am."

"She has no choice," Ernie said and sipped his drink. Ernie smiled again and again, Ernie shook his head. Did he get the point?

Of course his wife had no choice. She wasn't very good looking either. If ever two people settled into each other comfortably, it was these two, he thought. They deserved each other. He vaguely wondered if anyone who had seen him with Tanya had similar thoughts about him and her. He'd hate that.

"Oh shit," Ernie said returning. He was carrying a sealed eight and a half by eleven envelope. "I forgot about this. Some guy left it here a few hours ago."

"For me?"

"Yeah. See? He wrote your name on it."

Ernie took the envelope slowly and looked at Ernie.

"Who was he?"

"He didn't say. He was a pretty good lookin' guy. Never saw him before. He wore a jacket and tie, and, oh yeah, a pair of sunglasses." Ernie leaned over the bar to whisper. "He wasn't cleanly shaven. He looked like one of those guys you see in clothes catalogues or somethin'," he said nodding at one of his regulars. "Otherwise, he looked like an FBI agent or somethin'." He squinted. "Are you a spy? I always wondered what you did, Stoker."

"I'm a janitor. I clean up other people's messes," Stoker snapped back at him.

"Really? I thought you were the CEO of IBM," Ernie returned, but smiled.

Stoker studied the envelope. Skip would never send anyone like that around to give him an assignment. It wasn't his style. They were always extra careful about everything. Ernie stood there a moment more, watching him eye the envelope. Stoker looked up at him sharply.

"I didn't open it or nothin'. He was adamant about that."

"Huh? What do you mean, adamant?"

"He said make sure you don't open it, and when he said it, he took off his sunglasses and looked at me with eyes of cold steel. I think the guy could scare the shit out of Dracula."

He looked around his tavern.

"Creepy," he added.

'What?" Stoker asked.

"I could feel him watchin' me afterward, even though he left. I almost feel him watchin' me now."

Ernie turned quickly and studied the crowd again.

"No, he ain't here," Ernie said. "He's not the kind of guy who can get lost in a crowd. You'd spot him in Madison Square Garden during a Knicks game," he said and returned to the other end of the bar.

Stoker studied the envelope and especially his name. There was something weird about it, he thought and then realized, it was in his handwriting. It really did look like he had written his own name on the outside of this envelope. What the fuck. Whoever wrote this was good at forgery.

He started to open it, but stopped and looked at the man sitting two stools down. The man glanced at him and then looked away quickly. He checked his left. The two couples there were in loud conversations and didn't know he even existed. He looked behind him, too, but didn't see anyone taking any particular interest in him. The clump that had been laughing were now broken up into smaller groups of three and four and had moved away.

Confident it was all right, he began to tear open the envelope carefully. He separated it and slowly plucked out what were photographs.

Of people he had killed! Blood and all, lying dead at the scenes of the hits. These were like . . . police photos.

After he realized what the pictures were, he quickly shoved them back into the envelope and tried to seal it, but the glue wouldn't take. He felt like he had fallen into a vat of ice water.

He looked around again. Someone was obviously here watching him for his reaction. What the hell was this? Who would do it? If it was a cop, why didn't he just step up to arrest him? Was that coming any moment? He felt his heartbeat in his head. The pounding resonated that hard.

This was probably going to turn into some sort of blackmail, he concluded when no one stepped up after he had looked at the photos. Maybe someone from the police forensic teams had put this together. A police department was a rich garden in which to grow blackmailers. It puzzled him as to why there wasn't a note inside, a number for him to call, however. Was that coming later? He nearly jumped when he heard Ernie's phone ringing. He watched him talking, holding his breath the whole time, but Ernie's call wasn't about him. It didn't last long either. He wasn't going to wait for another.

As nonchalantly as he could, he put down the money for his drinks, took another gulp of his last drink, and then slipped off the stool. Ernie wasn't paying attention and Stoker didn't feel like saying good night anyway. He might hurry over to ask more questions about what was inside the envelope. Stoker turned and walked very slowly toward the exit, trying not to be obvious about the way he studied people on his left and right. No one was paying much attention to him. He was almost out, but what then? Would whoever did this be waiting for him? He hesitated at the door. Now he wished he was packing a revolver.

Stoker couldn't see it, but a half a block up from the far right corner outside Ernie's, John Milton's limousine was parked. John stepped out and walked briskly to the corner just across from Ernie's on the right. Two men in their early twenties with shaved heads and tattoos on the backs of their necks huddled and smoked while they stared at the entrance to Ernie's. They didn't see or hear John approach until he was practically on top of them. Then both spun around.

"Waiting for someone to come out, someone a little under the weather?"

"What's it to you?" the young man on the right asked.

"Maybe we're waiting for you," the other said.

John smiled and very calmly said, "You're always waiting for me."

"Wise guy," the first young man replied and took a step toward him. "Maybe too wise," he added and flicked a knife almost out the palm of his hand.

John looked at it. Suddenly, it began to glow like a horseshoe a blacksmith was shaping on an anvil. The young man dropped it and cried out. His partner stepped back, his eyes wide.

"What the hell?" His friend asked. "Why'd you drop it, Buzzy?"

"Didn't you see it turn hot, Jason? You pick it up," Buzzy said. Jason looked at John and then picked it up. It wasn't hot at all.

"What are you, a fuckin' idiot?" Jason turned to John. "Now where were we?" he asked.

John stared at him. Suddenly, as if his arm had a mind of its own, it started to bend toward him, moving the blade toward his throat. The young man's eyes bulged with terror as he struggled to keep his own arm from driving the blade into his throat.

"Suicidal?" John asked. He smiled. Jason's arm relaxed and he took a deep breath of relief. Buzzy still held his palm and stared in disbelief. They both turned back to John, who continued to smile.

"How'd you do that?" Jason asked him.

"I'm always learning new things here," John said, not really answering his question. "I'm going to call on you two again. I don't think you'll forget me." He nodded at Ernie's. "Keep watching. The next man who comes out is carrying thousands of dollars in his left pants pocket. He won't let you take it from him alive, however. Get my drift? You'll have more money than you could steal in a year."

Both looked at the front of Ernie's and then back at him.

"Who the hell are you?" Buzzy asked, sill rubbing his palms where they had been singed.

"I'm your guardian angel. Good luck, lads."

They heard the door open across the street, the laughter, conversation and muffled music spilling out on the sidewalk as Stoker emerged. He paused, looked both ways and then started to his right.

"Go," John said. "Now!"

Like attack dogs, both jerked around and started across the street. Stoker turned as they approached him quickly. Usually confident of himself, Stoker was still a bit shaken by what he was holding and how it was delivered. He assumed the two young men had something to do with it and braced himself. They didn't look that big. He didn't see the knife in time. The young man holding it never slowed.

"What the fuck," he cried. The creep looked like he would walk right though him, but instead, he caught Stoker right in the solar plexus. Stoker's eyes nearly exploded with the surprise.

"Sorry," John called out from the shadows across the street. "Sometimes, sacrifices have to be made for the greater bad."

He laughed and started walking slowly back to his limousine.

Buzzy and Jason were already rifling through Stoker's pockets, elated with their discovery and confused, too. But as they heard many times over, "Never look a gift horse in the mouth."

Cheered by their good fortune, they ran off into the darkness.

Stoker groaned.

He was still clinging to the envelope. His last thought was, at least they didn't get this.

10.

Fish parked at a no parking, no standing zone in front of the apartment building from which Warner Murphy fell to his death. He put their police identification emblem on the top of the dashboard in clear view.

"Some asshole will probably ticket us anyway," he told Matthew Blake. He might as well be talking to himself, he thought. Blake hadn't said two words since they had started out this morning. He had that far-off look that Fish was getting used to, but knew he would never be comfortable with. Cullen was right. There was something eerie about him.

Blake looked at him and then at the building as if he just realized they were there.

"Let's go," he said.

"You sure she's ready for this? You said you couldn't speak to her in the hospital. She's not out that long."

"It's as good a time as any. She'll never be ready for this," Blake said and got out.

Fish moved quickly to keep up with him, another thing he found himself constantly having to do. Sometimes, he thought Blake could glide over the sidewalk and fly up stairs. They stopped at the reception desk. Charlie Bivens looked up quickly from his newspaper. Immediately recognizing Blake and Fish, he snapped to attention.

"Officers," he said. "How can I help you today?"

Fish expected Blake would just ask him to announce their arrival to Sheila Murphy and then enable the elevator for them to go up to the apartment, but he stepped closer to the desk, practically leaning over it.

"How long have you worked here?" he asked Bivens. The question, although quite simple, seemed to throw him.

"Here?"

Blake just glared at him.

"Almost a year," he muttered. "I worked security for the TSA for nearly twelve," he added, now showing a little indignation. "I think I've been vetted pretty carefully. The board of directors for this building would make their own mothers go through the hoops. Besides, with all the backup systems installed, there'd be some evidence if I screwed up. As I told you and as you saw for yourselves, no one went up before Warner Murphy went down," he said.

"That's not funny," Fish said before Blake could respond.

"I don't like the implication of the question."

"What implication?" Fish asked him. He didn't think Blake had a particularly accusatory tone to his voice. It sounded very matter-of-fact to him.

"Sensitive," Blake said without changing expression. "You ever hear the expression, 'Me thinks the lady doth protest too much?'"

"What lady?"

Blake didn't reply and when he looked at Fish, he saw he was just as confused by the quote.

"Look. You know I can't turn the cameras off and I was at this desk the whole morning. There was only that five second glitch . . . hardly enough time for anyone to get by me. Besides, even if I fell asleep, it wouldn't matter. Why ask anything is all I'm saying?"

"That's what we're paid to do," Fish said, even though he couldn't help but agree with Bivens.

"Let Mrs. Murphy know we've arrived," Blake said with a commanding tone.

Bivens nodded at the camera above him and speed dialed Sheila Murphy.

"Lieutenant Blake and . . . sorry, what's your name again?"

"Detective Fish," Fish said. He didn't know why, but now he didn't like this guy. It was as if Blake had unmasked him with a simple question.

"And Detective Fish." Bivens hung up. "You can go up," he said. "Fish. Perfect name for a detective. You fish around, right?"

"And catch anything, even sharks," Fish said. He looked at Blake and thought he saw a slight relaxation in his lips, which was as close to a smile as he had gotten yet today.

They headed for the elevators.

"You suspect that guy of something?"

"There's something not kosher about him," Blake said. "I'm working on it."

They got into the elevator. Fish looked up, reminding himself.

"As we already knew, they even got cameras in here, Matt, and if he can't shut them down . . ."

Blake didn't respond. He stepped out as soon as they door opened enough and headed for the Murphy apartment. Sheila had the door opened before they got there. She had her hair down; her face was ashen. She wore no lipstick and was in a pink, floral robe and a pair of pink slippers.

Fish hadn't met her. He thought she was pretty and so young looking, so vulnerable, more like a little girl. Tragedy and sorrow aged people in his experience, but this woman looked like she had been thrown back years and needed someone to hug her and comfort her the way a child would. He wished he could do just that.

"I'm sorry to be bothering you again," Matt Blake said sincerely, perhaps moved by the same feelings moving Fish. "Thanks for seeing us."

"I'm glad you're here. I'm glad someone's investigating," she said, sucking in her breath, and stepped back to let them in. "Would you like some coffee? I've already made it," she added.

"Sure, thanks."

"Thank you," Fish echoed.

They followed her into the kitchen, noting that she had the curtains closed on the patio door. From what they could see, every window in the apartment had closed curtains. People in such sorrow were more comfortable in the darkness and shadows. Bright light screamed the ugly truth.

"My daughter is still at my parents' house. I'm afraid to bring her home. I just want to pack up and sell as soon as I can," she added and poured the coffee into two cups she had already set up on the kitchenette table. There was sugar and milk beside them. Fish sat first. Blake didn't sit until she did. They sipped some coffee. Sheila looked down at her cup ran the spoon in a circle.

"Understandable," Blake said. "Eventually, we become part of our surroundings and they become part of us."

What the hell does that mean? Fish wondered.

Sheila Murphy appeared to understand, however. She looked up, her eyes still bloodshot. It looked like tears were frozen under the lids and were just peering out.

"Exactly. I haven't slept in our bed yet. I sleep on the sofa. I'm afraid to look at any of Warner's things. When I do, I just start crying. I'm sorry. I know you're not here to hear any of this."

"Of course we are, Mrs. Murphy. We don't act in a vacuum. Terrible things happen to people and when we can't appreciate their sorrow, it's time for us to hand in our badges."

Sheila smiled.

"Thank you. I told everyone and I'm telling you again. My husband would never have killed himself. Not now, not ever."

"Can you think of anyone who would want to do your husband harm?" Blake asked.

She sat back and shook her head slowly.

"Neither of us have had anything close to a bad argument with anyone for years. I know he wasn't cherished by members of the district attorney's office."

"I doubt any of them take a loss that hard," Fish offered. She looked at Blake.

"Since Adam and Eve, no one is above suspicion," he said sounding like some prophet.

Sheila nodded.

"When you left the apartment and the elevator opened in the lobby, what did you see? Try to visualize it and tell me anything, no detail too small," Blake said.

She looked at them both and took a deep breath before she began.

"Megan was talking a blue streak like she always does in the morning. She wakes up and begins in mid-sentence sometimes, like she fell asleep before finishing a thought. She can be exhausting, despite her tiny size," she added, smiling and shifting from an aura of gloom to one of love and mother's pride. Both Blake and Fish smiled sympathetically, Fish happy he could have a reason to. "I wasn't paying all that much attention. I remember Mr. Bivens looked up. He was reading something. He said good morning."

"Did your daughter say good morning to him?" Blake asked.

Fish nearly choked on his sip of coffee. What the hell would that matter?

"No. She never said good morning to Mr. Bivens. He really never said good morning to her or said hello to her. I don't think he's comfortable with children."

Blake nodded. He looked like he had confirmed something.

"So you step out of the building. Your car is waiting?"

"Yes. We have a service to take Megan to school. Thank God we were off before . . . before . . ."

"No one came in right after you went out as far as you remember?"

"I didn't look back, but no one walked in while I was walking out."

"Do you remember anything at all unusual? Anything?"

She started to shake her head and then paused. "I do remember something."

"What?" Blake asked quickly, practically pouncing on her.

"It can't be anything. I'm sure it will sound silly, too."

"Sometimes what looks unimportant is important or what seems impossible is possible," Blake said. Again, Fish thought he sounded more like a philosophy teacher than a police detective.

"There was a man in a delivery uniform."

"New York's full of delivery men," Fish said. She looked at him and nodded.

"I was looking at this young woman though. She had on a very stylistic jacket and I was thinking about it when . . ."

"When what?" Blake asked when she looked like she would not continue.

"When this delivery man came out of nowhere. He was right behind her. I know it sounds silly."

Fish looked at Blake and then at her.

"I don't understand," Fish said. "So he was right behind her and you couldn't see him at first, right?"

She shook her head.

"It doesn't make sense, I know. But, he wasn't there and then he was. It all happened so fast. I forgot about it until just now."

"He wasn't there and then he was?" Fish repeated.

"Exactly."

"Maybe you were just looking at the jacket so hard that you didn't see him."

"Maybe, but . . . there was a space around her and between her and other people coming up the walk. He wasn't there and then he was," she repeated. "I sound crazy, I know. And everyone would expect me to."

Suddenly, she became more animated, more determined.

"Warner was getting ready to go to the office to receive the news that he was being made a full partner," she continued. "He was bursting with pride. We had made dinner reservations for a big celebration at Le Grenouille. My husband always had big ambitions. He wanted to become a judge someday, perhaps first as the judge for the New York Supreme Court in one of the jurisdictions and then up the ladder. This wasn't a man who just decides to take his own life. Someone killed my husband. Someone killed him but because of all the technology in this building, and no evidence of a stranger, nothing will happen," she added, now her voice full of rage as well as sorrow. "No one will do anything!"

"I'm here," Matthew said. She was growing hysterical, but his sharp, clear and firm statement stopped it in its tracks. "I'm not buying suicide," he assured her.

She took a deep breath, relaxed again and almost smiled when she sat back.

"Thank you," She said, but she had lost the look of a woman in mourning and had taken on the look of someone seeing vengeance as well as justice. Her face softened again. "I'm sorry. I don't mean to shout at you."

"That's okay," Fish said first. "I'm used to it."

"This might sound horrible for me to say," she continued, looking down now as if she couldn't look at them when she spoke, "but I'm concerned about the stigma of having your husband and your father known as a suicide victim. He's dead; he shouldn't be, but he didn't kill himself."

A pregnant moment of silence unnerved Fish.

"Sure, sure," he said, unable to think of anything else appropriate.

"Think about one other thing," Blake said. "During the preceding weeks, even months, did you or your husband meet a stranger that drew your curiosity? Did he talk about anyone?"

She sat back and thought.

"We've been to a number of parties over the past few weeks, parties with lawyers mostly. He met some new ones. I was introduced to wives," but nothing ever came of any of that. I mean, we made no new friends especially." She thought and then shrugged. "The only one that stands out for me, and mostly because of Warner's reaction, was this judge who's on the Criminal Branch of Supreme Court who tries felony cases in New York City. Warner didn't get along with him in court. They were like oil and water. Usually it was all over procedure and that sort of thing, according to Warner. He said he would pick away at him sometimes, hammering down on the smallest details. Warner wondered if he reminded the judge of someone he disliked or something.

"Anyway, he was at this recent party at one of the home of one of the senior partners, Bill Simon, and out of the blue this judge was very friendly toward Warner. He knew Warner was going to make full-partner and Warner said the man was as proud of him as his own father could be. He was gushing with compliments. Warner thought he might be bipolar or something."

"What's the judge's name?"

"Hunter. Daniel Hunter."

They were all quiet a moment and then she looked up.

"His sister lives in this building," she said. "Second floor." She divorced her husband years ago. Talk about stigma and embarrassment. Her husband, the judge's brother-in-law was convicted of pedophilia. He went to prison and, I believe, died there. Warner said he was murdered but no one cared. Convicts, he said, like to abuse pedophiles especially."

She paused. Fish looked at Blake. Was he just being polite? He looked very interested. What could that information possibly have to do with Warner Murphy's death?

"Do you have much to do with the judge's sister?"

"Little or nothing. A hello is about it. I haven't seen her anywhere but the lobby. She always looked terribly unhappy to me, depressed. Neither Warner nor I like being around people with negative energy," she said. "I mean, he didn't."

"What's her name?"

"She went back to her maiden name, Semantha Hunter. I'm sorry. I can't think of anything else. We've had wonderful years here. There isn't anything I can think of that would suggest a thing like this might happen to us."

"Okay. That's fine. I'll keep in touch with you," Matthew Blake said. He nodded at Fish and they both stood. "Thanks for the coffee." He paused and then asked, "Why isn't anyone here with you?"

"I have friends. I don't want to make it sound like I don't. Plenty of them offered, but I just needed to be alone for a while."

"Understood," Blake said.

"Sure," Fish added.

She followed them to the front door.

"None of this makes any sense," she said. "I keep expecting to wake up and realize it was all just a nightmare."

Blake looked at her and nodded.

"It will never end," he said. "It will just fade back under the weight of time."

Fish felt his mouth fall open. Why the hell did he say something like that to a woman in terrible mourning? However, she didn't look upset. She looked like he had confirmed what she had always believed.

And then, he hugged her, nodded at Fish and walked out. Fish pressed her hand softly, tried to smile and followed Blake. Hell, this was sad. For a moment, he couldn't speak. He just followed Blake to the elevator.

"I don't know what to make of any of that," he said when the door opened for them. "Some delivery man suddenly appears. A judge's sister lives in the building. Her husband was a convicted pedophile. The judge didn't like Warner Murphy and then was proud of him? And the stuff about Bivens? Her daughter didn't like him and he didn't like children? So?"

"It's helpful," Blake said.

"How?"

"There has to be a portal," Matthew Blake said.

"A portal? What's a portal?"

"An entry," Blake said.

"Entry?"

"A way he can get in."

"Oh. You're thinking basement, a window, what?"

Blake looked at him but didn't respond.

"What am I missing?" Fish asked.

"That's what we're trying to find out, Detective," he said.

The door opened on the lobby. Bivens looked up at them.

He paused, expecting Blake to say something else to the receptionist or ask another question, but he didn't stop to say anything to Bivens. He didn't even look at him.

Before they reached their vehicle that did have a parking ticket on it, Blake's mobile rang. He stopped while Fish went over and ripped the ticket off the windshield, tearing it up and cursing under his breath.

He looked back when Blake ended his call. He could see from the expression on his face that something was wrong.

"What?" he asked.

Blake walked slowly to the car. Fish stood there waiting, the shreds of the ticket in his hands. Blake seemed to suddenly remember he was with him.

"Lieutenant?"

"I'm going to disappoint someone, "I'm afraid."

"Who?"

"Assistant district attorney."

"Why?"

"I was putting the pressure on someone, expecting to break him today when I confronted him and help her nail down her case."

"What happened?"

"Someone confronted him and broke him ahead of me last night, broke him for good," he said.

11.

"I don't understand about the pictures in the envelope he was found holding," Michele said.

Blake looked like he wasn't listening to her. He was looking out the front window of the coffee café intently. She turned to look as well. All she saw was ordinary traffic and pedestrians, none of whom looked particularly interesting.

"What?" she practically shouted and he turned to her, took a sip of his coffee, and sat forward, turning those fascinating eyes into her rather than on her. She felt like he was reading her thoughts and the power of that penetration actually made her face warm. She knew her cheeks had flushed the way the cheeks of someone caught doing something not meant for anyone else's eyes might look.

"I was cornering Stoker Martin like a trapped rat," he said. "The pictures were pictures of his victims taken at the scene of the murders. I knew where he hung out and had the envelope left there for him. From what the tavern owner told me, after he gave him the envelope and he looked at the contents, he hurried out of the place. Fled was actually the word he used."

"How would that . . ."

"I wanted him to feel like he was being blackmailed, that he was vulnerable and that he would take the fall for all the people who had paid him to eliminate people. My expectation was that he would then go for the deal we presented and in this particular case, lead us to Heckett."

"How did Heckett find him originally? What, is there a help wanted column for hit men or something in New York? From what I know about him, Heckett doesn't live in that world."

"He knew someone who knew someone apparently. The someone he contacted acts like an agent. He gets a commission. You'll appreciate this. His name is Barry Tyler. He had more than five in his murder agency."

"What do you mean had?"

"Someone gave him a heroin overdose."

"Maybe he did it to himself. Isn't that usually the case?"

"Yes, but not in this case. He wasn't a heroin addict," Blake said and drank some more coffee. "Forensics confirmed that he was held down while the needle was inserted."

"Well, why was he murdered, too? Coincidence?"

"No. Nothing's ever a coincidence," he said. He thought a moment like someone who was trying to be careful about what he said and how he said it. "There's something bigger going on, perhaps."

"Bigger? You've said that before. What? Terrorism? What?" she asked, unable to disguise her impatience.

"I don't know yet."

She sat back, nodding.

"So what are you telling me, Lieutenant? It's going to be difficult if not impossible to tie Heckett to a hired gun?"

"I'm tracing some financial information to Tyler to establish at least the logical suspicion of a link, but this is all finally done in cash."

"No, I don't imagine hit men take credit cards or personal checks," she said, a little more irritably than she had intended, but he was telling her this was going to be much more difficult than she had hoped.

"No, they don't."

"Maybe we should forget about the hit man. We have motive. We have opportunity. We have an eye witness to his proximity to the event. We have the weapon used in his possession with his prints on it."

"I know he didn't do the actual shooting, Michele. Ignoring it because we're having trouble proving the connection to Stoker Martin worries me."

"Look," she said now leaning in on him, "you did your part of this. Now it's up to me. I'll run with the horses I have. It's how the system works."

Blake nodded.

"The ends justify the means."

"Never occurred to you, never played a part in what you do?" she asked.

He didn't answer. He finished his coffee and looked out the window again just as Fish pulled up.

"My ride's here," he said.

"Your ride? How did you get here? Taxi? Subway" Michele sat back. Maybe she had made a mistake putting so much faith in him or worse yet, letting herself become attracted to him. What did she really know about him? "Where do you live, Lieutenant?"

"I have a pied a terre in the East Village."

"Pied a terre? So where is your primary residence?"

He smiled.

"You sound like my accountant. I have a small house in Sullivan County."

"Sullivan County? I know it well. My family lives in Orange County, but we're not far. I've been to restaurants in Rock Hill, Monticello, even a small one in a village called Woodbourne. On cases, of course."

"I'm just outside of Woodbourne. Whenever I have time off, I go up for a country holiday," he said. "Nice place to kick back when things get a little overwhelming, which I'm sure they do for you as well."

His words hung in the air: a future invitation. She smiled.

"You mean, overwhelming like right now?"

"I'll see what else I can come up with," he said. His eyes seemed to freeze with a thought.

"What?" she asked.

"It's almost like someone is watching everything I do, hearing everything I say."

She just stared at him. Unfortunately, she shared the feeling. Was his understandable paranoia or did he really believe it?

"If anyone should know if he's being followed or his phone tapped, it's you."

"Yes." He smiled. "I'll figure it out."

He glanced outside again and saw Fish had spotted them. He nodded at him.

"That's my partner, Detective John Fish. He's a bit green under the gills, but he'll get there," Blake predicted.

"Fish, gills?"

Blake smiled again. She could count how many times he had since they had met, but she enjoyed each time. That was for sure. She hadn't felt this way since her first real schoolgirl crush on her English teacher, Martin Andrews when she was in the tenth grade. He had a smile that flashed like a neon billboard. All the girls were in love with him, but he floated above them like someone filled with helium, never losing that gap that kept them fantasizing but without real hope even though he was still a bachelor.

He stood up.

"Thanks for the coffee and bagel." He started to turn and stopped. "I'm on the Murphy case," he said.

"You still don't believe it was suicide?"

"No. I don't believe it was. However, I don't have anything that would cause anyone else to believe as I do."

"You really do have faith in your own instincts. Any other investigator I've met would be happy to peal it off and go on to easier cases."

"It's not in my DNA to take the easy way out. I'll be in touch if I come up with anything that will help with tying Heckett to Stoker Martin."

He turned and walked out of the café. She watched him walk to the vehicle and then signaled the waitress for the bill. It was funny. He hadn't brought her any information that would make her job easier. On the contrary, he had all but closed the door to a slam dunk conviction. She'd have to work the jury out of any reasonable doubt, but seeing him energized her. It was as if he had an energy that nudged her in places long dormant. She was so cheerful in fact that the droll waitress who obviously hated her job and had a difficult life, maybe supporting a couple of teenage children or something, brightened.

It was like passing on some magic. Now the waitress would and so on and so on until the sun would come out for everyone.

Aunt Eve would love to hear these thoughts, she mused as she walked out and headed back to the office, her confidence riding to the surface and boiling over like milk in an unwatched pot. She glanced back as if she expected Matthew Blake was still outside the restaurant, watching her disappear down the street and around a corner. But he was gone. She was disappointed.

Already a few blocks away, Fish followed Blake's orders and headed back to Murphy's apartment building. As usual, Blake was quiet. Sometimes, Fish felt like he was literally alone. He was imagining Blake being there. This was quite different from his last partnership. Sam Wisenberg hardly ever shut up. He would hear his voice in his dreams for the rest of his life. He knew Wisenberg was a nervous talker. He didn't have the personality for the job, but if Fish hadn't gotten promoted and away from Wisenberg, he was convinced he would be the one who had the nervous breakdown.

He wasn't sure, however, that he liked this dramatic contrast.

"Was that the assistant district attorney?"

"Michele Armstrong. She's prosecuting Lester Heckett."

"I couldn't see much, but she looks like she could be in the movies acting the role."

"We all act in roles," Blake said. "The only thing we don't know for sure is how it all ends."

"What, did you study philosophy or something?"

Blake smiled.

"Something," he said.

They drove on.

"Maybe if we park in the same spot, the traffic officer will get it," Fish said pulling into the same spot. "Or maybe it's just a role she has to play, huh?"

"Maybe," Blake said and got out.

"Who we gonna see?" Fish asked, again having to catch up. Whenever Blake got out of their car or started away from any place they were at for that matter, he walked so quickly that it gave Fish the feeling he wouldn't notice or care if he didn't catch up.

"Semantha Hunter first," he replied.

"The judge's sister?"

What the hell was Blake looking for in all this? Fish wondered.

They entered the lobby. Bivens was watching something on his smart phone, but the moment he saw them, he shut it down and sat up.

"If this keeps up, I'll put in for a job in the police department," he said as they approached.

"Why didn't you?" Blake fired back.

"Huh?"

"You went into security. That's police work. Why didn't you go whole hog and join the NYPD? You were in the military police in the army for nearly six years."

"And it was hard work, too. The military is full of social rejects and losers who couldn't make tea in civilian life. I've probably investigated as many crimes as you two have. I had enough of that. The TSA was child's play compared to it and this is child's play compared to the TSA."

Blake nodded.

"The easier way out is often the easier way in."

"What?" Bivens looked at Fish to see if he was as suspicious of him as Lieutenant Blake seemed to be, but he looked like a perennial tag-along, just as surprised as he was in how much interest in him Lieutenant Blake had.

"Where were you doing that short break in the recording?" Blake asked.

"Right here. The only time I leave this desk when I'm on duty is when I have to go to the bathroom. I didn't miss anything or anyone. If anyone had slipped in, he would have had to go up the stairs twenty flights. There's no one going up during that time on any of the elevator video. You guys saw that."

"Walking up twenty flights is not impossible," Blake said.

"It is for me," Bivens replied. He looked at Fish. "How about you?"

"Would you notify Semantha Hunter we are here to see her. I called her earlier so she knows," Blake said.

"Semantha Hunter?"

"203," Blake added.

"Oh, I know." He dialed and announced them and sent their picture to her monitor.

"What do you know about her?" Blake asked him.

He shrugged.

"She's some judge's sister. She's a kook. Everything is delivered to her apartment. She'll come down here like she's going out and then for no reason I could see, turning and go back up."

Blake and Fish headed for the elevator.

"I see you did do some research on that guy." Fish said.

"I started."

"How come you didn't tell me you were doing that?"

Blake looked at him as the elevator doors opened.

"I thought you'd realize from the last time that I have bad vibes about Bivens. You shouldn't be surprised," he said, sounding very critical.

Fish shrugged.

"I'm not surprised. I just thought I should know where you're going and be in on it."

"You're in on it," Blake said and pushed the button for two. "Relax. You'll be in deeply before you realize it," he added.

Fish didn't want to ask what that meant. The doors opened and they went to 203. Semantha Hunter was a tall, thin woman in her late forties. She had her chestnut-brown hair in imitation of Audrey Hepburn in Breakfast at Tiffany's, a hairdo that was as famous as the film, a chignon with French twist buns. She greeted them holding an unlit cigarette in a cigarette holder and wore a little black dress ankle length that resembled the iconic Givenchy design Hepburn wore in the first shot of the film.

"I'm afraid I can't give you more than fifteen minutes, darlings," she said. "I have a power lunch at the Four Seasons today."

"Fifteen is all we need," Blake said. "Thank you."

She stepped back, smiling, her attention focused fully on Blake. Fish felt as if she didn't even see him. She led them to the surprisingly Spartan living room consisting of two dark-brown leather settees, a glass coffee table with an empty glass bowl on it, a bookcase, and one matching brown leather heavy cushioned chair with a side table on which there were some glamour magazines. The marble title floor had no area rug and the coffee white walls had only a print of Matisse landscape.

"I know that Matisse," Blake said looking at it. "It's Matisse's Bonheur de vivre."

"Really?" Semantha Hunter said looking at it. "I failed French. What are you saying?"

"Joy of Life. You didn't know that?"

"No, it was a recent gift. I thought the colors worked well with my décor," she said. "So how can I help the New York police department? Does it have anything to do with the unfortunate incident involving Warner Murphy?"

She sat and nodded at the settee across from her.

"Did you know him?" Blake asked.

"Not really."

She glanced at her cigarette in the holder.

"I play this game with myself every day," she said, holding the cigarette holder higher.

"Game?" Fish asked.

"I've given up smoking, but I put the cigarette in the holder and parade about with it for hours. It seems to satisfy some urge, maybe to just look chic."

"Cheap?" Fish said, confused.

"Not cheap, chic . . . that's French, isn't it?" she asked Blake.

"Yes, but there's always an argument about the etymology of words," he replied and sat. Fish sat beside him quickly. Something about this conversation was oddly fascinating, but he couldn't put his finger on why. Blake turned to him. "It means stylish."

"Yeah, I knew that. I just misheard," Fish said sounding hurt by the implication. He looked at Semantha. "Sorry."

"No problem-o," she replied smiling. "So, how can I help you? I'm sorry I can't offer you anything to drink. I really am in a little bit of a frenzy. It took me all morning to get my makeup and my hair the way I wanted. You know how women compete with each other at a power lunch, I'm sure. We're all so self-absorbed."

"That's fine. Have you had much to do with Mrs. Murphy?" Blake asked.

"Nothing more than remarking about her clothes or that sweet little girl whenever I see them. How is she doing?"

"Not well. Yet," Blake added.

"Oh, how sad. How tragic. Life is a challenge, isn't it. We all have our little tragedies."

"Yes. Speaking of that, I'd like to ask you for something that might upset you."

"Please. What could my discomfort be in relation to that poor woman's horrible ordeal?"

She fluttered her eye lashes, put her cigarette holder in and out of her mouth and waited.

"I would like the most recent picture of your late husband," he said.

Semantha Hunter just stared at him.

"I don't have a recent picture," she said finally. "I haven't thought about him for years. You know he's dead, I'm sure."

"When was the last time you saw him?"

"I can't remember," she said quickly. Her entire mood was changing rapidly. "I haven't spoken his name or had anyone speak it to me for centuries."

"Have you seen him recently?" Blake asked. She looked at Fish and then at him.

"How could I see him? He's dead."

Blake reached into his inside pocket and produced a photograph. He rose and handed it to her.

"Did he look any different?" he asked her.

She looked at the photo and then up at him. Something in Blake's face told her he wouldn't stop.

"It's the way I remember him, yes. But I don't want to remember him."

"You see him in dreams though, don't you?"

"Nightmares," she corrected.

He nodded.

"How was he dressed the last time?"

She looked away.

"He was in a sort of disguise, wasn't he?"

"Ridiculous man," she said.

Fish sat back in awe. What was this? Why talk about a dead man? Was he humoring her for some other information?

"How was he dressed?" Blake repeated.

She spun on him.

"Stupid. Like a delivery man," she said.

12.

"What was all that? The woman's a nutcase," Fish said after they walked out of Semantha Hunter's apartment.

"She's quite unbalanced, yes," Blake said. The doors opened. Blake looked back at her door. "She's really not going anywhere today, no power lunch. She's living in her own fantasies and has been ever since her husband was convicted of pedophilia."

They stepped into the elevator, but instead of pushing lobby, Blake pressed four. Before Fish could ask why, Blake continued explaining what he meant, and because getting him to talk was so difficult, Fish wasn't going to interrupt.

"Her brother, Judge Hunter, was the one who was instrumental in getting her divorce effectuated. She was always a bit of a snob, you see, so when she had this tremendous embarrassment with her husband, she was actually so disturbed that she had to be in a clinic for a while. I suspect she was always rather high-strung, nervous. I have suspicions about her relationship with her brother, in fact."

"What?"

"After her time in the clinic," Blake went on, ignoring what he had introduced into the conversation, "her brother set her up in this apartment and has cared for her ever since. Bivens was right about everything being delivered to her. From what I understand, she's become an agoraphobic."

"An agora what?"

The doors opened.

"A kind of panic disorder. It's the fear of leaving your home, the safe zone, so to speak. In her case it developed from being afraid to face people after her husband's arrest and subsequent conviction. I doubt she's gone much more than down to the lobby and back."

"Just down to the lobby?"

"She thinks everyone or anyone could look at her and know she was married to a known pedophile. Luckily, she never had children with him."

"So her dressing up like that today is what?"

"She's dressing up like Audrey Hepburn in Breakfast at Tiffany's. It's another fantasy. I wouldn't be surprised if she dresses like Scarlet O'Hara tomorrow," Blake said.

"How do you know all this about her so quickly?"

"I have a terrific search engine," Blake said and pointed to his temple.

Fish smiled and shook his head. Then he looked up when he realized they were standing in front of Sheila Murphy's apartment.

"What are we doing back here?"

Blake pressed the buzzer and turned to him.

"She can see it's us before she opens the door, but we didn't have to go through the scrutinizing security checks we did coming into the lobby to visit someone," Blake replied instead of answering Fish's question.

"Well, we did a check of everyone who lives here, Lieutenant. I haven't been able to connect anyone to Warner Murphy or his wife except for Semantha Hunter. As Mrs. Murphy told us, they didn't have friends living in this building or business acquaintances. Everyone knows who they are, but no one socialized with them."

"Maybe he doesn't live here. Maybe he was just here."

"Huh? Who?"

"Whoever threw him off the patio."

"You mean he might have been in another apartment visiting?"

"Maybe. It's logical," Blake said, but he made it sound as if logic was the weakness in the explanation.

"How much before could he have entered the building?"

"No telling."

"Well, I'll go back and check the earlier video," Fish said.

"Exactly."

"But . . . there wasn't any of a man coming up in the elevator from any floor or down from any to the twentieth floor, Lieutenant."

"As Bivens said, there's the stairs?"

"But . . . twenty flights?"

"Only if he's coming directly from the lobby. He could have come from the second floor up, for example."

"That's not much less."

"If you're determined and you want to avoid detection, it's what you do."

The door finally opened.

Sheila Murphy looked a little more put-together. Her hair was brushed and she wore lipstick. Instead of a robe and slippers, she wore a pair of designer jeans, a white blouse with frilly cuffs and collar, and a pair of black shoe boots. Her eyes, however were still quite bloodshot. She had yet to come to the point where she would open them in the morning and not begin to cry.

"Sorry," she said. "I was just finishing dressing. I'm going out to my parents' home."

"We won't detain you. Just a quick question for you, Mrs. Murphy," Blake said. He reached into his jacket pocket and produced the picture he had shown Semantha Hunter. "I know you had a only a glimpse, but do you think this was the man you saw suddenly appear on the sidewalk outside of this building?"

Sheila leaned forward, took the photograph and studied it for a moment.

"It's hard to say," she said. "It was so quick, but, yes, he resembles him. Who is he?"

Fish waited with great interest to hear what Blake would tell her.

"We're looking into it," he said, taking back the photo. "As I promised, we're on this."

"Thank you."

"I'll stay in touch," he assured her and turned to Fish who stood there looking dumbfounded.

Sheila closed the door.

"What is this?" Fish asked with more authority. "You just showed her the picture of a dead man."

"Maybe."

"Maybe? You told me he was killed in prison, didn't you?"

Blake walked to the elevator, but paused before calling for it.

"Things in this world are not often what they seem, Fish. You ever put a stick in a pond and look at it?"

"Huh? What stick?"

Blake called for the elevator.

"When it's in the water, it doesn't look straight. It looks crooked even though it isn't."

"I don't get it. What's that have to do with the picture you just showed that woman?"

"What you see and what you hear are often not true, not in the sense we understand."

He stepped into the elevator. Fish hesitated and then stepped in. Now, more than ever, he wanted to know why Peter Thomas chose early retirement.

"Not in the sense we understand? So what are you telling me? The guy might not be dead?"

"Not in the sense we understand," Blake repeated.

"What other sense is there? You're alive or you're not," he replied, this time unable to hide the irritation.

"Maybe there's a third choice," Blake said calmly.

"A third choice?" Fish thought a moment. "What? A zombie?"

Blake stared ahead, already in that state of deep thought that Fish was unfortunately getting used to. They stepped into the lobby and suddenly, Blake turned to him.

"Would you call yourself a religious man, John?"

"Religious? Well, I go to church when I can, but it's never enough to satisfy my mother."

"The point is you go, John. You pray. You believe in things you can't see or feel or hear, right? Miracles, angels . . ."

"I guess. Yeah, I do, but that's . . ."

"There are many mysteries out there, John. Just keep an open mind."

An open mind? Opened to what? It sounded like more than simply evidence you could use in court. If he didn't know for a fact that Blake was a very successful police detective, he'd think he was with a real nutcase.

They paused at the receptionist's desk. Bivens had been watching them closely. Blake smiled at him. Then he took out the photograph again and put it on the counter. Bivens looked at it with obvious hesitation, the hesitation of someone who didn't want to be quoted or in any way involved.

"What's this?"

"You've seen him, haven't you?"

Bivens grimaced. He picked up the photograph and studied it a moment and then shook his head.

"No sir, I don't recall this man."

"All the people you have met? You're absolutely sure you've never seen or met him?"

Bivens looked at the picture again and nodded.

"Yes sir, I'm sure."

Blake took back the photograph. For a moment he just stared at him. Bivens shifted uncomfortably in his chair.

"He's not familiar," he said. Blake nodded.

"I'll see you again, Charlie."

"Don't doubt it," Bivens said.

They started out, Fish keeping a step or two behind. A dead man. He's showing people a dead man.

Maybe I better talk to Cullen, he thought. This guy is beginning to scare me. He's done outstanding police work, but maybe he's cracking up. Maybe that was what Peter Thomas saw happening, but didn't know how to deal with it.

When they stepped out, Blake paused and looked across the street at John Milton's limousine. He saw Charon come out of the café with two take-out lattes. The rear window went down and John took his. He kept the window down and smiled. Blake couldn't see the smile. He saw only the hand and the outline of John Milton's head, but perhaps because of the way the sunlight reflected off the street and the car, it looked like the passenger was sitting in a pool of fire.

Fish stunned him when he let out a loud, "I don't fuckin' believe it."

"What?"

Fish nodded at their car. There was another parking ticket on their vehicle.

"Oh. Relax. Didn't you ever meet anyone like whoever this parking enforcement officer is, John? Sticklers for the rules who'd give their own mothers a parking citation?"

"Yeah, and they all look like they have a stick up the ass," Fish said. He ripped off the ticket and tore it in two.

"You're not setting a good example," Blake said nodding at the pedestrians who watched him do it.

Fish didn't respond. He got into the car and stared ahead like a young, sullen boy, the knuckles on his fingers looking like they might just pop out of his skin. Blake didn't notice. He was watching the limousine across the street start up and pull away. Then he looked up at the Murphy's patio and envisioned Warner Murphy falling like an angel who had lost his wings.

He got into the car quickly.

"Make a U-turn," he ordered.

"U-turn? Here? Talk about breaking traffic laws."

"Quickly," he emphasized.

Fish shrugged and worked his way out, spinning around and inviting a chorus of horns that sounded like angry crows. Blake leaned forward.

"Catch up with that limousine," he said.

"What's it about?"

"I've seen it here every time we've visited the building."

"It's not so uncommon a limousine, Lieutenant. Maybe it's not the same one."

"With the same driver? Not easy to forget."

They drew closer to it and Blake copied down the license plate. The limousine made a right turn and slowed.

"What now?"

"Stop," Blake said. "Pull over."

Fish had to pull in front of a fire hydrant.

"I hope that idiot is writing tickets on this block," he muttered.

He watched the limousine. Nothing was happening and then a tall, stocky man in a drab gray suit got out of a car parked two cars in front of the limousine. He sauntered up to it as if he had all day to get there. Anyone watching would think he was going to pass it by, but the limousine driver stepped out, walked around the vehicle and opened the rear door for him. He glanced at the driver and got in. The driver closed the door, gazed around and then instead of returning to the driver's side, took a step back and stood there with his arms folded across his chest, looking like some palace guard.

"You recognize the man who got into the limousine?" Blake asked Fish.

"Yeah. Something familiar about him."

"It's the same Tom Beardsly I saw on Skip Tyler's block before we found him dead." Blake said.

"The ex-FBI guy? Really?"

Blake smiled.

"What?" Fish asked, sensing Blake had more to say.

"I have some of that precious logic you crave," Blake said after reading the feedback on his smart phone.

"Enlighten me oh great guru," Fish said. If he ever needed it, it was now, he thought.

"The limousine belongs to the attorney who has taken Warner Murphy's case defending Lester Hewlett, John Milton."

"No shit."

Blake stared a moment more at Charon and the limousine and then turned back to Fish.

"So much for coincidence. As I've been trying to tell you . . . in a universe designed with natural and supernatural laws, there is no such thing as a coincidence."

"Never?"

"Take heart my friend. If that was all it was, coincidence, we'd have little to do and most likely be unemployed."

"So you're telling me that nothing just happens in this world?"

"Nothing unintended by some natural force."

"Natural force?"

"Let's go. I have some calls to make and some more research to do through my search engine. Besides, we don't want to get another parking ticket," he added.

Fish tried to laugh. He really did, but something inside him kept him from seeing any humor in anything Blake said. Everything he said had some underlying second meaning. He felt like he was studying poetry in high school again. He tried really hard, but he always seemed to miss some other meaning, some vague reference or illusion. It frustrated him back then.

And that was just the way he felt now.

Only worse.

Now he thought, it might put him in some unnecessary danger, even though he had no idea what the hell that could be.

13.

"Go on, please, Tom. You're doing so well," John Milton said.

Tom Beardsly flipped the page of his pocket notepad. He loosened the top button of his shirt and then his tie. Why wasn't John Milton as hot as he was? The vehicle was stifling. This was proving to be one of the hottest springs on record in New York City. Skyscrapers looked like they were melting. Streets looked like stove tops. The combined sweat rising from uncomfortable pedestrians could cause a change in the weather. At least open a window, he thought, but didn't demand. From the start, he had an unmitigated fear of the man, and for someone with his experience and training not to fear any man, it was as puzzling to him as it would be to anyone. He sensed the fury behind those strangely dark eyes that at times seemed to resemble heated charcoal briquettes. They glowed and would suddenly look like two rubies. Of course, he thought he was imagining it.

He glanced out at Charon who looked like he had turned into a mannequin planted on the sidewalk, but seemed somehow to be watching him through the tinted window. The man looked capable of reaching through it and seizing him by the throat if he so much as suggested he might harm John Milton. He was ashamed at how shaky his voice sounded when he began to speak again.

"Her toughest case by far was getting a husband convicted for murdering his wife. The man seemed unapproachable. He was a county court judge, Shepherd Levine."

"A county court judge? That's like bringing down a bishop," John quipped. "Put a nice feather in her cap. Tell me about it," Milton asked, looking like a little boy about to hear a bedtime story. His face was full of glee.

Beardsly nodded obediently.

"He was having an affair with a woman in the county office building, Etta Hogan, and Shepherd's story was that Etta Hogan initiated and carried out the murder of his wife after he decided he couldn't go on with the affair."

"Admit to a lesser thought evil to get the jury to accept you were innocent of the greater sin. How, like a judge. How was the wife killed?"

"Etta Hogan shot her with a snub nose thirty-eight when she was returning home from visiting her mother in the hospital. Hogan claimed

Levine provided her with the weapon, even took her to a shooting range to give her instructions and practice and then planned where and when she should confront his wife. It was to look like a robbery, taking all her money and jewelry. She always wore expensive jewelry and expensive watches, even when she just went to the grocery store."

"Ostentatious. The Liberace Syndrome. I always thought humility was unnatural for either man or woman. If you have it, flaunt it or why have it?"

Beardsly nodded again. He was eager to get this secret session over. Despite the downward journey his career and his life had taken, he still clung to an iota of self-respect. What he was doing now for John Milton and others like him kept him from looking at himself too long in a mirror, not because he believed the work was immoral, but because he still saw himself as something more than a petty spy or facilitator. He didn't mind snuffing out a creep now and then. He had done it before, but for what he saw was a higher goal, a more justifiable motive. As nuts as it might seem to others, he believed he was doing good, doing it to effectuate justice. Now he was doing what he did solely for money.

"Hogan was waiting for her when she turned onto the road that led to the Levine home. It was on an unlit side street with only their home on the dead-end street. She had her automobile parked in the middle of the road, blocking it. I'm reciting directly from her testimony," Beardsly inserted. Milton nodded. "She then leaned against her car, pretending to be sick. Mrs. Levine stepped out to see what was going on and Hogan shot her point blank twice in the chest."

"How familiar a scenario," John said. "Quite classic, actually. Those wishing to do harm to others usually rely on the goodness they possess. I think there are as many scams exploiting human kindness as there are stars in the night sky. I just love it when Good Samaritans turn out to be the ones who suffer. Thank God for the weaknesses he created in them."

"Them?"

"Humanity, Tom. Don't try to be a lawyer. Go on. I assume Judge Levine found his wife's body soon after?"

"Yes, he was concerned when she was so late. He called the police first to see if there were any accidents reported in the vicinity between the hospital and his home."

"Rather brilliant, laying the foundation for innocence, but after all, he's a judge. If anyone should know how to do it, it would be he."

"A patrol car nearby was directed to his street and the officer found his wife's car and her dead body. A forensic team was on the scene quickly. They found Etta Hogan's tire tracks. She had gone off the road to turn around."

"Ah."

"Shepherd Levine then cooperated with the police and claimed Etta had become a stalker who wouldn't accept the end of their affair. As I said, he took on blame for having the affair. Became quite emotional about it, breaking down and blaming himself."

"Beating his chest quite convincingly, I imagine."

"They found the weapon in Etta's car."

"And the jewelry and watches?"

"Still on his wife's body, which strengthened Levine's version of things. Etta claimed he was supposed to walk down to the scene of the murder and take the jewelry off his wife's body to make it look like a robbery, but apparently, if we're to believe Etta, after she left, he didn't take the jewelry, thus framing her."

"That is brilliant," John Milton said. Beardsley paused and stared at him. The man really did look like he appreciated what the judge had done. "So Etta left thinking he had provided the police with the theory it was just a robbery. He really sold her on the plan. She must actually have been in love with him. Fascinating. Sorry. Go on, Tom."

"Levine gave the police all the information they needed to convict her as a rejected lover, but Michele Armstrong didn't buy it, buy his innocence. He was in line now to inherit his wife's estate, inherited from her father."

"Greed. It's such a reliable motive," John said. "But kudos to Michele Armstrong for being suspicious. She has good instincts. Too good, maybe. And?"

"Etta fired back immediately when she realized she was taking the full fall. She agreed to be a prosecution witness and turned over some gifts the judge had given her, a note he had written to set up a rendez-vous."

"But our judge had already admitted to the affair?"

"He did it then. He hired a defense attorney from Goshen, Gerald Orman, one of the best in the region who was actually a friend of Michele Armstrong's father."

"I know of him. He's good, but not good enough for any firm I'll have."

"Armstrong went on a relentless pursuit of the weapon's history, tracking back to a petty thief fifteen years prior who was convicted of possessing an illegally obtained pistol. The pistol was missing from the police archives. Levine, by the way, sentenced him to five years."

"How deliciously ironic or maybe not."

"Maybe not? That would be one helluva plan that far in advance of it all."

"Some destinies are written in indelible ink, Tom. Still, locating the origin of the weapon and the fact that it was missing surely wasn't enough to get past reasonable doubt."

"Armstrong knew that. She was smart. The pistol had only Etta's prints on it. That was suspicious. Why wipe the pistol clean first? But Judge Levine wasn't up on forensics or a bit sloppy about it. Remember, he took her for those shooting lessons."

"Someone saw them on the range?"

"No. It's one of those out in the country areas where pistol practice is permitted. They only went a few times anyway, I believe. No one saw them there."

"And so . . . what's the second shoe dropped?"

Beardsly smiled. He couldn't help it. It brought back memories of cases he had helped solve when he was a top agent.

"He put the bullets in the gun for Hogan and she didn't use them all. His print was on four bullets. As I said, Armstrong was relentless and always suspicious."

"The main characteristic of a good prosecutor. Brilliant pursuit."

"From what I was told, she had a way of pushing the investigators," Beardsly said. "Initially, the case looked so slam dunk. You know what happens then when it comes to the investigators when there's a shortcut."

"Sloth kicks in. I am so grateful for the lazy and uninspired in important places, especially law enforcement. It gives my clients an edge. Excellent work, Tom. I'll have more for you to do in the near future," John added. "We're just beginning what will be a mutually profitable relationship. In many ways, I promise."

He leaned forward and tapped on the window. Charon opened the door and handed Beardsly an envelope. Beardsly opened it and quickly visually counted the hundreds. There was more than he had been promised. He looked up, surprised.

"A little bonus," John said. "Enjoy it. Get greedy. You'll work harder for me."

"Yeah, well, I'm not exactly rolling in it these days."

"You will," John said.

Charon held the door open and stepped back. Beardsly reached out to shake John's hand. John looked at his hand as if he had to first inspect it for germs or something. Then he seized it so quickly and held it so hard that Beardsly winced. He didn't want to show fear or pain so he didn't move or speak. Milton turned his hand around in his and with his other hand, stroked the top of Beardsly's as though Beardsly's hand was unique, the hand of a famous artist or pianist.

"'Oh what a piece of work is a man! How noble in reason, how infinite in faculty . . . in action how like an angel and in apprehension how like a god!'" He smiled. "Don't look so amazed, my friend. "You must constantly remind yourself that you are the 'paragon of animals.'"

John laughed and let him go. Beardsly's hand stung, but he said nothing. He just nodded and stepped out. Milton leaned over to look out at him.

"I don't know what the hell you said."

"I was quoting from *Hamlet*. Didn't you pay attention in literature class?"

"I was absent that day," Beardsly said and Milton laughed.

"I like you, Tom. You're a man after my own heart. We'll know each other a long, long time, I'm sure," he added and sat back.

Charon closed the door and then went around to get in the limousine.

"We have some real competition this time, Charon," John Milton said angrily when Charon returned to the driver's seat. His mood changed instantly, and just as instantly, however, changed back. He smiled. "Someday, I hope she'll come to work for us. It's not out of the question, you know."

Charon knew but he didn't say anything. John looked at his watch.

"To the hoosegow," he ordered. "I have to see my new client. I have work to do, but when don't I, huh? The purpose is to develop my new army to do all this for me. I'm tired of being an instigator, whispering in people's ears, urging them to break their convenient with you know who. How can I lose though? He promises them eternal bliss in some ethereal paradise only He appreciates, Charon. I offer them all the pleasure and contentment here where they can see, feel, taste. Do you think He's just stupid? Or is it arrogance? I'm supposed to be the one with arrogance," he continued.

He knew he was ranting, but sometimes, he couldn't help himself. Actually, he rather liked the sound of his own voice. That was why he was so good in court, especially at summations.

"Oh, I'm not flawed because of that, Charon. Don't for a moment believe it. The only thing wrong with me is . . . there is nothing wrong with me."

He laughed.

Charon didn't make a sound.

John Milton grimaced.

"I think I need someone again, Charon, another companion. I shouldn't be the only one who appreciates me, now should I?"

"No," he answered for himself. He looked out the window. "No. I need something more. I always will.

"Maybe that's the curse I bear, but it's not a bad one," he quickly added.

"Look at all the brilliant things I'm saying. It's wasted on you, Charon. It's like screaming in Grand Canyon or something. I hate echoes. I never liked anything that came back at me."

He sat back and for a moment, sulked.

It was times like this when he wondered if this world was worth it.

He was always driven by one deep fear. What if God retreated? It was just as easy for Him to start somewhere new. What if God decided they weren't worth it after all and left the battlefield? He'd be left with a world of sinners. That was like a great artist doing a great painting with only blind people to show it to, or like a great actor doing an award winning performance for an empty theater.

Or worse yet, making a great summation to a jury of the deaf.

Stop worrying, he told himself as he watched a young boy helping an elderly lady cross the street. He's given them just enough conscience to make my work difficult. He's too confident to give up. He's got the bigger ego.

"We're fine, Charon," he said as if he had been having this debate aloud. It didn't matter. Charon heard his thoughts. "Beardsly's report has given me a wonderful concept for my defense. I wonder if MS Armstrong will realize it."

At the next red light, Charon turned and smiled even though it looked like doing so might shatter his face.

"You think she will. Yes. So do I. She'll come to appreciate me. I'll be quite fascinating to her, and confusing, too. Oh, her ego might hold her back, but eventually, it will turn. I'm confident. Besides, it's something new and wonderful to live for, Charon. I think she might be my best prize in decades.

"And the son that we have together, my best prince in centuries."

His laughter seemed to propel the vehicle forward into the traffic where he could mingle easily with the masses.

14.

Lester Heckett was frightened and his fear exhausted him. He wasn't sleeping; he was eating poorly, and worse of all, he felt like he had aged years in months. Places ached in his body that had never ached. There were dark rings deepening under his eyes. He was sickly pale and for no reason at all, he would suddenly break into a shiver. *I look as guilty as hell*, he told himself. *Forget the assumption of innocence concept. The jury will convict me the moment they see me. There doesn't even have to be a trial. I have no chance.*

He looked up from his clasped hands in the conference room as his new attorney stepped in. Something about him was terribly familiar, and for the first few moments, Lester raked his memory to realize where he had met him or seen him. Unlike Warner Murphy, John Milton did not look all business. He was quite relaxed and smiled as if they were meeting at a bar to enjoy a close friendship, interesting gossip and jokes. He was just as impeccably dressed and if anything, was a better looking man, but Lester had assumed he'd be older, too. He hoped the firm, believing he was a lost cause, especially now that his lawyer was dead, didn't throw some newcomer at him simply to build some experience.

"Sometimes my clients remind me of expectant fathers," John Milton said still standing and looking down at him. "They have that same worried expression you now wear like a mask. Will their wives survive? Will the baby be born healthy? That sort of thing. Of course, my clients are wondering if they'll survive, not their children.

"Fear not," John added finally sitting across from him. "You will. I am John Milton." He extended his hand and clasped Lester's. He was handcuffed to the table so he didn't have much leeway to move. John nodded at the cuffs and shook his head. "We're so intent on chaining everyone to something in this country now, either to protect ourselves or help ourselves seem more powerful. Nothing like enslaving others, eh?" He laughed, but Lester just stared at him.

How can he be so light-hearted? He acts as if this is nothing more than a parking ticket, Heckett thought.

"So, I've read Warner Murphy's file and studied the evidence against you."

"Did they find out what happened to Warner Murphy?" Lester asked instantly. He was like someone in a coma who had heard something that triggered consciousness.

John Milton smiled and shook his head slowly.

"You're worried about him now? You should be worrying only about yourself, Lester. He's dead. What happened was he leaped off his patio and badly damaged a Mercedes S-class twenty flights below."

"Why?"

"Maybe he thought he'd lose your case, Lester. You don't mind my calling you, Lester, do you, Lester?"

"No. Am I going to lose my case?"

"Now you're thinking properly, Lester. Concentrate on yourself. No. You're not going to lose or more appropriately, I'm not going to lose. I don't lose."

"That's what I was told, although you look kind of young for the story they gave me," Lester Heckett said, his skepticism practically streaking out of his eyes.

John Milton smiled.

"I'm not as young as I look. I take good care of myself and I have good genes. My father is actually still alive, although we haven't had a conversation for what seems to be a few millennia. You never got along that well with your father either, as I understand it."

"How do you know that?"

"Oh, I do my research, Lester. I don't like being surprised, especially by prosecutors. I just love wiping gleeful smiles off their faces."

"Is it true? You've never lost a case?"

"Not really. I made some compromises that pleased the prosecution in the past, but in the end, I was pleased more and so were my clients. I mean if you're caught red-handed, it's not easy getting you acquitted; although, I did have two cases where eye-witnesses were so discounted, the client walked.

"Now," John Milton continued, finally letting go of Lester's hand so he could open his briefcase and take out a small packet of papers. Lester hadn't realized he was holding onto John Milton like someone holding on for dear life. John Milton didn't seem to mind. "There is an eye-witness to neutralize, and I think you can help me do it very effectively.

"If you're honest," that is, "about everything," he added.

Lester squinted.

"What do you mean?"

"Well, I exaggerate a little when I say everything. I don't need you to be too honest. Remember, I'm an officer of the court. I have an absolute ethical duty to the judges to tell the truth." He smiled again. It was more like his eyes twinkled. "I just have the skill and talent to pick and choose the right truths to tell. Anyone trying to survive in this world has to do that, Lester, and goodness knows, you're trying to survive."

"How come you're so . . ."

"Happy to defend you?"

"Yes."

"I love a real challenge and you present one." He leaned in to whisper. "To be completely honest on my end, Lester, I don't believe Warner Murphy would have won your case or even compromised on a plea that would have satisfied you. He would have disappointed us both. He had reached that point where he was more interested in building his own career. Lawyers like that are more willing to make unsatisfactory compromises. But don't misunderstand me. I take interest in the success of other defense attorneys. Don't look so surprised. I love my work. You lucked out getting me. I promise."

For a moment Lester was speechless. He rarely had seen such unmitigated arrogance. It brought a smile to his face.

"From the way you're putting it, I should be happy Warner Murphy leaped off a patio?"

"So happy that you might as well have been the one to help him over. You know, like telling him, do me a favor and drop dead. Quite a drop, I'll admit."

"That's cold."

"Fighting to survive sucks all the warmth of human kindness out of you, Lester. Even Adam betrayed Eve. You know the story . . . she made me do it. Women have had men wrapped up tightly and neatly ever since. Well, maybe not world over, but close. I know you agree.

"Actually, I could have defended Adam successfully, if the judge would have permitted it. I would have pointed out that there were extenuating circumstances . . . what today we call entrapment."

Lester shook his head. What the hell was this new attorney talking about? Who cares about Adam and Eve?

"I understand you don't think we need a postponement," Lester said.

"No. I know the case inside and out as if I had been there from the start."

"How can that be?"

"We ask ourselves that question about so many things, Lester. Trust me. I know all I have to know to defend you successfully."

Lester wanted to believe him. He took a deep breath. What choice did he have really?

"Well, what do we do now?"

"We talk. We get to know each other, but most important, we get to develop your defense together. It takes teamwork, Lester. You're as important to all this as I am. They'll be looking at you as much as they look at me. Well, maybe not quite as much, but enough to make a difference. I want you to spruce up, get this defeated look out of your face. Shave, eat, exercise, and show them you love life, love it so much you wouldn't want to take it away from anyone, least of all a good friend and a partner. Understand?"

"Yes."

"Good. Not that I think I'll need to put you on the stand, but when you enter a courtroom charged with murder, you're on the stand the moment you set foot in the room. Don't let anyone tell you otherwise."

Lester nodded.

"Yeah, I was just thinking about that before you came in, thinking about the impression I would make on a jury right now."

"Were you? See? Great minds think alike. Okay, let's begin with the real reason Elliot Strumfield didn't turn you in when he realized what you were doing with the money, actually had been doing for some time. It helps if you confess what I need you to confess, but to me only for now. So. Why was he so disappointed in you and don't tell me because he thought you were such an honest man. You and he weren't strangers to bending rules."

Lester felt the heat rise from somewhere behind his heart, flow up his neck and into his face. Who was this man? He couldn't have been on his case very long, and Warner Murphy never asked any question with such an underlying implication. He would never suspect Murphy had anything remotely resembling this in his notes for John Milton to read.

"I don't know what you mean," Lester said.

"Oh dear, dear," Milton said. "You're a coward as well as a liar. How disappointing."

"Fuck you," Lester said, his face now so hot, he felt as though he would burst into flames, his head the tip of a torch.

John Milton simply smiled. He didn't show an iota of vexation or take offense.

"That's good," he said instead. "You still have self-respect and pride. I simply can't stand having a mealy mouth client who looks desperate and frightened. People enjoy having power over others. If you look meek and terrified, the jury will enjoy their life and death authority and might even find you guilty simply for the mere pleasure of doing so."

"Huh?"

"I know human nature, my friend. Let's get back to our defense. In a real sense, it's going to be offense, which as you have heard, I'm sure, is the best defense."

Lester Heckett knew his life was in jeopardy. He wouldn't get a death sentence, but he couldn't imagine life in a maximum security prison. Even life with a chance of parole wouldn't matter. He would die there not long after he was imprisoned, and possibly at his own hand, too. The tension he felt right now was so severe, he thought he might have a heart-attack, but his new attorney seemed almost impish. He behaved as if he enjoyed every moment of Lester's anxiety.

"All right. We'll do some preparation. Let me set the table," John Milton said. He shuffled a few papers. "During happy days you and your wife and Strumfield and his wife were good friends, correct?"

"So?"

"You and Elliot Strumfield knew each other from college, but you didn't start the business together. You went separate ways for a while."

"I worked for a brokerage firm."

"That went out of business. It was then that Strumfield came to your rescue."

"I had something to offer. It wasn't an act of charity," Lester replied with a flare of indignation. After all, this wasn't the first time that he was accused of riding on Strumfield's coat tails. Cisley, for one, was always accusing him of doing that.

"Oh, you had something to offer all right. No denying that. We'll get to that in a moment. This money you invested in your shell company outside of the U.S. wasn't all embezzled, correct?"

"None of it was embezzled."

"Well, let's not debate definitions. That's what I do in court. However you made the money, you socked away what you could. You have over three million dollars in this account," John Milton said and produced a bank statement.

"How did you get that?"

"What's the difference? Just know that if I could get it, Michele Armstrong can get it or has."

"Who's Michele Armstrong?"

"She's the ADA who's going to prosecute you. She's a hotshot, bright and very attractive. Men on the jury will fall in love with her. The judge might as well."

"Great."

"Cheer up. The women will fall in love with me," John Milton said. His eyes were so dazzling that they looked like July Fourth sparklers. Maybe it was the reflection of the lights in the room. He sat back. "Now that we know I know you more than you imagined, we'll get into your defense. It's a lot like getting into a hot bath, slowly. You have to get used to people the same way, Lester, my Lester," he added, sounding as if he was his father. "Let's continue pealing the onion."

He took out another set of papers. In between some pages, were some pictures. He moved them out slowly and displayed them as if he was proud of them.

Lester Heckett looked at them and found he couldn't breathe for a moment.

It was as if that warning his grandmother whipped over him frequently when he was about ten and doing forbidden things came true.

"God sees everything, Lester," she had admonished.

"How did you get these pictures?"

"What's the difference, Lester? You were going to use them to get Elliot Strumfield to back off. You had something to do with setting him up, didn't you? It was your insurance from the start. Doesn't make you look too nice, I know," he said and picked up the pictures of Strumfield and Lester's wife. "Don't worry about it," John Milton added. "I have control of them and will use them when and if I have to. And the man you hired for this, has a bad case of memory loss until or unless I need him to be otherwise.

"Now, the question about your hiring someone else, someone to shoot with more than a camera will probably come up."

Lester didn't speak. He had never admitted this to Warner Murphy. The prosecution must have found out something recently.

"Well, I didn't . . ."

John Milton held up his hand.

"No confessions please. I hate confessions more than I hate sobbing prayers. All I said was the prosecution might bring that up. It doesn't mean they will succeed in attaching you to an assassin. If you did use the seventy-five thousand dollars you withdrew from your Cayman account for that purpose, you most likely felt confident no one would be able to trace it. However, all these foreign accounts are proving to be less and less sacrosanct. I mean this hypothetically, of course. It's one thing for them to prove you withdrew that sum, but another for them to prove you used it to hire a killer. Implications don't eliminate reasonable doubt."

"But what are we going to do to . . ."

"To defend against that accusation? Oh, we'll handle it. No worries," John Milton said. "We'll handle it all."

The room seemed to brighten and radiate with new hope and confidence. Lester looked at John Milton for a long moment, and in that moment, for reasons he couldn't quite understand, he thought that this man could very well save his life. He would uncover every rock necessary to confuse and distort the truth, and in doing so, he would win.

He finally felt a smile on his face. It was like smiling after you had a terrible sunburn. It hurt a little, but it was wonderful knowing you could still do it, smile.

And all because of this attorney. The self-pity he suffered when he had heard about Walter Murphy's death dissipated. He could feel the blood returning to his face, his complexion improving. His posture improved as if he had just been injected with optimism and self-respect. He wasn't sure why it had come so quickly, but the thought was vivid. John Milton would save his life.

He was that good and had that kind of power.

15.

"Why are we going to this prison again?" Fish asked Blake. They had just gone over the George Washington Bridge and turned onto the Palisades Parkway.

"I told you. I want to follow through on Keith Arthur, Semantha Hunter's ex-husband."

"But . . . Mrs. Murphy wasn't really sure there was a resemblance between the delivery man she saw and the picture of Hunter's ex. And there's no capture of any delivery man on the lobby CCTV."

"That five second black out bothers me," Blake said.

"Even if he crossed the lobby and got right into an elevator, there's no delivery man on the elevator CCTV."

"I thought you'd mention Bivens not having ever seen him either," Blake said.

"What difference does it make anyway? The guy was killed some time ago, wasn't he? I mean, I don't get all that mumbo jumbo about things not being what they seem, another choice beside life and death . . . I've got an open mind, but not open to anything and everything, Lieutenant."

"I know. Don't feel bad about it."

"Feel bad? Why should I feel bad? I don't feel bad," Fish said firmly. He had been thinking about all this and having trouble sleeping. Twice, he came close to talking to Deputy Inspector Cullen about Blake.

Blake smiled.

"Look, maybe it was someone who resembled Keith Arthur. I'll give you that, but it couldn't have been Keith Arthur so shouldn't we be looking elsewhere? Use the picture you have of Keith Arthur to see if we have anything on anyone resembling him? I can see doing that, but this is really a waste of time the way I see it."

"I told you when we started out that you didn't have to come along," Blake said.

"I don't mind coming along. I just don't get it. Why are we doing this?"

"I work on instinct," Blake replied. He turned to him. "So far that's not been a bad thing to do."

"Sure, sure. I know you've got quite a record, Lieutenant. I'm just trying to get my mind around all this."

"Think of it this way, Fish. We've got ourselves a conundrum. As far as I can tell from everything I've learned about Warner Murphy, he was the least likely candidate for suicide. He had no mental issues, no bi-polar symptoms, was productive and successful in his work, loved his family and was going to be given a full-partnership in one of the most prodigious defense law firms in New York City on the day he died. In a scale of one to ten assigning suicide for cause of his death, I think we're somewhere around minus ten. You've been party to all this research and information. Do you disagree?"

"No. I admit that bugs me, too."

"Good. Now, we can rule out the second cause of death, accidental. The way the railings are on the patios in that building, it's impossible to trip and fall off of one, correct?"

"Yes, yes," Fish replied. He didn't intend to be spoken to like this, but he couldn't deny anything yet.

"So we come to the last cause of death, murder. Physically, it seems quite impossible for anyone to have gotten into his apartment and committed the act. We have the time of the murder nailed down. We know exactly when his wife and daughter left and exactly when he hit the top of that Mercedes. No security camera, no live witness puts anyone going up to his floor just before he was killed, and your check of the visitors a day before hasn't turned up anything or anyone we could suspect."

"You forgot to mention that my review of the video cameras in the elevators don't show anyone going from another floor to the Murphy's floor during the time period involved anyway."

"Correct. We'll continue to look into it, but so far, no other tenant had any motive for doing him harm, and from what we've learned, none of them were very close to the Murphys, close enough to get into an argument with Warner, and none are directly involved with the criminal court system in New York.

The only way to tie anyone else in that building to them or to Warner Murphy in particular is to cite his acquaintance and professional relationship to Semantha Hunter's brother, Judge Hunter. It's the only thread we have to follow so far."

"But to what? It's a dead end. Literally. Keith Arthur was killed in prison before Warner Murphy died. Not that it would matter. He was in prison and even if he wasn't killed in there, he'd be in there when Murphy died!" Fish felt the blood rise to his face with the frustration.

"I'm not sure it's a dead end," Blake said calmly.

"Your instincts tell you something else?"

"That's what I said."

Fish thought a moment.

"How did you get into this?" he asked.

"Pardon?"

"Police work? I learned you really were studying to be a priest."

"It's not exactly a secret. I was surprised at how long it took you to learn that."

"Right. I was lazy. So what happened? You had an affair with some girl and decided you couldn't be celibate?"

Matthew Blake smiled.

"That's the usual reason people ascribe to my decision. I even had a bishop so much as accuse me of it. He wouldn't accept my reason."

"Which was?"

Blake turned to him.

"I had a calling."

"What the hell's that mean?"

"You know," Blake said smiling at him, "like people get a calling to join the clergy. It's not all that different when you think about it. We're all trying to defeat evil."

Fish shook his head.

"So you had a calling to become a police detective? Some voice called to you and said, 'Matthew Blake, go be a police detective?'"

"Something like that, yes. The good guys don't always rely on prayer alone, Fish. In the New Testament, the angel Michael is said to have lead God's armies against Satan's forces. God has an army and it's not soldiers carrying prayer books." Blake turned to him again. "Don't you feel like you're in God's army sometimes, Fish?"

"If it's God's army, we should have a better budget," Fish said.

"Good point, Fish. I'll tell the Captain to use that argument next time he tries to increase the budget."

Fish looked out at the scenery as they flew along the Parkway. He still didn't know what the hell they were doing.

"I don't know whether you're just a lucky nutcase or someone with a special talent, Lieutenant."

"You'll know soon enough," Blake said.

They drove on.

"You seem to know your way around here pretty good," Fish said when they left Route 17 and began to wind their way through small hamlets a little over an hour and a half later.

"I have an escape up here."

"An escape?"

"Old farm house I picked up. Good R and R."

"I wondered if you had any other life but police work, Lieutenant."

"I claim it's an escape, but the real truth is that you can step out of the room, but not out of yourself," Blake said.

"Not out of yourself? Do I get college credit in philosophy for being your partner?"

Blake laughed the hardest he had since they had met. Fish smiled.

"Let's get some lunch," Blake said. "I know where there's some home cooking in this hamlet."

"Where are we?"

"Pulling into Woodbourne. The maximum security penitentiary is here."

Fish looked around. It was basically a one street village with a garage on one end and a bar and grill on the other. Blake made a right onto the street that led to the prison and pulled up to what was called Richard's Pot House, a small luncheonette that was nearly packed with customers. There was little pedestrian activity in the village so these people were obviously familiar with the place, he thought.

"Pot House?" he asked looking up at the sign.

"Sal specializes in chicken pot pies, shepherd's pie. That sort of thing, but he makes other things. It's a prison town. It makes all its money off the employees and businesses that service the penitentiary. Years ago it was one of the hamlets that was supported by the Catskill mountain resort industry."

They got out and Fish paused for a moment and looked around.

"I like the quiet and the fresh air. They need cops here?"

"They need them everywhere, Fish. Even the Eskimos have some law enforcement."

They entered Richard's Pot House. It wasn't that big a restaurant. There were a dozen and a half tables and a counter with ten stools. It had chestnut brown painted walls and a white tile floor. Two large front windows had silvery white shades. Because the place had a low ceiling, the conversations echoed over each other making it all sound like people at the Tower of Babel. Blake nodded at the counter where there were two seats available. Three waitresses served the tables, and the owner, Sal Richard and another man worked the counter.

From the look on Sal's face when he saw them, Fish realized he knew Matthew Blake. When they began to talk, Fish could see that he was fond of him, too. Blake remembered everything about the man's family, where his children were living, even what they did for a living. Sal assumed Blake had come up to go fishing, which was another thing Fish never suspected he had any interest in doing. He realized that Sal Richard knew Blake was a New York City detective, but he didn't ask him anything about his work.

"I know I told you about the pot pies, but the chicken and cheese sandwich he makes is the big secret. He has his own special sauce on it," Blake told him.

Two of the waitresses paused to say hello to him and he asked them about their families.

"You're like some old timer here, a local yokel or something," Fish said.

"People are our business, Fish. You have to be interested in them to do the work we do. We win trust. That's how we get what we have to get done, done. I know we have the toilet bowel view of humanity, but there are really good people, too, which is why we have to work hard at this."

"You do sound like someone who had some kind of calling," Fish remarked. "Maybe you should have stuck it out and become a priest."

"Forget about what I should be. What got you into it?"

"My father. He wanted me to be a policeman, but he pushed me to go to detective school. He and I used to watch mysteries on television together. He loved to read Raymond Chandler, writers like that. Got me reading them. Got it into my blood."

"It was probably already there, Fish."

"Probably."

"You'll get very good at this. I can sense it."

"Instinct?"

"Yep," Blake said.

He didn't know how to think of Blake anymore. He couldn't help respecting him, but at the same time, he was so damn weird.

"What about your family?" Fish asked him.

"What about them?"

"Where are they?"

"I don't know."

"Huh?"

"I was born in Pennsylvania, but I was an orphan until I was four. I had foster parents for two years, but that didn't work out and I returned to the orphanage. Three years later, I went to another foster home."

"You never located your real mother and father?"

"No. My foster family adopted me and I took on their name."

"How'd you get the name, Matthew?"

"One of the Sisters at the original orphanage named me."

"Sisters? So you were in a religious orphanage."

"Most of them are," Blake said smiling.

"Well, don't you want to know who your real parents are?"

"I feel like I do know them," he said, finished his coffee and wiped his lips.

"Huh?"

"We gotta get going. Sal, great sandwich as usual. Best to Rose."

"I'll tell her. She's always asking me if you stopped by."

"I'll be back," Blake said. "Got some vacation time coming."

"God bless," Sal said and they left.

"You take vacation time? Didn't know you were this human," Fish half-kidded as they got back into the car.

"We all have some weaknesses," Blake replied.

He had called the warden and the warden, as promised, set them up to meet with one of the head guards, a man named Donald Wilson. He was a heavy six-footer with curly light brown hair and had the face of an ex-prize fighter, which they discovered he was. He had hard, bony hands that looked like they had been broken on a face a few times.

"What'cha tryin' to determine, if the bastard raped some other child?" Donald Wilson asked without saying hello. He had the air of someone who was annoyed with everything, including himself.

"Not exactly," Blake said. "How'd he die?"

"Don't tell me some bleedin' heart is trying to blame that on us."

The warden cleared his throat and Wilson dropped his indignation.

"The way I figure it is someone raped him for a change and he tried to take revenge and got himself killed. No one knows nothin', of course. Right, Warden?"

"Just answer the questions please, Donald."

"Did he have any visitors, frequent or otherwise?" Blake asked them both.

"I'd have to check on that, but from what I remember, he didn't. Donald?"

"He was shit. Who'd come to see him? Even the creeps here thought he was creepy."

"Who claimed his body?" Blake asked.

"I did get that information for you," the warden said and opened a slim file. "Someone paid for his cremation anonymously. Here's the name of the funeral parlor that carried out the instructions."

Blake looked at it and copied down the name. Then he looked up at Wilson.

"I imagine you have quite a collection of human garbage here, Mr. Wilson, but was there anything about him you remember?"

"He was a conniving, sneaky, reptile. I don't know if he developed some kind of a nervous condition or what, but he started jetting out his tongue like a snake. It bugged everyone. No other prisoners want to eat with him. He sat by himself in the cafeteria and curled up around his food like a wild dog. I can take anything any of these assholes can throw at me in here, but I don't mind admitting that that creep gave me nightmares."

"You found his body?"

"Yeah. I heard the screaming and found him, but there was no one around. Maybe he strangled himself."

"So he wasn't beaten to death? Or stabbed? He was strangled?" Fish asked. The question occurred to him so quickly that he had to ask it. He had assumed more than one inmate had committed the killing.

"That's it," Wilson said. He smiled. "Might have been suicide."

"You're not serious about him strangling himself?" Fish said.

Wilson looked at him.

"Maybe he was trying to get someone's hands off his neck, but his were on his neck and the fingers were very tight."

"Fingerprints on anything lead to any suspects?" Blake asked the warden.

He shook his head.

From the way the two men looked, Fish thought there had been little interest in who had killed Keith Arthur. They probably saw it as a form of relief, especially Donald Wilson.

"Okay. Thanks very much," Blake said rising.

"I hope you guys are getting good overtime," Donald Wilson told them.

"Oh. We don't work for the money," Blake said. Wilson's eyebrows went up. "We work for the pleasure of meeting people like yourself." He smiled. "Thanks, Warden," he added.

Fish followed him out.

"That guy's enough to keep me from breaking the law."

"Probably broke it as much as the men he guards," Blake said.

"So what do you make of that idiotic idea that he choked himself to death? You can't strangle yourself with your hands. At best, you'd starve your brain of oxygen and pass out. Your hands would relax."

"At best," Blake said as they got into the car. He paused and then shook his head.

"What?"

"Maybe he didn't have control of his hands," Blake said, started the car and drove out.

"You mean, someone put his hands over Keith Arthur's?"

"Could be."

Fish was quiet.

"I don't even know why we're thinking about it," he finally said. He noticed they were taking a different highway.

"Where are we going now?"

"To the funeral parlor," Blake said.

"Why? You think his ashes might still be there?"

"I doubt it," Blake said. "I doubt it very much."

"Who the hell would want his ashes?"

Blake didn't respond. Fish sat back and closed his eyes. Take a short nap, he told himself. It's the only thing that makes any sense.

Twenty minutes later, they pulled into the Foster Funeral Home in Ferndale. The funeral home was a large, three-story Queen Anne style house that obviously had been expanded to accommodate a chapel and a showroom for coffins. It had pristine white aluminum siding and black hardwood shutters. There were beautiful maple trees standing like Roman columns on both sides of the building. Their leaves were claret, like the color of a rich, red wine. A hearse parked in the front. To the right was a likewise expanded parking lot. Great care had been taken to create attractive landscaping on the property with flower beds and well-trimmed hedges. There were two dozen automobiles in the parking lot.

"Maybe we're interrupting something," Fish muttered. He was never fond of funeral homes or cemeteries, for that matter. It came from his grandmother threatening him that if he didn't eat his vegetables, the dead would rise out of their graves in the nearby cemetery and dance around the house at night joyfully. "Because you'll be unhealthy and die and join 'em."

"The guest of honor won't mind," Blake said and got out. He looked back when Fish didn't get out. Reluctantly, he opened his door. "You don't have to come in if the place bothers you. I just have a couple of questions for the funeral director."

Fish stood, but didn't close the door, thinking about it. Then he shrugged.

"And miss any of this? No way. I want to be able to tell my grandchildren," he said and joined Blake. Mourners were gathered in the chapel. A man about twenty, dressed in a tuxedo, smiled at them.

"You're not that late," he said. "Just starting."

"We're not here for the funeral. I need to speak to the funeral director. Is it Mr. Foster?" He showed his identification.

"Oh. Yeah. That's my Dad," the young man said. "I'll get him. You can wait in his office, if you want," he added nodding to their right.

"Thanks."

Blake and Fish walked to the office door and entered. It was very neat, immaculate in fact. There were brochures on the dark-cherry wood desk, a vase with real pink and white roses on the table in front of the settee, and plaques on the walls with some letters of appreciation framed. Blake read a few. He paused when he moved a vase and saw a picture of a cross, only on this cross, Jesus was upside down. He picked it up and looked at it.

"What'dya got?" Fish asked.

Blake showed him. Fish studied it a minute.

"Weird."

Blake nodded and put the picture back. He looked at another framed document.

"Business has been in the family nearly a hundred years," he told Fish.

"Yeah. I imagine it's like the cemetery. Everyone's just dyin' to get in it."

Blake smiled.

"I grew up next to a cemetery," Fish explained. "Never got used to it, seein' the funerals, the people visiting graves. Kept me indoors at night until Packy McDermott described makin' love to Jillian Robinson on some cool slab one summer night. 'course, Packy didn't have all his wires connected. Died in Afghanistan in a copter crash. It was his fourth rotation."

"Gentlemen," they heard and turned to greet Morgan Foster, a thin fifty-eight-year-old man with a full head of chalky white hair neatly styled. He was lanky with long arms and hands that looked transplanted from a man a foot taller. "How can I be of assistance?" he asked. Whether it was a characteristic of his work or not, he spoke in a loud whisper.

However, Fish had the feeling he rarely raised his voice. Maybe he didn't want to wake the dead and lose a commission, he thought and nearly laughed at his own private joke.

"We can see you're busy, Mr. Foster. We don't want to take up much of your time. I need to know what you can tell me about the cremation of one Keith Arthur. He was killed at the prison in Woodbourne."

"Oh yes," he said moving quickly to the file cabinet on the left of his desk. "I remember it because everything was done anonymously. I received a bank draft to pay for it all."

He pulled out a file and opened it. He read some papers and then turned to Blake.

"Here's a copy of the bank draft. Here's the letter of instruction." He handed them both to Blake. He looked at them, nodded and handed them back.

"Who picked up the urn?"

"As you can see from the instructions, he was identified as a Mr. Don Martin. When he arrived, he had the letter of authorization described here in the instructions. Is there some kind of problem? A family complaint?"

"What can you tell me about Don Martin?" Blake asked in response.

"Not very much, I'm afraid. He looked to be about mid-forties, perhaps six feet tall."

"Dark brown hair?"

"I believe so, yes. Nicely spoken, wore an Armani suit and Beluti shoes. He was all business. Signed the paper work, took the urn and left."

"Beluti?" Fish asked.

"I'm quite up on styles, designers, but not because of my own taste in wardrobe. Some of my clients want their loved ones in what they consider the best, even though in life they never would spend the money on such things."

"Seems like a waste," Fish muttered.

"Not to their loved ones. In many cultures, people are buried with riches."

"They don't dress them up for cremation, do they?"

"Some do, yes. You say 'they' as though you're not one of us," Foster said smiling. "We're all mortal and all capable of great sorrow. We take great pleasure in easing the pain."

Fish grunted. Forster looked at Blake.

"Is there anything else?"

"May I see that signature again?" Blake asked. He studied it a moment as if he was committing it to memory. "Thanks. Oh. We couldn't help wondering about that picture of a cross you have there."

"Oh, yes." Foster lifted it gently and held it as though it was a valuable artifact. "This was something my son found on the Internet. He printed it out to show me. He thought it was a big mistake some church had made."

"Was it?" Fish asked.

"I don't know. Someone had egg on his face, I bet."

"Maybe," Blake said. "Thanks for your time and information. Sorry to have bothered you."

"You're welcome. No problem. I have a well-oiled machine here. Practically runs itself," Foster said. He nodded at Fish who obviously couldn't wait to leave. He was outside ahead of Blake who followed talking on his phone. Blake held up his hand. Fish watched and waited.

"I appreciate it, Warden," Blake said. He listened and then his face seemed to harden right before Fish's eyes. "I see. Yes. Thank you."

He ended his call.

"What?" Fish asked.

"Keith Arthur was the fourth inmate killed or who died in prison who was cremated during the past three years."

"So? Who the hell wants to visit the gravesite of a murderer or mother rapist or whatever? They probably dumped their ashes in a sewer."

"They were all requested and paid for anonymously," Blake said. He turned and looked back at the entrance to the funeral home.

"What?" Fish asked.

"They were all done here," Blake said.

16.

He was starting to get under her skin. Every time Michele Armstrong finished with her witness and he was supposed to begin his cross examination, John Milton prolonged the pause in court activity with little annoying tactics. Sometimes, he would lean over and whisper in Lester Heckett's ear, often laughing before Judge Philips addressed him with what Michele thought was a too nice, "Mr. Milton, would you like to cross-examine this witness?" It was almost as though she wanted to be differential to the defense attorney instead of vice versa. There was no sarcasm or even a note of irritability.

Michele was used to the opposing attorney's attempts to throw her off balance during a trial, but up until now none she had come across was as good at it as John Milton. His irritating manner began before the trial had started. She was standing at her table and looking down at her notes when she sensed him beside her. Only, he wasn't simply beside her; he was very close, closer than someone would normally stand beside her, even someone she had known. It was what any New Yorker would call, "In your face." Surprised, she stepped back. For a moment she thought he had been smelling her, inhaling her perfume. He had his eyes closed and then opened them quickly.

"Hello," he said. "I thought I'd introduce myself and get us off on a professional footing. John Milton."

He offered his hand. She couldn't help but notice the onyx ring. It seemed to glitter and in the glitter there was the image of the peace sign or what she knew was considered a broken cross.

"Oh," she said and took his hand. He didn't shake. He held her hand and kept his eyes fixed on her face, the smile sitting on his lips anticipating something more from her. "Please to meet you," she added.

He let go of her hand and looked around the courtroom.

"Why do you suppose this is called a courtroom?"

"Because it's where we hold court?" she replied. "You think?"

"Yes, but a court can be so many things. It almost makes it sound as if this is just another game, simply another competition."

"I doubt the judge and jury will feel that way, not to mention the wife of the deceased," she said. His smile widened.

"I'm the one who's supposed to be defensive," he said.

"I'm the one who's supposed to be more sensitive," she countered and he laughed.

"You and I are both freshman in a sense. This is my first defense as an associate in the Simon and James agency and your first prosecution as a New York district attorney. Something of an occasion neither of us will soon forget, two rookies doing battle."

"I would hardly consider myself or you, for that matter, a rookie, Mr. Milton."

"Please, call me John."

She started to nod and realized that in her left hand she was clutching the magic eye amulet her aunt Eve had given her. It seemed to radiate warmth reminding her it was there. Maybe Aunt Eve was starting to rub off on her. She would never have paid heed to anything like this. She even walked under ladders and didn't care if a black cat crossed in front of her, but for some reason, especially for the first day of trial, she made certain to bring the amulet with her. She placed it on the table beside her papers.

John Milton stepped back, his eyes fixed on the amulet.

"Very pretty," he said. "Some sort of good luck charm?"

"They're bringing in your client," she said nodding at Lester Heckett's entrance instead of answering. His comment was full of ridicule.

"Oh. So they are. Well, I'd wish your charm brings you good luck, but that would be hypocritical and I never believe in luck anyway. Everything happens for a reason, don't you think?"

"Exactly," she said.

"I hope we'll still be this friendly when it's over."

"I don't see why not. What's between us isn't personal."

"Yet," he added, widening his smile and then left to join Heckett.

She stood there looking after him and now she vividly recalled how suddenly very twisted and nervous she had become that first day. She watched the way he greeted his client and spoke to the police guards. Whatever he said to them made them laugh. He seemed to be enjoying himself far too much. She could think of nothing funny about any of this, but for a moment she wondered if he took more delight in his work than she took in hers. After all, right up until now, the one accusation she couldn't throw off was that she was too serious and too uptight about her career.

Maybe so, but she was determined to boost that career considerably with this prosecution. However, both the district attorney and Eleanor Rozwell looked a lot more nervous about the case after she had confirmed that Lieutenant Blake was now unable to make the connection between Heckett and the hired gun.

"If Lieutenant Blake is right, and I'm confident he is, the actually killer is dead," she told them. "But Lester Heckett pulled that trigger, too, and I want to go after him straight on. Obviously, the defense won't introduce the possibility of a hired killer."

"Not one hired by Heckett," the district attorney said, "but he could develop there was one and claim Heckett isn't tied to him. The burden of proof for that, if the jury seems to be accepting it, is entirely on us."

"But Heckett has the motive and was at the crime scene and had the weapon in his possession. No jury can overlook all that."

They both looked thoughtful.

"It could be enough," Eleanor Rozwell suggested. "We got the indictment. We can't just walk off or postpone forever, hoping Lieutenant Blake will eventually find a way to tie him to the killer, who we haven't established at the crime scene anyway."

The district attorney nodded.

"Sorry about this. We thought it was a good first case for you, Michele."

"I wasn't looking for a milk run. I'll win the guilty verdict," she said, perhaps too confidently. Was that arrogant? They talked a little about the defendant's counselor, John Milton, but she didn't get the feeling that they thought he was overwhelming, despite his experience and record. Apparently, Warner Murphy had been seriously considering a plea deal. There was some informal, off-the-record chats. John Milton, however, was sending no such signals. They would have to go to battle.

At this point in the trial, she already had done what all her associates considered an excellent opening, laying out her case, and methodically establishing Heckett's motive through the testimony of both of Strumfield's partners, the financial documents and the Grand Cayman Island bank statements. She had brought in the real estate agent who had arranged for his rental in Hong Kong, but she was holding back on Cisley Strumfield. That was her piece de resistance, and by now she was showman enough to know when to play the best cards in this legal drama.

Milton had done little to challenge any of it so far, and in fact, was willing to stipulate for the record that Heckett did not deny shifting funds for some personal reasons. She corrected him for the record by stating it wasn't simply shifting funds, "It was embezzlement."

Milton's come back was a smile, a nod, and replying, "For which he is NOT being tried today." The implication was that it was all he should be tried for at maximum. "And if he were, we would be ready to show, he wasn't underhanded about it."

She was tempted to respond, but one look at the judge's face told her that the exchange was enough.

She moved on to the weapon found in Heckett's apartment, calling on forensic to testify that it was the weapon used in the Strumfield murder. She then called up Matthew Blake to describe where they had found the pistol and Heckett's reaction to the discovery.

When Matthew took the stand, she couldn't help but take note at the way John Milton's face changed. His impish, almost joyful look, dissipated and was replaced with an expression of dead seriousness. He looked angry, in fact.

"We found it under towels in the master bedroom bathroom closet of his home during the first fifteen minutes of our search, and when he was confronted with the news, he said he knew nothing about it and had never seen it until then. He accused us of planting evidence and then refused to say any more," Matthew testified.

"Were Mr. Heckett's fingerprints on the gun?"

"No, but it was obviously wiped clean. There were no fingerprints on it. Not even dust," Matthew Blake said glancing at Lester Heckett.

"Were you able to trace the weapon to any previous owner?" "Objection, your honor," John Milton said. "It has not been established that my client was the current owner or ever the owner of the pistol in question at the time of this discovery."

"Objection sustained. You'll have to prove more than possession to establish ownership, Ms. Armstrong," the judge said.

"Were there any serial numbers on the pistol, Lieutenant?" she asked quickly. It was always wise to move instantly off an objection sustained against you. You didn't want the jury thinking about it at all, if possible. Not recognizing the judge's reprimand made it seem insignificant anyway. She had learned all this quickly in law school from Professor Lasky who was considered a jury expert and employed often by attorneys to help choose juries. None of it had to do with right or wrong. All of it had to do with changing the odds to make winning more possible.

"There were, but they had been filed off."

"So we can conclude that there was an illegal weapon in Mr. Heckett's possession and that weapon was used to kill Mr. Strumfield?"

"All true, yes," Blake said.

"When you confronted him with the pistol, what was his explanation?"

"He didn't know how it had gotten there."

"Under towels in his bathroom?"

"Yes, that's what he said."

"Was there any evidence showing someone had broken into his apartment to leave a pistol under towels in his bathroom?" she asked, nearly smiling as she spoke.

"None."

"Did you ask him where he was the night Mr. Strumfield was murdered?"

"We did. He claimed he had a headache and was home all night. There were no calls, no visitors, and therefore no confirmation."

"Did Mr. Heckett claim to have had visitors in his home subsequent to the murder of Mr. Strumfield?"

"He made no such claim."

"Did he claim to have had maid service subsequent to Mr. Strumfield's murder?"

"According to his own record, the maid would not have been there and he did not claim she was. He then said he would not answer any more questions without any attorney."

"How did he react to the news of his supposedly best friend and partner being shot to death?"

"He looked . . . pensive. Like someone contemplating what a terrible sin he had committed."

"Objection, your honor," John Milton said rising. "That's reaching. Lieutenant Blake has not been trained as a forensic psychologist. I don't think he's qualified to make such a judgment."

"I'm only ascertaining the opinion of a seasoned police investigator who has confronted many villains in his life, your honor. Whether he is right or not the jury will determine."

"Exactly. The jury makes that determination and not your witness. Objections sustained," the judge said.

Michele felt the pang of another reprimand, but did her best not to look disappointed. Just be all business, she chanted to herself.

"Did Mr. Heckett say anything to indicate he was sad, upset?"

"Just one 'Oh, my God,' I believe."

"Nothing else?" she asked and looked at the jury to show them her shock. "Didn't he inquire after Mrs. Strumfield's health? Whether or not she had been injured, too, or how she was doing? Anything?"

"Not a word. He fell into his 'I'll talk only through my lawyer mode.' Immediately after that."

"In your experience, is this the behavior of an innocent man?"

"Objection," John Milton cried.

"Withdrawn," Michele said. "No further questions for this witness, your honor." She nodded at John Milton and walked to her table.

Obviously, he wasn't going to waste time before cross-examining this witness. He practically flew out of his chair. Finally John Milton became aggressive in his cross-examination. Michele had been wondering if he wasn't taking it all too lightly and losing before he had even begun. She couldn't help feeling that he was lulling her into over-confidence, however.

As soon as he began, it was clear to those watching, especially to the jury, that there was something different about the way John Milton addressed Lieutenant Blake from the way he had addressed any other witness. There was a sharp, angry tone in his voice. His relaxed posture was gone. He lost that impish smile he was carrying throughout the trial up to this point and looked more like a soldier on guard duty reacting to a threat. Anyone watching couldn't help wondering if the two hadn't crossed paths a few times and both come away upset, if not enraged. They assumed John Milton had done courtroom battle with this detective at least once. He honed in on Blake, ready to pick on his words or his intonation.

"Didn't your forensic report include an examination of the remaining bullets?"

"It did."

"And were Mr. Heckett's prints on them?"

"No. They were wiped clean of prints just as the gun was."

"Since Ms. Armstrong has made a point of your being an experienced investigator, Lieutenant, as an experienced investigator who has carried out many warranted searches, would you consider the hiding place for this pistol, under towels in a bathroom, very sophisticated?" he asked.

"Not very."

"Not the act of a cold-hearted killer?"

"I wouldn't come to that conclusion."

"You just told us that whoever used this gun was careful enough to wipe it clean and all the bullets clean and not leave any new fingerprints. Why take so much care with that and then do something so amateurish with that weapon? Hide it under towels in his own bathroom?"

"Killers aren't perfect," Matthew Blake said. He fixed his eyes right back at John Milton. Now John offered his wry smile.

"Neither are police detectives, Lieutenant. But that's why the accused have a right to a defense. You weren't on his heels, were you? He had plenty of time to get rid of the pistol, didn't he?" he followed quickly.

"He had time, of course. He could have tossed it on the way home."

"Why didn't he? Despite your implication because of the lack of fingerprints on the weapon and bullets, Lester Heckett's not a career criminal, Lieutenant. He doesn't rob banks, mug people. He has no criminal record, correct?"

Blake glanced at Michele. This was the time to suggest a hired killer, but without the clear proof, he was naturally hesitant. They had talked about it before trial and he could see that she had not changed her mind.

"He robbed his own company." Blake said instead.

"As we've said, that's to be determined yet. In any case he replaced the funds, did he not?"

"When he was caught having stolen it."

"I prefer borrowed with permission, which we'll establish later if necessary."

Michele's eyebrows went up. If necessary? Why wouldn't that be necessary for the defense? What did he have up his sleeve? She wondered.

She looked back at the audience. Aunt Eve had just arrived and had taken a seat. This was the first day she had attended. She had done it quietly, but Michele felt her presence. They smiled at each other, but then Aunt Eve looked intense, even a little upset when she focused on John Milton.

And then something odd happened. John Milton paused as though he was trying to understand either a thought or a feeling, paused long enough to alert the judge who wasn't as gentle this time.

"Mr. Milton? Are you finished with the witness? We have a trial to complete."

John Milton turned and looked back toward Aunt Eve and then said, "Hardly finished, your honor. Sorry."

He stepped toward Matthew Blake, his cold smile now more like a mask made of ice.

"Was this pistol registered to Mr. Heckett?"

"I've already said no."

"Was there any pistol registered to Mr. Heckett?"

"No."

"In your vast experience as a detective, if someone attained a weapon illegally and used it, wouldn't he be more inclined to get rid of it rather than keep it and hide it practically in plain view?"

"Unless he had to return it?" Blake blurted. Milton smiled. Blake had fallen into the trap.

"Return it? Where? To the gun library?" John Milton asked, turning to the jury.

Blake looked at Michele again and shrugged. Neither of them had believed Milton would raise the possibility of a hired gun. They believed he couldn't be absolutely sure they had no definitive proof, but here he was doing just that. Reluctantly, Matthew Blake continued.

"No, but if he had hired someone to commit the murder, the killer could have told him to keep the weapon."

"For what? A souvenir?"

"No, but I've investigated cases where the hired killer did things like that to keep the person who hired him from confessing and revealing him. In one similar case, he had the individual keep the pistol in his safety deposit box. He accompanied him to the bank to make sure."

"Oh how conniving. What a waste of brilliance. He could have been a . . . police detective," John Milton said. Some in the audience laughed. The judge rapped his gavel.

"Stick to your questions and leave the comments for the journalists, Mr. Milton."

"Yes, your honor. Sorry. So, Lieutenant Blake, following your implication, do you have any evidence to present to us today that firmly establishes Lester Heckett hired a hit man?"

Blake looked at Michele. She had introduced the Cayman Bank statement, but had not yet presented the withdrawal of the seventy-five thousand right before Strumfield's murder to establish the possibility of a payment to a hit man. As she had told Matthew Blake, she didn't want to open the door through which John Milton could introduce the argument that the murderer had to be more of an expert with pistol. She would rather deal with it when he presented his defense. By then, she would have established a great deal with the jury, and perhaps, he would look like he was desperate.

But John Milton had led Lieutenant Blake into it and she knew Blake wasn't going to go along with her and try to avoid it anymore. She was disappointed, but she couldn't fault him for his honesty. He wouldn't compromise with the truth. She had hoped he wouldn't have to go there, but that was exactly where John Milton had taken him. How could he be so confident that he wasn't giving the prosecution an opportunity?

Blake's hesitation encouraged him.

"So you cite cases where hit man made their employers hold onto the weapons as some sort of insurance. Are you then saying Lester Heckett is incapable of having committed this act himself, Lieutenant?"

"I didn't say that. Anyone is capable of murder."

"Anyone? Even priests? Even the Pope? Even Jesus Christ?"

Blake didn't answer. He looked at the judge. She wasn't demanding an answer.

John Milton widened his smile.

"We understand your hesitation there, Lieutenant. Isn't it true that you were a seminary student on his way to becoming a Catholic priest?"

Michele felt her mouth fall open. She had sensed something like this about him. She had felt it, but he didn't volunteer the information. Why not? Blake glanced at her and then turned back to John Milton.

"Yes," he said.

"That's quite unusual, isn't it? A man nearly a priest quits and becomes a police detective?"

"Objection, your honor. This line of questioning has nothing to do with the case or the facts."

"Oh, I think it does, your honor. It goes to Lieutenant Blake's credibility. Are his observations made from facts or faith? Does he hear voices? How did he come to these conclusions that he can't substantiate today?"

"Objection sustained," the judge said. "However, I see nothing stated by the witness that comes solely from faith, counselor."

"Perhaps," John Milton said, throwing the jury an impish smile. "Let's get to who did and who didn't commit this murder, Lieutenant. Isn't it fair to say that when it comes to Lester Heckett performing the actual murder, you have your doubts?"

Before Blake could respond, John Milton asked, "Can you enlighten us why? Oh, please, Lieutenant. Pretty please."

Matthew Blake's face turned a bit crimson. Anyone could see that he was subduing a rage fermenting inside him.

"I haven't said anything to indicate I have doubts about your client's guilt," Blake replied. "I just gave you a possibility as to why someone might not get rid of a weapon."

"Oh, you must have doubts, Lieutenant. You almost became a priest. You know what it's like to look into the human soul."

"Your honor," Michele said.

"Mr. Milton, you have laid no foundation for such a comment."

"I thought it was self-evident, your honor. Sorry. Okay, Lieutenant. You're an experienced investigator," John Milton repeated, now making it sound like experienced was something undesirable. "You just related how careful the killer was to clean off fingerprints, even from the bullets. Can we conclude that such action is beyond the scope of your average amateur killer?"

"No."

"No?"

"Not with all the forensics on television these days," Matthew Blake offered.

John Milton laughed.

"Sinners have it so much easier thanks to the media, is that it?"

"Something like that, yes."

"So, our killer learning from CSI or something, makes a brilliant attempt at a cover up when it comes to the pistol and the bullets, but hides the weapon in an obvious place, so obvious that you found it in fifteen minutes. Correct?"

"It took about that long, yes."

"Long? You call that long? Lester Heckett knew he was going to be what you call a person of interest because of the money issues and Mrs. Strumfield's testimony, and yet he doesn't cover up the most important clue? You have him brilliant on one hand," John Milton said holding up his right hand, "and pretty dumb on the other," he added holding up his left. With his hands in the air like someone surrendering, he asked, "I repeat. Isn't it possible he didn't know it was there? Possible that someone put it there without his knowing?"

Matthew Blake had anticipated that John Milton would use such a possibility as a defense argument, but without any definitive tie-in to a hit man, he couldn't dismiss it. For a moment he looked confused. John Milton was about to suggest that the actual killer could have done that to throw off the scent that would lead to him? It would go right to reasonable doubt. He glanced at Michele again. Now, she looked very worried. This was starting to slip away from her.

"Lieutenant?"

"Possible yes, but not probable when you consider the other facts."

"Ah, that probability thing. It keeps coming up in our world, especially the world of a good detective. But probability is not certainty, is it?"

"Bigger chance that it is than not," Blake said.

"That's not what I asked, but it's all right. We all know the answer," John said, winking at the jury. "There is then the possibility that the actual killer might have planted the weapon in Mr. Heckett's home, correct?"

Blake just stared at him.

"I'm only suggesting the possibility, Lieutenant."

"In an infinite universe, anything's possible," Blake said. Eyebrows lifted, even the judge's. Milton smiled.

He went to his desk and picked up some papers. Both Blake and Michele Armstrong knew what was on them.

"Let's consider it then. Speaking of probability which you just said has a better chance of certainty than not. We have the analysis of the angle of the two shots indicates the killer shot Mr. Strumfield from the landing above the living room where he was sitting and found dead. There's a distance of nearly twenty feet. Why would my client attempt to shoot Mr. Strumfield from so far away when he could walk right up to him and pump two bullets in his heart? They were still friends at the time, weren't they?"

"I don't know that they were. Mrs. Strumfield told us her husband had given Lester Heckett an ultimatum. Their friendship had to be strained to say the least."

"So strained that Mr. Strumfield wouldn't let him in the apartment?"

"I don't know."

"If he had let him in the apartment, he wouldn't have had to shoot him from a distance, correct?"

"Probably not."

"That old probability again. If the friendship was so strained and my client shot Mr. Strumfield, then he probably broke into the apartment, yet there's no sign of a break in, correct?"

"No, but . . ."

"Are you saying Strumfield gave him a key to his apartment so he could come by and shoot him from a distance that would require some expertise with a pistol?" John looked at the report in his hands. "Yes, it's nearly twenty feet. That requires some expertise with such a pistol, doesn't it?"

"That distance is an estimate."

"An estimate? We know where Strumfield's body was found. We know how far the chair is from the landing. But okay, even if it was only reasonably accurate, Lester Heckett still would have to have to perform something like some Wild Bill Hickok circus sharp shooter, right?" He glanced at the sheet again, "two wounds less than an inch apart. It would take a marksman to achieve that, correct?"

"Not necessarily."

"But probably?"

John Milton turned to the jury and glanced at Michele.

"Which means, according to your own definition of probability, we would pay heed to your conclusion that it's more likely someone else besides Lester Heckett committed this murder."

"Objection, your honor. The witness has not stated that conclusion."

"Objection sustained."

John Milton turned sharply on Blake. He stepped toward him, looking like he might leap at him.

"Did you discover any evidence to indicate Lester Heckett was familiar with guns, pistols in particular?"

"No, but he could have practiced secretly, I suppose."

"Could have, might have, not very definitive for a detective presenting evidence in a murder trial. Something more customary for a priest, wouldn't you say?"

Before Matthew Blake could respond, John Milton turned to Michele. "Probably your friendly witness," he said and walked back to his table.

Michele rose slowly. She knew she had to follow this line of questioning now. Blake looked at her apologetically, but clearly ready to do whatever he could to help.

"Since defense counsel has introduced the possibility of a hired assassin, let's follow that for a moment, Lieutenant Blake. As you have stated, you've been involved in murder cases in which someone hired an assassin, have you not?"

"Yes."

"When you have this suspicion and investigate this probability, what is one thing you might check first?"

"A withdrawal of funds with which to pay the killer."

"Yes, and according to the bank statement I entered into evidence, Lester Heckett withdrew seventy-five thousand dollars just before the murder of Willard Strumfield. Is that in line with what you've seen paid hit men?"

"Not that much necessarily, but very credible. Especially to hire a dependable and experienced killer."

"You had a lead in this regard, did you not, Lieutenant?"

"Yes."

"Can you explain it to the jury, please."

"One of my informants lead me to an individual who brokers murderers for hire. He told me this man had told him he had been offered nearly double his usual fee to assign a killer to a case. He specifically said, seventy-five thousand dollars."

"Which is exactly what Lester Heckett withdrew in cash right before Mr. Strumfield was shot. A man who hires someone to kill for him is still a murderer, is he not?"

"Absolutely."

"Thank you."

She headed back to her seat, unable to feel confident. She felt more like she was in retreat.

"A few more questions," John Milton said. "Did this informant specifically mention Lester Heckett?"

"No. As I said, there was a middle man. I followed up on it and was able to determine through my informant whom in his stable of killers he might have put on this killing."

"Did you arrest the middle man, bring him in for questioning?"

"I couldn't. He was found dead from a drug overdose before I could get to him. We know now that he was murdered, deliberately injected with a drug overdose."

"How unfortunate. What about the probable assassin? Did you get a lead, follow up on him or her?"

"He was killed in a mugging?"

"A trained killer killed in a mugging? Who's safe on our streets these days?" Milton offered and smiled at the jury. "Okay, where is this informer, Lieutenant? I don't see him on the witness list?"

"You can't have an informer testify in court. Not only would he no longer be of any value to the police, he'd probably be killed."

"Then I move that Lieutenant Blake's testimony regarding the payment of seventy-five thousand dollars to employ a hit man be considered hearsay and stricken from the record, your honor," John Milton said.

The judge nodded.

"Sustained." He turned to the jury. "You will disregard the testimony concerning the payment of seventy-five thousand dollars for a hit man."

John Milton smiled at Michele, but it wasn't a smile of arrogance. It was more like a look of regret, an apology. It made her angrier.

It was time to call up Cisley Strumfield and establish Lester Heckett's motive and presence at the murder scene. With the motive, the weapon in his possession and the eye-witness account, she was still very confident of a win.

But when she looked at Cisley Strumfield, she paused. Her face was trembling.

She looked like she was made of thin china.

And in seconds, she would crumble to the floor.

She then turned to look at Aunt Eve. Her face was more disturbing. She looked like she had seen one of her ghosts.

And when Aunt Eve looked back at her, she shook her head the way she did when she predicted something dark and sad for anyone she had confronted long enough to establish a view of his or her future.

17.

Cisley Strumfield walked so slowly to the witness chair, Michele thought she wasn't going to make it, that she would simply fold up like a dress dropped from a hanger and spread herself out on the floor. She clutched her Judith Leiber purse against her body like someone who feared it being snatched, squeezed it under her arm and against her breast as protectively as a football player heading for the goal posts when she was sworn in, and sat with her hands over it as if she was drawing some sort of power and stability from it.

Michele regretted not being firmer about how she should dress. She certainly didn't need the gold over Sterling silver diamond bangles on her left wrist to compliment her nearly two-carat diamond wedding ring along with the expensive purse, and she could have worn a black or gray pants suit outfit and not an Armani tailored pearl Lurex Melange jacket and skirt. Michele thought however, that this was who Cisley Strumfield was. She was literally uncomfortable in less expensive clothes and probably felt naked without her diamonds.

Michele smiled at her, hoping to keep her calm and secure.

"I know how difficult this is for you, Mrs. Strumfield. It hasn't been that long since this tragedy," she said, fully aware that to the jury, a woman who took pains with her make-up and wore clothing and jewelry most of them couldn't afford, didn't rise to that expectation of difficulty Michele was implying. Time had passed and mourning her husband could have diminished in its intensity, but surely the trial was bringing it all back in spades.

"I can't get the sight of him out of my mind," Cisley Strumfield said, following Michele's lead. Her voice was thin, obviously on the verge of cracking into sobs. She glanced at Lester Heckett and quickly turned back to Michele. "I'll do my best. I want to see justice for my husband."

"Of course. We all do. Thank you."

"You've known the defendant Lester Heckett for some time as did your husband?"

"Yes, a long time. I've known him nearly nine years."

"And you knew that your husband knew him years before he had become involved with his company?"

"Both of them often talked about their days at college."

"Why did your husband offer Lester Heckett a position in his company?"

"Lester wasn't doing that well. He had failed in his entrepreneurial efforts. He was in debt, matter of fact," she said as if the word 'debt' was a profanity. "He came to Elliot for work and Elliot hired him." She turned and looked at Lester Heckett. "He made him a wealthy man, but he was very greedy and jealous of Elliot's success."

"How do you know he was jealous?"

"I could see it whenever he was with the both of us. Elliot mentioned it to me often. It bothered him, made him sad, disappointed."

"Did your husband often bring home his work, tell you about the ups and downs in the business?"

"Never. He knew I didn't like finance. It was always too boring and complicated for me."

"But he did tell you about Mr. Heckett's embezzlement."

"Objection, your honor," John Milton said. "We have not established any illegal activity on Mr. Heckett's part."

"Shifting of funds into his own account," Michele corrected. She looked back at John Milton. He flicked his wrist at his forehead and smiled.

"Please answer the question, Mrs. Strumfield," Michele said.

"My husband was heart-broken about that once he discovered what Lester had done. Not only did he feel betrayed, but he felt he had betrayed his two other partners by bringing Lester into the mix, as he would say."

She opened her purse, took out a tissue, and dabbed her eyes.

"Were you present when your husband confronted Lester Heckett about this transfer of company funds to his own private account?"

"I wasn't in the room, but I could hear everything. My husband was shouting a lot, and he was always a soft-spoken man, even when he was angry."

"What did you hear?"

"I heard Mr. Heckett breakdown, claim he was under great pressure because of his divorce. I heard him promise to restore the funds."

"So there is no doubt in your mind that your husband did not give Lester Heckett permission to take this money?"

"No, no doubt."

"What did you hear your husband say after Lester Heckett promised to return the funds?"

"He told him how terribly disappointed he was in him, how much the betrayal pained him, and how embarrassed he was to have brought him into the business. He told him he would not press charges against him if he returned the money in two days, but he wanted Lester to resign."

"And what was Mr. Heckett's response?"

"He was grateful and apologetic, but he pleaded for his job. He begged for another six months at least."

"And your husband's reaction?"

"He was adamant that Lester resign immediately after restoring the money."

"Okay. Let's fast forward to that infamous and horrible day, Mrs. Strumfield. You had gone out to do some shopping, correct?"

"Yes, and to meet some friends for lunch."

"Was there any way Lester Heckett would know you weren't home at the time planned for your husband's murder?"

"Lester had called me the day before. He wanted to meet with me to convince me to work on my husband and convince him to give him more time to earn more money. He asked to meet me for lunch and I told him of my plans already made. I also told him I would not approach Elliot on his behalf anyway, that I was just as disappointed and disillusioned with him. I warned him to get the money returned and I hung up."

"It started raining right after your lunch ended so you took a taxi cab home?"

"Yes, but I normally take a taxi."

"Describe what you saw then?"

"I got out of the taxi and started toward the front entrance when I saw Lester look back at me and then hurry away."

"How far was he from the building?"

"Maybe fifty feet at most."

"So there is no doubt in your mind, you saw Lester Heckett moving away quickly from your building just before you went up and found your husband had been shot dead?"

"None whatsoever," she said firmly.

"And when he saw you, he didn't approach you to talk. He continued to flee?"

"Yes."

"Thank you, Mrs. Strumfield."

She glanced at John Milton and then at her Aunt, who still didn't smile despite the good testimony Michele had drawn from Cisley Strumfield.

John Milton rose so slowly, he seemed to be unfolding into his true height and for a moment, Michele thought he did look a little taller. He moved slower, too, his head down, looking like he was struggling to come up with a question, and then, just as suddenly as ever, he raised his head and smiled.

"How long had your husband known of your affair, Mrs. Strumfield?"

Cisley Strumfield's whole face trembled. Michele felt a terrible sick feeling come over her. This came completely out of thin air. She looked at Matthew Blake. He shook his head.

"I have had no affair," Cisley said as soon as she regained her breath.

John Milton held his smile.

"You swore to tell the truth and nothing but the truth, Mrs. Strumfield."

"I'm telling the truth."

"We're going to have to subpoena a Mr. Bob Middleton, Mrs. Strumfield, and then the clerk at The Dew Drop Inn in Fort Lee, New Jersey. Clark is his name, I believe. Short, stout red-head man of forty or so? He's seen you and Mr. Middleton at least, what, five times?"

Cisley Strumfield didn't reply, but it was obvious that she was shocked with the details John Milton was proposing.

"Mr. Middleton is the husband of one of the women you lunch with on a regular basis, isn't he?"

"Yes," she said, barely audible.

"But you don't feel too guilty about it, right? Your husband had an affair with someone you knew not that long ago, correct?"

She shook her head.

"I don't know of any . . ."

"Of course, you do. How did you find out about that? A friend saw them, I believe? Actually, to show you of your husband's affair, you were given photographs, were you not?"

Cisley looked toward Michele, but she had no reason to object. It would look bad to do it and be overruled. She would look like she was trying to prevent the truth.

"We can produce the photographs, enter them in the record, if you like? I have copies. I don't want to bring you any additional pain, Mrs. Strumfield. I don't want to ask you to identify your husband with the wife of someone who was supposedly a good friend."

Cisley Strumfield's face began to crumble, crinkle up as if it was made of cellophane.

"Shall I produce the photographs?" John Milton asked softly.

"No. Yes. I knew about his affair," Cisley admitted.

"The truth feels so much better, doesn't it?" he asked, but didn't wait for an answer. "Did you have your affair as a way to get even?" John Milton asked. "I think a lot of us might sympathize with you if that was your motive," he quickly added.

Michele felt she just had to object. It was weak.

"This line of questioning has nothing to do with Mrs. Strumfield's testimony, your honor."

"Oh, I think it does, your honor. I think it speaks to truth and consequences, as well as motive. It certainly speaks to the validity of this witness, especially when established that Eliot Strumfield was seeing Lester Heckett's wife before and after their divorce."

There was an audible gasp in the audience and even from some of the jury members.

"I'll allow it," the judge said.

"This affair?" John said. "To get even then?"

"No. It was just something that happened. It's over. It's been over so long that I don't think about it anymore."

"That's convenient. Loss of memory when it comes to our indiscretions, our sins. Since we all sin, how lucky are those with Alzheimer's after all," John Milton said and looked at the jury. "Okay, now that we have restored your memory somewhat, can you tell us how your husband reacted when he found out? He knew Middleton, right?"

"We came to an understanding," she said. "Neither of us spoke of it after I ended it."

"Spoke is one thing; shared your bed is another," John said. "In fact, when was the last time you slept together? And don't tell me the night before he was killed."

"I object, your honor. The defense counsel is on some kind of wild fishing expedition. There is no possible way he can substantiate the Strumfield's private love life."

"Oh, it's not so wild, your honor," John Milton said. "And I'm afraid our esteemed assistant district attorney is incorrect. I can substantiate it if Mrs. Strumfield treats us to the truth. That's why I'm asking her."

"I want to see pretty quickly where you're going with this, Mr. Milton."

"Understood, your honor. Okay. I'm sympathetic to your horrible situation, Mrs. Strumfield. We don't need to explore your husband and your sexual relationship. However, you're the one who has had the real money in this marriage, aren't you, Mrs. Strumfield. You financed your husband's business and you've always owned seventy-five percent of his share. You had this written in your prenuptial, didn't you?"

"Yes," she said.

"Of course, now that he's dead, you have one-hundred percent of his share and his share of the company is fifty-five percent, so you have control of the company now, correct?"

"Yes. I believe that's so."

"Oh, you know it's so. You're not as oblivious to finance as you're trying to get us to believe. Do you have money overseas for example?"

"Elliot invested in some overseas properties, I believe."

"I'm asking if you personally have money in a Swedish bank account, Mrs. Strumfield?"

It was clear Cisley Strumfield was astonished. How could John Milton know this? Her husband didn't even know it. Michele could almost see her mind at work. Should she admit it or deny it? He's just guessing. He can't prove it.

"Didn't Mr. Middleton help you set that up?" Milton followed.

Now the look of shock was trembling through her face and brought trembling to her hands. She fumbled with her tissue. Bob, Cisley thought, had betrayed her. But he had money there, too. Or did.

"I'm not doing anything illegal," she said in response.

"Ah, so you do have considerable funds in a Swiss bank account. It's better just to tell the truth at the start, Mrs. Strumfield. It makes my work easier for me," he added and gave the jury another one of his impish smiles.

Cisley looked toward Michele, but she didn't want to prolong this subject with an objection. John Milton looked at her as well. It was as if he was challenging her to do it. She pressed her lips together and he gave her a slight nod. She was sure of it. Then he turned back to Cisley Strumfield.

"Did you withdraw seventy-five thousand dollars recently?"

"No," she said as firmly as she could, but she glanced at the jury. They looked skeptical. People were always hiding their investments in and their withdrawals of money in Swiss banks.

"When you overheard the argument between your husband and my client, you saw an opportunity, didn't you?"

She shook her head.

"I don't know what you mean. What opportunity?"

John Milton moved in closer.

"You're actually the one who hired the hit man and you lied here today about seeing Lester Heckett near your building on the day of your husband's murder, didn't you? Because of what had happened between him and your husband, you saw a wonderful opportunity, didn't you?"

"No."

"You had the man you employed hide the pistol in Lester Heckett's apartment and in a place where the police would find it, didn't you?"

"No."

"In fifteen minutes," John Milton said and glanced at Matthew Blake. "Perhaps the police had an anonymous tip."

He let that hang in the air for a moment and nodded slightly at the jury.

"You had no love for your husband anymore. You haven't slept with him for years now. You suspected him of being unfaithful all the time. You wanted to start a new life," he continued.

"No, that's not true. We were comfortable together."

"Comfortable? How can two people who live with such a compromise call themselves comfortable?"

Tears were clouding her vision. She tried dabbing her eyes, but it didn't help. And then . . . John Milton seemed to metamorphose right before her eyes and become her husband.

"You hated me," she thought she heard him say. It was her husband's voice, but slow, the words stretched and sounding like a recording playing too slowly . . . "Youuuuuu hatttteedd meeeee. Youuuuuu waaanteeed meeee killeddddddd. Youuu neverrr forgave meeeee!"

"NO!" she screamed. "I didn't hate you. I didn't have you killed!" She stood up. The Judith Leiber purse fell out of her hands. She looked around at all the people, their faces stretching, their eyes oozing. She brought her hands to her ears and screamed again. "NO!"

Michele was up calling for a recess. The judge was banging her gavel.

To Cisley Strumfield, John Milton became John Milton again and her heart stopped pounding.

But she couldn't battle back the darkness. She couldn't help herself. She collapsed in the witness chair.

The courtroom was in a state of bedlam. Michele and a female officer rushed to Cisley Strumfield. The judge called for a recess and ordered the courtroom cleared. When Cisley Strumfield began to regain consciousness, they took her to an office near the courtroom. A physician was requested. It all happened so quickly that it was like some mystical power had fast forwarded time and events.

Michele, dazed a bit herself by now, met her aunt out in the lobby. She was sitting on a bench staring at the wall. The moment Michele appeared, she turned to her and shook her head.

"How is she?"

"She had to be sedated."

"This is bad for you, isn't it?"

"Yes. I made a bad strategic mistake."

"I must tell you what I saw just before that poor woman fainted, Michele," her aunt said and reached for her hand. Michele could feel her trembling.

"What, Aunt Eve?"

"That man, that attorney, when he was questioning your witness, he became a large, thick dark shadow."

"What?"

"Just for a few moments and then he returned to himself, but I saw it. I've seen it before, always just before something terrible is about to occur."

"You were probably just as angry and upset as I was, Aunt Eve. I should have done a better job of vetting my witness. We fell into a trap. He's just a very clever attorney."

"No. I saw it," Aunt Eve insisted.

"Okay. You're upset, too. You might as well go home. The trial won't resume until tomorrow. I don't expect it to last much longer anyway," she added mournfully.

"You have to be more careful, Michele. There's something bigger happening here. I'm sure of it now."

She let go of her aunt's hand.

Bigger? That's what Matthew Blake had told her, twice.

"What? Why do you say 'bigger'?"

"I'm not sure yet."

That was Matthew's response, too. She sucked in her breath and tightened herself, recapturing her nearly perfect posture.

"Well, whatever it is, we'll get to the bottom of it," she said.

Her aunt rose.

"You don't want to get to the bottom of it. That's not a good place to be," she said. "I'll have something comforting to eat when you get home."

"Oh don't prepare anything, Aunt Eve. Thank you, but I'm not going right home," she said and kissed her cheek. Never had that cheek felt as cold as it did then, she thought and watched her walk away, for the first time looking her age, looking older than her mother.

When she turned, she was facing Dave Duggan. He shrugged. Here it comes, she thought.

"The district attorney called me. Looks like we'll have to discuss the wake," he said. "The stench of reasonable doubt in that courtroom is pervasive."

"Heckett was responsible for this murder," she said definitively.

He shrugged.

"Once the jury rules, you can't run around saying that, Michele. You win some; you lose some. The trick is knowing how to lose gracefully."

"You're the second person who's been in that courtroom who has made it sound like a game," she said.

"Who's the first?"

"John Milton," she replied. "I'll talk to you tomorrow. Let me lose the damn trial first," she added. "He still has to present a defense."

"My guess is he won't bother," Duggan said. "But I'll wait. Unless you just want to go somewhere and cool down. How about The Advocate Club?"

"Thanks but no thanks, Dave. I don't want to look at any lawyers right now or anyone or anything that has to do with them."

He nodded, disappointed.

"Okay. Stay cool," he said, sounding like a high school boy. He smiled and walked off. She felt bad about it, but right now, all she wanted to do was have a strong martini somewhere everyone or anyone but lawyers hung out.

As if he could hear her thoughts, he stepped into the hallway from the men's room and waited for her.

"Take me to a quiet bar," she told Matthew Blake. "No. Take me to a noisy one. Preferably frequented by blue collar workers."

He nodded.

"I know just the place," he said, offered his arm, and walked her out of the building.

18.

"How did he know all that about Cisley Strumfield?" Michelle asked Matthew Blake as soon as they were served their drinks. "Her husband's affair? Her own affair, who with, where they had gone to . . . make love and how many times?" She had almost said, fuck, but hesitated. Was it because she now knew he had been a seminary student? She suddenly realized that he had yet to use profanity with her, unlike just about every other policeman and detective she had met in her short but busy career.

"Nobody on my side had any idea obviously," she continued, unable to contain her frustration. It was pouring out of her nose and ears like steam. "There was nothing in the file. Neither the district attorney nor Eleanor Rozwell mentioned anything mitigating about my chief witness."

She felt she was ranting, but she couldn't help it.

"I mean, John Milton just recently came onto this case. He claimed he didn't need a postponement. He could have gotten one. I feel like I'm the one who should have asked for a postponement now, not him."

Blake reached out and touched her hand.

"Easy," he said.

She took another sip of her martini and looked around. He had taken her to a blue collar establishment all right, a watering hole called, The Easy Hour. They sat in one of the three booths available, each one looking well worn, faded with small rips in the artificial leather. It looked like the clientele were New York City water and electric workers, toll booth employees and taxi drivers. It was noisy with its muffled music, chatter and laughter, but there was energy. Everyone was letting off steam and acting like he had just been released from solitary. She didn't want to be anywhere sedate. If anything, she didn't want a place that suggested a wake.

Michele fingered her martini glass. She could see her face reflected in the glass. It looked like the reflection she would get of herself in one of those fun mirror places in entertainment parks. But for the moment, everything looked and felt distorted to her and not just her face. It was as though all the laws of physics had suddenly been suspended, even gravity. She felt like she might just rise and float to the ceiling at any moment.

"I mean, how could he get so much secret personal information in so short a time? Why didn't I think of the possibilities and ask the right questions of her before I put her on the stand?"

"You had no reason to have considered her a person of interest, Michele."

"But I should have had one. Skepticism and suspicion are essential ingredients in any prosecutor. I didn't do a good job of vetting my witness at her deposition."

"You asked her if she and her husband had a good relationship?"

"Yes, but I didn't pursue it. I should have continued and asked, good relationship when? Any reason why that statement might be challenged in court?"

"But you had the suspect almost instantly. Thanks to me."

"I didn't cast a wide enough net of doubts and suspicions," she replied. "It's the first time I've been so narrowly focused. A good prosecutor has to challenge his or her own evidence, case strategy. I was too damn anxious to nail him and chalk up a victory, impress everyone. Ambition and vanity can be deadly."

"Blame it on me," he said. "I should have been the one to widened my net to include the possibilities. I was confident we had the man who ordered the killing and the killer. I still think we did; we do. Look, John Milton had more reason to find holes in the witnesses. That's his whole job."

"But how was he able to do it so quickly and so well? The bank information from Switzerland, too. He had just started at a new firm. It's like he had begun this case months ago, like he knew Murphy would die and he'd step in to take his place."

Blake looked like she had given him an idea.

"What?" she demanded. "What are you thinking?"

"Nothing. Look, he has an ex-FBI agent working for him personally," Blake said. "Tom Beardsly. I don't know how long he's employed him."

"Beardsly? Why do I know that name?"

"National headline maker. He killed two innocent people in a shootout with two suspected terrorist that was off the charts, something like a wild west show on Wall Street, crowded and busy at the time. One of the innocent victims was the mayor's personal friend, a billionaire, international financier and philanthropist. The whole thing embarrassed the Bureau. Beardsly was often a loose cannon, the FBI's Dirty Harry. The ends justify the means kind of guy. There was even some talk about him having taken vigilante action a number of times. People he was investigating met with odd accidents."

She nodded.

"I remember the story."

"Thing was he was good at conducting an investigation," Blake said. "When it comes to information, he knows where to go and how to get it and fast. He probably taps on people who still owe him favors, open otherwise locked doors. Very smart of John Milton to hire him. However, I suspect he might have done more than just dig up information for him. He might also be employed to bury information."

"Bury? What do you mean?"

"I'm trying to tie him to the death of the hit man broker or agent."

"Barry Tyler?"

"Yes. We arrived very soon after at the scene and as I was entering the building, I was fairly sure I had seen Beardsly driving away. We're running fingerprints, testing material, all of it to see if he left something of himself behind, but if anyone should be good at a cover up, an ex-FBI agent should."

"What are you saying, Lieutenant? Are you suggesting John Milton hired him to stop us from reaching a witness who could tie the killer to Lester Heckett?"

"It smells like it."

She sat back, thought a moment and then shook her head. She was beginning to get a queasy feeling about Lieutenant Blake. Maybe it was because of the work he had to do, or maybe it was because of his religious education, but he seemed to see evil conspiracies everywhere. An 'evil lurks in the hearts of all men,' sort of thing. The old Original Sin argument.

She recalled him proposing that Warner Murphy's death was somehow tied to what was happening in the Strumfield trial, for example. She shook her head.

"How tempting, but no. That's too easy for me to accept. Good excuse for my failure in there. Why would John Milton care that much and risk so much for a man he barely knows?"

"Ambition. He wants to win."

She thought, drank and shook her head again.

"No. That's too much. I read John Milton's resume. He's good. He doesn't seem to need to stack the deck. I must admit that I didn't see him coming. Maybe I'm just not as good at this as I think I am."

"Not the time to start self-doubting," Blake said. "Remember. What doesn't kill me makes me stronger."

"You? Quoting Nietzsche?"

"Why not?"

"A former seminary student? Didn't Nietzsche believe that religions were simply a way of re-empowering the weak at the expense of the strong?"

"I always liked to read and understand the opposite point of view, the challenges to faith. You have to know your enemy to defeat him."

"I recall Nietzsche also said 'Be careful when you fight the monsters, lest you become one. You are fighting monsters, aren't you?"

Blake smiled.

"Yes. And I worry about that all the time."

"So do I," she said.

"Then don't be so hard on yourself. You're still one of the good guys no matter what the outcome of one trial."

"Thanks, but are you comforting me now as a priest or as a policeman?"

"I'm not a priest. I couldn't be one."

"Why not? What stopped you?"

"Before you say it, it wasn't celibacy."

"I don't know if I like that. I can't help wishing it was."

"Okay, it was to some extent," he said. "Maybe to a larger extent than I was prepared to admit, but what stopped me was turning the other cheek."

She nodded.

"An eye for an eye sort of guy now?"

"As long as it's for justice and not revenge; otherwise, Gandhi was right. It just leads to blindness on both sides."

"So now I know why you were in Rome and why you're different from any other cop I've met."

"Different, but I hope not less effective."

"No, I think I can believe you have better instincts than most. You don't see it all as just black and white, facts and figures, do you? You operate almost as much on feelings. You're more like a profiler. You get into the mind of the perpetrator."

"Exactly. You read me well," he said. "But most of the time, that's hard to convey, which bugs my new partner. I don't know if he'll last with me too much longer. I think I scare him sometimes with my predictions that look like they're coming out of thin air."

"Is that what happened with your previous partner?"

"Not exactly. There were other extenuating circumstances when it came to him that didn't come out of thin air."

"Like what?"

"Let's just say he didn't appreciate my having good instincts."

"I see. Whatever. I wish I had some of that power of good instincts right now. Maybe, I would have known what to expect from Mrs. Strumfield."

"You have it. It just has to grow stronger and it will with time and experience."

"Yes, Father."

"Please."

"Sorry. I'm not in the mood for encouragement."

"You should be. Get her back in there and try again with Mrs. Strumfield," Blake said.

She sipped her drink and shook her head.

"Would be a waste of time."

"Why?"

"You heard what she was screaming. She's incoherent. I don't know when I could get her back in there and even if I did, I have no idea what she would say now. Frankly, she might need professional help."

"What did she say when she regained consciousness?"

"She still claims that at one point it wasn't John Milton cross-examining her. It was her husband."

"Maybe it was."

"What?"

Blake stared at her or rather, right through her.

"Is this one of those out of thin air sort of things?"

"No, not exactly."

"This isn't going to that comment you and my aunt now have made, is it? Something bigger is going on here? You won't believe the things she told me in the hallway afterward."

He seemed to return to earth and forced a smile.

"What did she tell you?"

"Something about John Milton becoming a large dark shadow."

"About the time Mrs. Strumfield claims he turned into her husband?"

She drank and thought and then nodded.

"I guess." She squinted. "You think that means something, something beyond reality?" She hummed the famous theme music from jaws. He could see she was feeling her drink quickly, probably because she had begun drinking it with such anxiety and frustration. She had downed it quickly and signaled for another.

"Well?" she demanded. "Are you going to start seeing things no one else can see?"

"Maybe," he said. "I have to check on some ashes."

"Ashes?"

"Forget it."

She was given her new drink and began to sip it immediately.

"So what are you going to do? Ask for a postponement because of Mrs. Strumfield?"

"Postponement? No. I suspect I won't get it anyway. The jury is not going to believe anything she says and John Milton could have it all repeated. I'd rather the jury forget she was even on the stand. Of course, that weakens my motive and presence at the scene arguments. You're sure the doorman at the hotel didn't see him, right?"

"I'm sorry," he said. "Remember it was raining. He wasn't hanging out outside and was talking too much to the receptionist. I don't blame him. She was quite attractive."

"Wonderful. More gets by men because of their floating eyes than anything." She took another long sip of her second martini. "I have no second witness to corroborate her sighting of Heckett."

"No one else has come forward. You're not the only one with some regrets. I should have moved a little faster linking things up. Maybe I would have gotten to the hired killer in time to make a difference."

"I'm not going to use you or anyone in the police department as a scapegoat. Don't try to fall on a sword for me, Lieutenant. You're not to blame. I'm the one prosecuting the case. I chose to go forward with what I had. The buck stops here," she said pressing her right hand against her breast.

"Not a bad place to stop," he remarked. Her eyes widened.

"Why Lieutenant. Are you hitting on me?"

"Would you like me to?"

His comeback was so fast, she lost her breath for a moment.

"Ask me again when I'm not drinking and feeling sorry for myself," she replied. "Right now I'm too vulnerable."

"Duly noted," he said and then perked up with a new thought. "How about we go get something to eat at a nice restaurant? Sober you up a little. You'll feel better and then I can ask you again."

She thought a moment.

"No, I think I'm going home. My aunt will have something emotionally and psychologically soothing for me to eat even though I told her not to bother."

"Emotionally and psychologically soothing food? What's that?"

"Something made with a magic potion, I'm sure."

She finished her second martini. He had yet to finish his first.

"Something the Shirley McLaine of Soho often does?"

She laughed and nodded.

"She became like this after she and her husband had that terrible car accident? She was in a coma."

"Yes. How do you know that?"

"I took some time to learn about you."

"For professional reasons?"

"No," he said.

She stared at him a moment and then smiled.

"I never suspected. You have always been very . . . professional."

"I'm just out of training."

"Remnants of pursuing the priesthood?"

"No, just bashful."

She laughed and then instantly changed to a serious expression.

"It's true. Nothing seems to be what it looks like. All of a sudden, I feel like I've entered another world, and I don't mean because I've come to New York. There are so many more mysteries in my life now. I'm getting so I don't know what to believe is real and what isn't. Maybe my aunt isn't so off-the-wall as I think."

He nodded.

"There are more things in heaven and earth, Horatio, than are dreamt of in your philosophy," Blake recited.

"Nietzsche and now Shakespeare. I won't lack for education working with you, Lieutenant." She thought a moment. "Hamlet was talking about the ghost of his father at that point in the play, right?"

"Yes."

"Do you think Cisley Strumfield saw her husband's ghost in the courtroom?"

He thought a moment and shook his head.

"Might have been something more," he said.

She nodded, now a slight smirk on her face.

"Might have been something more? Okay, Lieutenant. I changed my mind. I will have something to eat with you."

"You will?"

"Yes. You'll take me home and eat whatever my aunt serves. You might need it more than I do," she said, and Blake laughed harder and longer than she had seen him laugh up until then.

Maybe it was the martinis or maybe it was just Blake's company, but the sheet of dread that had fallen over her was lifted away. She didn't think she would be laughing again this soon after the day's courtroom disaster, but here she was feeling young and carefree, hanging her arm on his as they left the tavern and started toward Matthew Blake's car.

He opened the door for her and got in. As he was coming around to get in on his side, he stopped. He seemed to freeze for a moment. She looked in the direction he was looking. There was the usual traffic and pedestrians. Nothing was happening across the way that she could see, but she could see that he was intrigued about something. He moved but slowly to the driver's side, looking back as he opened the door.

"What's wrong? You look like you just saw one of America's most wanted."

He got in.

"There's a familiar black limousine across the street," he said and started the engine.

"Oh? Whose?"

"I think it's John Milton's," he said.

She felt a trickle of ice down the back of her neck. It ran along her spine. She leaned over to look. There was a black limousine. It started away, moving in the opposite direction.

"It's not an uncommon car, Lieutenant. Could you see the license plate?"

"No, I didn't catch it," he said.

"Why would he be following me?"

"More like he'd be following me," Blake said. "Or maybe now, he's following both of us," he added and pulled away from the curb.

19.

"You know what I fear the most, Charon?" John Milton asked in the tone of a hypothetical question as they headed uptown to the restaurant where he was to meet Alexander James for a pre-victory celebration. He had already arranged for it to be a wild night for the senior partner. Charon stared ahead just the way someone who knew that if he waited patiently, the answer would be told.

"What I fear most, Charon, is déjà vu. Can you even begin to imagine what that must be like for someone like me? This is why it is so important for me to recruit. I mean He's got thousands, tens of thousands, running around proselytizing and convincing all who walk this planet of His celestial existence, right? Once you're convinced He exists, you're then worried that He might not approve of your behavior. That's an unfair advantage," Milton said, raising his voice.

"I'm not complaining, even though it sounds like it," he added quickly. "I won't succumb to sniveling and crawling. I'm just pointing out facts. If anything, these facts mean I should be appreciated even more for my accomplishments. I will admit to being disappointed from time to time, but in my case disappointment only leads to more determination. I do not get discouraged, Charon." He paused and then said, "Drive a little slower. I want him to wait a bit. I never want any of them to think I need them, even for a moment."

Charon eased his foot on the accelerator. For a moment John Milton was distracted by the sight of the city coming to nocturnal life, populated by those who enjoyed the darkness more than the light, those with faces full of expectations, fantasies and in so many cases, a desperate need for some form of sexual satisfaction. What would his world be like without sex? Greed, sloth, vanity, all the rest would not be enough, and even combined into one powerful force would still not become a big enough key to open the vault of all the souls he needed to plunder. Talk about vampires and blood. Their hunger was nothing compared to his. How could an occasional feast on hemoglobin rival his thirst for the embodied spirits of God's imperfect creations?

"Where was I?" he muttered. "Oh, yes, not discouraged. On the other hand, witness poor Michele Armstrong. By now she's full of self-doubt, wondering whether she had made a mistake choosing to do what she does and be what she is. Ordinarily, I would move on someone like that quickly, Charon, and take advantage of the moment. Disappointment and disillusion, especially with yourself, opens windows and doors. I can slither in so much easier, but she is being buoyed up a bit by her clergyman policeman right now, the famous Saint Matthew, I'm sure.

"That's all right. We'll let that go forward because when she loses faith in him, sees how inconsequential he really is, impotent in fact, she'll be like a babe in my arms. She will suckle on my sympathy and curl up comfortably against my chest, welcoming my kisses and caresses and begging me to accept her into my fold. Don't you think?"

Silence thundered in his ears. He roared and pounded the seat so hard that the limousine lifted and fell the way it would if it had gone too quickly over a sleeping policeman, a rise in streets to keep traffic slower. Charon finally turned and glanced at him.

"Yes, yes, you can speak," John Milton told him.

"Your plan is wonderful," Charon said in a deep, mechanical voice. John Milton shook his head.

"I need to spend more time on you, Charon. I'm not saying I don't want to hear compliments. I just want them to sound . . . more authentic. I'll work on it. I know I have neglected you. I, too, get distracted sometimes. It's my passion for the things I do and enjoy. It overwhelms."

Charon looked forward, reassuming his cement posture.

"Okay. You don't have to drive so slowly anymore. Drive normally. We can get there now," he said.

Ten minutes later they pulled up in front of the East 80's upscale restaurant called The Garden of Earthly Delights, a restaurant so special there were no prices on the menus and tables were reserved months in advance unless you had some in with the manager, which meant forked over a considerable bribe. At the end of the meal, the one paying for everyone's dinner was given a bill, and if he or she didn't like it, they didn't have to come back. John Milton loved the arrogance of the place, the indifference to anyone's opinion about the cost of food and wine. You didn't come here if you worried about fifty, even a hundred dollars. You came here to impress your guests and feel like royalty, for the service was impeccable and the food, although at least two or three times costing what it should, was excellent. Two of the best chefs in New York, if not the country, prepared the meals.

When John Milton's limousine pulled to a stop, the rear left door of a black Town Car across the street opened and a dazzling, five feet ten inch New York escort with silky black hair floating over her shoulders stepped out and began to cross the street. Charon got out and opened the door for John. He sat there watching his woman walk as if she was parading down a designer's fashion show runaway. Drivers of passing cars nearly lost control. Horns sounded. John Milton laughed.

"I can see his bones turning gray and decomposing already," he muttered to himself. "All in due time. No mistakes. No rushing. Not this time," he told himself.

With a look of indifference, Charon, too, watched her approach the car. "John," she said. "I'm here."

"So you are, my dear, so you are."

He stepped out and held out his hand. She came to him obediently and took it.

"You feel . . . earthly," he said. She brightened.

"I hope that's a compliment."

"Oh, you know it is, Magdalena. I want you in every way to be human, to be secular."

"I know what you want, John."

"Yes, you do. You always do. Shall we?" he asked offering his arm. She took it, glanced at Charon and smiled, but he didn't smile back. "Don't ever give him a working prick. He'll drill for oil," she said and John Milton laughed all the way to the entrance where the doorman, a tall thin, light-skinned African American with a nearly luminous pair of ebony eyes, waited, those eyes so fixed on Magdalena, it was as though he was committing every cell in her body to his memory.

"Good evening, sir," he said. "Ma'am."

"Bon soir," John said. Magdalena left him with a caress on his hand and a movement in her lips that would take him to an orgasm in his fantasy this very evening. She looked back at him with that knowledge in her face. He tried to swallow and then just turned away quickly and began counting passing cars to get his mind off her. It was futile.

The cozy restaurant had subdued lighting, but reeked of elegance and savoir faire. The waiters and busboys looked like they were tiptoeing around tables. There were four special booths at the far right, reserved for those who demanded total privacy. Three were filled with movie and sports celebrities. Alexander James sat alone in the last one, nervously drinking his vodka and soda, his eyes fixed on the entrance and then brightening with his wide smile the moment John Milton and Magdalena entered.

He looks as anxious as a little boy on Christmas morning, John thought. *Let's bring him presents and promises.*

All eyes were on them, as a matter of fact. Even the celebrities sitting with beautiful women themselves couldn't keep from looking lustfully at Magdalena. The tight black dress she wore over her full round breasts, flat inviting stomach, perfectly proportioned hips and long legs that flashed up to the inside of her thighs through the slit in the dress had an even greater impact on the men than full nudity would have had. Every inch of her was full of promise. Unwrap her and discover the phantom woman every male chased since puberty. Lips moistened and dicks practically moaned in anticipation. Wives and girlfriends flung darts of envy. Some reflexively pulled their shoulders back and their breasts up. The ones caught in mid-sentences flashed crimson rage at their partners who tried desperately to look like nothing had happened to turn their libidos on full blast.

"Alex, please meet my friend Magdalena," John said.

Alexander James was afraid he might literally have a heart-attack when Magdalena extended her hand. It was thumping that hard under his breast bone. Although he felt like he was imitating some courtesan in a royal court and therefore looked silly, he didn't attempt to shake it. He brought his lips to her delicious fingers and held them there just a second too long. Magdalena smiled at John who raised his eyebrows and then moved to sit beside Alexander James.

"How do you know so many extraordinarily beautiful women, John?" Alexander James asked, not taking his eyes off Magdalena.

"I see no reason to really get to know any other," John said and Alexander James laughed. John sat across from him.

"I heard every detail of the trial, blow by blow, brilliant, John. You wiped them out so badly that they might just throw in the towel before the judge takes her seat tomorrow."

"One must not count his chickens before he hacks off their heads," John replied. It wouldn't have mattered what he had said. Alexander James could hear nothing but his bubbling testosterone. He realized, however, that John had said something.

"Bill sends his congratulations and his regrets. He had a pressing family matter to attend to," Alexander James said, again looking mostly at Magdalena. He couldn't take his eyes off her long. She was as enticing as John Milton's private secretary, if not more so.

"Families can be oppressive at times," John said. "Even a family of angels," he added and Magdalena laughed.

The waiter took their drink order.

"Yes, well Bill's also having a hard time with the O'Hara defense, speaking of families."

"Killing your adulterous wife should simply be a recognized blood sport, not a crime," John said. "Of course, there should be different rules for adulterous men. Men have always been more apt to wander from the loins of the ones they pledged to love and cherish until death do them part. Look world over and you'll find married men and mistresses taken for granted. Puritanical America is just uncivilized when it comes to all that."

"Here, here," Alexander said raising his glass. "So tell me about yourself, Magdalena."

"I'm here. What more is there to tell?" she replied in a voice so sultry it made Alexander James's head spin for a second. He actually put his hand on the table to steady himself. John Milton saw it and smiled.

"Easy, Alex. There's a whole night ahead."

"Well, I do have a trial tomorrow," Alexander said, unable to hide the disappointment in his voice. "And so do you, matter of fact."

"Oh, you will do fine no matter what and we already know I will. There are many ways to build your strength, you know, all sorts of nourishment men who are married a while too often forget."

"What? I've never heard it referred to as nourishment." Alexander looked from Magdalena to John Milton. "You're a rogue, John, an instigator of the first order."

"Oh, I've been called many things, haven't I, Magdalena."

"Yes, he has, but never call him late for dinner," she told Alexander, and John Milton laughed. He laughed so hard that Alexander James found he had to join in.

Moments later, the waiter approached looking apologetic for being there and having to interrupt them to take their dinner order. It almost seemed to him like these three people didn't care if they ate or not.

"Permit me to order for you. Is there anything you don't like?" Alexander James asked Magdalena.

"I was never happy about the taste of Communion wafers," she said, and again John Milton roared.

Alexander James leaned over to whisper.

"I haven't taken Communion since I was eleven."

"It's cannibalistic," John said. "Even thinking of it figuratively. You're eating the body of Christ. It's probably where Hannibal Lecter got the idea."

"Who?"

"One of my favorite fiction villains, Alex. You've got to read other things than legal briefs."

"Right, right. Back to the food. What about Lobster Fra Diablo?"

"I can't believe it," Magdalena said looking at John. "It's my favorite."

"Mine, too," John said.

"Done," Alexander James said and ordered two bottles of what he knew was the best and most expensive wine. He was sure he would drink practically all of one.

John Milton brought up only one serious issue during dinner.

"Have you spoken to Bill about my ideas for expanding the firm?"

"Oh, yes, yes. I liked your proposed candidates, too, and told him so."

"That's good, Alex. I'll follow through then. We will definitely justify the expansion."

"Sure, sure," Alexander James said.

John smiled. He could have suggested they repaint all the offices and fire every secretary but his own tomorrow and Alexander James would have nodded, not that he would need his support much longer anyway. It was all going to be easier than he imagined, he thought, and then sat back, enjoying the food and letting Magdalena run the show. She had done it many, many times and he was never disappointed.

After dinner, John insisted Alexander see Magdalena's penthouse apartment. It was really his, but there was nothing in it that would tip that off. Alexander James made a weak attempt to pass it up, referring to his early court date, but Magdalena was too persuasive. When they got into John Milton's limousine, she was all over the senior partner. Minutes after they drove off, Alexander realized they were in a limousine. He was that much under a cloud.

"Excuse me, John, but is this your car service?"

"Exclusively," John Milton said. "It's one of the perks I insist upon for myself, but no worries. I'm not billing the firm for it."

"Oh no, I wasn't worried about that," Alexander James said even though he would never extend such a personal service to himself or the firm. They called for cars when they needed to and had none exclusively. Both he and Bill Simon did very well, but it wasn't until Alexander James stepped into the penthouse apartment he had been told was Magdalena's that he realized he might be just a little too frugal in his life. He knew for sure that Bill was and that Bill's parsimony was always ripe fruit for an argument between himself, his wife and his two daughters attending college, one a sophomore and one a senior, both a Vassar.

The penthouse blew him away. He stood gaping at the large rooms and the flow of them moving from the wide entryway to the living room into the dining room and the open kitchen. It had rich marble floors, red velvet curtains, and upscale modern furniture to fit an otherwise minimalist décor. They continued into the apartment. There was a separate media room and then came what was oddly only one bedroom.

"No room for guests in this Citizen Kane apartment?" Alexander asked.

"My guests stay with me," Magdalena whispered. She was holding onto his arm. He wobbled a bit. Her lips were touching his earlobe. He could feel the delightful chill churning through his heart and quickly turning into delightful warmth.

"How about an after dinner drink?" John Milton suggested.

"I thought we had one," Alexander James said. He tried to look at his watch, but Magdalena put her hand over his wrist and turned him toward her.

"One can't be enough, Mr. James."

"Oh, you can call me Alex by now," he said.

"Alex," she whispered. Her face as so close, her lips lining up with his.

"I'll go make a drink," John Milton said and left them just as Magdalena kissed Alexander James and sealed him firmly in the promise of her body.

Nevertheless, John Milton poured himself a glass of Sambuca on the rocks and sat back on the rich leather sofa in the living room. He didn't have to be there to hear and see what was happening. He had only to close his eyes. The sound of the door buzzer interrupted the scene unfolding. Alexander James was undressed and in bed with Magdalena about to slide in beside him.

John rose and went to the door.

"I'm not late, am I?" Lilith asked.

"How could you be? I summoned you," John Milton said smiling. "You're a tease, you are," he said pinching her silky soft cheek.

"How do you like it?" she asked him and spun around to show him the sexy lace low V-neck tight-fitting hip evening dress. Her platinum hair flowed down to the wing bones. It emphasized her dark complexion and made her stunning blue eyes absolutely luminous and radiant.

"It's times like this when I really question who makes the more beautiful creatures, me or Him?"

Lilith giggled.

"Do I get to vote?"

"Hardly," he said. "Only He can stuff the ballot box. Okay. They're in the bedroom."

"Already? Without me?"

"Magdalena is more horny than usual, I fear. Be gentle at first, but drive him to the point of exhaustion. Pull back after that. I don't want him to die tonight in bed. I have other plans for that event tomorrow. Here," he added and gave her a packet of cocaine. "Use wisely later. It comes with instructions."

She laughed.

"You always save the best for last," she said and sauntered in and through the apartment. She paused before turning toward the bedroom, raising her arms and pretending she was about to dive into a pool.

"Go on. Stop showing off," he said smiling.

"Yes, Daddy," she replied and went into the bedroom. He looked at his watch.

It was so extraordinary, this thing called time, measuring it so precisely. He wondered if he would ever get used to it. How could anyone used to measuring centuries in seconds ever get used to the hands of a clock?

To him it looked like a frivolous waste of energy and attention.

Oh, the sacrifices and accommodations he made to carry out his eternal revenge.

He laughed.

He doesn't understand, he thought, *just how much I enjoy it.*

20.

"I can believe she has some spiritual powers," Michele said when she and Matthew Blake entered the loft apartment and saw the table had been set for three.

Blake looked at her askance.

"You texted her when I wasn't looking."

"You were always looking," she came back and he smiled.

"Yes, I was."

"My aunt doesn't have a smart phone. She gets her messages from another system operating in another world."

Blake laughed and Aunt Eve came out of the kitchen carrying a large casserole dish.

"I heard you come in," she said. "Perfect timing."

"Why doesn't that surprise me? This is Lieutenant Blake, Aunt Eve. Will you confirm that I did not call ahead of time to tell you we would be coming for something to eat," she said.

"She didn't call. She didn't have to call. There are things anyone who has patience and really pays attention to what and how people say things can tell. Please, have a seat."

She put the casserole on the table.

"Yes, but how about . . ." Michele nodded at Blake. Aunt Eve smiled.

"Now you don't want me to reveal, to describe the little hints and indications I read that told me you would be with the Lieutenant tonight, do you?" she teased. Matthew Blake laughed.

"I almost feel it's unnecessary to introduce you to him," Michele said.

"Hello, Lieutenant. Welcome," Aunt Eve said.

"What is in that casserole, Aunt Eve?" Michele asked.

"It's top secret. Please." She nodded at the chairs. "I have some wonderful white wine that was given to me recently by a man who owns and operates his own vineyard in Napa Valley, California. I helped his sister get over her fear of flying so she can visit him more often."

They sat and Aunt Eve began to serve what looked like a parmesan cheese crusted meatloaf, but Michele knew she was a vegetarian. Steam rose from the servings and the aroma was enticing. Aunt Eve gave herself some and sat across from them. She handed Matthew the bottle of wine and the wine screw.

"If you please, Lieutenant Blake. Do us the honors."

"Love to," he said and went about opening the bottle. Then he poured some in their glasses and his own. "May I offer a toast?"

"I expected no less," Aunt Eve said and winked at Michele.

Michele had sobered up during the trip home. She really didn't know what to make of Matthew Blake's suggestion that John Milton had followed them to the tavern. Why would he? How could it possibly matter or impinge on the trial to spy on her and Lieutenant Blake, unless he thought Lieutenant Blake was going to give her some new evidence. But how could he tell anything by sitting in a limousine and watching for them? It just didn't make any sense, but what made her concerned was how concerned Matthew Blake seemed to be.

"To better days to come for all of us," Blake said and they clunked their glasses. "Was that okay?" he asked Aunt Eve.

"Oh, perfect. It's important to wish for things, but when you do, try to envision them," she replied. "It puts us on a path we might otherwise not travel."

Blake nodded and looked at Michele, impressed.

"See? Your aunt and I speak the same language."

"That's what I'm afraid of," Michele said.

They started to eat, the two of them slowly and carefully at first and then, they looked at each other and smiled.

"It's delicious, whatever it is," Blake said.

"Yes, it is, Aunt Eve. You better give me this recipe one day."

"One day," she said. She looked at Matthew Blake for a long moment. "I heard what was said about you in court. You left the spiritual life?"

"Not spiritual life so much as a career in it," he replied.

"But you had doubts. You still have great doubts."

"Here we go," Michele said. "I warned you."

"That's all right. Yes, I do, Aunt Eve. I have doubts."

"Doubts are a burden, a burden sometimes too heavy to bear."

He ate some more and nodded.

"Yes, they can be heavy."

"You didn't just wake up one day with these doubts. You saw something that opened the door to them. Most who choose to be members of the clergy, regardless of the religion, build a fortress of faith that's practically impenetrable. Am I right?"

"Yes, you are."

Michele sipped her wine, looked at Aunt Eve and then at Blake. It was the first time since she had met him that he looked vulnerable. There were times when a man becomes something of a boy again, no matter how old he might be, and his face will reveal it. He could look frightened, helpless or suddenly terribly dependent. Any woman worth her femininity who cared for him reached out, tried to offer some motherly soothing touch or words.

She felt like reaching out to Blake, but hesitated. She didn't want to embarrass him.

"It's not important for you to reveal it now, Lieutenant, but someday, it might be important to reveal it to Michele," Aunt Eve added nodding at her.

"What the hell are you two talking about?" she finally asked. "You do speak another language."

It broke the heavy moment. Blake smiled and Aunt Eve shook her head, shrugged and ate some more of the casserole.

"Maybe neither of us really know," Blake offered. He continued to eat as well. They drank more wine. Then he paused and obviously thinking about something carefully, looked at Aunt Eve.

She smiled.

"Go on, Lieutenant. Ask me what's on your mind to ask," she said.

"You told Michele that you saw John Milton metamorphose into a big, dark shadow?"

"I did. It was not an unfamiliar shadow, as I said. Be wary of him," she warned.

"As I am of all high-priced, media centered defense attorneys," Michele said.

"Don't become bitter about your work, Michele," her aunt advised. "It will spread like a plague into every aspect of your life. At the moment, I don't see that happening to you," she added smiling.

"How did this come about, this visionary power you possess?" Blake asked.

Aunt Eve talked about the traffic accident, the loss of her husband and the subsequent coma she had been in.

"I believe I crossed over and back," she told him. "And when I returned, I brought the power of the vision with me."

"Makes sense to me," he told Michele. He didn't look like he was humoring anyone either.

"I guess I'm the only one who isn't a little nuts here," Michele said.

"How lonely that must make you," Blake said and they both laughed.

"I have some illegal brownies to serve with my herbal tea," Aunt Eve told them after they finished the casserole. "One of my clients brought it to me as part of her payment. Can I risk it?" she asked Blake.

"I'm not on the narcotics squad. I specialize only in murders, rapes, armed robberies, the easy stuff," he replied. Aunt Eve laughed.

"I like a man with a sense of humor."

"I like a man with any sense," Michele countered.

Under the table, she felt the urge strongly now to reach for Matthew's hand. He took it and smiled at her. When Aunt Eve went into the kitchen, he leaned over and kissed her.

"Maybe we don't need the brownies," he whispered.

"Power of suggestion, but I feel like there was something soothing in that casserole."

"A little more than soothing. I'm floating."

"Aunt Eve," she called. "We don't need anything more. Thank you."

"I really didn't think you would," she called back. "Maybe it would be overkill."

They laughed, giggled like children, and stood up. She was still holding his hand. Neither spoke. She turned and led him through the loft to her bedroom. As soon as they entered, she stopped.

"This is insane," she said. "I should be crying in my beer, not acting like I'm celebrating."

"Maybe you can cry in your beer later," he told her and turned her to him. "Right now, I can think only of champagne."

She smiled and they kissed, slowly, gently at first, but quickly turning it into a more demanding kiss, their hands moving like four small animals that had been unchained, pressing, exploring, pulling and stroking in a delicious frenzy.

On her bed their clothing became intolerable. Anything that lay between their naked bodies was quickly discarded. The rush of desire that consumed them wouldn't even let them speak. There was no time for words, for promises, or for pledges. Nothing was needed to convince either of them that they should search and discover the wonder of each other's bodies. Her breasts craved his lips as much as his lips craved them, her nipples, her neck, the small of her stomach, the warmth between her thighs. Her moans were demanding, her legs locking around his hips. He pressed his mouth to hers and entered her, first seeming amazed at himself and then finally unable not to speak, whispered, "You're wonderful, beautiful, everything."

She didn't want to speak yet. She didn't want to do anything that might interfere with the lift he was giving to her spirit, her ego, her desperate need to feel pleasure in the midst of her depressions and fears. He was taking her away with every stroke. She could feel herself climbing, coming, building toward more and more. It was different. It was better than any other time with any other man. Something magical was happening. Just before she finally cried out her exquisite pleasure, she laughed to herself thinking, maybe it was Aunt Eve's casserole after all.

Afterward, they lay beside each other silently. He held her hand and they stared up at the ceiling like two teenagers overwhelmed with what they had just discovered about themselves as well as each other. The only sound was the ticking of a miniature grandfather's clock Aunt Eve had brought into her room recently.

"So, when do you tell me?" Michele finally asked.

"Tell you what?"

"What you saw that opened you up to doubts and drove you to leave the seminary school and pursue a career as a detective."

"Your aunt was right. I believed that those who were devoted to their faith and wanted to pursue a role in it were so fortified by their beliefs that they formed an impenetrable wall around them, a wall that the devil could not breach."

"Not everyone can be a saint, Matthew. Saint Matthew," she added smiling and turning to him.

"I know that. I expect we all have some weaknesses and commit some minor sins in our lives, but not mortal sins, and even if someone commits a mortal sin, there is supposed to be room for redemption if there is repentance, confession, a firm resolution to sin no more. What I saw was a prince of the faith commit a mortal sin, and instead of repenting, cover it up and blame it on someone lesser who suffered severe punishment."

"Someone was framed by a priest?"

"A bishop actually, yes. I suppose I always had a talent or predilection for solving problems, crimes. I put together the proof and presented it."

"And you were ignored?"

"What I had accomplished was shelved for a supposed higher good."

"So the doubts began?"

"In spades," he said. "I found myself thinking more like a deist."

"Refresh my memory."

"Deism is basically the belief that God does not involve Himself with what happens in the natural world. He allows it to run according to the laws of nature. Such a belief denies the existence of miracles. I tossed this around in my mind for a long time, even after I left the religious world. And then . . ."

"Then?"

"I began to wonder if leaving it all to the laws of nature didn't essentially turn it over to evil. I started to think that there are supernatural forces at work, but not the forces they preach in church."

"And so you see conspiracies, evil conspiracies?"

"And so I don't reject any possibilities, no matter how farfetched they might seem. That willingness to consider what most would call supernatural events is disturbing to others. Although I didn't die and come back like she claims, I think, however, I have a third eye, just like your aunt might."

Michele began to hum the theme from Jaws again.

"What I sense from that is your frightened," he said. She stopped humming.

He sat up quickly as if he had heard something only he could hear.

"I have to get going," he said.

"Why? You could stay over."

"Perhaps another time."

"I don't like the sound of a promise, never have. It's usually a way to avoid something unpleasant, something better ignored."

"It's not a promise. It's a fact. I want to know you more, laugh with you, share regrets, hopes, explore every sound and every sight we can together."

"Be careful. Any other woman would consider that a commitment."

"You don't scare me," he said and she smiled, reached up to touch him almost as if she thought he was unreal for a moment. He took her hand and kissed it. For a moment neither of them said anything. He glanced at the clock and let go of her hand.

"Are you coming to the trial tomorrow?"

"Now I am," he said reaching for his clothes. She pulled the thin blanket over herself and watched him dress. He smiled at her when he was finished.

"Don't look so damn pleased with yourself. I had something to do with this, too," she said.

He laughed and leaned over to kiss her.

"Your aunt going to be waiting for me out there?" he asked in a whisper.

"You're the one with the third eye. You tell me."

He smiled, messed her hair and walked out. She listened, but didn't hear him say anything to Aunt Eve. She rose and reached for her silky robe. After putting it on, she went to the window to watch him get into his car. Maybe he did have a third eye, she thought, he looked up just as she peered through the curtains and waved.

Moments later, he drove away. She stood there and gazed down at the street. A sudden chill came up her legs and embraced her around her waist.

Just beyond the corner, its front peering around like a cat was a black limousine.

21.

Dave Duggan was right on target with his prediction.

John Milton offered no real challenge to the prosecution's case. In an almost paint by numbers strategy, he paraded three character witnesses for Heckett, none of whom offered her the slightest reason to cross-examine. He didn't bring up any witnesses to counter the evidence she had presented, not even to confirm that Lester Heckett had no experience or even knowledge of guns. The character witnesses were sickly-sweet with their testimony. Two of them were secretaries at the company and another was a broker, who looked like he thought he was testifying in the O.J. Simpson case or something. He never stopped smiling for the artist drawing pictures of witnesses. In the end it was almost as if Milton was presenting Heckett for a job and had brought along substantial references. Of course, she hoped beyond hope that the jury would see that as either arrogant or his belief it was futile to put up a real defense, but deep inside she knew that it was too much wishful thinking.

She made what she could of her trial summary, hanging hard on motive and the possession of the murder weapon. She was careful about Cisley Strumfield's testimony, implying that the entire gruesome event was mentally disturbing and her behavior on the stand was understandable. But she stressed that what she had witnessed outside her apartment house on the day her husband was murdered was irrefutable. Cisley was too familiar with Lester Heckett to mistake someone else for him and any implication to suggest she was responsible for her husband's death bordered on the ridiculous.

"It's reaching for straws," she declared. "Mrs. Strumfeld had a comfortable relationship with her husband and had no financial reason to see him harmed. What she has now, she had before."

Michele hammered on Heckett's lack of any alibi and lack of remorse, but toward the end, she felt like she was stopping in mid-sentence, her words hanging in the air for a few moments and then dropping and smashing at her feet.

Milton, she had to admit, was brilliant. He took the perfect tone with his summary, no longer behaving impish or satirical, but instead implying that the prosecution had no choice but to follow through on a very weak case. He practically had the jury feeling sorry for Michele and almost as a side issue, urged them to consider Lester Heckett's guilt or innocence and find him innocent. In fact, Michele actually believed in the end that the jury took a day and a half simply out of respect for her. All of them had left the courtroom to deliberate with reasonable doubt tied in a bow around their necks.

Nevertheless, when it came, the not-guilty verdict felt like a punch in her stomach. Aunt Eve didn't attend the final days. Each morning she wore the look of sympathy a parent might give her child when she had lost a contest or didn't get the choice part she wanted in the school play. "There's always next time," although unspoken, still rang through the loft.

Matthew Blake, on the other hand, was more angry than sympathetic. She knew the anger was aimed at himself and was so sharp that she almost felt sorrier for him than she did for herself. He looked like a little boy sulking and threatening to do himself harm.

"I let you down," he told her after the jury's verdict was announced and the judge had gaveled the case closed. "I know I keep saying it, but it's true. I should have moved faster. All I had to do was connect the dots and bring it in, but I got distracted. I'm taking on too much."

"Let's not start assigning blame," she said, probably more sharply than she had wished. She didn't have a chance to soften it because she was immediately inundated with media and began working with Dave Duggan to put the best face they could on a dramatic defeat. More than one reporter was suggesting she might not be ready for the big time. Matthew Blake stood by wincing at the innuendos and questions. Finally, he mouthed, "I'll see you later," and left the courtroom quickly, his head down.

Michele observed that John Milton did not spend much time with his client. Of course, Heckett was bursting with glee and gratitude, but she saw that Milton was dismissive. It was almost as if he was eager not to have anything more to do with his client. At one point it looked like he literally turned his back on him while Heckett was in mid-sentence, laying oodles of thank you's on his attorney. She could see that John Milton was more interested in her and suddenly headed directly for her. The reporters stepped back like the waters of the Red Sea for Moses and grew still for a moment so they could hear and witness his comments to her.

"You have nothing to be ashamed of, Ms Armstrong," he began. He raised his voice an octave or two when he added, "You kept me on my toes. I couldn't relax a moment. If you had been handed better evidence to work with, you would have steam rolled over me."

Now that it was over and she was face to face with him again, she realized how handsome he was and felt the light of his eyes like dazzling reflectors on her. His impish little grin was suddenly darker, sexier, more mature. She became conscious of how foolish she looked admiring him, her face softening into an appreciative smile. Instantly, she stiffened her posture and changed expression.

"Are you telling us that your client was guilty then and got away with it, Mr. Milton?"

He laughed, nodding at the reporters.

"See? Don't underestimate this one, ladies and gentlemen. She has taken a place on the New York legal stage and she will make headlines soon, I'm sure."

Cameras clicked.

He leaned toward her.

"May I take you to dinner tonight?" he asked. "We don't have to discuss the case, I promise. I think we can share many common experiences. We both deserve a relaxing evening."

The question was so out of her realm of expectation that she found herself tongue-tied for a moment.

"I don't think so," she finally said. "It might take me a little while to regain my appetite."

"Oh, don't be so hard on yourself, Michele. You're stunning. Please. I would be so grateful. After all, there was nothing personal here. We were both performing the parts we were cast to perform. It might very well turn out differently the next time."

Dave Duggan heard some of it and stood back in awe. She looked at the stupid expression on his face, at the reporters still impressed with Milton, and then at him again. Oddly, he looked vulnerable all of a sudden, even desperate for approval, like some errant young boy who wanted to be forgiven, in this case for winning. His eyes were full of pleading. She felt herself weaken.

"I'm returning to my office," she replied instead of a definitive yes or no. "Call me in an hour."

"Absolutely," he said and stepped away.

"You'd go to dinner with him?" Dave asked instantly.

"Don't you remember the Godfather's advice?" she asked, gathering her materials and turning toward the doorway.

"Huh? No. What?"

"Keep your friends close and your enemies closer," she said and started out, the reporters still trailing behind her like determined car exhaust.

She was nearly out of the building when Duggan caught up with her again.

"Well at least we got some good news today," he said. "I was just told."

"What?"

"Alexander James, one of the senior partners in the firm Milton has joined fell flat on his face today in court."

"What's that mean?"

"Just what I said. He collapsed in court just before beginning his cross-examination of one of our witnesses. They took him away in an ambulance. One for the good guys," he added.

Michele watched John Milton getting into his limousine and shook her head.

"Don't be so quick to count a new victory," she said. "You don't know who will replace him," she added and continued to her waiting vehicle.

Inside her car, she watched Milton's limousine disappear around the corner. Aunt Eve thought there was something dark and foreboding about him. Matthew suspected him of being underhanded. Both thought there was more at stake than the murder trial suggested.

Maybe I'm the only one who can discover what that is, if it is anything at all, she thought. Was she attracted by the challenge or by Milton's extraordinary good looks? Was it the woman in her thinking or the defender of the public good? More important perhaps, was she arrogant or just plain stupid after all?

There really was only one way to find out.

She was happy not to find an atmosphere of doom and gloom at the district attorney's offices. Sophia Walters did her best to hide her disappointment for her. "I'm sure you'll do better next time," she told her, her smile as buoyant as ever. Michele collapsed in her desk chair and paused to catch her breath. Despite her effort to remain positive, the ride over did feel like the ride to a cemetery. She sucked in her breath, closed her eyes and clenched her fists. It had seemed so easy at first. She would gracefully slip into success. She felt like a homerun hitter whose big hit was stolen at the last moment by a dynamic outfielder.

Oddly, what she wanted to avoid the most was not professional criticism, but the phone call she anticipated from her mother as soon as the news reached into her protected little world outside of the city. Maybe her father would hear about it first. She knew he was trying to keep up with the day to day reports on the trial. She could just hear him telling her mother, "Don't make her feel bad." Her brother was sure to call, but at their father's request with the words dictated to make her feel better. No matter what they said, she knew they all would now have doubts that she could compete in the big show, which was how her father had put it. "You're going to the big show."

Michael Barrett stepped into the office so quietly that she didn't realize he had entered until he stood before her. She blinked and then sat up.

"Oh. I didn't hear you enter, Mr. Barrett."

"By now you think you'd be calling me Michael, Michele." He took the seat in front of her desk. "This is my fault more than yours. I should have gone along with the plea deal Warner Murphy was suggesting. I should also have known we'd be in trouble once we knew there was a professional killer involved and we didn't tie it up neatly. This Lieutenant Blake had brought us three solid prosecutions before you arrived. Every case was so well put-together, I assumed this one would be similar. Everyone was a little too overconfident."

"Except John Milton," Michele said.

"Yes. Interesting man. There's just enough of his past vague enough to make him a mystery. I don't want you feeling sorry for yourself. I brought you on because I saw something exceptional in you and I still believe it's there. I like the way you handled a difficult situation. You'll fare far better next time. Eleanor and I are looking over the assignments. I want you busy right away. It's better not to have too much time for regrets. My brother's a screen writer in Hollywood. Did you know that?"

"Yes. Garden of the Dead, Life Sentence, The Dark . . ."

"You do your homework. Those are his last three, but he's had plenty of disappointments along the way and I always remember what his agent told him when they had a disappointment."

"Which was?"

"One word. Next. That was it," he said standing. "We'll have next on your desk by tomorrow morning. Whatever you do, don't spend the night alone, Michele. Do something interesting," he advised, smiled and left her.

Right on cue, Sophia buzzed her.

"I have a Mr. Milton on the line," she said, obviously trying to contain her own surprise.

Michele hesitated. Then she thought about Michael Barrett's advice and picked up the receiver.

"Michele Armstrong," she said. "Aren't you the prompt one?"

"I was a teacher for a while and I found that if I wasn't on time, my students wouldn't be so concerned about lateness. Forget about that do as I say not as I do stuff. They do what you do. Always," he said.

"You were a teacher? I didn't see that in your resume."

"I've been many things that I haven't bothered to acknowledge. I hope to dazzle you with my biography," he said. "I have reservations for us at a very special restaurant, one you might not have heard of yet, but will, Angel's Lair."

"No, I haven't heard of it."

"It's a little bit of gourmet heaven."

"How is your senior partner?"

"A victim of over-indulgences, I'm afraid."

"Shouldn't you be more concerned?"

"Oh, I'm concerned, but a long time ago, I learned how to walk and whistle," he added.

She nearly laughed. She looked at her watch.

"I'll need about two hours to clean up my wounds."

He laughed.

"Wounds? You take everything too personal, but in my book, you are a winner, Michele. Pick you up at seven-thirty then?"

She thought a moment.

"Yes," she said.

"Great. See you then."

"Wait. You know where I live?"

He laughed again.

"I guess I walked into that one. You are a good trial attorney. Yes, I know. I make it my business to know as much as I can about my opponent. I hope you're not offended."

"No, but I want to see a lot of quid pro quo at this Angel's Lair," she said.

"You will. Promise," he said. "I'll be an open book."

After she hung up, she sat there amazed at herself and how fast it was all moving. Why was she doing this? It was as if she had lost control of herself. Was she on a mission? Was that how she would or could explain it to both Aunt Eve and Matthew? She didn't want either to be offended. Perhaps for now it would be better not to reveal her intentions.

Her mother called less than fifteen minutes later. Despite the warnings she was sure her father had given her mother, her mother's voice was full of pity. She just had to add, "You could always come home, dear. Never forget that."

"You should have read more Thomas Wolfe, Mom," she told her.

"Thomas Wolfe? Why?"

"He wrote You Can't Go Home Again."

"That's ridiculous. I came home, didn't I?"

"Yes, yes you did, Mom. Exactly. Thanks. I'll call you later in the week. I'm getting another case tomorrow. We win, we lose. It's the nature of the American legal system. If it was always a sure thing, there would be no need for trials."

"It's all too complicated for me. My sister must be driving you nuts about this."

"She's fine," Michele said. In no way would she ever complain about Aunt Eve, and especially wouldn't mention her fixation on the spiritual world. "I'll see you soon," she added even though she had no intention to do so. "Love to Dad and Bailey," she said. "Bye. I love you," she added with the usual nonchalance she knew irked her mother.

They had once had an argument about it. "Love," Michele insisted, "was a diamond word. You banter it about too easily and like an overabundance of diamonds, it loses its value."

"Nonsense," her mother insisted. "Love can never lose its value if it's sincere. You're too pedantic, Michele. Like a lawyer you parse every word to death. You were always like that, Michele, even when you were only four."

Actually, her mother made her think about herself. Her comment was surprisingly accurate. She wondered if she wasn't taking her too much for granted and not giving her more credit for some wisdom.

So many exchanges between us and the ones we love are regrettable, she thought. The more we love someone, the more apt we are to wound them in little painful ways. Love really means the power to forgive. That's what we spend most of our time doing, forgiving each other and mostly, ourselves.

She rose and quickly bounced out of the maudlin mood. This spurt of energy was definitely unexpected, but instead of leaving the courtroom despising her opponent, she had left fascinated with him. Who was he really? Like her he had come out of the hinterlands to take a place on the Great White Way of the American criminal justice system. The tide of time had washed them both ashore almost simultaneously. He was on the more lucrative side of things so he came better equipped perhaps.

After she left the office, she hailed a taxi but kept thinking about John Milton. And Matthew Blake, who was in so many ways almost as much a mystery. They had similar early lives. It was understandable for Matthew to distrust and even dislike John Milton. A police investigator builds a case for the prosecution to carry forth in a courtroom and the defense attorney sole reason for existence there is to destroy that case, even destroy the credibility of the investigation and investigator.

Of course, Matthew would warn her about him, but he seemed more intense than he possibly should be, suggesting John Milton did underhanded things to win his case and make him seem especially malevolent, following them, spying on them. How could that possibly matter for the trial? So the assistant district attorney spent more than usual time with a police investigator on the case . . . how does that help the defense? Why would John Milton even care?

Aunt Eve's reactions to him were understandable. She saw evil loitering about as it was; she would surely see evil in the man who would or could damage her niece's career opportunities. And of course, she would like Matthew Blake. He was helping her niece to succeed and he was apparently into similar things and beliefs.

It's time to make conclusions for herself, she thought. She wanted her independence; she wanted her opportunity, didn't she? Well then she had to strengthen herself and not be dependent on anyone else entirely. If that be hubris, so be it. In the end I will either congratulate myself or blame myself.

Actually, she was feeling way better than she had anticipated she would when she entered the loft.

But her aunt put that to rest quickly.

"You're making a mistake," she said the moment she set eyes on her.

22.

John Milton stopped at New York Presbyterian Hospital on his way to pick up Michele Armstrong. He had called her from the limousine when that hour she wanted was up. Nora had informed him of Alexander James' collapse in court moments after he had left the Heckett trial.

"I'm surprised he lasted that long in court," John quipped. "I always underestimate the staying power of my sinners. What's that wonderful saying, 'Only the good die young.'" That's as it should be."

He laughed with such glee that Charon turned to look at him.

"Showing surprise? You're starting to come to life, Charon. Considering it's been only a thousand or so years, that's good."

Charon turned back to the street and pulled up to the entrance to the hospital.

"I won't be too long," John Milton told him when he stepped out. "Just long enough to plant the seeds for our new Garden of Eden."

Walking briskly, he entered the hospital and joined Bill Simon and Alexander James' wife and children in the waiting room. It was crowded and noisy, the hum of sorrow and tragedy circling like angry bees, but the James family looked up with surprise and interest as he drew closer. The children hovered around their mother who, John thought, looked more frightened and concerned than he would have anticipated. Everything he had learned about Alexander James led him to believe he had one of those marriages held together like spider webs. A brisk wind could blow them apart. They shared the lives of their children but more like two business partners than husband and wife. He found that so common with married couples today. How easy it was to make a joke of their oaths and the priests and rabbis who extracted them from their wells of fantasy at the ceremonies.

Perhaps Alexander James' wife thought she would be punished for not being sad enough. Women endure so much more abuse than men, especially from their own men, and carry on like good soldiers. Women can be so much stronger when it came to pain, but not when it came to vanity. Just ask Eve, he mused and laughed.

"I came as soon as I heard and was able to," John told Bill Simon. He nodded and turned to Alexander James' wife and children.

"This is John Milton, our new associate, who had a very successful day for the firm today," he said.

James' wife forced a smile. His children just stared, the boy looking annoyed by the intrusion of a man with such an aura of power and success draped over him. This was a time only for depression and sadness, no accolades and certainly no smiles. They would tolerate no smiles. They glared back at him like imps chained to dungeon walls. They were obviously caught between hating their father for bringing them to this and concern for his survival.

"I'm sorry to have this occasion as our first time to meet," John said.

"Thank you," James' wife said. The kids said nothing.

He and Bill Simon stepped away.

"She doesn't know it all yet," Bill Simon said. "There were significant traces of cocaine which definitely contributed to his heart attack."

"Cocaine? I suspected a little too much alcohol, perhaps, but cocaine? He doesn't strike me as the type."

He shook his head and captured a look of disbelief as if he could pluck it as it passed by on the face of someone else. He caught his reflection in the glass of a nondescript landscape print. He could take on any emotion and convince even one of His angels that he was sincere.

"I didn't think so either, but you never really get to know anyone, do you, no matter how many years you've been together and what you've gone through together," Bill Simon said, now unable to hide his bitterness. John could see he was sinking into a deep depression. Soon, he'd be beside himself and talking to him would be a waste of time.

"No, you never do. The best you can hope for is fifty percent. What's his condition now?"

"He's fallen into a coma." Simon looked back at Alexander James' family. "The prognosis is not good." He kept his eyes on James' wife. "I knew they were having their troubles, just like any married couple, but I just learned that they slept in separate bedrooms for some time now. That's why she didn't know what time he came home the night before."

John Milton nodded. He ratcheted up his concern.

"I wonder why people don't realize that their personal lives will affect their public and professional lives. If you're miserable at home, you'll bring that with you and infect others who depend on you."

"Very true," Bill said. "All these other people will have tough days tomorrow.

John nodded. Looking around at all the obvious misery, he concluded that there were no angels here. None but one rebellious bastard, himself. He pulled himself up into the posture of an obedient soldier.

"I assume you want me to step into James' current case."

"We have a postponement, of course."

"Bad timing for all this. I was about to inform you of three other cases crossing my desk today when I was told about Alexander. My secretary handled it all well."

"Three?"

"All highly lucrative, clients that can easily afford us, I might add. Alexander's condition is bound to get out, Bill. I think it's time we talked about taking on some more associates and in particular, I'd like to see the firm have its own public relations officer. We're going to need him, not only for the negative news, but for the upcoming jolt to our business."

Bill Simon nodded, not failing to hear the "we" and "our" clearly stated. He sighed.

"We've done well with our boutique firm up to now."

"Absolutely, but well enough now to gracefully and naturally expand. You have room for more offices and there will be no question about earning the finances to do it all. I hate to talk about the future when we're sitting in this tragedy, but sometimes events dictate themselves, don't you think?"

Bill Simon nodded.

"Sometimes, I think I'm too old to have any more ambition."

"Age is a funny thing. People tend to think it can be measured only by time, but events crowd days into weeks, weeks into months and months into new years."

"Yes," Bill said, a little taken by John Milton's observation. "Lately, I've been thinking just that. Many of my professional friends look older than they are."

"Well, I don't think you're ready to be led out to pasture, but you might think about slowing down. That's why taking on more professional help is a good idea, too, don't you think?"

Bill Simon looked at him with a little suspicion.

"You're a fast mover, John."

"It's all a matter of prospective, Bill. To me, it's taking me far too long to get where I am, and I've set some high goals for myself. I have a ways to go. It's only natural to be a little impatient."

"Probably. Okay, let's talk about it all in the morning."

"Of course. I have some excellent young and talented attorneys to suggest and some very good secretarial help." He leaned into him. "I'd like to bring in one young attorney for an interview this week. I've worked with him. He's with a small firm in the city and we can easily steal him away. His name is Paul Scholefield. I'm eager to see your impression of him."

"If you're recommending him, he must be good."

"Thank you. You won't be disappointed. We should also discuss redoing the offices. Unfortunately, most do judge a book by its cover."

"Whatever," Bill Simon said. Out of the corner of his eye, he caught the doctor moving toward Alexander's wife and children. "This doesn't look good," he muttered and started for them.

John Milton hung back.

"On the contrary," he muttered. "It looks absolutely perfect."

He waited to hear the definitive news. The James's family was quickly escorted to a private room. Bill Simon started out with them and then turned and hurried over to him.

"I'm calling my wife to help out here. Take charge at the office tomorrow. This coming so soon after Walter Murphy . . . they'll all be devastated.

"I understand. Don't worry about anything. Nora and I will handle it all. Take all the time you need."

Bill Simon nodded, pressed his hand appreciatively and started away.

John Milton looked at the faces of the family and friends concerned for one of their own. How vulnerable He has made them, he thought. Was it a mistake or did He do it so I'd have more ambition? You'd think He'd be bored with all this testing of faith. He smiled and glanced at the ceiling.

"Hello? Did You ever think it's a symptom of low self-esteem to continually insist on total devotion?"

He hid his smile under a feigned look of sadness as he walked out and to his waiting limousine.

"You know, Charon," he said after he got in and they started away, "if it continues to be this easy, I might just lose interest."

His laughter seemed to accelerate the vehicle. Less than twenty minutes later, they pulled up to the curb in front of Michele's aunt's loft apartment. He started to get out and stopped. He could sense it, a very thin-veiled veil of antagonistic energy. He felt like Superman about to enter a garden peppered with Kyptonite. Why suffer even the smallest pain? He sat back and closed the door. Then he took out his mobile phone and called her.

Michele heard her phone vibrate in her purse on the vanity mirror table. It wasn't hot, but it felt warmer than usual when she plucked it out and answered. She had decided to wear a strapless beaded bodice tulle gown she had bought herself for her last birthday. It was fitted with wrapped tulle from the waist to the knee and then had a trumpet skirt. She wore the thin diamond choker her father and mother had bought her for that same birthday. She thought the black silk shawl would be enough.

"Armstrong," she said.

"Oh, I'm so sorry. I think I'm running a little late. There's not much time for the small talk. Will your aunt be upset?"

"I doubt it," Michele said.

"Would you, could you . . ."

"Come out?"

"Yes. I'm ashamed of my bad manners."

"I'll be out in a minute," she said. "I'll let you know what I think of your manners at the end of the evening."

John Milton laughed.

"See you soon then," he said.

He started to smile and then stopped. Of course he was aware of his powers of persuasion, but he had anticipated a little more resistance or at least some anxiety on her part. It wouldn't surprise him to learn that she had told Lieutenant Blake about her date and that he had her wired or something. He hadn't walked into traps often, but he had done so. This battle was all still quite ongoing. The biggest irony of all was that he enjoyed all the sins that characterized the souls he won. Normally, he could control them all when it came to himself. The hardest to control wasn't sloth or lust or greed, however, it was vanity. The defeats he had suffered through the ages were usually in some way or another a result of that because it blinded him to warnings he would otherwise easily realize.

He had intended to reveal something of his super abilities to Michele Armstrong tonight. He wanted to sweep her off her feet and win her over so completely that she would become his Fifth Column, his spy, his eyes and ears in the district attorney's office. He would have to do it more slowly now, he thought, more carefully.

She appeared and Charon instantly stepped out and opened the limousine door for her. She paused when she set eyes on him.

"It's all right. He's asexual," John Milton said leaning out and smiling.

"What?" She still hesitated, obviously not sure whether or not he was joking.

"Charon, will you smile, please and kindly take the lady's hand properly."

He did so and John pulled back to make room for her.

"I'm afraid he makes Boris Karloff look like George Clooney," she said and John Milton laughed.

"You're absolutely brilliant," he said. "You don't know how refreshing your self-confidence is."

"Over-compensation perhaps, especially tonight."

"Hardly," he said. They were off. "May I say you look as beautiful as I envisioned you could be."

"You mean I wasn't beautiful in court?"

"No, no. I meant . . . look, at this. You have me on the defensive so quickly."

"You are a defense attorney."

He laughed.

"Okay. So tell me, what convinced you to accept my invitation?"

"The quid pro quo. I want to know how you learned all those things about my witness so quickly, know more about your techniques in court. What are your secrets?"

"All that in one dinner date?"

"Journey of five thousand miles begins with first step," she said imitating a Chinese prophet."

"Well, as long as you realize it's a journey of 5000 miles," he replied.

She laughed and glanced behind them. She had noticed a car start up and start after them when they had pulled away from the curb, and wondered if it could be Matthew Blake. She had been anticipating his call after things had settled down, and when he didn't call, she was tempted to call him to explain why she had decided to accept John Milton's dinner invitation. At minimum she intended to tell him about it when she saw him again, but right now she was afraid he would convince her not to do it, or even be angry and hurt that she was even considering doing it. However, he kept so much from her that she didn't see why she couldn't keep something from him for a while. Maybe it was a delayed reaction emerging because of the trial outcome, but she was annoyed at all the mystery boiling around her. It was time to make some discoveries for herself.

"You seem suddenly in very deep thought," John Milton said.

"Maybe that's the effect you have on people."

"Oh, no question," he replied.

Michele was surprised at some of the turns they made to weave uptown to this restaurant. She had tried to find it on the Internet, but to no avail.

"How long has this restaurant been around?" she asked.

"Angel's Lair? Oh years. It's very low key by design, however. That's what makes it special and enables it to hold onto its cache. It's one of those places that doesn't have to advertise. The manager, Gabriel David, takes pride in the clientele."

"Who owns it?"

"Some corporate entity. I think it was created more to have something extraordinary for their clients and the like than to make money, although with the prices they charge, it looks like they can't help but make money."

She glanced back again.

"I think someone's following you," she said.

"Maybe he's following you," he replied and smiled.

"Doesn't bother you?"

"Someone's always following me, Michele," he said.

The restaurant truly seemed to appear out of nowhere. They turned down a dark street and stopped in front of a door with subtle if not indistinct lighting. There was no sign, nothing that indicated it was Angel's Lair.

"This is it? They really do want to keep under the radar," she said.

"Yes. Gives it that mysterious, private speak-easy feel, doesn't it?"

Charon opened the door for them.

"Thank you," she said and turned to John Milton who stepped out after her. "Doesn't he talk?"

"Say something she'll never forget, Charon, please."

"I'm pleased to meet you," he said.

John Milton shrugged.

"He's an excellent driver and loyal employee so I forgive him his social failings."

He took her arm and they headed to the restaurant's front entrance.

"Does he live on this planet?" she whispered. John Milton laughed.

"If I can, he can," he said and pressed the button.

The door opened automatically and they entered a ruby entrance way with a thick black and gold Persian rug, a large oval mirror in a mahogany frame on the left and a coat-check desk on the right. The walls were a woven silk fabric. Above them, a tear-eye chandelier rained down most of the light. Ahead of them was the oval-shaped entrance to the dining room. She recognized Mozart's Requiem in D-Minor playing as light background.

The woman behind the coat-check counter seemed to rise up rather than step out of a corner. She was older than most coat-check personnel Michele had seen, and she was dressed in what was more like a business suit. Maybe she was covering for someone, Michele thought.

"Want to surrender your shawl?" John Milton asked her.

"Not particularly. It's my security blanket right now."

He smiled and nodded.

"Thank you, Rosemary. We're fine," he told the woman behind the counter. She nodded and stepped back into the shadows.

When they turned, a tall, thin man with dark-brown curly hair appeared instantly in the dining entrance. He was dressed in a tuxedo, and when he smiled, revealed two prominent gold molars. Everything about him was long, from his narrow face and neck to his arms and hands. In fact, she thought he was spidery, but he had warm light-blue eyes.

"Mr. Milton, what a delight to see you again," he said, "and with so beautiful a woman."

"Michele, this is Gabriel David. He means whatever he says. He hasn't been as kind to other women I've escorted here for business reasons."

Gabriel shrugged, but reached for Michele's hand and brought to his thin, somewhat pale lips.

"Welcome to Angel's Lair," he said.

"It looks very special," she said.

"Now that you're here, it will be," he replied.

"Oh boy. This is the place to cheer up a loser," she told John Milton. His smile widened.

They entered the dining room.

The vibrant ruby shades in the entryway were carried through the swirls of it in the milky white floor tiles and into the otherwise coffee white panel walls dressed with sconcesthat were classical Greek and Roman. Many of the paintings on the walls looked like originals or at least copies because she recognized Giorgione's *Sleeping Venus,* Tintoretto's *Adam and Eve,* and Salvidor Dali's *Christ of Saint John of the Cross.* The other paintings were obvious Medieval works of art depicting plagues and fires.

"Not the most cheery art for a restaurant," she quipped.

"But great art nevertheless and great art will please you in one way or another," John Milton said as they followed Gabriel David to their table in the far right corner.

Michele realized all eyes were on them in the nearly full restaurant. The clientele looked like people whose pictures were always in those magazines featuring participants in the high social life in any city, photographs of the super wealthy enjoying what looked like perennial spring, decked out at galas ostensibly for charity but really organized for the well-to-do to exhibit their new designer clothes, fashionable hair styles and expensive jewelry. The side effect was some charity enjoyed an uptick in funds and thus justified all the ostentation and vanity. Although many of the men seemed to know John Milton and nodded at him, while some of the women smiled, he didn't acknowledge anyone.

"Why is it I get the feeling that the combined net worth of the people in this room is more than the net worth of many third world countries?" she asked when they were seated.

"Your feelings are probably accurate," he replied. "Would you mind having a bottle of Dom Perignon to start?"

"Why would I mind?"

"You might think it coarse of me to celebrate, considering . . ."

"You have a reason to celebrate," she said. "Why deny it?"

He nodded at the waiter who stood a few feet back waiting.

"I have two reasons to celebrate tonight. The court victory, yes, but having you join me for dinner as well."

"Not quite of equal points."

"Speak for yourself," he said. He glanced around. "You don't know all the players yet, but there are three New York Supreme court judges here tonight."

She looked at the clientele.

"I know one, I think. Judge Cornbleau. Nassau County?"

"Correct."

The waiter brought the champagne and poured two glasses.

"I'd like to make a toast a la Humphrey Bogart," John Milton said holding up his glass. Michele held hers.

"I think I know it," she said.

"Then let's make it together. He touched her glass and she and he said, "Here's looking at you, kid."

She couldn't help but laugh and sipped her champagne.

"Before you charm the hell out of me," she began, "tell me how you acquired all that personal data in the short time you were on this case."

"My, you are all business first, aren't you?"

"Why do I get the feeling you are, too?"

He laughed.

"Okay. One of the first things I acquired when I had the money to do so was hire a personal private investigator."

"Tom Beardsly?"

"So you do your research too. Why did you ask then?"

"You seemed to me to know more than what one investigator could bring you that quickly."

"I might have a few others on the payroll. I like to cast a wide net when I take on a case. I'm sorry."

"Hardly something that requires an apology. When did you decide to become a lawyer?"

"Oh, I think I always was. It was in my blood to defend the accused when I was younger. I always felt . . . needed. Shall we consider the menu? You must be hungry by now."

He nodded and the waiter handed them the menus.

"I recommend the lamb shank. The chef here does wonders with it. It will melt on your plate."

"Why don't you just order for me," she said and put her menu down.

"All right. I will."

She watched him order in French.

"Doesn't he speak English?"

"It makes it taste better," he replied and she laughed again.

"How did you get Cisley Strumfield to believe she was being questioned by her husband?" she asked, aiming her question like a pistol at his eyes and pulling it on him abruptly so she could catch him unguarded.

"What makes you think I did anything to make her think that?"

"I have some good instincts."

He laughed.

"Absolutely. I wouldn't find you as fascinating if you didn't."

"So?"

"You want me to tell you? What happens to a magician who reveals the secret of his tricks?"

"You consider yourself a magician?"

"There is all kinds of magic in this world, Michele. The kind performed in Las Vegas, your aunt's kind, and Mother Nature."

"So you know about my aunt?"

"I said I did my research on you. I absolutely adore people like your aunt. I just didn't think she'd be in the mood to see me tonight. It's a little too soon."

"You were right about that. In fact, I can't guarantee she'll ever be in the mood to see you."

"I'll find a way to charm her, appeal to her sort of magic."

"What kind do you perform?"

"Something between Mother Nature and Las Vegas. I ordered a favorite red wine of mine. I hope you like it."

"You're a magician. Make sure I do," she said.

"Abracadabra," he said waving his hand over the table.

"So I'm not getting my quid pro quo when it comes to Cisley Strumfield?"

"Whatever I did stimulated her guilt."

"You don't seriously think she had her husband killed?"

"No, but she had guilt over her affair, I believe and maybe that was exacerbated by his death."

She sat back and sipped her champagne. The waiter had practically leaped to refresh her glass. After another moment, she slipped off her shawl. He smiled.

"I was actually afraid that you'd have an unfair advantage with the jury. I've seen juries show more favor to beautiful attorneys like yourself. Even the women on the juries do. They're more concerned with what you're wearing than what you're saying."

"That's very chauvinistic."

"Am I chauvinistic? So I'm chauvinistic. I contradict myself. I am large. I contain multitudes."

"Playing with Walt Whitman? You're still chauvinistic."

He smiled. Two waiters were bringing their salads, bread and he wine.

"I can see there's no point in trying to fool you," he said.

"Try anyway. I enjoy it."

How he laughed.

I will win this woman, he thought. She's very special.

And when I do, it will be like stealing an angel.

23.

Fish was surprised to find Blake at his desk so early in the morning. From the way others looked at Blake and then at him, he got the impression they already knew Lieutenant Blake was in a very bad mood. They made a point of keeping their distance, widening the circle around his desk. He was just staring ahead, not even aware that Fish was there standing in front of him.

"Hey," Fish said. "What'dja do, sleep here last night?" Blake blinked his eyes rapidly for a moment and then nodded.

"Matter of fact, I practically did," he said. "I was here at six."

"Why? What's up?"

"I had some work to catch up on, but we've got a new homicide," Blake said rising. "Call just came in from toxicology. Forty-year-old white male, arsenic poisoning."

"Married?"

"Yes. Let's go."

They started out.

"Wife in the frame?"

"And mistress," Blake said. "Either one got fed up. Whoever we tag, we'd better have an open and shut case. Reasonable doubt is more and more like unreasonable doubt these days," Blake added, not disguising his bitterness.

"Yeah. Sorry about the Heckett outcome," Fish said as they continued out. "The newspapers are having a field day blowing up this John Milton into some super lawyer."

"Sorry about the outcome?" Blake said pausing. "Yeah, I guess we can all say we're sorry about it. A dark shadow has moved over this city."

"Seems to me it was always over this city," Fish said.

Blake walked faster. They got into the car.

"Not like this," Blake said. He just sat there for a moment, his hands on the steering wheel.

"What makes you say so? The Heckett case? Lots of bad guys walk, Lieutenant. I'm sure this wasn't your first bad experience with the legal system."

Blake didn't move, didn't speak. He looked frozen in fact. Fish saw the way his knuckles reddened as he tightened his grip on the steering wheel. It was as if something was boiling inside him and could overflow in a wave of hot blood.

"There somethin' else you're not telling me, Lieutenant?" Fish asked.

"There was a note waiting for me on my desk when I got in," Blake said. He turned to him. "It was from Aunt Eve."

"Aunt Eve?"

"Ms. Armstrong's Aunt."

"Oh. Oh yeah. What about it?"

"She said Michele had gone out to dinner with John Milton last night."

"Last night? After the verdict? No shit?"

"That's not the worst of it in my mind."

"What is?"

"She didn't come home and she doesn't pick up on her mobile," he said. He started the engine and drove in silence.

Fish wondered. Was he worried about her or pissed that she had gone out with someone else? He turned the words over carefully in his mind so he could ask the question without enraging him?

"You don't think John Milton's capable of hurting her, do you?"

Matthew Blake smiled. Fish thought it was a maddening smile. It actually put a little chill in his spine.

"John Milton is capable of committing evil you haven't even imagined," he said.

"He's a bad ass lawyer who's hired a bad ass ex FBI guy as his personal investigator, but I wouldn't give him credit for too much more."

"He's depending on that," Blake said.

Fish nodded. What the hell was he talking about now?

They drove on in a heavy silence until they reached the apartment building on West 57th.

"So what is this? What do we know?" Fish asked.

"Victim's name is Dylan Kotter. Accountant at CNN. Wife's name is Melody. They've been married twelve years, no children. She claims she was at her sister's apartment in Brooklyn last night looking after her two cats. Her sister's on holiday in Puerto Rico."

"I don't think you have to babysit cats all night. My grandmother always had cats. They're pretty damn independent."

"I'm sure there's more to the story. She claims she came home early this morning and found her husband stone dead on the sofa. Uniformed officers and paramedics first thought it was a heart attack. Medical examiner estimated time of death about one in the morning. Wife says he had his mistress in the apartment while she was away. Claims it wasn't the first time. She told the uniformed patrolmen that she could smell the scent of her perfume in the air and on the sofa.

"She said the mistress's name is Marie Longstreet. Nevertheless, she claimed she didn't want a divorce. She wanted to 'open his eyes' and save their marriage. She told the officers on the scene that they were talking about adopting a child before all this.

"Maybe that's true, maybe not. The mistress was possibly disgusted with his failed promises to divorce his wife and marry her. If she's the perp, I imagine she felt used and wanted to stamp her displeasure on his soul. I had time to check her out. She's a twenty-two-year-old hostess at the Dew Drop Inn just over the GW Bridge in Fort Lee."

"Well, it's probably one of them," Fish said. "Poison is usually a woman's MO, and spies, of course, but he doesn't sound like an undercover agent."

"Yes, usually a woman's MO," Blake said. "However, my guess is nothing will be usual in this city anymore. I'm telling you all this because you could be on this one more than I will. I'm waiting for a phone call that might take me away any moment."

"Take you away? How long?"

"I don't know. Some doors are opening."

"Doors?"

"Let's go," Blake said getting out of the car. Fish followed him.

"Doors?" he repeated.

Blake stopped at the apartment building entrance. He looked back at the street as carefully as someone who feared he was being followed, and then entered, leaving Fish unanswered. Fish shook his head and caught up. Blake said nothing in the elevator. He glared ahead, the tension and rage in him palpable. When the door opened, he charged out of the elevator and down the hallway to the Kotter apartment.

Both of them were surprised to be greeted by an attorney named Paul Scholefield when they buzzed. He introduced himself quickly and handed Matthew his card as soon as Matthew had presented his. He was a little over six feet tall, light brown-haired man, slim in his tailor-made dark blue suit. Maybe in his late twenties, Scholefield looked as well put together as a store-front manikin, his fingernails manicured, his coiffeur cut with surgical precision.

Blake looked up from the business card.

"I've heard of ambulance chasers, but you're almost ahead of that. What, do you anticipate crime?" Blake asked in an accusatory tone.

Paul Scholefield didn't even blink. He smiled softly, giving himself an innocent, school boy look. He had the sort of face that would take multiple decades to reveal his true age.

"I specialize in preventative legal medicine," he replied. "I don't anticipate crime, just the need for a criminal attorney. I know what happens when you guys confront an unattended death, especially when there is a wife or husband involved."

"You know what happens?" Blake muttered. "Are you a family friend?"

"My relationship with Mrs. Kotter is not pertinent to your investigation, Lieutenant."

"I think I'll know what's pertinent and what isn't," Matthew Blake countered. "Where's Mrs. Kotter?"

"She's resting at the moment, but we don't want to stir up your policeman's natural suspicions so I'll let her know you've arrived. Have a seat in the living room," he added and stepped back to let them in.

They entered.

"Living room? Hasn't that been sealed off?" Matthew asked. "It's an unattended death," he emphasized for Fish's benefit as well.

"Oops. Someone's already screwed up the chain of evidence, I'm afraid. This is why lawyers are needed. Excuse me," Scholefield said and went down a short hallway to knock on a door.

"Screwed up the chain of evidence?" Fish asked. "Why lawyers are needed?"

"Yes, he's working for the public good," Matthew Blake said. "Don't you know people have to be protected from the police as much as from criminals?"

He and Fish entered the living room. It was small with two large cushion easy chairs and a matching sofa. A single tumbler was still on the hard wood coffee table in front of the sofa. There were some magazines and a book about U.S. economic history on the table. There were no signs of any physical confrontation. Nothing looked disturbed.

Melody Kotter walked in with Paul Scholefield not only at her side, but holding her at the elbow, ostensibly to keep her steady.

Here's a full service lawyer, Blake thought. If he didn't know her before or he wasn't recommended by some friend, he's one smooth worker.

Melody was dressed in a light pink, terrycloth robe and wore a pair of matching pink slippers. She looked like she had just recently had her hair done. It was finely brushed and she wore lipstick, a little rouge and some eye shadow, looking more like she was getting ready to go out for the evening and not just rising from a state of depression and sadness.

"Mrs. Kotter, I'm Lieutenant Matthew Blake and this is Detective John Fish. I'm not sure you know it yet," he continued, glancing at Paul Scholefield, "but a toxicology report has confirmed that your husband's cause of death was arsenic poisoning."

He waited for her reaction, but she just stared silently as if she were anticipating him to add, "You're under arrest."

"Do you have any specific question, Lieutenant?" Paul Scholefield asked.

"Were you aware of this before now, Mrs. Kotter?"

"No," she said. "But I'm not surprised to hear it. She was here. That bitch was here."

"Easy," Paul Scholefield said in a loud whisper. She sucked in her breath, closed her eyes and then opened them again as if she had just repowered the computer in her head.

"Did you touch the glass that's on this table?" Blake asked, nodding at it.

"Do you mean ever or recently?" Paul Scholefield countered.

"Obviously, recently."

Melody Kotter looked at the glass as if she had not seen it there before this moment.

"It's part of a set of glasses we keep in our liquor cabinet," she said. "I did not touch it recently, but I have washed and dried the set and put it back a few days ago."

"There wasn't any other glass on the table?"

"I don't remember," she said. "I was more concerned with Dylan than the room when I entered."

Matthew nodded at Fish who put on his gloves and then put the glass carefully in an evidence bag.

"This entire apartment is now a crime scene," Matthew continued. "A forensic team is on the way. We're going to have to search the entire apartment. If you have somewhere else to go for a while . . ."

She looked at Paul Scholefield.

"That's not necessary. Mrs. Kotter will stay out of your way. She is obviously in a state of shock at the moment. I have her doctor coming up to see her to give her a sedative. I suggest you have your team search the master bedroom while we wait in here so she can retire to it when they're finished."

"I'd rather nobody wait in here," Matthew said. "We don't want to disturb the scene."

"Too late for that, don't you think?" Paul Scholefield said. "From what Mrs. Kotter has told me, at least four uniform patrolman were in this room and two paramedics."

"Nevertheless . . ."

"All right. She'll wait in the guest bedroom."

"Nothing can be touched or moved anywhere in this apartment right now," Blake warned, "even in the guest room."

"You or your partner can witness her lying down," Paul Scholefield said. "She might peal back a blanket."

"Did you and your husband have a fight recently concerning this other women you mentioned to the police and just made reference to, Mrs. Kotter?" Blake asked, ignoring him.

"We discussed her, yes," she said.

"Amiably?"

"I might have raised my voice," she said.

"You were obviously angry at him, weren't you?"

"I wasn't happy with his behavior, no, but I didn't poison him. She poisoned him in more ways than one."

Her face finally began to crumble, her lips trembling, her arms shaking. Paul Scholefield put his arm around her shoulders. "I'm afraid that's all she can do at this point, Lieutenant. You'll have to work around her," he concluded and turned her to walk her back to the guest bedroom. Blake nodded at Fish who followed them. He returned a moment later.

"Her lawyer put her to bed and is sitting at the bedside like a relative. He's still holding her hand."

The door buzzer sounded.

"That's probably forensics," Matthew said. Fish went to the door and the team entered. While Fish was explaining the situation to them, Matthew felt his mobile vibrate. He stepped away and answered it when he saw who was calling. "Matthew Blake," he said.

"One moment for Ms Armstrong, please," Sophia Walters practically sang.

It was nearly thirty seconds later when she came on. He was tempted to hang up.

"Matthew. Sorry I couldn't get back to you sooner, but they handed me my new case practically in the lobby of the building this morning on my way in. It's a rape case. My first, actually. A man named Jerome Rand raped his sister-in-law, Carol Kyle, an unmarried cocktail waitress who was staying in an apartment close by that he supposedly found for her. She was looking for new work in New York. I feel like I'm going to try Marlon Brando in *Streetcar Named Desire*. Like everything else, it got a little complicated. The wife backs her husband and accused her sister of sick sibling rivalry. I was hoping for a teenager robbing a grocery store. You know a Detective Fern Littletree? She's been on the case and gave me her file. I believe she's the only female native American in the NYPD," she said, rattling it off like someone high on cocaine.

"I know of her. She just started."

"You sound tired."

"Didn't sleep that well. I called you, but you didn't answer my calls." He waited for her response, but she was silent.

"I had a message from your aunt waiting for me very early this morning," he continued. "She was concerned about you when realized you hadn't come home last night," he said rather than come right out immediately to ask her about John Milton.

"Yes, well you know my aunt, how she can be."

"You went to dinner with John Milton?" he finally asked, unable to wait for her confession.

"Yes, to an interesting restaurant, Angel's Lair. Ever hear of it?"

"No. How could you go to dinner with him? How could you spend any time with him at all outside of that courtroom?"

"I wanted to know more about him. Besides, I don't think you should be questioning me in that tone of voice, Matthew. We're not exactly engaged," she added. Her voice became dramatically different, testy.

"I didn't say we were, but I thought you found him obnoxious to say the least."

"Everyone is different in court from what they are outside. Everyone," she stressed, the implication clear.

"I see. Okay, I'm on a new case now, too."

"More work for me?"

"Hopefully, it will be tighter wrapped before the district attorney gets it. I'll call you, if you'd like."

"Why not? Call when you can and I'll pick up when I can. Good luck on the investigation," she said. She didn't say goodbye. He heard the line go dead and hung up himself.

It felt like his face was on fire.

"Lieutenant?" Fish said standing in front of him. "I told them to start in the guest bedroom. I thought you'd appreciate that."

"Whatever. Just don't give that attorney any reason to file any complaints and complicate it all, John. There's something unusual about him. Despite that crap about protecting people involved in an unattended death, I think he knew Dylan Kotter was poisoned before we arrived." Blake looked at his watch. "It's not two and a half hours since I got the call. How did he know that quickly?"

Fish shrugged.

"Spy in the lab? Everyone got someone earning extra bucks."

"Maybe."

"What else could it be?"

Blake just looked at him as if he had asked a very dumb question. Fish actually felt a bit uncomfortable and was happy to see Blake get another call and put his attention on something else. While he talked on his mobile, Fish returned to the bedroom to watch forensic working around Mrs. Kotter. Her attorney stood off to the side, his arms folded over his chest, glaring at them.

"You could have started somewhere else in this apartment and let her get some rest until her doctor arrives," Paul Scholefield said.

Melody Kotter kept her eyes closed.

"Does Mrs. Kotter have a job beside taking care of her sister's cats?" he asked Scholefield.

"She's on a leave of absence from a secretarial position at a parochial school," he replied.

"I just wondered why she was wearing so much fresh makeup," he said. Marie Kotter opened her eyes.

"Why did you take a shower this morning or did you?" Paul countered.

The two forensic men stopped searching through drawers and turned to them.

"I never saw an attorney so attached to his client, but I forgot that you guys get paid by the hour." Fish said.

Paul Scholefield smiled.

"Everyone gets paid by the hour," he replied.

"We don't."

"Sure you do. You just get less when you divide your pay by the hours you put in. But you don't work for the money. You work for justice, right?"

"Justice. There's a word you should look up. Maybe for the first time," Fish replied, proud of his comeback.

Paul Scholefield continued to smile. Then lost it when Matthew Blake came up behind Fish.

He pulled him aside.

"I got the call I was telling you I might get, John. You're in charge here until I return. When you're finished here, pay the mistress a visit. Maybe she won't be as lawyered up."

"Where are you going, Lieutenant? In case I'm asked."

"To our favorite funeral parlor," he replied and hurried out.

Fish stared after him, not moving until he realized his mouth was wide open in astonishment.

On his way out, Blake's mobile vibrated again. He paused in the apartment house lobby.

"I got the text you just sent, Lieutenant," Kay Billups said. "You were right on with your inquiry so I thought I should call you rather than text back."

"Oh? Thank you. What do you have for me?"

"Mr. Milton has arranged for Mr. Scholefield to have an interview day after tomorrow with him and Mr. Simon."

"Okay. Thanks, Kay."

"It's my pleasure," she said with such feeling that it was clear to Blake that she was truly happy to cooperate.

"I know," he replied.

It was a good day to make discoveries, Matthew Blake thought as he continued out of the apartment building to his vehicle. The sky was washed of all the gray clouds he had seen scattered when the sun had come up in the morning. The sunlight was dazzling, unwrapping shadows and exposing the homeless who had been entrenched in every nook and cranny the city offered to protect them from the elements. There was a crispness in the air that infected the traffic and the pedestrians. No one could hide from the activity around them. They rushed about as if all their imperfections were exposed and they needed to get to where they were going, inside, comfortably disguised in their jobs and professional identities. Even the inanimate parts of this urban world seemed to reveal their cracks and faded surfaces.

There was a timing to everything, he thought, and his task was to realize when the moment had come, the opportunity had raised its head, and the voices had sounded like trumpets. He was going to make a difference today. He was going to seriously wound the beast that scratched on cathedral walls and carried Cain on its back as it trampled over the souls of the innocent and faithful. He went forth like the knight in shining armor he envisioned himself to be.

A little less than two hours later, he was parked across the way from the Foster Funeral Home in Ferndale. He fixed his suspicious eyes on the building and the parking lot and waited patiently to confirm what he knew anyone else would think was farfetched enough to be insane. However, what prophet, what inventor, what theory or great idea wasn't first thought to be crazy, including electricity? The average person didn't fully understand electrons and protons, yet believed that if he or she flipped a switch, a light bulb would glow, a machine would start, and a television or radio would go on and continue what people two hundred years ago would believe was magic, maybe evil magic.

Perhaps two hundred years from now, this would be just as accepted, just as believable. He was just a different sort of Columbus finding a different world. He was without doubt, confident and not fearful of any ridicule.

While he waited, he thought about Michele Armstrong. All this had become quite personal now. He could motivate himself with lofty goals, but there was also this very particular objective. He had to rescue her from any danger. He had to protect her not as one of many, but as someone for whom he deeply cared. Dare he say loved?

He envisioned her. He relived their kisses and caresses. He felt the warmth and the hope their lovemaking had given him. Admittedly, it had taken him off course, but it was a detour he needed in order to sustain himself. Love in any form nourished the soul. It was impossible to survive without it, not in the sense of survival he believed in. Maybe he was fighting for himself as much as he was for her.

The arrival of a familiar vehicle snapped him out of his musing. Tom Beardsly parked his car and got out. He stretched, spit out whatever he was chewing, and headed for the funeral parlor entrance. Blake shifted in his seat so he wouldn't be visible if Beardsly turned his way, but the man never did. He entered the funeral parlor quickly. A little more than fifteen minutes later, he stepped out, carefully carrying what was clearly an urn. With just as much care, he put it on the floor by the passenger's seat in his car. Then he paused, looked around and got into his vehicle.

He drove out slowly and turned right.

Blake started his engine and followed him. He remained far enough behind not to be obvious, but they were soon taking roads with little or no traffic. Houses became few and far between and many of those he saw looked abandoned. The grounds were overgrown, and like most areas of America where degeneration had taken hold, there were also abandoned vehicles and trucks. When he did see a house that looked still lived in, he didn't see anyone outside. He felt almost like he was entering a netherworld. Even the vegetation began to look odd, trees leaning, bushes invading each other, and most curious, no signs of wildlife. Where were the rabbits and deer? Eventually, he didn't even see birds.

Ahead, he saw Beardsly make a turn down an unpaved road. His vehicle swayed from side to side as the wheels navigated holes and short ditches and then he disappeared around another turn. Blake brought his vehicle to a stop and considered the road. His intention was to remain undiscovered, but if he started down this road, the dust cloud would reveal him. Instead, he pulled his vehicle off the paved road and followed some flat, solid looking ground to move behind some large oak trees with bark that looked like warts.

He got out and started down the dirt road, walking at least three-quarters of a mile before the farmhouse appeared ahead. He saw no crops in the fields, nor any livestock. The afternoon sun weakened behind birch and maple trees to the west casting long shadows over the scene before him. Beardsly's car was in front of the farmhouse, but Beardsly wasn't in it. Blake hesitated and then he cut to his left and ran through the woods so he could look around the West corner of the farmhouse. When he moved farther left, he saw the rear end of John Milton's black limousine.

Beardsly emerged from the farmhouse and got into his vehicle. He backed up and then turned around and headed away from the farm-house, down the dirt road and away. Moments later, Blake heard what sounded like women wailing in a rhythm, the volume rising and fall-ing. He moved closer to the farmhouse and kept moving left so he could get a better view of the rear. A half dozen women wearing black shawls and the hollowed out heads of black crows above their own heads were gathered around a pile of dried branches. They continued their chant-ing. It was Latin, the Lord's Prayer, but something was very different about it, Blake thought and then realized it was being sung backwards.

The branches burst into flames, the fire building. Milton and his driver stepped out of the rear of the farmhouse. His driver was carrying the urn. The women parted, breaking the circle and John Milton took the urn from his driver and stepped close to the fire. One of the women let out a shrill scream and they all stopped singing.

Milton opened the urn and stepped closer to the fire. For a long moment, there was silence and then he tipped the urn and muttering something Blake couldn't hear, dumped the ashes into the fire. A cloud of black smoke rose and drifted to the right. The women stepped back and then the smoked gradually began to take the shape of a man who finally stood naked in front of John Milton.

Milton raised his arms and held them out to embrace the man and the women began to chant again. John Milton led the resurrected man back into the farmhouse and the women gradually lowered their voices and stopped singing. The fire died down as they turned and entered the farmhouse, too. John Milton's driver shoveled dirt over the remaining embers before joining the others in the farmhouse.

For a moment Matthew Blake thought his feet were frozen to the earth. He willed himself to turn and start away, but he didn't move. Then he struggled again and his feet lifted and fell as he ran, as fast as he could, back through the woods all the way to his car.

It was as if a nightmare he had when he was a child had just materialized in front of his eyes. He was chilled and couldn't get warm for a good ten minutes before he felt confident that his fingers would work, that indeed the rest of him would obey his commands.

Then he started the engine and slowly pulled out and back onto the road. He didn't drive fast until he realized he had returned to the world he knew.

All he could think of was Michele, telling her what he had seen and warning her how close she was to becoming one of the women wearing the black shawls.

24.

Michele Armstrong suddenly felt exhausted. It washed in and over her like a cold breeze. She didn't know from where or how she had garnered all the energy she had begun with today, anyway. A good part of the evening before was a blur. She couldn't swear to getting any sleep at all. Maybe it was because of her fatigue, or maybe it was due to something else working its way inside like a tape worm, but some paranoia had begun to seep in around the edges. It was always like her to be sensibly skeptical, but the flow of all this negative energy and suspicion was something different.

Had Eleanor Rozwell really handed her what everyone thought was going to be a fairly easy prosecution with the Heckett case or had she anticipate a dramatic failure? She knew from talking with Sophia Walters, who was one of those office personnel who made it her business to dip into everyone else's business, that Eleanor believed she was not involved enough in Michele's being offered the position. In fact, when she did meet Eleanor that first time, she thought the interview had gone badly. The woman had ice in her voice and gave off negative vibes. She recalled her making the point that the New York District Attorney's office was a much more complex and sophisticated agency than anything in the other New York counties. She actually asked her if she thought she was ready for this and made her feel that every syllable in her response was being judged.

Meeting with Michael Barrett was night and day different. It wasn't hard to see why a man with his personality would rise so quickly to the top prosecutor in the city. He was very bright and as knowledgeable as any U.S. Supreme Court justice, but he had the warmth to telegraph sincerity and concern as well. Maybe because he had three daughters, two in their twenties and one nineteen that he was so comfortable with a woman her age. She felt his nurturing abilities and left really wanting to work for him.

However, she knew, even more so now, that he trusted and depended on Eleanor Rozwell a great deal. Perhaps she wasn't his cup of tea socially or personally, but he respected her and believed she was the spine in the district attorney's office. Michele imagined he went out a bit more than usual on a limb to offer her the job. Eleanor accepted his decision, but surely kept a cloud of probation hovering over it. Michele didn't have to have anyone actually voice it, but she could hear it whispered through the walls. "You could lose once in a while. Everyone does, but you've got to start racking up successes pretty quickly, especially when you're being evaluated by Eleanor Rozwell."

In many ways this second case she had been handed was even more difficult than the Heckett case, but Eleanor didn't present it that way.

"You've got great DNA evidence. There's no question he had sex with her. You have the pictures of her traumas, bruises your expert witness will testify are associated with unnecessary force. You have the situation, the place being her apartment, the event occurring at a time of night no one would usually entertain a guest, and you have evidence of his drinking heavily. Dig into his past and see what you can find that will help develop the case. She'll be a good witness, too. Okay. Go to it," she concluded.

Sounds good, Michele thought, until she discovered the animosity between the two sisters. Instead of pointing her rage completely at her husband, the wife was accusing her sister of wrecking her marriage. She discovered this today and debated going in to Eleanor's office to tell her or tell Michael Barrett about it. Eleanor might take it as a show of weakness by setting up an excuse for failure before she had even begun. She could convince the district attorney to assign another AD to the case, and moving her off something this soon into it, would surely set the stage for her doom, especially after her initial defeat.

But her new, raw paranoia which she would readily admit seemed to blossom out of thin air this morning got her to thinking that Eleanor Rozwell knew all this before she handed her the assignment. She was the type of person who when contradicted might visibly accept it, but never forget it and work to prove herself right.

Of course, at my expense, Michele thought sadly. She glanced at herself in the mirror she had brought to her office. When she went to wipe something off her right cheek, John Milton's face appeared just behind her, smiling lustfully. She spun around, but there was on one there.

"I am tired," she told herself and gathered her things together, the file especially, to leave and go home.

Sophia looked up surprised. She was leaving an hour before the end of the day.

"I have something I have to do," she told her. "I'm on my mobile if you need me."

"Yes, of course," Sophia said, but watched her leave, her own face full of concern.

Michele had just stepped out of the building when Matthew Blake seemed to come out of nowhere. She had the feeling he had been waiting at the entrance, anticipating her. She jerked herself back the moment she saw his face. His hair was disheveled, looking like he had run his fingers through it from every direction, and his eyes were wide, as wide as someone who had just seen a violent death. Ordinarily, he was immaculate, but she could see mud stains on his pants and even a small tear in his suit jacket. His tie was jerked loose, the top buttons on his shirt undone.

"I've got to talk to you immediately," he said. He didn't want for her to accept his invitation. He seized her firmly at her left elbow and started to pull her along, heading for his car at the curb.

"Matthew, what's come over you? You're hurting me!" she cried, pulling her arm out of his grip.

"Sorry, but we must talk now. Please," he begged. He stepped forward and opened the car door for her.

She looked back and around her as if she wanted to be sure someone witnessed her getting into his car under some duress.

"He's not here. Don't worry," he said with an icy smile.

"Who?"

"Please, get in, Michele," Blake urged, the desperation clearly in his voice.

She got into the car. He closed the door and ran around the vehicle to get in. He looked back and then shot away, his tires squealing. He beat out a red light and turned a sharp right. Michele snapped her safety belt in quickly.

"Why are you driving so crazy? What is it?"

He put his hand up for her to wait and when he saw an open place to park, he pulled in and shut off his engine. For a moment he just sat there looking ahead. She waited, afraid to make any demands. He turned to her slowly.

"Wanted to get us away from there."

"Why?"

"There's someone or someone's in your offices who are not shall we say friendly to my efforts."

"What? Who?"

"Let me start at the beginning," he said, his voice forcibly controlled and calmed. "A little less than a year ago, I sensed a different energy come into the city. I did my work, solved my cases, and delivered solid evidence to the district attorney's office. But suddenly, the shadows were deeper, the darkness in the souls of people I once trusted got thicker. I knew something was happening. I had sensed something similar years ago when I was seriously thinking of devoting myself to God, and what happened, happened. It was then that I knew I had a special gift, a gift I had to use where it would most be effective, and that place was in police work.

"I know it will sound crazy to you, but I can see him."

"Who?" she asked.

"Satan, Lucifer, whatever name he goes by."

"So you're as good as my aunt Eve?" she asked, a slightly satirical smile on her face.

"Your aunt Eve is one of those people who can read energy well, sense things, but she can't do as much as I can, see as much as I can. Nevertheless, you shouldn't ridicule her."

"I don't ridicule her. I humor her and she knows it. Where is this going, Matthew? Are you just upset about my going on a dinner date with John Milton?"

"You didn't go on a dinner date with John Milton. You went on a dinner date with Lucifer," he said.

Michele stared at him a moment and then turned away and shook her head.

"When I was in high school, I had a boyfriend for a while and then I started with another boy, and my first boyfriend came to see me and told me the new boy was really AC/DC. He was having sex with other boys as well as girls, sometimes. When that didn't work, he spread a rumor that he had herpes. I'm not saying it's something males do more than females, but it is natural to be jealous."

"I'm not jealous. I mean, I am, but that's not what motivates me to tell you all this. I think you're in terrible danger."

"I know. Like I would be if I was seeing someone who had Syphilis."

"NO!" Matthew said pounding the steering wheel. "Take me seriously for a moment, will you."

"Okay, okay. Calm down. What do you want me to know?"

He relaxed a bit.

"From the moment I began to investigate Warner Murphy's death, I knew something very dark and deadly had come into the city. Everyone wanted to declare it a suicide, and to everyone else, that would seem most logical because there was no evidence of anyone entering the building and his apartment to do him harm. The witnesses, the video replays, forensics, you name it, there was nothing to suggest anything but suicide."

"And as far as I know, that's where it stands."

"It wasn't suicide. He was murdered. I tracked to a man who was killed in an upstate prison in Woodbourne. After he died and was cremated, John Milton brought him here to kill Warner Murphy. I can't prove it yet, but the attendant in the lobby was part of it all. I'm not finished fully investigating his past, but I'll make the connection eventually."

"Let me understand you, Matthew. You're saying that John Milton brought a man to New York City after he died and was cremated to kill Warner Murphy?"

"Michele, think about this. Who took Warner Murphy's place at the law firm?"

She simply stared at him for a moment and then shook her head.

"Have you been drinking?"

"Stop it."

"You're going to feel like a fool after I tell you what you said. Go home, Matthew. Take a nap."

She turned to get out. He grabbed her arm.

"Ow."

"Michele, I need to know what you did with John Milton last night. There are changes going on inside you that you might not understand or even be aware of. You spent the entire night with him?"

"If you have to know, we had dinner and we went for a ride and talked. I don't know where the time went, but he was very interesting. He's traveled to many fascinating places in the world, speaks seven languages, and met people in high places. We just talked, or he talked and I listened. I don't think you need to know more than that, Matthew."

"You will when I tell you the rest. After I tracked Warner Murphy's killer back to the Woodbourne prison and learned how he died, I followed the chain of events to the funeral home where he was cremated, paid for by supposedly an anonymous benefactor. It's called the Foster Funeral Home. They've cremated a number of hard case prisoners from that penitentiary. You can check that out for yourself."

"So? That proves what?"

"One of the things I discovered in the owners office was a picture of Christ on the cross upside down."

"Upside down? What's that?"

"It's an icon for Satanists, those who worship the devil."

"Michael . . ."

"No, just listen. I asked the warden to let me know when another death in the prison came up, one that had a similar arrangement involving the Foster Funeral home, and one did come up today. I went to the funeral home and waited and guess who came to pick up the urn, Tom Beardsly, John Milton's private investigator."

She sat back.

"Interested now, huh?"

"I don't know where this going, but go on."

"I followed Beardsly to a farmhouse in an area that could be the setting for *The Grapes of Wrath*. It looked forgotten. The whole area was . . . defeated. Even the vegetation looked unhappy."

"The vegetation?"

"When Beardsly continued down an unpaved side road, I parked and walked through the woods. Milton's limousine was there. After a few minutes, Beardsly left without the urn so I got in position to see what was going on and saw a Satanic ritual during which John Milton resurrected the cremated criminal through fire and took him into the farmhouse. It was blood curdling."

"Resurrected?"

"He rose in black smoke and took form."

"A man who died and was cremated?"

"Exactly. A distortion of Christ's raising of Lazarus. Satan likes to mimic God's miracles."

She shook her head and sat back.

"Even you should admit that this is a lot to digest and believe, Matthew."

"Of course it is. It's supposed to be."

"Excuse me?"

"Someone once said the devil's greatest asset was the fact that so many don't believe he literally exists."

"Did you take any pictures of this ritual?"

"No. I won't need them. I'm not looking to have him indicted and tried for resurrecting the evil dead."

"What are you looking to do?"

"I'm looking to stop him and throw him out of this world the way he was thrown out of heaven," Blake said. "All I ask is you stay away from him."

She nodded.

"Stay away from John Milton," she said. "That's where this is going?"

"This isn't jealousy, not in the sense you're thinking, Michele. I wouldn't be afraid of competing with him for your devotion if he were really just a man."

"Okay, Matthew. I need to go home. I'm very tired and as it turns out, I have more of a challenge facing me in court than I first thought. I'm being asked to sink or swim. I have my own problems at the moment."

"You don't believe anything I've told you, do you? Not a word."

"I'm too tired to believe anything right now. All I wish is for you to be careful, to think through anything you do or say to anyone else, Matthew. You've had a great disappointment, too, maybe in more ways than one. You're probably very tired, too. We both need some rest."

"Right. Some rest." He started the engine. "I'll take you home," he said. "You don't seem to be taking whatever I tell you seriously so I hesitate to add anything."

"What else?" she asked, closing and opening her eyes, like someone in a dentist's chair.

"We have a new homicide. I left John Fish on it, but I know now it's not a coincidence. Nothing ever is."

He pulled away from the curb and turned around.

"Why do you say that? What's not a coincidence?"

"The young attorney representing the chief suspect, Paul Scholefield, someone who was at her side moments after it was determined her husband was murdered, already is being considered for a position at Simon and James."

"How did you find that out?"

"The receptionist at Simon and James, Kaye Billups. She never liked John Milton. She's my inside man," he said. "He replaced Warner Murphy's personal secretary with one of his own, and has hired two researchers for the firm already."

"That's not unusual, Matthew. New people suggest new people."

"You heard about Alexander James collapsing in court and dying. It wasn't a natural heart attack. He ingested cocaine."

"I'd like a dollar for every attorney who does."

"Now he's bringing in this Paul Scholefield. Don't you see? He's taking over this prestigious law firm with a gold reputation. The cases are flowing in."

"It could easily be just a coincidence, Matthew. People are naturally drawn to a winner."

He smiled at her.

"There are no coincidences, Michele. Something happens because of good energy or bad. That's all there is to think about."

She was silent.

"He's coming for someone else," Matthew said, nodding and sounding more like he was talking to himself now. "That's why he performed the ridicule of Lazarus. It's like rubbing salt in a wound, a spiritual wound." He turned to her. "He's deliberating letting God know, challenging Him."

He smiled.

"Okay, Matthew."

"That's all right. Only this time I'll be there."

"Don't do anything stupid, Matthew. Talk to someone else about all this, maybe a priest you respect."

He pulled up to the curb in front of her aunt's loft.

"Will you promise to do that?" she asked, putting her hand on his arm. "Will you?"

He shook his head.

"You're already in great danger, Michele. You won't tell me about last night. Maybe you really don't remember, but I fear he's already gotten into you."

She pulled her hand away as if his arm burned it.

"That's uncalled for, Matthew."

"I don't mean sexually, although I wouldn't be surprised."

"Get some serious help," she said and opened the door.

"Michele!" he called.

She hesitated and looked back at him.

"Michele. It's more than your life that's in danger."

"Right now, I'm only worrying about my career," she said, holding up her briefcase, and then she closed the door.

He watched her walk away and drove off, the feeling that he had to do something and do it quickly, more intense.

His vibrating mobile snapped him back to the moment.

"Blake," he said.

"Forensic came up blank with any traces of arsenic anywhere in the apartment, but found evidence of it in the remnants of the drink that were in that glass. I got everyone possibly involved to give me samples of their prints, but Melanie Longstreet gave me the hardest time. I had to bring her in and guess what. There were two sets of prints on the glass we confiscated," Fish said, "Dylan Kotter's and Melanie Longstreet's."

"So you think she poured him his lethal drink."

"I'd say so."

"What was the drink?"

"Jack Daniels and soda."

"Did you check the contents of the Jack Daniels bottle?"

"The contents? No."

"Do it. You'll find the arsenic was already in the bottle. What else did you find out?"

"Melanie Longstreet admits to being pissed off at him, but she claims she refused to see him. She was off during the time of death. Medical examiner puts it at about nine P.M, and Dylan Kotter was seen earlier at the restaurant she works in. She told us she went home and sulked, but didn't go back to this apartment with him. She has no one to confirm her being home at the time of Dylan Kotter's death. Her prints are on the glass, Lieutenant and she has motive and opportunity."

"Do you have any witnesses who saw her at the scene, the building at around 9 P.M.?"

"Not yet. We're bringing her in again, now that the prints are confirmed. She'll break."

"No, she won't."

"Why not? She doesn't have an attorney yet as far as I know."

"It's a waste of time."

"What? Why?"

"I don't even have to hear any of this to know who killed Dylan Kotter," Blake said.

"Who?"

"Whoever Paul Scholefield represents."

"But the wife looks clean."

"She killed him, Fish."

"Really? And you're convinced of this how?"

"Her lawyer, Paul Scholefield is going to work with John Milton. I'm sure he always has."

"What?"

"Don't worry. I'm on the bigger picture. Check that bottle of Jack Daniels. Check other glasses in the cabinet to see if Melanie Longstreet's prints are on others. Prints could last a while in that environment if the glasses weren't wiped or cleaned. We don't know those prints were made last night. Poison in the bottle would indicate the wife knew he would drink it and then set up the mistress."

"And you figured this all out because Paul Scholefield is her attorney?"

"Exactly. You'll see," Blake said. "You'll see," he muttered to himself. "I gotta go. Do what I said."

He hung up.

He never thought it would become something personal. He had no family that could be threatened, but saving Michele Armstrong had suddenly become just as important as saving mankind.

He had no doubt he could do it.

25.

John Milton stood back in the belly of a wide shadow and smiled at his favorite street toughs, Buzzy and Jason. They were sitting in their late model BMW Park watching many couples walking hand and hand, some people with dogs on leashes, and some obvious homeless people thinking they'd find a comfortable place early for the evening. The two were shopping for an easy mugging to make some extra spending money.

Automobile traffic was building as it always did this late in the afternoon. Taxi drivers were racing to deliver their current passenger quickly enough to get another fare. Estate cars and limousines as always seemed to smoothly thread themselves through the clog of nervous private drivers and buses. The city's habitual heartbeat moved into a more characteristic atrial fibrillation with all the irregular stopping and starting, horns sounding warnings and complaints, and pedestrians challenging the changing traffic lights.

John Milton took pleasure in the commotion that was building around him. Chaos was a fertile garden in which he could plant the seeds of his favorite sins. Egos flared; jealousies flourished and charity was trampled under the hooves of self-preservation. A rich investment of contradiction had been installed in this creature, man. How easy it was to affect the balance and tilt them in his direction. Love your neighbor but beat him to the finish line? Work hard but pretend you don't want to be rich? Stroke the church with your dollars, but cut the competition's throat? It is easier for a camel to go through the eye of a needle than a rich man to enter the kingdom of heaven? The super-rich are shaking in their leather boots? I doubt it, John Milton thought as he looked around and smiled. He was tempted to put up a billboard that read: *God made it impossible for you to be the creature he wanted and then punishes you for failing. He's sadistic!*

John got into the rear seat of the BMW easily even though the car doors were locked. Jason and Buzzy spun around, Buzzy reaching for his knife.

"What the fuck . . ." Jason said.

"Don't tell me you're relying on that knife again," John told Buzzy, who looked at it, relived the memory of it scorching his palm, and quickly dropped it on the seat.

John Milton ran his hands over the black leather.

"Nice ride. You get it legitimately with the money I helped you raise?"

"We used some of it, yes," Jason said. "Let's say it was hot off the market so we got a discount."

John Milton laughed.

"I'm glad to see you're both doing so well. Now it's time for you to repay me, although, I'll never ask you to do something that won't in some way benefit you even more. Start the engine."

"What for?"

"We're taking a ride, Jason. Best you don't ask too many questions."

Jason looked at Buzzy whose face reflected his own terror and then started the engine.

"Make a left at the next street and follow my directions," John Milton said.

He had them drive to a West Side apartment building, warning Jason to drive carefully all the way.

"You don't want any accidents with this car, even fender-benders. You don't want to draw any attention to you. In fact for the rest of your life, you must think of yourselves as invisible."

"Invisible?" Buzzy asked.

"Of course. My advice now is that you clean up your act, buy some better clothes, better shoes, stop with these stupid haircuts and avoid getting any more tattoos. You're like two rattlesnakes shaking your tails and hissing constantly. You invite attention and send out warnings. How do you expect to mine the richer veins of fortune? The moment you walk into a building, a bank, or even step onto a street, alarms go off."

"Who are you?" Jason asked.

"I'm your father and your mother. I've given birth to you and I'm going to care for you as long as you listen to what I whisper in your ears."

"You look like some rich businessman," Buzzy said.

"That's what I am; that's what all this is, a sort of business. Okay, park here. A woman is coming out of that subway station in five minutes. I want you to help her keep traveling."

"Keep her traveling? Where?" Jason asked.

"To her eternal destination. Where else? She doesn't have a lot of money in her purse. About one-hundred and ten dollars, but she wears a wedding ring that her husband passed along from his grandmother. It's worth about thirty-thousand dollars. You can fence it for fifteen easily. I'll tell you whom to go to. Problem is, the ring is practically part of her finger now. I hope that knife is sharp, Buzzy boy."

"I can cut a pubic hair in mid-air with it," he said.

Jason laughed.

"He has and not his own."

"You guys take such pleasure in domination. It's joyful to see you, but I'm expecting bigger and bigger things for you, so you'll do what I tell you."

"Well, I do need new clothes," Jason said. "So do you, slob face," he told Buzzy.

"Whatever. I'm just not dressing like some fag."

"Oh, that's exactly what I'd like you two to do. Come off gay. People trust gay men more."

"Fuck that," Buzzy said, but when he looked at John Milton, he lost his bravado. "I'm never kissing him."

John Milton laughed and then nodded.

"Here she comes," he said. "Mug her fatally, get the ring and take the pocketbook. I'm leaving an address on the seat. Bring the ring there. Get rid of this car and find another," he added.

"What? I like this car," Jason said. He could feel the fire in John Milton's eyes. It was as if he was only inches from a blow torch.

"Your fingerprints are all over it. Someone in one of these buildings probably saw you parked here. You don't have foresight. I'll provide that. Am I making myself clear?"

"Yeah, sure," Jason said.

"Go," John Milton commanded with a voice that seemed to puncture their ear drums. They got out of the car. Jason looked back and saw he had stepped out and stood by to watch. They walked quickly.

Kaye Billups was thinking about some groceries she needed. She had brought her bags with her to work, three folded into a large one. It was her contribution to the environment, reusable grocery bags. She had promised Lee she would get the already prepared lemon chicken breast. He would have their salad prepared before she arrived. Her mind was on what other necessities they needed and what sort of a surprise she could bring him for dessert.

They were very comfortable in their marriage now. Although she fell in love with Lee Billups when she was twenty-two, she had come to believe that people can grow to love each other even if they hadn't had that rush of passion in the beginning. Being comfortable in marriage meant just that. They fit each other in so many ways, anticipating each other's pleasures and displeasures, making that extra effort to please and support each other especially when they had a common disappointment or concern. Lee liked to tell everyone that they were a team and what made them successful was neither knew who was the coach. But what was more important, neither really cared. The truth was she was content with herself, with who she was. Maybe she infuriated some of her feminist friends, but she was never concerned about being just as good as a man in every way.

Lee was a retired accountant. He had worked for a big firm for the last twenty-five years and had reached the highest pay level and promotion he could. He was the first to admit that his work wasn't very exciting, but he was one of those who drew pleasure out of organizing numbers and figuring out small maneuvers that made significant differences. Nothing pleased a customer more than being told there was a way to reduce his financial burden. He was just egotistical enough to believe that he was as affective when it came to helping other people find happiness as was a good therapist or even a doctor. "I'm Doctor Numbers," he told his children and grandchildren. "I know just when something doesn't add up and is sick."

He was a very soft-spoken, gentle man who loved his family and made sacrifices when it came to providing more for them. He wasn't very athletic, but watched his diet and took grand and what he called historic walks in the city religiously every weekend. He knew every ethnic neighborhood in detail and knew what buildings had significant architecture. She had gone many times with him, smiling to herself as he lectured about the demise of what was classic and the coldness of what was modern.

She wondered what he had in mind for this weekend. Today, she was going to tell him that she was seriously thinking of retirement, too. The brutal and still inexplicable loss of Warner Murphy never stopped haunting her and now they had the death of Alexander James. For her the piece de resistance was the arrival of this new, far too suave and he her mind, dishonest man. He disturbed her in ways she never anticipated. What's more, she could see and feel his growing grip on the firm. Now, with Mr. James gone, she had little faith that Bill Simon would halt John Milton's growing influence and power. What was worse in her mind was the man seemed to feel and believe he was entitled to it. The interest this police detective had in him reconfirmed her feelings and fears.

Perhaps most important, she would never get over John Milton's innuendo that first day she had met him, his eerie knowledge or suggestion that she had undergone an abortion. There was no secret deeper buried in her heart. No one in her family, knew, not even her parents when it occurred. Yet somehow, he had stirred up the memory and gave her the feeling he shared the secret. It actually made her feel a little sick. From that moment until now, she couldn't look at him without a chill gripping her heart. She smiled, spoke as calmly and friendly as she could, but she knew he wasn't pleased. She was happy to tell the detective anything she knew, but she couldn't help being afraid, too.

No, she wouldn't stay on much longer, not now. It was time to join Lee and graze on the same or new pastures they would find together, do some of that extra traveling they had talked about so long that they almost faded into memories. "Weren't we there?" Lee might joke when they looked at the brochure.

She smiled to herself. Just out of the corner of her eyes, she saw the two unpleasant looking young men walk toward her and then split so each would walk on the other side of her before she had a chance to move to the right. Neither looked at her, but she couldn't help feeling they were well aware of her. She hadn't looked at them very long, but just a glance made her cringe. It was as if her heart had closed like a hand into a tight fist under her breast. She quickened her pace and glanced around. No one took any special notice of her, which was not particularly unusual on the streets of New York. Most people were afraid of making eye contact with anyone they didn't know, and she wasn't close enough to her building to run into any other tenants with whom she was familiar.

"In the old days," Lee was fond of saying, "all our friends were horizontal. Now they're all vertical. Our friends are stacked under and over us."

Everyone would laugh at that; everyone would laugh at Lee's humorous commentary about the lives we all led, but they would nod and think he's right, too. She was very proud of him. She wasn't simply comfortable with what they had, she decided. She was proud of it. They had survived. They were special. Thinking these thoughts and concentrating on what she liked to call important trivia when she was out in the streets kept her from thinking about any of the dark and dangerous things people confronted daily in a city as big and diverse as New York. Of course, because of the nature of the work at Simon and James, the defense of people accused of serious crimes, she couldn't completely avoid the dark world around her.

Lee didn't mind her bringing it home. He looked forward to it almost as if she was really a storyteller spinning the oral history of modern American society. No matter what the crime, he was always astounded people could commit them. A little fudging of finances to ameliorate taxes was one thing, but physically harming another human being, especially someone you had supposedly once loved always rang with the tone of science fiction. His face would register the shock and disbelief, but he always wanted her to elaborate on the details. He knew it wasn't nice to want to know those things.

"It's why those supermarket rag papers sell so well," he admitted. "I do read their headlines when I pass them by. There's a little voyeur in us all. Do you think admitting your weaknesses makes you any stronger, Kaye?"

She thought a little more about that one. Goodness knows, most of the clients at Simon and James expected their weaknesses to be swept under the rug. They weren't ready to admit anything, no matter how inconsequential. If she were to believe the defenses the lawyers created, angels walked into the office, offended that they were even accused.

"I suppose in the end the worst person to lie to is yourself," she had replied, thinking about all that.

Lee had smiled.

"I like that, Kaye. You're a lot smarter than your bosses know."

She almost laughed aloud thinking about all that now. She quickened her pace, wanting to get home and in his company as soon as possible.

But then, she felt it.

It was like a needle, the point was that sharp.

"Don't scream or I'll push this right through you," Buzzy said. His breath was a mixture of cigarette smoke, garlic and something with the scent of death, something as nauseating as rotting flesh.

She felt her legs wobble and her lungs ache. The young man who had been on her right stepped up beside her and took her hand as if he was going on a Sunday stroll with her.

"Walk," Jason said with a smile that could freeze the flame on a candle.

"What do you want?" she managed. "Take my purse."

"We will, but it's nice of you to offer," Buzzy said. He had pulled the knife up into his right sleeve so that just the edge of it showed. "Turn," he ordered and with the other man tightening his grip on her hand until it hurt, she turned with them into an alleyway between two buildings. Two scrawny cats leaped off an open garbage container and a third emerged, looked at them, hissed and leaped out.

"Keep walking," the man holding her hand said.

"Please."

"No need to be polite," the other man said. "Your purse," he added and slipped it off her shoulder.

Thank God, she thought. That's it. That's all they want.

Buzzy opened the purse and took out her wallet, tossing the purse into the open garbage container.

"Two points," Jason said. He still held onto her hand very tightly.

"Let me go. You have what you want," she said. She tried to turn, but the man who had taken her purse seized her left hand and held it up.

"This ring belongs to us," Buzzy said.

"No, please," she cried.

Buzzy made an attempt to slide it off. She cried out in pain.

"He was right," Jason said. "Anesthesia first. We're not inhuman," he added.

Buzzy stepped behind her and pulled her head back to cut a neat incision in her throat. She gagged and collapsed. Jason reached for her left hand, her ring finger up.

"Doctor?" he said.

Buzzy smiled and then sliced it, amazed at how easily it went through her finger. Jason wrapped the finger and ring in a dirty handkerchief and shoved it into his pocket. Kaye Billups folded into a fetal position and died in small gasps at their feet. They looked at each other to see if either had even an inkling of remorse. Neither did.

"Let's go," Jason said.

They walked out of the alley.

It was like rising out of a swamp. No one passing by did more than glance at them, obviously fearful of them looking back and noticing. They walked faster and reached their car in less than a minute.

John Milton was gone.

"Where the hell is he?" Jason asked.

"I'm not complaining," Buzzy said. "Let's go."

They got into their car and drove off. Buzzy reached back and looked at the slip of paper.

"Got the address. The guy's name is Murdock."

"Let's go collect," Jason said.

"I wonder if he'll give us more for the finger," Buzzy said and they both laughed.

John Milton watched from his limousine across the way. As soon as they disappeared around a turn, he tapped the front seat and Charon started off. John sat back and took out his mobile. He speed dialed Michele Armstrong. Her voice mail picked up after only one ring.

"I imagine you're a little tired," he said. "No worries. Only, I've done some digging around. You have good reason to believe someone is setting you up for another fall. You're going to lose this rape case."

He hung up.

"I love the courting process so much, Charon," he said. "Almost more than I do the result. In fact, if I had to be honest, which as you know, I hate to be, I would have to admit that I deliberately prolong it sometimes. Of course, you might think I'm simply teasing Him, giving Him the impression He might just win one. It's sort of a win-win for me, Charon.

"Are you absorbing all this?"

Charon turned back to look at him.

"Yes, I'm serious. I keep track of everything. Someday, I hope to have my biography written, or rather, my autobiography. Who else would I trust with it?"

He laughed.

Charon turned back to look at the street ahead.

John Milton sensed something and leaned forward to look.

"Well, I'll be. You're actually smiling, Charon. I do believe you will evolve into something or someone worthwhile yet. I'll be like Dr. Frankenstein and run around screaming, 'He's alive! He's alive!'"

Charon accelerated on John Milton's laughter. The black limousine slipped into the city traffic seamlessly and continued along as if he had always been there, always walking to and fro through the earth and up and down in it.

26.

Blake was standing by the printer in his office and waiting for the picture the warden at the Woodbourne maximum security prison was sending him. According to the warden, it was a relatively recent picture. Of course, he wondered why Blake wanted the picture of a dead convict and what was the interest in his final arrangements anyway, but Blake satisfied him by simply replying, "To close up some loose ends."

As the photo began emerging, John Fish hurried over to him. Blake didn't notice him. He was concentrating on the face he had just printed.

"Before you start, this is definitely just a coincidence," Fish began. He had just arrived himself and had assumed Blake wasn't in yet. He hadn't answered his mobile all night, and Fish thought he was still out of town.

Matthew turned to him slowly. His eyes looked cloudy, confused. For a moment Fish had the eerie feeling that Lieutenant Blake had forgotten who he was. He seemed to be struggling with recognition or so deep in thought, he really didn't see him.

"Lieutenant?"

He blinked rapidly. *Coming back to this world?* Fish thought.

"What is it, Fish?"

"Just in. A mugging victim was identified as Kaye Billups, a receptionist at John Milton's new firm, Simon and James."

"What?" Blake's face came fully back to life, his cheeks reddening. "When?"

"Late yesterday. I knew you'd be interested, but it looks like a random mugging for sure. She was led into an alleyway and . . ."

"How is she?"

"She's dead, brutally murdered, Lieutenant. Throat cut and apparently the mugger or muggers couldn't get her wedding ring off, so they cut off her finger and took it as well. No sign of it in the alley. Of course, a cat or a rat could have carried it off, but. . . ."

Blake's face turned a pale shade again.

"That's definitely no coincidence, Fish. She was giving me information."

"Information? About what?"

"About John Milton."

"What sort of information?"

"Information about what he is doing at Simon and James. That's how I knew Paul Scholefield was going to work for them, for him, I should say." He looked distant again. "He knows I'm on his trail."

"What trail? Why investigate a defense attorney and who he hires? Are you out to get some sort of revenge for the Heckett acquittal? What?"

"Revenge? Hardly. He's going to do something more significant than the Heckett acquittal anyway."

"Who? Milton? What's more significant? Wait a minute. Why isn't this a coincidence? You think he's responsible for Kate Billups mugging?"

"Of course he is."

"To stop you from finding out who he's hiring?"

"Oh, much more, Fish, much more. I think this proves it," he said taping the picture he had just printed.

"Who's that?" Fish asked nodding at it.

"A convicted killer, Sam Lonegan, The latest resurrected," Blake said. He folded the picture and put it into his jacket pocket.

"The latest resurrected? How do you mean? Does it have something to do with that funeral home? What are you saying, Lieutenant?"

"I haven't got time to explain it all right now, Fish. I have a few things to confirm, but I'll be calling you later. Stay alert. There's a storm coming," Blake said and started away.

"Storm? But what about . . . the Kotter case?" he asked, his voice drifting off as Blake rushed out of the offices.

Blake wouldn't have heard him if Fish had shouted it, but even if he had heard it, he wouldn't have turned back. He could understand easily why many would think he was suffering serious paranoia, but at the moment, anything or everything that would interfere with his goal was highly suspicious. Even too much traffic on the city streets looked suddenly created.

He'll throw everything he can in my path to stop me, Blake thought, *but nothing will.*

He turned on his bubble light and worked around the traffic, through red lights and even took a one-way street for a short distance to get to the East Village, the neighborhood adjacent to Greenwich Village, and what he knew was Tom Beardsly's apartment building. Just as he got out of his car, he saw a young woman leaving the building. He thought he had seen her in the courtroom during the Heckett trial, sitting right behind John Milton. He sensed that she had spent the night with Beardsly. She was an attractive, light-brown haired woman no more than twenty, but dressed in a light blue designer skirt suit more characteristic of a Madison Avenue business woman. As soon as she reached the sidewalk, a black estate vehicle pulled up. She got in quickly and the car drove off as Blake reached the front steps of the building. He watched it disappear around a turn.

Fringe benefits, he thought, convinced he was right, and started up the stairs.

He didn't expect Beardsly would let him in and he was thinking he would buzz some other tenant and identify himself to get in. He wanted to surprise Beardsly. As he reached to push someone else's button, however, he noticed the front door had not closed when the young woman had left.

"Nothing happens by coincidence," he muttered, repeating his favorite mantra. He opened his jacket and put his hand on his pistol as he walked into the building. Beardsly's apartment was on the third floor, a corner unit. He looked at the elevator and then decided instead to go up the stairway, drawing out his pistol as he turned to the first landing. He paused and listened. Someone was playing his television too loud in one of the second floor apartments, but other than that, there was nothing unusual. He continued up and turned slowly to look down the third floor hallway to see if anyone was waiting for the elevator door to open.

He saw no one nor heard anyone. Stepping out slowly, he walked quietly up to Beardsly's apartment door. He heard what sounded like him walking around just inside. Talk radio was on. He heard Beardsly laugh at some political sarcasm. Looking back and around the hallway first, he knocked rather than push the buzzer button. The walking stopped and the radio volume was lowered. He knocked again and then he heard the handle being turned.

"Comin' back for something?" Beardsly said as he started to open the door. He opened it enough to see it wasn't his woman, but Matthew Blake. Blake took advantage of the look of surprise on Beardsly's face by putting his shoulder to the door and slamming it back at him. Beardsly fell backwards and sat hard on the area rug in the entry. Blake stepped in and closed the door.

"What the fuck . . . what the hell is this?" Beardsly asked, now more embarrassed than angry at how foolish he looked and how easily he had fallen.

Blake reached into his pocket and produced the photo of Sam Lonegan. He held it out.

"You know who this is?"

Beardsly stood up, brushed himself off and looked.

"No. What the hell you think you're doing bustin' in on me like that?"

"It's the man whose cremated remains you delivered to John Milton at that old farmhouse."

Beardsly squinted at the picture and then looked at Matthew Blake. "Farmhouse?"

"Don't try to deny doing it."

"What'dja do, follow me?"

"You brought another urn to him not that long ago, the urn containing the remains of Keith Arthur. He killed Warner Murphy."

"Warner Murphy?" He put his hands on his hips. "I know that case. That was a suicide. Besides, that happened recently. Keith Arthur was already dead himself. What the hell are you talking about asking about the cremated remains of people in urns anyway?" He smiled coldly. "You trying to freak me out like Popeye in The French Connection? You going to ask me if I pick my toes in Poughkeepsie next?"

Matthew Blake hesitated. Could it be that Tom Beardsly didn't know who John Milton was and what he could do?

"Keith Arthur killed Warner Murphy after John Milton resurrected him from the ashes you brought him and then sent him to do it. He threw him off his patio."

Beardly's rubbed his rear end and flopped back on his sofa.

"Resurrected killers, huh?" He nodded. "I know who you are now. You're that wacko detective, the one they call Saint Matthew, ain'tcha?" Beardsly asked smiling. "Peter Thomas told me about you, about how you forced him out of the department, threatened and blackmailed him."

"How do you know Peter Thomas?"

"Due diligence," Beardsly said. "I was asked to speak with him."

"Milton sent you to him. That makes sense," Blake said thinking aloud. "Peter was tired and corruptible. He fabricated evidence to convict someone."

"Who are you, Serpico?" Beardsly laughed. "He got the creep. What difference did it make how he got him?"

"When you behave like them, they win," Blake said.

"Great. I'll remember that when I attend my philosophy class later." His rage and embarrassment returned. "What the fuck do you want anyway? Why'd you come bustin' in here? You don't have a warrant? You're behavin' like them yourself."

"This is different. There's no time to waste."

"No time to waste for what?"

"I want to know what John Milton has in mind for Sam Lonegan to do? He must have given you some indication? You're in this pretty deeply. You'd better talk."

"In what pretty deeply? Delivering urns? You're a real nutcase. Get the fuck out of here before I call the police myself."

Blake didn't move. Instead, he smiled.

"You work for John Milton, but you're afraid of him, Beardsly, aren't you? He pays you, but I'd bet you'd work for him anyway, do anything he asked. Did you ever ask yourself why? It isn't just that monster of a driver he has. You carry a 357 Magnum. How you get away with still carrying I don't know, but you do."

"Fuck you."

"You've been working for him longer than you think. The first time you did something illegal, you invited him in."

"Invited who in?"

"I don't have to tell you. You know. You've always known."

Beardsly smirked and shook his head.

"I was told you always have a stick up your ass when it comes to defense attorneys. If John Milton's too good for you guys, find another line of work."

Beardsly stood up and stepped closer to Blake, his face only inches away from Blake's.

"If you walk out of here now, I'll forget how you came in, but get out now," he said, "before I stop being charitable to a mental case."

If he thinks I'm unstable, I might as well behave as though I am, Blake thought.

He turned as if he was going to leave and then, with his pistol flat in his palm, spun around and struck Beardsly on his left cheekbone. He went down again, rolling onto his back. His cheekbone was fractured, but the shock overcame the pain. He looked up at what he now believed was surely someone who had gone stark, raving mad. Blake knelt, his knee on Beardsly's stomach, and pointed his pistol at his face.

"I saw you leaving Skip Tyler's street just as we had gotten there. John Milton sent you there to do him so I couldn't prove Heckett had hired a hit man. You made it look like he overdosed on heroin. You're about as dirty as a law enforcement agent can get. After your dead, I'll make sure he doesn't get your ashes, Beardsly. You're never coming back."

He cocked his pistol.

"Wait, you crazy bastard. What the hell do you want?"

"Where's John Milton going to be today? What is he planning to arrange and to witness? You're the backup, aren't you? You're always there now."

"Shit," Beardsly said looking at his palm. He was bleeding profusely now.

"That's nothing to a corpse," Blake said. He leveled the pistol.

"Wait. I'm to be at the St. Regis at two."

"The St. Regis?"

"Yeah. Two o'clock."

Blake looked at his watch.

Beardsly saw his attention shift and seized Blake's wrist, twisting his arm so the gun was no longer pointing at him. Then he shifted his left leg and with his free arm, he turned and threw Blake off him, still holding onto his wrist so he couldn't aim it at him. He threw a punch with his other hand and caught Blake on the side of the face, driving him onto his back and then getting on top of him, but Blake didn't release his grip on his pistol. When Beardsly reached back to throw another punch, Blake was able to reach up and seized his throat.

Beardsly's effort went to getting Blake's steel-like fingers from closing on his windpipe. He could feel his body start to cry for air. He tried to turn Blake's gun around and in the process, lost his grip on his wrist. Instantly, Blake got off a shot that drilled through Beardsly's chest and cut off the wires and arteries that delivered the blood to his head and his arms and the neurons to his muscles. In moments he was like a ballooned version of himself leaking air rapidly and closing in and down on his skeleton. Blake easily tossed him over and then stood up.

He should call it in, he thought, and then thought, there isn't time to get soaked in this right now. He took out his mobile and found the number for the St. Regis Hotel. As soon as he had a live person on line, he identified himself.

"What's happening at the hotel around two, today?"

"We have a New York State District Attorney conference," he was told.

When he hung up, he dialed Michele Armstrong's office.

"I'm sorry, Lieutenant," Sophia Walters said, "she's in a do not disturb meeting with her new client. Can I take a message?"

"I've got to talk to her now!"

"Unless there is a personal family crisis, Lieutenant, we're not permitted to interrupt when a victim is being interviewed by a member of the district attorney's staff. I'm sorry. I promise . . ."

"You make sure to tell her to call me as soon as she's finished," he said. "It's not a family tragedy for her, not yet, but it's urgent."

"I will do," Sophia replied. "I'm sorry. I'm . . ."

He didn't have time to waste on the phone. After he hung up, Blake stared down at Beardsly's lifeless body. He wasn't the first man he had shot and killed in a police action, but he was closer to his target than he had ever been. He could see the light slip from his eyes, his soul slipping from his body. He felt this death more than any other. He was close enough for the dark shadow to brush against him and make him sense his own mortality.

Shaking it off, he left the apartment. Someone in the apartment across the way opened his door and peered out, but as soon as Blake appeared, he shut his door. Blake figured he had heard the gunshot, but he wasn't about to stop and explain. He didn't even try to wait for the elevator. He bounced down the steps and shout out of the building, hurrying to his car. Moments later he was off, his bubble light going again, heading for the St. Regis Hotel.

27.

Aunt Eve's warning this morning that this was going to be a very dark day haunted her, but her aunt had been in a gloomy state of mind ever since Michele had gone to dinner with John Milton. She had lit candles, put up talismans and other charms to ward off evil, and in fact, put some of them on the door to her bedroom. Now she was reciting her own spiritual incantations, inserting her name into her special prayers. This morning she was dining it right outside her bedroom door. Michele found herself deliberately avoiding her and for the first time since moving in with her, Michele wondered if her mother hadn't been right to warn her off of living with her aunt. When her aunt went into this melancholy and woeful state of mind, she seemed to age right before Michele's eyes. The bottom line was she was very depressing.

Michele sat back in her chair, now even more depressed. Carol Kyle, the woman for whom she was going to seek justice wasn't just going to be a disappointment as a witness for herself and the case against her brother-in-law. She was going to be a disaster. Michele had no doubt that Jerome Rand forced himself on her, but maybe it was only this one particular time, and as bad at that was, as violent as the photographs revealed, she was afraid Carol's obvious equivocation of previous assignations with her brother-in-law as testified to by her own sister, no matter how innocent Carol made them seem, would diminish and excuse his recent sexual attack.

Pictures of bruises weren't enough. The defense would surely make the point that people can abuse themselves with what some would call overly passionate, even violent sex. There were those who actually claimed to enjoy it more that way. Toward the end of the interview, Carol's revelation that this wasn't the first man she had accused of sexual assault added to her depression about pursuing the case.

"How many were there?" Michele asked, tensing in anticipation of the answer. Carol had made this claim as if it had been some sort of an accomplishment, something that proved how attractive she was.

"Two, three," she said shrugging. She brushed back her shoulder-length dark-brown hair. She had come to the office made up enough for a magazine photo shoot. Maybe she thought they were going to take more pictures and one or more of them would find its way into newspapers. How could Eleanor think this would be a good witness?

"What is it, Carol. two or three? You can't estimate something like that?"

"Three. Because other women let them get away with it, they thought they would with me," she said petulantly. "They were in for a surprise."

"Charges were filed?"

"Yes, but only one actually resulted in a court hearing," she said. "The others were settled."

"Settled? How settled? With money?" she asked, grimacing.

"Well, they paid," she said, her eyes wide. She'd certainly have to insist she cut down on make up when and if she was in court. She had enough mascara on to last a week in the rain. "I wasn't going to let them get away with not paying somehow."

"And the one that had the court hearing?"

"He settled for community service or something."

Michele could feel the bottom falling out of her self-confidence. It literally felt like she was sitting on an inner tube that was deflating. John Milton's admonition left on her voice mail was ringing in her ears, "Someone is setting you up for another fall."

"We'll talk again before we decide how we'll go forward," she told her victim. Could she feel comfortable even calling her that? "Don't talk about this case with anyone else, not even your sister now."

"Oh, we're not speaking," she said. "Actually, she was the one who stole boyfriends, not me," she added. Now what, Michele wondered, a revelation of sibling rivalry when it came to men? This could raise the question in the jury's mind concerning whether or not Carol enticed her sister's husband to prove a point or better her. She raised her hand like a traffic officer.

"Okay, that's enough," she said.

Carol Kyle could see the skepticism in Michele's face.

"Well, everyone believes me, not him and certainly not my sister," she ranted. "I'm not the first woman he cheated on her with."

"We'll talk again," Michele said forcing a smile. She stood up and practically escorted her out of the conference room, closing the door quickly behind her and returning to her seat.

For a few moments, she just sat there staring at nothing, dazed. Then she nodded to herself and started to get up to go see Eleanor Rozwell. She was going to tell her that the best she hoped for was a plea deal. If Eleanor refused to let that happen, she was determined to go to Michael Barrett and plead the strategy. There was no question that it would look like the retreat it was, and after a dramatic loss, she knew it didn't bode well for her future, but it was the sensible way to go. Maybe Michael would respect her for that.

Before she could stand, Sophia entered, her face telegraphing something serious enough to justify her bursting in rather than buzzing her.

She looked like the words were ready to explode in the inside of her cheeks. Michele settled back in her seat.

"What?"

"Lieutenant Blake called ten minutes ago. He wanted me to break in on your session with Carol Kyle. He insists you call him immediately. He sounded very disturbed. I'm sorry. I hope I wasn't wrong not to interrupt you, but . . ."

"No, you were right," she said, releasing the fear and tension that had seized her body. All she could imagine was something terrible had happened to a member of her family, but it was just Matthew being overly dramatic. After the way he had behaved and the things he had said the day before, she was sure of it. "I'll take care of it. Thank you, Sophia."

The moment she stepped out, she called Matthew Blake, actually a little annoyed that she had to take the time to do it right at this moment. She almost hung up and put it off before he answered, but she had no idea what he might do to get her attention next time. He might even drive over and burst in her while she was talking with Eleanor or Michael.

"Thank God you called," he said instantly on answering.

"What's happening, Matthew?" she asked. She was unable to hide the fatigue and depression in her voice. To her surprise, he didn't jump on that as she anticipated. He was obviously very excited about something new.

"Good, good. I see from the number that you're still at the office. Good."

"Yes, Matthew, I'm still here. I just finished with interviewing a victim."

"The rape case? The one you thought was more complicated?"

"Yes, yes. So what is going on? You nearly scared my secretary to death," she said, now not hiding her visible annoyance.

"She should be frightened. We all should be."

"Why? Where are you?"

"I'm almost to the St. Regis Hotel. I was calling to tell you that if you were coming here, don't."

"Why would I be going there?"

"There's a New York state prosecutors' conference there."

"What? Oh, damn. I forgot," she said. She'd have to wait to talk to either Eleanor or Michael Barrett, probably until the morning. "Why are you going there?"

"John Milton has sent Sam Lonegan there. I'm sure of it."

"Who's Sam Lonegan?"

"The man who died in prison and was cremated and just resurrected, the one I just told you about yesterday."

"What are you saying? You're making my head spin. Why would John Milton send anyone there, much less a what? Resurrected man? What are you going to do, Matthew?"

"I'm going to stop him. Don't worry. I figured it out. It all makes sense to me now."

"What does?"

"He's going to have Michael Barrett assassinated and he's going to put up his own candidate for district attorney in a special election soon after."

"Who? John Milton? He's going to have the district attorney assassinated? Is that what you're saying, Matthew? Do you know how ridiculous this is sounding?"

"Didn't you hear what I said? It makes sense. He'll control it all. I never told you all of it when I told you about my religious studies, Michele, and what changed my mind about my future. I had discovered that the Satanists had infiltrated the Vatican. Eventually, he'll have the Pope, too."

"The Pope? Michael, you're not making sense. Look," she said taking a deep breath, "I'll meet you somewhere. We'll have coffee and talk. I promise."

He surprised her by laughing.

"What's so funny?"

"Of course you would suggest that, Michele. You don't realize it, but you're already in his control. Don't you see? He wants you to stop me from getting to the hotel in time. You don't even realize what you're doing."

"Stop you? How does he know you're on your way there, Matthew?"

"Oh, he knows now. I've already eliminated part of his plot."

"What part? How? What have you done? What do you mean by eliminated?"

"Mark my words, Michele, one way or another, you'll be working for John Milton if I don't stop him. I'm saving you as much as I'm saving Michael Barrett."

"Matthew, please listen," she began, but he hung up. She redialed but his voice mail came on. "Damn," she said and marched out of the office. She didn't stop to tell Sophia anything. She just ran down the hallway to the elevator to see if she could get to the St. Regis Hotel in time to stop something terrible, whatever that was.

As soon as he hung up on Michele, Matthew Blake pulled his car to the curb on Fifth Avenue near 55th Street and sat there for a moment. The sky had grown overcast. The air smelled like rain was coming. He could almost hear the shadows unfolding in alleyways. Evil was rising out of the earth like steam from hot springs. Everything he saw and heard reconfirmed his suspicions. This was to be a day when tragedy emerged from wherever it had been incubating and put its Mark of Cain on the face of mankind, unless, of course, he could stop it.

Think, he told himself. Get ahead of it.

Sam Lonegan surely would be properly dressed in a suit and tie. There would be nothing about him to alert anyone's attention. In fact, he would probably look like another prosecutor. That would be John Milton's little inside joke. He might even have the proper name tag. What Matthew had to do was determine where the assassination would occur. It wouldn't matter that Sam Lonegan would be caught right afterward or shot. His body would disappear somehow, some way. He was confident of that. Keith Arthur hadn't been seen again.

For dust you are and to dust you will return, he thought. *Everything he does is in one way or another a mockery of scripture.*

He studied the picture of Sam Lonegan and then he got out and walked slowly to the hotel, looking at every man he passed and who passed him. He stepped into the lobby and paused. The famous King Cole Bar/lounge looked crowded. Every seat at the dark, lavish wood bar with the famous Old King Cole mural was taken. There were enough suits in there to tell him that there must be a break between sessions going on. It was an opportune time for Lonegan, a man no one but he would recognize.

The desk clerk and hotel security personnel looked curiously at him standing there, turning in a slow circle, studying everything and everyone with an unusual intensity. They could see some people were disturbed at the way he scrutinized them. One of the security men stepped up to him.

"Sir? You looking for someone? Are you here to register?" he asked.

Matthew Blake took out his identification and showed it to him.

"Oh. Well, what's up, Lieutenant?" he asked.

"There's going to be an attempted assassination here, maybe any moment," he replied.

"What?" The man's face paled.

"Don't worry. I have it under control," he said and stepped toward the bar. He could see Michael Barrett at a corner table talking to two other men. He panned the crowd. No one resembling Lonegan appeared to be in there.

"Sir," the security man said coming up behind him, "are more police personnel on the way? Should I clear the room? Is there anyone to alert?"

"There's no time to get any more help now," Matthew said.

He started walking into the bar but stopped. Something made him turn around and looked toward the entrance.

"I don't understand,' the security man said.

Blake put up his hand, his gaze fixed on the man who had turned to the right so he couldn't see his face clearly, but the man was in a black suit and black tie.

"I'll call the manager," the security man said. Blake didn't respond.

Sam Lonegan turned slowly, looked at Michael Barrett and then turned to leave the hotel. Blake shot out after him. He might have stopped him now, he thought, but he'll be out there waiting for another opportunity. He paused at the entrance and saw Lonegan hurrying east. He was walking fast, almost gliding over the sidewalk. Matthew hurried after him, walking fast and then breaking into a run when he saw him turn between a truck and a taxi cab and head into a narrow alleyway.

Blake held up his hand to bring a vehicle to a stop, the driver leaning out of his window to scream profanities. He didn't look back. In moments he was in the same alleyway. It wound around behind a restaurant. He took out his pistol and moved slowly. When he made the turn, he saw Lonegan just standing there, smiling. He had his gun out.

Instinctively, Blake went to one knee and got off his first shot, a perfect shot drilling a whole right in the center of Lonegan's forehead. He looked surprised for a moment and then returned to his smile as he literally folded like an accordion in slow motion, his head and neck sinking into his chest, his chest into his hips, his hips into his legs, and all of it into his feet before he settled in a pile of ashes on the ground. Blake stared astonished. It was almost like killing a vampire with a silver bullet.

The sound of his pistol unloading still echoed in his ears, seemingly bouncing off the alley walls and back before spilling into the busy street and merging with the cacophony of car horns, the sound of a drill breaking up cement in a street repair and what he distinctly believed was a shrill cry of rage and sorrow rising from the sewers.

He rose slowly and as he approached the ashes, recited the Lord's Prayer. He holstered his pistol, took a deep breath and called John Fish. As soon as Fish answered, he told him his location.

"I need a back-up team here ASAP," he said. "I was just in a shoot-out, a very unusual shoot-out."

"What's that mean?"

"Just move quickly," he replied. He ended the call and took out a handkerchief to wipe his face. He could feel the layer of cold sweat covering his forehead, cheeks and his neck. As he stared down at the ashes, he wondered just how much information forensics would be able to determine. Certainly not any identity since all DNA was destroyed in cremation. Maybe all he could get determined was it was the ashes of a human. He remembered that sometimes a tooth might survive and with the barrel of his pistol, he moved the ashes around, searching. The bone-colored material was as fine as sand.

Who would believe him? He couldn't bring in Beardsly now and through interrogation get him to confess to picking up the ashes. He knew Malcom Foster would be sufficiently vague about who had picked up the urn, and although John Fish had accompanied him to investigate the funeral home, he could confirm nothing that would relate to this. Neither he nor Michele believed anything he told them. He knew that.

He spun around when he thought he heard someone laughing. For a few moments he stared at the alleyway, half-expecting John Milton to come sauntering toward him, wearing that same wry, confident smile he had worn in the courtroom when he had cross-examined him. No one came. He heard the sound of police sirens and breathed some relief.

And then it happened.

Seemingly out of nowhere, a rush of air spun around him and scooped up the ashes. He turned quickly as they rose in a funnel and began to scatter at least a dozen or so feet above him. Another breeze swooping down from the tops of the surrounding buildings picked them up and swept them away, scattering them in the air before it all became totally calm again. He looked down at the empty place where once the small pile of ashes had been, just as he heard the first patrolman call to him from the alleyway. Two more uniform patrolmen came rushing behind him, guns drawn. The three paused and looked around. Blake holstered his pistol again.

"What's going on, Lt.?" the first patrolman asked.

Matthew reviewed his response before replying. He could start to explain this to them, but they'd end up being witnesses to establish he had lost his senses. John Milton would grab victory from the jaws of defeat, for after all, he did stop the assassination. He had beaten him this time, and it was most important to be able to beat him another.

"I had a tip that someone was going to assassinate the DA," he replied. "I spotted a man who looked suspicious to me and he ran out of the St. Regis."

"Where is he?" the second patrolman asked, glancing around.

"I thought he went down the alley and I'd be in a shoot-out, but he must have slipped out or got into a car or something."

The patrolmen looked at him, at each other and then holstered their pistols.

"I'll make a report," he said. "Thanks for getting here quickly."

"No problem, Lt.," the first patrolman said. The three hesitated as Matthew gazed around and then up at the tops of the buildings. Milton's resurrected assassin was back in hell at least.

At least he knew that they could die twice.

He nodded and followed his back-up patrolmen out of the alley.

He walked back up to the St. Regis. Whatever break the conference participants had taken had ended. The bar had only a half dozen people in it. One of them was Michele Armstrong. She had apparently just arrived and was speaking with the security man who had first approached him when he arrived at the hotel looking for Lonegan. The moment she saw him, she broke away.

"Where have you been? What did you do, Matthew?" she asked.

"I stopped him," he replied. "Let's get a drink."

He walked over to the bar. She stood back, hesitant and then joined him.

"What would you like?"

"Nothing, Matthew. She slipped onto the stool next to him. "Just tell me something . . . sensible."

"Grey Goose and soda," he told the bartender. "Sensible," he repeated as if he was turning the word around and around, checking it like a jeweler determining the value of a diamond.

"Yes, sensible, for Christ sakes."

He smiled.

"I guess in a way it all is for Christ's sake. When I finish this drink," he began after the bartender put it in front of him. "I'm going to report my having a life and death struggle with Tom Beardsly."

He turned to show her the bruise on his cheek.

"About that business with the urn?"

"Yes, that business. He admitted to picking it up and delivering it to John Milton, but apparently Milton kept him in the dark about what he would do with it, what it all meant. Our discussion got . . . how should I put it . . . out of hand. He attacked me and we struggled. He almost killed me, but I was able to get off a shot and . . ."

"You killed him?"

"For now," he replied.

"What?"

"I'll bet you and anyone else a thousand dollars that he'll be cremated and probably at the same funeral parlor."

"Matthew, you have to report this now. It's a fatal shooting. It needs to be properly investigated."

"I know the drill. I'll take care of it. It will put me down for a while until everything is stamped Kosher. The important thing is I'll be back. You can deliver that message if he takes you out to dinner again."

She shook her head, looking at him with far more pity than sympathy. It made him smile.

"I told you. The devil's greatest asset is the fact that so many don't believe he literally exists."

She looked down at her hands clasped together on the bar.

"I really like you, Matthew. You're a very bright and interesting man. Maybe you're just working too hard. This shooting review will give you an opportunity to step back, get some rest."

"It won't change anything."

"Just give it a chance. Go up to your mountain retreat and don't do anything that remotely relates to law enforcement. Read, cook, fish, whatever. Do it for a while and I'll try to come up for a weekend."

"That would make me happy, but I repeat, it won't change anything, Michelle. You're good. You're still dedicated and idealistic enough to believe you can make a difference. You only can if you're aware of those who will try to stop you from doing that. Unfortunately, a good dose of cynicism and distrust is very important in this world. It's just the way it is."

"Okay, Matthew."

"No, it's not okay, Michele. I hope you'll realize that soon. Outside of the halls of justice, which is a misnomer to start with because what goes on inside doesn't have as much to do with justice as it does with power or money, there is the statue of Lady Justice. She supposedly wears the blindfold to be objective and impartial, but I've come to believe that she wears the blindfold because she can't stand seeing how the scales are tipped with much more than facts and truth. The rich get their version of justice and the poor get punished for being poor. It's almost as though he designed it. No wonder he's here now. No wonder he's deeply entrenched in it."

"Milton?"

"Whatever name he goes by at the time. It's all humorous to him, Michele. Do you know who John Milton was, what he wrote?"

"Yes. Paradise Lost."

"In which Lucifer is a tragic hero. 'Better to reign in hell than serve in heaven.' He's doing a good job of turning this into a suburb of hell."

She put her right hand on his arm.

"I can't believe you believe all this, that you've become such a paranoid."

He shrugged.

"A good detective has to be paranoid."

"Certainly not to this extent."

"What's happening with your rape case?"

"We're dropping the charges. After more research I found that there were even more complications."

"But you were out front on it. She put you there. Get a little paranoid, Michele, before it's too late."

"Cynical and paranoid."

He shrugged.

"It's survival."

"Okay. I won't give up on you. My aunt wouldn't permit that anyway."

He nodded.

"When you do, he's won a big victory," he replied.

She stared into his eyes for a moment and then leaned over, kissed him on the cheek, and slipped off the stool. He watched her walk out.

And he wondered.

How far away would she be the next time he saw her?

EPILOGUE.

John Milton watched Bill Simon sign the papers that essentially turned the firm over to him. Milton had added three more attorneys and replaced every secretary. As they sat there in the conference room, the designer John Milton had hired was beginning the renovations of the offices. Milton had bought out the leases on the adjacent offices as well and the work had begun to tear down walls and expand. Bill Simon was astonished at how quickly John Milton was getting the building permits and approvals. When he mentioned that, John shrugged and smiled.

"Isn't all life a matter of who you know more than what you know, Bill? Surely someone who has reached your age and had your experiences knows that."

"No, what I've learned is it isn't who or what you know. It's who or what you can buy," he replied. "Exhibit A," he added lifting the papers with his signature on them.

John Milton laughed.

"I'd wish you good luck," Bill Simon added, "but somehow I don't think that ever mattered to you."

"Every successful man knows you make your own luck, Bill, or rather, when a fortunate opportunity arises, you have to have what it takes to make it beneficial. That's my definition of luck."

"Yes." He sat back. "As you did after Warner Murphy's inexplicable death."

"The king dies. Long live the king. Nothing's new about that."

Bill Simon stood and looked around.

"I didn't think I would get so tired of all this so soon, but when you're mired in the uglier side of things daily, you can't take a shower hot enough or long enough to feel clean."

"Cleanliness is overrated," John Milton said.

"My mother used to tell me that cleanliness is next to godliness."

"Exactly. Overrated," John said standing. He extended his hand. "Good luck to you in your retirement, Bill, and thank you for preparing a great foundation for a great firm."

"What will you call it now?"

"What else? John Milton and Associates."

Bill nodded.

"Good lu . . . I mean, make good use of your fortunate opportunities."

"I will. Thank you."

He watched him leave. Then he went to the window and looked down at the city, at the lines of traffic moving like lines of snails, the pedestrians rushing over sidewalks and across the streets. He saw only vulnerable souls, people looking over their shoulders suspiciously at strangers.

"How frightened they all are. Why did you make them so frightened? They fear being hungry, being cold, being tired, and being sick. They fear failure and most of all, they fear death. You created them with lust and jealousy, sloth and vanity. You challenged them to be angels after you failed even with the angels you had created. Don't you realize how easy you made it for me?

"Or is this all part of your grand scheme. Am I walking into another trap?

"Don't reveal it. If I knew where I was heading, it would take away the joy of the trip."

He laughed and heard a knock on the door.

"Yes?"

Nora entered, looking sexier than ever. Her red silk dress was more like a second layer of skin. She looked bright and excited and that excited him.

"What delicious thing are you here to tell me, Nora?"

"The Jacob twins are here," she said.

"Ah, my teenagers accused of patricide. Did I ever tell you that it's one of favorite to defend?"

"I wonder why," Nora said. Her eyes narrowed and her tongue thinned and emerged to taste his scent. He smiled.

"I'll be right there," he said.

In the moment, in the silence that followed he had his first feeling of doubt in a very long time. It was like a cold, passing breeze. He shook it off quickly.

Then he opened the door and, holding himself as regally as he once was, returned to the battlefield like a soldier who could live nowhere else.

ABOUT THE AUTHOR

Andrew Neiderman was born in Brooklyn and grew up in New York's scenic Catskill Mountains region. A graduate of the University at Albany, State University of New York, from which he also received his master's in English, Neiderman taught at Fallsburg Junior-Senior High School for twenty-three years before pursuing a career as a novelist and screenwriter. He has written more than forty thriller novels under his own name, including *The Devil's Advocate*, which was made into a major motion picture for Warner Bros., starring Al Pacino, Keanu Reeves, and Charlize Theron, and is in development as a stage musical in London. Neiderman has also written seventy *New York Times*–bestselling novels for the V.C. Andrews franchise. He lives with his family in Palm Springs, California. Visit him on Facebook at www.facebook.com/AndrewNeidermanAuthor.

ANDREW NEIDERMAN

FROM OPEN ROAD MEDIA

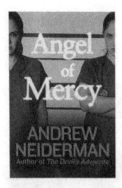
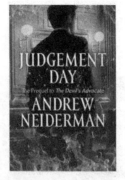

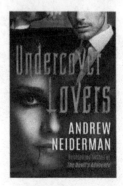

OPEN ROAD

INTEGRATED MEDIA

INTEGRATED MEDIA

Find a full list of our authors and
titles at www.openroadmedia.com

FOLLOW US
@OpenRoadMedia

CPSIA information can be obtained
at www.ICGtesting.com
Printed in the USA
JSHW052115010922
29991JS00001B/90